A life adrift...
A home rediscovered...

Praise for the Novels
of Karen White

On Folly Beach

"Heartwarmingly tender, with a bit of mystery and intrigue, and the feel of the Carolina ocean breezes, *On Folly Beach* makes the perfect summertime reading choice." —*The Wichita Falls Times Record News*

"If you crave a tale that will have you burning the midnight oil in order to get to the next chapter, then make *On Folly Beach* one of your must reads this summer." —Jackie K. Cooper, *The Huffington Post*

"Known for her exquisite prose, which delves into the inner core of her characters' emotions, [White] delivers a superb story. . . . She has proven her prowess as a storyteller by demonstrating her unique combination of history with intrigue and love in order to create an unforgettable novel. Without a doubt, *On Folly Beach* is White's crowning achievement." —Fresh Fiction

"*On Folly Beach* is a terrific book with a thoughtful plot, a dash of history, and the promise of future happiness. It's the perfect story for an escape from the heat or to stick in your suitcase as you head off for vacation." —*The Conroe Courier* (TX)

"*On Folly Beach* is a perfect summer read—heck, a perfect read for any time of the year. Karen White knows how to spin a perfectly crafted story and/or mystery, and readers are sure to love this soon-to-be bestseller." —The Best Reviews

"Karen White weaves history (some little known), daily living, love, deceit, sorrow, and survival together in *On Folly Beach*. She bombards the senses with vivid imagery, poignant metaphors, and analogies. . . . Emmy's and Heath's personal battles entwined with the historical characters' battles mak[e] *On Folly Beach* compelling. It is a KEEPER!" —Long and Short Reviews

continued . . .

Written by today's freshest new talents and selected by New American Library, NAL Accent novels touch on subjects close to a woman's heart, from friendship to family to finding our place in the world. The Conversation Guides included in each book are intended to enrich the individual reading experience, as well as encourage us to explore these topics together—because books, and life, are meant for sharing.

Visit us online at www.penguin.com.

"White has a clear, sweet voice, and the ability to mark occasions from multiple viewpoints. Her characters are rich and captivating." —*RT Book Reviews*

The Lost Hours

"Reads as an intricately plotted mystery. . . . White makes a good case for why new generations should sustain ties with the old—and why certain stories have to be told, no matter how long it takes."   —*The Atlanta Journal-Constitution*

"Wonderful phrasing . . . leav[es] readers with a slice of history too haunting to be forgotten."   —*Charleston* magazine

"An interesting look at family. . . . Readers will enjoy this deep Savannah River family drama."   —The Best Reviews

"Through vivid details and emotionally charged characters, White creates this year's must-read novel. Without a doubt, *The Lost Hours* is most definitely a labor of love."   —Fresh Fiction

The House on Tradd Street

"Engaging. . . . The supernatural elements are not played for scares, but instead refine and reveal Melanie's true character. . . . A fun and satisfying read, this series kickoff should hook a wide audience."   —*Publishers Weekly*

"*The House on Tradd Street* has it all, mystery, romance, and the paranormal including ghosts with quirky personalities."   —BookLoons

"Brilliant and engrossing . . . a rare gem . . . exquisitely told, rich in descriptions, and filled with multifaceted characters."   —The Book Connection

"Has all the elements that have made Karen White's books fan favorites: a Southern setting, a deeply emotional tale, and engaging characters."
                                        —A Romance Review

"Karen White is an extremely talented and colorful writer with tons of imagination. If you are not a believer of paranormal, you will be after reading this novel."   —Fresh Fiction

The Memory of Water

"Beautifully written and as lyrical as the tides . . . speaks directly to the heart and will linger in yours long after you've read the final page."
—Susan Crandall, author of *A Kiss in Winter*

"Karen White delivers a powerfully emotional blend of family secrets, Low-country lore, and love in *The Memory of Water*—who could ask for more?"
—Barbara Bretton, author of *Girls of Summer*

Learning to Breathe

"White creates a heartfelt story full of vibrant characters and emotion that leaves the reader satisfied yet hungry for more from this talented author."
—*Booklist*

"Karen White has gifted readers with another masterpiece, touching every emotion in her novel *Learning to Breathe*! White captures the essence of small-town living and the nuances of family life, making all her characters leap from the pages. . . . White adds another wonderful story to her fans' keeper shelves!"
—Reader to Reader Reviews

More Praise for the Novels
of Karen White

"The fresh voice of Karen White intrigues and delights."
—Sandra Chastain, contributor to *At Home in Mossy Creek*

"Warmly Southern and deeply moving."
—*New York Times* bestselling author Deborah Smith

"[A] sweet book . . . highly recommended."
—*Booklist*

"Karen White is one author you won't forget. . . . This is a masterpiece in the study of relationships. Brava!"
—Reader to Reader Reviews

"This is not only romance at its best—this is a fully realized view of life at its fullest."
—Readers & Writers Ink Reviews

"*After the Rain* is an elegantly enchanting Southern novel. . . . Fans will recognize the beauty of White's evocative prose."
—WordWeaving.com

New American Library Titles
by Karen White

Falling Home

On Folly Beach

The Lost Hours

The Memory of Water

Pieces of the Heart

Learning to Breathe

The Color of Light

The Tradd Street Series

The House on Tradd Street

The Girl on Legare Street

The Beach Trees

KAREN WHITE

NAL Accent
Published by New American Library, a division of
Penguin Group (USA) Inc., 375 Hudson Street,
New York, New York 10014, USA
Penguin Group (Canada), 90 Eglinton Avenue East, Suite 700, Toronto,
Ontario M4P 2Y3, Canada (a division of Pearson Penguin Canada Inc.)
Penguin Books Ltd., 80 Strand, London WC2R 0RL, England
Penguin Ireland, 25 St. Stephen's Green, Dublin 2,
Ireland (a division of Penguin Books Ltd.)
Penguin Group (Australia), 250 Camberwell Road, Camberwell, Victoria 3124,
Australia (a division of Pearson Australia Group Pty. Ltd.)
Penguin Books India Pvt. Ltd., 11 Community Centre, Panchsheel Park,
New Delhi - 110 017, India
Penguin Group (NZ), 67 Apollo Drive, Rosedale, Auckland 0632,
New Zealand (a division of Pearson New Zealand Ltd.)
Penguin Books (South Africa) (Pty.) Ltd., 24 Sturdee Avenue,
Rosebank, Johannesburg 2196, South Africa

Penguin Books Ltd., Registered Offices:
80 Strand, London WC2R 0RL, England

Published by New American Library,
a division of Penguin Group (USA) Inc.

First New American Library Printing, May 2011
20 19 18 17 16 15 14 13 12

 REGISTERED TRADEMARK—MARCA REGISTRADA

LIBRARY OF CONGRESS CATALOGING-IN-PUBLICATION DATA:

White, Karen (Karen S.)
The beach trees / Karen White.
p. cm.
ISBN 978-0-451-23307-3
1. Self-realization in women—Fiction. 2. Women artists—Fiction. 3. Family secrets—Fiction.
4. Missing persons—Fiction. 5. Biloxi (Miss.)—Fiction. 6. New York (N.Y.)—Fiction. I. Title.
PS3623.H5776B43 2011
813'.6—dc22   2010052283

Set in Bembo Regular
Designed by Alissa Amell

Printed in the United States of America

PUBLISHER'S NOTE
This is a work of fiction. Names, characters, places, and incidents either are the product of the author's
imagination or are used fictitiously, and any resemblance to actual persons, living or dead, business
establishments, events, or locales is entirely coincidental.
   The publisher does not have any control over and does not assume any responsibility for author or
third-party Web sites or their content.

This book is dedicated to the residents of the Gulf Coast and New Orleans who know better than most why we rebuild.

ACKNOWLEDGMENTS

A huge thanks to my alma mater, Tulane University, and to my dear friends and New Orleans natives, Nancy Mayer Mencke and Lynda Ryan Casanova, for showing me the Crescent City and all of its beauty and some of its secrets. Thanks also to my father, William Lloyd Sconiers, Biloxi High School Class of 1950, for many things but especially for his stories of growing up in Biloxi, Mississippi, and for teaching me the correct pronunciation of "Tchoutacabouffa."

To friend and home builder, Julie Kenney of Kenney-Moise, Inc., for taking pictures of the gulf in winter and describing flora and fauna long-distance—not to mention telling me about the ins and outs of beach house construction—my undying gratitude.

And, of course, thank you to Wendy Wax and Susan Crandall, for all of your wonderful insights and critiques, and for reading this book as fast as I could write it!

When I have seen by Time's fell hand defaced
The rich proud cost of outworn buried age;
When sometime lofty towers I see down-razed,
And brass eternal slave to mortal rage;
When I have seen the hungry ocean gain
Advantage on the kingdom of the shore,
And the firm soil win of the watery main,
Increasing store with loss, and loss with store;
When I have seen such interchange of state,
Or state itself confounded to decay;
Ruin hath taught me thus to ruminate,
That Time will come and take my love away.
This thought is as a death, which cannot choose
But weep to have that which it fears to lose.

—William Shakespeare,
Sonnet 64

The Beach Trees

CHAPTER 1

The little reed, bending to the force of the wind, soon stood upright again when the storm had passed over. —AESOP

Julie

SEPTEMBER 2010

Death and loss, they plague you. So do memories. Like the Mississippi's incessant slap against the levees, they creep up with deceptive sweetness before grabbing your heart and pulling it under. At least, that's what Monica told me. Monica had been the one with the memories of the great muddy river that cradled the Crescent City, and of the sparkling water of the gulf and the bright white house that sat before it.

My own family settled in Massachusetts about one hundred years after the Pilgrims, and my sturdy New England upbringing left me unprepared and a little in awe of Monica, with her strange accent that curled some words and mispronounced others, that was neither Southern or Northern but a strange combination of both. Her stories of her childhood were seasoned with the dips and waves of her accent, almost making me forget that Monica had abruptly turned her back on these places that existed so vividly in her memories, and never gone back. Like me, Monica was a self-imposed orphan living and working in

New York City, both of us trying very hard to pretend that we belonged there.

I leaned forward in the minivan's driver's seat and glanced in the rearview mirror at Beau, Monica's motherless little boy, and the fear and anxiety that had been dogging me took hold again. In the last two months I had gone from being a workaholic at a reputable auction house, with no other responsibilities except for my monthly rent and utilities, to the broke, unemployed guardian of a five-year-old boy, possessor of a dilapidated minivan, and apparently the owner of a beach house in Biloxi, Mississippi, with the improbable name of River Song. Despite almost a lifetime spent collecting things, I was at a loss to explain my recent acquisitions.

Beau stirred, and I found myself hoping that he would remain asleep for at least another hour. Although we'd stopped overnight in Montgomery, Alabama, listening for endless hours to Disney music was more of a strain on my already raw nerves. For nearly twenty hours we'd been traveling south in a van built during the Reagan administration, through towns and scenery that made me think I'd taken a wrong turn and stumbled into a foreign country. After recalling some of the stories Monica had told me about growing up in the South, I realized that I probably had.

"Mama?"

I looked into the rearview mirror and into greenish blue eyes so much like his mother's, offset by remarkably long and dark eyelashes. Monica said the lashes were from all the Tabasco sauce Louisiana mothers put in their baby's bottles to get them used to hot food. The memory made me smile until Beau looked back at me, his eyes repeating his question.

"No, sweetheart. Your mama isn't here. Remember what we talked about? She's in heaven, watching over you like an angel, and she wants me to take care of you now."

His face registered acceptance, and I looked away before he could see what a fraud I really was. I knew less about Monica's Catholic heaven and angels than I did about raising young children. There was something about this whole experience that was like on-the-job training for a career I'd never wanted.

Beau lifted his left thumb to his mouth, a new habit started shortly after his mother died. In his right hand he held Monica's red knit hat that he placed against his cheek, and began to softly scratch a hole into the knit. It had become his constant companion, along with the dozens of Matchbox cars and LEGOs he managed to secrete in his pockets, backpack and pillowcase. Although just barely five, he'd seemed to regress to almost three-year-old behavior since his mother's death, and I didn't know the first thing about how to fix it. Letting him keep his mother's hat had simply seemed a necessity.

"Julie?"

My eyes met his again in the rearview mirror.

"I need to go pee-pee."

I glanced over at the portable GPS that I'd purchased secondhand on eBay. We were in a place called D'Iberville, Mississippi, only about thirty minutes from our final destination. I could picture the beach house Monica had described so clearly in my mind: the wide porch, the rocking chairs, the columns that had always made me think of welcoming arms. My foot pressed heavier on the gas pedal. "Can you hold it just a little longer, Beau? We're almost there."

Scrunching his eyebrows together, he nodded and began to scratch his mother's hat in earnest.

Focusing again on the road in front of me, I began noticing the signs for the Biloxi casinos: Beau Rivage, Isle of Capri, Treasure Bay. None of Monica's stories had included mention of the casinos, leaving me to wonder if it were because they'd been built after Monica left, or because they were as alien to the Gulf Coast as their names.

I took the Biloxi exit off of Interstate 10 and onto Interstate 110, and the GPS showed the van on a narrow strip of road and surrounded by water on both sides as we crossed the Back Bay of Biloxi toward the peninsula nestled between the bay and the Mississippi Sound. I felt hot despite the air-conditioning, my heart pumping a little faster as it suddenly occurred to me the enormity of what I was doing. Heading into the unknown with a five-year-old child no longer seemed like the sanctuary I'd at first imagined as I'd sat in the lawyer's office on Lexington Avenue as he'd handed me a set of house keys, and the name and address of a woman with the unusual name of Ray Von Williams. From twelve hundred miles away, it had all seemed so much more promising than the bleakness of my current situation. Death and loss, they plague you. I sighed, finally beginning to understand what Monica had meant.

The September sun skipped and danced over the water as the road rumbled under the minivan's tires, the constant rhythm doing nothing to dissipate my increased heart rate. The chipper voice of the GPS, whom Beau had named Gertie, instructed me to exit onto Beach Boulevard, the Mississippi Sound running parallel to the road.

High-rises and casinos dominated the landscape to the east. Driving west, I passed the hotels and restaurants with empty parking lots, owing, I assumed, to the time of year. A wide apron of sand banded the sound to my left as I continued west, where on the right side of the road empty lots with only stunted trees and steps leading to nowhere sat next door to houses with new roofs and brightly flowered hedges. The garish colors looked defiant against the scrubby grass yards and plywood windows of their neighbors. A tall, white lighthouse sat nestled between the opposing traffic lanes of the highway, leaning slightly inland.

I recalled a photo of Monica, her brother, and assorted cousins gathered in a pyramid in front of the base. A photo that could belong in any family's album—any family's except for my own.

Nervously, I watched the flag on the GPS show that I was nearing my destination on the right, my thoughts confirmed by Gertie's enthusiastic voice. Flipping on my turn signal, I turned blindly into a driveway and stopped. We had arrived.

I blinked through the windshield, trying to comprehend what I was seeing; trying to understand if the bare boards of wall frames were brand-new, or the hollowed-out guts of a house that had once stood on the site, its porch columns like welcoming arms.

Without looking down, I reached inside my purse for the piece of notepaper where I'd written down the address for the house, to make sure I'd plugged the right one into the GPS: 1100 Beach Boulevard.

Trying to quell my panic, I turned around to face Beau with a forced smile. "I need to check on something. Can you watch the van for me for a minute?"

He hesitated for only a second before nodding. Removing his thumb from his mouth, he said, "I still need to go pee-pee."

I patted his jeans-clad knee. "I know. I'll hurry, okay?"

Leaving the van running, I climbed out onto the crushed-shell drive and slammed the door behind me a little too hard. I smelled the water, then: salty and something else, too, that I couldn't quite identify. Something that reminded me of my own desperation.

Sending Beau a reassuring smile, I walked to the spot where the drive met the road, looking for a mailbox, a painted number—anything that might tell me that this wasn't where I was supposed to be. Not that I hadn't had that exact thought about one hundred times since climbing into the van in New York the day before.

There was an empty lot next door, with short cement steps leading up to nothing but air, and a For Sale sign swinging in the barren and sand-swept yard. On the other side of it sat a modest yellow clapboard cottage with new grass and a freshly swept front walk. More important, it had a mailbox at the end of the driveway. Walking quickly, I stuck to the side of the road, squinting until I could read the house number: 1105.

Using my hand to shield my eyes, I counted off the lots to make sure I'd really found number 1100. I stole a glance across the street that ran perpendicular to Beach Boulevard and noticed the For Sale signs on empty rectangles of land nestled alongside midcentury homes with thinning trees and new porches. An empty lot near the corner had brick pilings sticking out of the sandy soil like grave markers, casting shadows on the landscape.

Staring back across the street to where I'd left the van, I spotted the old oak, the ancient tree of Monica's stories and paintings. There had once been a tire swing hanging from its thick limbs, leafy branches granting shade on hot Mississippi afternoons. It still stood, but its arms were shorn and stunted, the sparse leaves making the tree look like the balding pate of a man too vain to shave his hair all the way off.

I stumbled back to the car, the enormity of my situation colliding with the pent-up grief and the years spent searching for all I'd lost. I was blinded by it, could barely see the door handle, and fumbled three times before I was finally able to open the door and pull myself into the driver's seat. I grasped the steering wheel, oddly relieved to find something solid beneath my hands, wondering—and hoping—that I might pass out and wake up anywhere else but here.

"Julie?" the little voice called out from the backseat. "I don't need to go pee-pee anymore."

I smelled it then, the sickly tart smell of urine as it saturated the small space inside the van. I sat in shocked silence for a long moment, and then I began to laugh, because it was the only thing I could think of to do.

CHAPTER 2

Landfall: The intersection of the surface center of a tropical cyclone with a coastline. —NATIONAL HURRICANE CENTER

After using nearly a full box of hand wipes to clean the seat and Beau, and then putting a clean pair of pants on him while apologizing for not taking him to the bathroom when he'd first told me that he needed to go, I had calmed down enough to think. I handed the little boy a juice box and a bag of Goldfish crackers, then scrambled in my purse and found the notepaper again with Ray Von's name and address on it. I wished there had been a phone number, too, since showing up at a stranger's front door unannounced with a little boy in tow wasn't something my New England upbringing had prepared me to do.

As I plugged the address into the GPS, I thought again of how very far from home I really was, and how doing what I'd previously considered unthinkable had become an option only because there was no plan B.

I pulled the van back onto the road and drove east as mapped out on the GPS, Gertie's chirpy voice making me grit my teeth. There was a lot of new construction on this side, mostly of what looked like high-end condos mixed in with the large casinos, and I wondered what had happened to all the houses that had once sat here by the water before gambling had become legal and before the storm.

I took a left onto Bellman Street and the area became residential again, with as many houses as vacant lots lining both sides of the road. At Gertie's direction, I found myself in front of a tiny but neat pale pink house, its single front door painted a glowing yellow and covered by a shingled portico held up by wrought-iron posts. A wreath of green, gold, and purple flowers graced the front door, giving the small house a touch of grandeur. Pots of bright blooms I couldn't name spilled over planters and window boxes. It relaxed me somewhat; I figured that anybody who could do such beautiful things with flowers had to be the kind of person who didn't mind strangers asking for help.

I helped Beau out of his seat and spent a few minutes wiping orange cracker crumbs off of his face and shirt before combing his hair. I wet my thumb as I'd seen Monica do a thousand times and used it to clean green Magic Marker from his chin. I knew better than to ask him to leave the red hat in the van and instead held out my hand for him to take as I led us to the front door.

I stood still for a long moment, feeling the warm September air that seemed saturated with the scent of salt water and damp vegetation. I couldn't find a doorbell, so I gave a brief knock on the yellow wood and waited. A loud meow caught my attention, and I turned my head to see a fat black cat perched on one of the flowerpots, staring at us with calculating green eyes.

"Kitty cat," Beau said around his thumb.

The cat regarded him silently before leaping from his perch, pausing to brush against Beau's legs before darting off to the side of the house.

"You shouldn't let a black cat cross your path."

Beau and I turned at the sound of the clipped voice with perfect diction, spotting an old woman with skin the color of ash standing in the open doorway. From her hunched back and sticklike arms and legs that were more sinew than flesh, she had to be at least ninety years old. I wasn't sure what I'd been expecting, but it certainly hadn't been an old black woman who didn't seem at all surprised to see me.

I placed my arm around Beau's narrow shoulders, feeling protective. "I'm sorry to bother you, but I'm looking for Ray Von Williams."

The old woman didn't seem to hear me. She was looking at Beau so intently that the little boy pressed his face against my leg, covering his cheek with the hat.

The woman's eyes sharpened, but her voice was soft when she spoke. "That boy's a Guidry." She touched Beau on the shoulder and he shrank back.

Even though he was way too tall and heavy, I bent down and scooped him up. "Are you Ray Von?"

The woman looked steadily at me with eyes that reminded me of clear green marbles. "Yes, I am." She squinted, leaning forward. "Are you Julie Holt?"

I started as unexpected relief settled on me: relief at knowing that I wasn't alone in this empty place of leveled lots and real estate signs. Relief at knowing that somebody knew who I was. It didn't even occur to me to wonder or care how the old woman knew my name. "Yes. Yes, I am. And this is Monica's son, Beau."

The woman smiled, white dentures showing between her lips. "I got something for you." Without another word, she turned into the little house, leaving the door open. Not really having any other options, I squeezed Beau against me and followed Ray Von inside.

I closed the door behind us and we entered a small living room where a soap opera played on the television and a collection of papier-mâché masks covered the wall next to the large front window. As I followed the older woman to the back of the house, I paused for a moment, not able to name what was missing.

The next room was the kitchen, with a row of gleaming pots and pans hanging from the ceiling, along with bunches of dried herbs, grasses, and flowers. Something bubbled on the stove, the smell reminding me of Sunday afternoons in Monica's apartment. My stomach grumbled, calling to mind that I hadn't eaten since breakfast and that Beau would need more than crackers and juice.

Ray Von was already stacking telephone books in a sturdy wooden chair at the table, her movements swift and strong, belying her years. "You put Miss Monica's boy here, and I'll get you some red beans and rice."

I placed Beau in the chair after reassuring him that I'd stay next to him, then sat down at the table. Everything seemed so surreal, but I felt myself giving into it as I relaxed against the back of my chair, letting slide the weight of responsibilities and uncertainties, and allowed myself to be taken care of, if only for a short while.

Ray Von stood at the stove using a large ladle to pour red beans over beds of rice she'd already heaped on two plates. When she placed them on the table in front of Beau and me, I noticed that Beau's plate was an old plastic one showing faded images of Mickey Mouse and Donald Duck, and I suddenly realized what had been missing from the living room: family photos. I stared at the plate for a long moment, the cartoon characters at odds with the rustic kitchen and the old woman with no family photographs.

Ray Von filled two plastic tumblers with water from a watercooler by the door and placed them by our plates. "Blow on it first, you hear? I'll be right back."

My stomach rumbling loudly now, I leaned over and stirred Beau's quickly and blew on it, trying not to smell too deeply the heavily scented steam that rose from the plate, because it would make me even hungrier than I already was. After testing Beau's to make sure it was okay to eat, I stuck a fork in my own plate and ate quickly, burning my tongue and having to take a gulp of water to cool it off. But it didn't matter. Nothing seemed to matter anymore.

When Ray Von returned, both of us had nearly empty plates. After leaning a brown-paper-wrapped rectangular package about the size of a place mat against a low cabinet, Ray Von retrieved our plates and scooped second helpings onto them before returning them to the table.

Ray Von sat and folded her hands. "Why are you here with her boy but without Miss Monica?"

My last bite of red beans and rice lodged somewhere in the back of my throat. Slowly, I took a drink from my glass, taking my time to form an answer. It hadn't occurred to me that I'd have to tell the story again. I glanced over at Beau, who had finished eating and was drifting to sleep in his chair, his finger working a hole into the red hat.

I took a deep breath, letting the air fill the space where grief and loss had taken up residence so long ago, then let it out again. "Monica died almost three months ago."

Something flickered in Ray Von's eyes, but she didn't look away. Finally, she said, "I suspect it was her heart."

I looked at her in surprise. "How did you know that?"

Her face remained impassive, but her bottom lip trembled. "She was dying from the moment she was born. I suppose we all are, but some of us are scheduled from the start."

"I don't understand."

"She was always delicate that way. They called it 'congenital heart disease,' and it's not the first time that family's seen it."

I sat back in my chair, my breath coming so fast that I felt light-headed again. "So she knew she had a weak heart? And didn't do anything?"

"Oh, I don't know if she knew, but I did. I was there when she was born, and I could see it even though the doctors couldn't. Her mama had her tested, too, to be sure, and those doctors still couldn't see anything."

Ray Von stood and took their dirty plates to the sink before she continued. "Some, they can tell when they're born. But others, they don't find out until they're older, and then the heart is so damaged that they need a new one. I'm thinking Miss Monica didn't get her new one in time."

I thought of the last year of Monica's life, of how weak and frail she'd become, of the wait for a new heart. Of how she'd gone to sleep one afternoon and never woke up. But Monica had known long before that, I could see now. She had known and not told me until she couldn't hide it anymore.

Glancing at the wrapped package, I was struck by a thought. "How did you know my name?"

A thin eyebrow went up. "Miss Monica sent it to me with a note. She said the package was for Julie Holt and asked me to hold on to it until you could come and pick it up."

Laughter shouted at us from the television in the other room. "When did she send it?"

Ray Von turned to face me, her back against the sink, her head bobbing in her effort to hold it up high despite her hunched shoulders. "This past February. I hadn't heard one word from that girl for ten years, and then this package arrives with a note that I'm not to open it, and that Julie Holt might come by sometime to pick it up."

I slid my chair back. "Can I see what it is?"

Without answering, Ray Von moved to Beau's chair, where his head had fallen back in sleep, his mouth slightly open. Gently, she smoothed the hair from his forehead. "I loved his granddaddy like he was my own, and then his mama and her brother, too. Hardheaded people, but I loved them. Especially Miss Monica, who was more hardheaded than the rest. She had a sense of right and wrong that would have put a saint to shame. She didn't give a second chance to anybody who didn't live up to her high moral standards." She picked up my glass and moved to the watercooler to refill it. "Especially to those she loved the most."

She kept her back to me for a moment, as if trying to decide whether to tell me anything more, then turned around and placed the tumbler on the table before sitting.

I closed my eyes, trying to corral all the questions that were flitting through my mind, too many to count. "Monica told me stories about her family. About you. They were all happy stories, good memories. They helped me forget. . . ." I shook my head, not wanting to veer down the old path. "But she never told me why she left and never came back. Or why she broke off contact from everyone."

Ray Von was silent for a moment, and I waited, hoping for an answer that would at least explain why I'd driven so far to find something that no longer existed. Instead, Ray Von said, "She used to paint. At first it was just the Guidrys' house here, and the beach and the lighthouse. And then she started painting people—anybody who'd sit still long enough for her. Don't know what happened to all those paintings."

I swallowed, remembering all the landscapes and portraits Monica had painted from memory, like illustrations for her stories. "I think she was on the verge of breaking out. She was scheduled for a big show at a major gallery in New York when she got sick. They had to cancel it." I took a sip of water, needing to wash down the loss that clung to the back of my throat. "We both loved art. That's how we met, actually, at an exhibit of early-twentieth-century American portraitists. My great-grandfather, Abe Holt, was one of the featured artists, and he was one of Monica's favorites." Smiling at the memory, I continued. "I was on an awful blind date, and she came up and spilled her drink on him." A small laugh burbled in my throat. "She reminded me so much of my little sister, so petite that her clothes hung on her. I sort of adopted her right then, because she looked like somebody needed to take care of her."

"And the boy? Where is his daddy?"

I paused. "Monica didn't know. The relationship was . . . temporary. He wasn't a part of her life." I clasped my hands tightly in front of me but managed to meet Ray Von's eyes. "Why did she leave? She convinced me to drive all the way down here just from the stories she told me about this place. About her family. But she never told me why she left them."

Ray Von looked away, her eyes shadowed again. "I can't tell you that, because I don't know."

I stared at the older woman, not sure whether I believed her. Finally, I nodded, realizing I wouldn't get another answer. I felt close to tears again, having traveled so many miles, yet arriving no closer to my destination than when I'd left.

"Monica left me her house here, in Biloxi, and guardianship of Beau. I'm not really sure why, because I know she has family. And the house . . ." I stopped, not wanting to revisit it even in my mind. "I guess Hurricane Kat—"

Ray Von held her finger to her lips and shook her head. "We don't say her name out loud around here. Not ever."

I nodded. Even five years later, the hurricane's reminders were everywhere. "I thought that I could just move in with Beau, find a job, and live happily ever after." I pressed my hand over my mouth. The exhaustion of the last months pushed at my head and heart, my isolation suddenly intolerable. Monica had gone to confession every week, and for the first time I could understand why.

I looked up, recalling the Ray Von of Monica's stories, the Ray Von who listened without judgment, and I could no longer hold back the need to unburden myself. "I've never done anything so unplanned or reckless in my life. And I've got this little boy to think of now, and I've brought him here to where we don't even have a bed to sleep in. How could I be so irresponsible?" I bit my lip, wishing now I'd said nothing.

Ray Von leaned toward me, her accent thickening as her diction dropped. "You ain't dead yet, so you ain't done." She stood and retrieved the brown-paper-wrapped package, struggling slightly from the weight of it. I somehow knew that Ray Von would resist any assistance and remained seated. "Don't you go opening it here, now. Miss Monica didn't want me to see it, and I don't want to stir up spirits." She indicated Beau, whose eyes were now open but bleary as he looked around the kitchen as if wondering how he'd gotten there. I almost laughed, thinking that I must have the same look.

The old woman placed the package in front of me. "You got family around here?"

I shook my head, unable to find brief words that would explain my family or why I'd been so eager to adopt Monica—a girl as lost as I was.

"Then you need to take this boy to New Orleans to see his great-grandma Aimee. She'll know what to do."

My finger plucked at the edges of the packing tape, and I recognized the delicate handwriting on the front of the package. "But there had to be a reason why Monica didn't tell them about Beau. What if she didn't want me to take him there? She sent me here, to Biloxi, not New Orleans."

Ray Von leaned closer, her eyes darkening. "Are you going to take that boy and go sleep on an empty lot? Monica's boy needs more than that. You take him home first, then figure out what to do after."

I sat still, listening to dim voices from the television in the other room, and knew I had run out of choices. "I don't have an address."

Her white teeth showed as Ray Von straightened. "Fifteen Twenty First Street. In the Garden District. The pink Victorian with the beautiful garden with the statue."

I took a deep breath, then stood. "Thank you. For the food. For this." I indicated the package. "For the advice. Monica always spoke fondly of you, so I figure you wouldn't tell me wrong."

Ray Von didn't smile. "She left me behind just like she did everybody else. I'm thinking about that boy. He doesn't deserve to be cut off from his family."

I frowned. "Will it be okay with them that, well, that . . ." I wasn't sure how to continue.

"That he doesn't have a daddy? There's some who might care, but not Miss Aimee. She'll love him like he was a prince just because Miss Monica was his mama."

I lifted Beau from the chair, my back feeling the strain. "I'm glad to hear that." Ray Von leaned over to pick up the package, but I stopped her. "Please don't. You've done enough for me already. Let me go put Beau in the car, and I'll be right back to get it."

It looked at first as if the old woman would refuse, but then she jutted out her chin instead and nodded. When I returned, Ray Von was in the living room watching another soap opera, the absence of any type of photos or family memorabilia oddly unsettling. I walked past her toward the kitchen to retrieve the package, feeling the solid wood of a frame beneath the paper. I hesitated for a moment inside the doorway. "Thanks again, Ray Von. I appreciate all of your help."

Ray Von didn't raise her gaze from the television, where a blond woman with heavy lip gloss was starting to cry.

"One last thing," I said. She didn't lift her head. "I was wondering if you had the deed to the Biloxi house. If Monica might have sent it to you with the package. She only gave the lawyer the keys."

"I gave you everything I had." She lifted a remote control and raised the volume. "You can close the door behind you on your way out."

Knowing there was nothing else to say, I juggled my load to grab hold of the door handle, then pulled it shut. The black cat that had greeted us on our arrival sat waiting by one of the flowerpots with his tail waving languidly, standing sentry to make sure we left.

Turning my back on the cat, I slid the package into the back of the van, then pulled out of Ray Von's driveway, eager to get away from the odd little house and even odder woman. Remembering the directions to what remained of the beach house, I returned to the street running along the side of it, unable to bring myself to pull into the drive again. Leaving the car running and the air-conditioning on, I slid into the backseat next to Beau and lifted the package onto my lap.

Carefully, I slid a finger under a flap and gently ripped the tape and unfolded the sealed flap at the top. Peering inside, I could make out the top of a thick gilded frame, but nothing else. Placing it on my lap, I continued gently prying off tape and unfolding paper until it was completely unwrapped. I found myself staring at the back of a framed canvas. The whole thing was no more than fifteen inches by eighteen, but it suddenly felt incredibly heavy in my lap. Gingerly, I grasped the edges of the frame and turned it over.

I stared at the portrait, not comprehending exactly what I was looking at, realizing that I'd been expecting to find a painting of the beach house as Monica had remembered it, instead of the ruin it was now. I tamped down my disappointment as I stared instead at the portrait of a beautiful woman with black hair and blue eyes, creamy skin, and a Mona Lisa smile. It showed the woman only from the waist up, but it was clear that she wore some type of ball gown, the material shimmery and midnight blue, an incredible necklace at her long, elegant throat, and earrings of sapphires and diamonds at her ears. Even more remarkable was the stunning brooch of what looked like emeralds and dark green enamel in the shape of an alligator, its tail in an exaggerated point and the eyes glittering red jewels.

It was a striking portrait that seemed to capture the essence of the unknown woman, made her seem alive with active thoughts as her half smile, half smirk regarded me from the canvas. There was something else there, too, something familiar to me that I couldn't quite place. I tried harder, trying to harness the stray thought that wouldn't stop flinging its way through my head like a fish thrown on dry land. And then my gaze came to rest on the artist's signature.

Lifting the frame higher to see it better in the light from the window, I squinted at the florid signature in red paint, not to see it better—my eyesight was perfect—but because I was sure there was some mistake.

"Julie, I'm thirsty."

The voice seemed to come from very far away as I lowered the painting back down to my lap and looked at the little boy sitting next to me, not really seeing him.

Abe Holt. The bright red lines of my great-grandfather's well-known signature danced in my peripheral vision. Abe Holt.

I knew from my experience at the auction house that the painting, assuming it was an authentic Abe Holt, would be worth a considerable amount of money. But why did Monica have it? Monica was always broke; surely she would have sold it at some point. Like when she and Beau were evicted from their apartment for failure to pay their rent. And why would she have left it to me? Monica knew of my family connection to the artist; surely she would have told me about its existence. Unless there was a reason she couldn't.

Slowly, I began to wrap the painting again, even more careful now that I understood its monetary value. Why? The one word continued to reverberate through my head. I slid the painting carefully under the front seat, then gave Beau a juice box.

"I want to go home."

I brushed Beau's dark blond hair from his forehead. "I know, sweetie. Me, too. But we're not done with our adventure yet, okay? But soon."

Not able to stand to see his look of disappointment, I slid up front to the driver's seat and flipped on the GPS. Very carefully, I input the New Orleans address Ray Von had given me. One and a half hours to my destination. After putting the car in drive, I pulled forward onto the road, heading once more to a place foreign to me and away from a past I was beginning to discover didn't want to be left behind.

CHAPTER 3

Come rain or high water, there's no place like home.
—Krewe of Muses Mardi Gras Float, 2006

An old police detective once told me that it wasn't the mountain ahead that wears you out, but the grain of sand in your shoe. I'd thought at the time that I understood what he meant, but soon came to realize that I hadn't, not really. Because the grain of sand is different for everybody, and some people can never figure out what it is.

I wasn't sure if it was the sight of the demolished beach house, or the still-visible signs of Katrina's passage as I neared New Orleans, and the gleaming roof of the Superdome visible from the highway, that made me remember those words, but I found myself reaching for my cell phone and punching in the familiar numbers.

"Detective Kobylt."

I could hear the sounds of other phones ringing and people talking in the background, the familiarity of it doing nothing to quell the sick panic I felt every time I heard it. The first time, I'd been twelve years old and I'd walked into the police station to tell somebody that I couldn't find my little sister.

"Hello, Detective. It's Julie Holt."

There was a brief pause. "Hello, Julie. We haven't heard from you in a while."

"I know. I've had some . . . changes. I'm not in New York anymore, at least not right now. I'm traveling, actually, which is why I called. I wanted to make sure that if you needed to reach me you wouldn't use my landline, because it's been disconnected. You still have my cell number, right?"

I heard him breathe out before he answered. "Yes, Julie. I know we do. I'll make sure that I make a note in the file about your old number."

"Thank you." I pressed on the brake as a rusted-out brown sedan, even older than my own vehicle, changed lanes by swerving in front of me without a signal. "I was wondering if you followed up on that article I sent you. The one about the girl abducted in Worcester. It's not that far from my hometown, and the girl was the same age as Chelsea."

"I did. The guy in Worcester was in prison when Chelsea was taken, so his alibi's pretty tight."

"Oh." I nodded into the phone. "It's just, well, I thought you'd call to let me know."

Detective Kobylt's voice sounded tired. "Look, Julie, I've got other cases I'm working on. That doesn't mean that I'm not keeping Chelsea's case active—because I am. It's just that I don't have time to call you with every dead end. I know Detective Johnson did before his retirement and my being assigned to your sister's case. But things are different now. They've combined departments and doubled my workload. But I haven't forgotten you. Or Chelsea. I promise to be in touch if there's anything new."

"I know. I'm sorry. It's just, well, it's been a while."

"It's okay. Look, I've got to go."

"All right. Thanks for talking to me."

"It's my job. And, Julie?"

"Yes?"

"Keep sending me information. You never know what I might have missed or what might turn out to be a lead."

I smiled into the phone. "Thanks, I will. Bye." I clicked off the phone, then turned off the highway and followed signs to St. Charles Avenue. For a few blocks I drove parallel to a streetcar with open windows and passengers with bored expressions. A tourist leaned out of a window to take a picture, then ducked quickly back inside to avoid getting hit by a light pole.

The houses and businesses here were more intact than what I'd seen from the neighborhoods visible from the highway on my approach to the city, but I found myself swerving to avoid enormous potholes in the road, making Beau giggle from the backseat. I made another exaggerated swerve just to hear him laugh again.

The commercial buildings gave way to grander houses as I traveled into the residential area of the Garden District. I took a left on First Street, crossing the streetcar tracks on the grassy median and the opposing lane of traffic, and nearly missed being clipped by a Jeep Cherokee with New York plates and a Tulane window sticker. Despite the cooler temperature, I found myself sweating. Four years in Manhattan without a car had left me out of practice for the evasive maneuvers required for city driving.

The canopy of large oaks on St. Charles gave way to gated gardens of flowering trees and shrubs, none of which I recognized, decorating the mansions behind them like frilly aprons. I slowed to take it all in, accepting that my knowledge of New Orleans had consisted mostly of what I'd seen of Hurricane Katrina news footage and Monica's references to Mardi Gras parties and her years spent at Sacred Heart. But none of that had prepared me for the fantasy of it. I couldn't think of another word that would adequately describe the exotic, historic otherworldliness of what I was seeing.

A car honked behind me, and I realized I'd stopped completely in the middle of the one-way street. I pulled ahead, searching for the house number, then slid into an open spot at the curb as I approached the right block. Iron gates in rose patterns and fleur-de-lis tops separated the gardens from the cracked and uneven sidewalks, roots of nearby oaks showing their impatience with human encroachment by pressing against the flagstone and brick pavers.

I rolled the window down a few inches and breathed in, smelling air that was green, moist, and fragrant. For the first time in my life, I wished I could paint, or draw, or somehow capture this street with its marred roads and walkways, the pristine houses with their eccentric gardens of overabundant flowers and foliage. Chelsea could have. Chelsea would have known how to translate all of it onto paper or canvas.

Glancing across the street, I spotted the chipped blue tile numbers embedded in the sidewalk: 1520. I should have recognized the house from Ray Von's description of the pink Victorian with the beautiful garden, but I'd been too busy gawking at its neighbors to notice. Wide front steps led up to a gracious front wraparound porch dotted with wicker rocking chairs and more plants hanging from the porch ceiling. Matching turrets framed the front of the house like parentheses, giving it the dubious impression of a castle. Large double wooden doors sat in the middle, long rectangular windows in each polished door like drooping eyes staring warily at the encroaching garden.

Switching off the ignition, I turned to look at Beau, who'd fallen asleep with his thumb in his mouth and his mother's hat balled into a pillow for his cheek. Wanting to assess the situation first, I decided to let him sleep for another minute. Carefully, I cracked the windows, then opened the door and locked it quietly, not wanting to wake him. Checking for traffic, I crossed the street to the house and stopped. Monica had never painted this house for me, and for that I was grateful. Because if I'd known what to expect beforehand there was no way I'd have found the courage to park in front of the house and expect to walk up to the door and knock.

It wasn't just the grandness that I found imposing. It was intimidating, yes—but I had interacted with wealthy investors many times in the art auction business. But the news I carried with me, of the death of an absent granddaughter and the existence of a great-grandson, made me pause on the sidewalk outside the gate. A fountain tinkled softly in the middle of the brick walkway, soothing my jittery nerves.

A sound brought my attention to the front garden. A man wearing faded overalls and a straw hat squatted in front of a flower bed, pulling out dried and withered flower stems. He wore no gardening gloves, and the skin on his arms and hands was caramel brown.

As if sensing he was being watched, the man turned to face me. The first thing that struck me was that he was a lot older than I'd thought. And then it occurred to me that I was staring, and he was staring back at me—his one good eye a piercing green. The other eye was invisible beneath the scarred and mottled skin of his eyelid that seemed to melt into the disfigured skin of his cheek.

Unsettled, I lifted a hand in greeting, then stepped back off of the sidewalk before turning and jumping back into the van. From the corner of my eye, I watched the man return to his gardening as I rolled the windows up and started the ignition.

I looked in the backseat and found Beau watching me quietly as he sucked softly on his thumb. He was too old to be doing that, but he'd lost so much recently that I wasn't about to make him stop now.

"I want to go home," he said around his thumb.

If only I knew where that was. For about the millionth time I wondered how I got here, how the meticulous Julie with all her organized plans had become this woman whose only home seemed to be an old van and whose prospects for upgrading her current position were slim.

"We're going to a hotel tonight. Won't that be fun?"

Beau kept sucking his thumb without speaking, his silence incriminating. Moving my gaze back to the GPS, I punched the button for "nearby places" in search of a hotel. There were several bed-and-breakfasts in the Garden District, but I felt the need to be farther away from the house on First Street, and away from the piercing gaze of the man with the ruined face and clear green eye.

After selecting a middle-of-the-road chain hotel with a name I recognized, I headed back the way I'd come on St. Charles Avenue, toward the downtown area. I navigated around large potholes as I made the loop around Lee Circle and the statue of General Lee. Monica had once told me that the Confederate general's statue faced perpetually northward because he had once said that he would never turn his back on the North again.

The houses gave way to businesses as I crossed the two main thoroughfares of the central business district, Poydras and Canal Street, then turned onto the famed Bourbon Street and entered the French Quarter. I drove slowly, not wanting to hit pedestrians, who not only seemed to think they could cross the streets anywhere with impunity, but who also seemed to move unhurriedly, their movements soft and liquid and so different from Manhattan pedestrians'. A brass quartet played jazz on the corner of Bourbon and Iberville, a trombone box in front of them with a spattering of coins in the bottom, the music like a sound track to my strange and new adventure.

I turned right onto Royal Street and found the valet parking for my car. As they loaded up a baggage cart, I had Beau hold on to my belt with one hand while I clutched the wrapped painting in my arms. I glanced around, trying to get my bearings and find the T.G.I. Friday's I'd spotted on the drive in. Beau loved the chicken fingers, and I figured he deserved some kind of treat after being stuck in a van for more than two days with only me and my pathetic attempts at making believe that everything was going to be all right.

My gaze paused on the storefront across the street, a wall of windows with framed art lit with expert spotlighting. Even though I'd never been to New Orleans, I knew of Royal Street, with its array of world-renowned antique stores and art galleries. This particular store, Mayer & Ryan, seemed to be a mixture of both. Feeling the weight of the painting in my arms, I turned my back on the store and entered the hotel.

Our room was small but clean, the room rate reasonable. Still, with my limited finances, I'd have to figure out pretty quickly what to do next. After tucking the portrait under the clothes in my suitcase, I took a smiling Beau, and his mother's hat, to T.G.I. Friday's, where we both had chicken fingers, then returned to the hotel and went to bed early.

Beau fell asleep immediately, but despite my own exhaustion, my eyelids seemed to be held open by springs. I tossed and turned, the glaring numbers on the bedside clock mocking me as they marched forward.

Eventually, I climbed from the bed and moved a chair to the low window. Pulling the curtains aside, I could see into Royal Street, not completely deserted even at this late hour. It was comforting to me, reminding me of my apartment in New York, and the busyness of a city that never slept. It made me feel in solidarity with all those souls down on the pavement, awake like me, avoiding the dark that chased their nighttime dreams.

I pulled the painting from my suitcase and unwrapped it, then returned to the chair near the window. The dim glow of the streetlights cast shadows on the portrait, erasing all of the features of the woman except for the glittering jewels of the alligator brooch and the piercing blue eyes. The woman seemed to be watching me, taunting me about my indecisiveness.

Leaning the portrait against the chair legs, I rested my elbows on the windowsill and pressed my forehead against the cool glass. The windows of Mayer & Ryan were still lit, the gilt-framed paintings and dark wood furniture glowing like a mirage.

I knew I had choices to make, decisions about my future. Beau's future. About money, and a job, and the ruined River Song. But before I could make any decisions, I had to figure out what I wanted. And that was the real problem. Since the age of twelve there had been only one thing I'd wanted, one thing I'd prayed for daily, one thing I'd ever allowed myself to hope for. I'd been afraid that a different want would make my desire to find Chelsea less powerful, would fling me in the wrong direction entirely.

Everything I'd done or accomplished in the past seventeen years had been accidental and circumstantial. From choosing a college to starting my career, it had all been happenstance, because I never allowed myself to want.

I looked down at the portrait, toward the lower right-hand corner, where I knew my great-grandfather's sprawling signature was splashed against the canvas. If I could sell it, the proceeds would mean security, more time to allow the right opportunity to show itself, money to support myself and Beau for a period of time. As I carefully wrapped the painting again, I thought of Monica, dead at the incomprehensible age of twenty-eight, and tried to think of why she'd left me the painting.

If I had been more settled in my life, with a home I owned and someone permanent to share my life, I could imagine that Monica had wanted me to hold on to it: an investment piece and a part of my family's history rolled into one. Something with which to impress dinner guests.

But I had none of those things. Even Beau's presence in my life was temporary, I realized now. Despite whatever had driven Monica away from her family and home, her directions for her son's guardianship and her gift to me of River Song—such as it was—must have been an indication that she wanted Beau here, in the South. And the portrait was perhaps a temporary means of support.

For me, though, there was no such sanctuary. I'd never allowed myself to hope that there was one: a sanctuary from my endless searching for something that seemed to be growing less and less obtainable.

I stood and tucked the painting back in my suitcase, feeling more settled now that I'd made my decision, confident with relative certainty that I'd reached the same conclusion Monica had when she'd decided to leave the painting to me.

My mind made up, I returned to bed, hoping to find a few hours of sleep before Beau awoke. I lay down in the bed next to his, facing him, and fell asleep listening to the occasional rasp of his finger worrying a hole in his mother's red hat.

★   ★   ★

At ten o'clock the next morning, I took Beau and the painting across the street and an hour and a half later emerged with a written contract to sell the painting on commission. The negotiations with one of the owners, Nancy Mayer, had been straightforward once she realized that I was knowledgeable not only about the painting and its artist, but also about its value. Ms. Mayer had been guarded about offering assurances of when she thought it might sell, citing the economy and the shrinking number of tourists, but I had seen the excitement in her eyes when she told me that she had a number of long-term clients who might be interested in it. She'd also promised to place it in the front window, as the colors were eye-catching, the alligator brooch something that would attract locals and tourists alike.

As we stood on the sidewalk facing our hotel, I considered getting into the van and driving back to the pink Victorian on First Street to confront Aimee Guidry with news she wouldn't want to hear. But I hesitated, feeling Beau's soft hand in mine as we stood on the sidewalk waiting to cross the street. For some reason, Monica had made me Beau's guardian, his protector. The irony of it was hard to escape. And as unprepared for the job as I believed myself to be, I wanted to find out who these Guidrys were before introducing Beau.

I knew the Guidrys from Monica's stories: their names, their hobbies, their favorite foods, their pasts. But I didn't know what they'd done to make Monica leave, to force her out on her own at the age of eighteen. Monica had spent the next ten years of her life re-creating the good parts of her past with stories and pictures, but none had ever explained the unforgivable. Despite what Ray Von had told me, that one unexplained reason was reason enough to be cautious where Beau was concerned.

We headed into the hotel and to the business office with the computer for the use of the hotel's guests. I did a Google search for the name of an hourly day-care chain that Monica had used in emergencies in New York. It wasn't cheap, but it was safe, and, I was relieved to note, they had one on Magazine Street, not too far from First Street.

After I filled out all the necessary paperwork and got reassurances that he wouldn't be separated from his hat, Beau made a tearful good-bye. I promised I'd make it up to him. Somehow.

I drove around the Garden District for curiosity's sake as much as an admitted desire to procrastinate. Grand mansions sat before cracked sidewalks, Greek Revivals posed comfortably next to Italianate villas and Queen Anne Victorians. I lost myself in the grid of one-way streets, ending up on Washington Street by a cemetery with raised tombs that called to mind a city for the dead.

Slowly, I meandered my way back to First Street and slid the van into the same spot on the curb where I'd parked the previous day. I sat inside it for several minutes, the sun through the windows warm on my skin, and stared at the house across the street. After taking a deep breath, I exited the van, smoothing down my blouse and skirt in the hopes I'd be found presentable. Beau had told me that I looked nice, but he was five.

Pausing at the garden gate, I peered inside to the yard, relieved to find it empty except for the fountain and the statue of a little boy. The handle turned easily, the gate swinging open without protest, as if daring me to find another reason not to go farther. After carefully closing the gate behind me, I stood in the quiet garden, marveling again at the riot of color in pots and flower beds, and listened as a car passed by on the street behind me.

Climbing the porch steps, I imagined I could feel the weight of the air, leaden and moist and carrying with it too many memories that weren't my own. A crescendo of insect sounds shouted out from the short hedge that lined the walk, but I was unable to translate what they were trying to tell me.

I spotted a doorbell set in an ornate brass plate and raised my hand, then paused. What would I say? *Hello, I'm your long-lost granddaughter's friend. She's dead, but I have her little boy with me because she made me his guardian. I know he belongs with you and not me, but I don't know what kind of people you are. And I don't really know if I can part with him.*

This last part came as a surprise to me. I loved Beau, but I'd never thought of him as mine. I collected things: teacups, spoons, sewing machines like the one my mother had once used—all now boxed up in a storage unit in New Jersey. But I'd never wanted them enough to be unable to part with them. I imagined that, subconsciously, it had been a deliberate thing. But with Beau I could sense the rending rip, like tearing fabric, that would accompany his leaving.

My hand dropped to my side, and I found myself staring at the polished wood of the door, wondering absently how many times it had to be refinished in this climate to keep it that way. I wasn't sure how long I stood there, listening to the relentless rhythm of a thousand invisible insect wings, filling my head with so much noise that I couldn't think straight. Taking a step back, I turned and moved to the bottom of the porch steps before stopping again. I needed more time. Beau needed more time. One more day. One more day of sparing the Guidry family, of fooling myself into believing they were better off not knowing. Because I knew, from my own long years of searching, that I'd give anything to just know.

I'd nearly reached the garden gate when I heard the front door open behind me. I put my hand on the knob and turned it, irrationally hoping that I hadn't yet been spotted, already envisioning myself running across the street to the van.

"Can I help you?"

The voice was male, startling me. I'd imagined, somehow, that Aimee Guidry lived alone. Slowly I turned and stared at the man in front of me. He was about my age, and he was looking back at me with the same curious expression I imagined was displayed on my own face. He carried a cup of steaming coffee and had a rolled-up newspaper under his arm. He wore a dress shirt tucked into trousers, an undone tie draped over his shoulders, and dark loafers. But his hair was a light sandy brown streaked by the sun, and his eyes were an unusual greenish blue. Like Beau's. Like Monica's.

I knew his name was Wesley John Guidry III but that he was called

Trey, that he loved jazz music and had played the trumpet as a teenager but had never been that good at it. He loved fishing and domestic beer, and had gone to Tulane for undergrad. He was a whiz at chess, hated losing, loved to hide insects and small reptiles where they'd be discovered unexpectedly. And he was Monica's older brother.

I froze, holding back all the things I wanted to say. *Did you miss her? Did you ever look for her?* And then, *Why did you make her leave?* Unexpectedly, I said, "No. I'm sorry. I just realized I'm at the wrong house."

"I know all the neighbors. If you give me a last name, I can tell you which house is theirs."

I opened the gate, my hand trembling, not at all sure why I'd lost my courage. Maybe because, as I'd stood staring at the door, I'd imagined them taking Beau and my never seeing him again. "Never mind. I'll find it." The gate shut loudly behind me as I hurried to the van and got in. Keeping my gaze averted from the pink house, I started the engine and pulled into the street. With a final glance, I noticed that the front door had closed, and that the old man I'd seen the previous day now stood at the corner of the ornate fence, watching me from his ruined face, his single-eyed gaze following me as I drove down the street.

CHAPTER 4

When you lose your sails, row. —ROMAN PROVERB

A shaft of light filtered from the maple tree in the side yard of my childhood home, landing on the grass between Chelsea and me, restless as it lifted itself again in the early autumn wind. I watched as it skittered across the lawn and into the sandbox we were too old for, yet which remained where it sat under the redwood deck, collecting leaves and shovels and Barbie heads—the detritus of a happy childhood.

Chelsea pointed to a cloud high above, its whiteness fierce against the dark blue of the sky, its sides layered and angular. "It looks like a man holding a baby, doesn't it?"

I stared hard. "No. It looks like a cloud."

"See—there's his face." Chelsea pointed, but I still didn't see. I never did. "He's wearing one of those old-timey hats and a long coat. The baby's head is on his shoulder."

I sat up, frustrated. Chelsea had always seemed to live in a different world: a better, more colorful one. I saw black and white where Chelsea saw rainbows. "It's just a dumb cloud." I stood, then headed for the house, tired of the stupid game. "I'm going inside."

Chelsea turned her head, blocking the sun with her hand. "Mom said you were supposed to watch me."

"Then come inside. I want to watch TV."

Chelsea returned to studying the clouds. "But it's so nice outside. And it's going to be turning cold soon and we won't be able to."

I hesitated, looking upward again, trying to see anything besides condensed water droplets. I knew that was all clouds were, because I'd learned it in my earth science class. But I'd never been able to convince Chelsea: Chelsea with her wild imagination where nothing was really as it seemed. I stared hard again, but saw only sky.

"I'm going inside," I said, walking away and not waiting to see whether Chelsea followed.

But my feet seemed suddenly mired in mud, each step harder than the last, my legs unable to lift my feet high enough to move forward. I heard a telephone ringing somewhere and I turned to look at Chelsea, to ask her whether she'd heard it too, but Chelsea was gone, the grass where she'd been now moving silently in the wind. And still, the sound of the telephone ringing and ringing.

I sat up in my hotel bed, my eyes wide, my nightshirt sticking to my back, the ever-present feeling of having lost something important—a hand, or a foot—the feeling that it was still there, but every time I reached for it, I grabbed only air.

Sun streamed in between the curtains, brightening the room with daylight. I fumbled on the nightstand for my cell phone, glancing at the clock that read eight thirty. I blinked my eyes, wondering how I could have slept so late, then remembered I hadn't fallen asleep until after the last time I'd looked at the clock at four. I sat up as the phone vibrated in my hand, then glanced toward the next bed to find Beau watching me, his blue-green eyes reflective as he sucked his thumb and scratched at the pilled red hat.

I smiled at him, then felt the familiar quickening of my heart, realizing that the only person who would be calling my cell number would be Detective Kobylt. My trepidation changed to curiosity as I looked at the phone and recognized the 504 New Orleans area code.

"Hello?"

"Is this Julie Holt? This is Nancy Mayer from Mayer and Ryan. I apologize for calling so early, but I have some very exciting news that couldn't wait."

It took a few moments for me to become fully awake. Finally, I managed, "Exciting news?"

"Yes. We have a strong interest in the Abe Holt painting you brought in yesterday. I knew putting it in the window would do the trick." I could hear the woman's smile in her words, but there was something else in her tone, too. I didn't have to wait long before I figured out why.

"There's a small catch, however."

I held my breath. "Yes?"

"She'd like to meet with you first to discuss the portrait. I don't think this will be a hard sell, and you're even more knowledgeable than I am about the painting, so I'm sure this is just a formality. But the woman is an old and frequent customer of ours, so I was hoping you'd be agreeable to a meeting."

I watched Beau, his finger now protruding through the first hole he'd made in the hat, and who was now busily scratching through another. "Yes. Sure. I can do that. When?"

There was a brief pause, making me squirm. "Actually, she's here now and would like to meet with you as soon as possible. I know you're staying across the street from the store. Would you be able to be here in fifteen minutes?"

I glanced at the clock, then back at Beau. "She's there now?"

A small, tinkling laugh came through the phone. "As I said, Mrs. Guidry is a longtime customer and friend. She called me at home last night, too late to call you, and asked me to set this up as early as possible."

My hand froze on the phone. "Mrs. Guidry?"

"Yes. She's from an old New Orleans family, so you might recognize the name. She's apparently quite the fan of Mr. Holt and is intrigued by your family connection to the artist."

"She's there now? In your store?"

"Yes. Can you be here in fifteen minutes?"

I forced my voice to stay calm, my gaze resting on Beau as I spoke. "Can she come here to the hotel lobby instead?"

After only the briefest of pauses, Nancy Mayer said, "I'm sure that won't be a problem."

"Great. Then give me twenty, and I'll meet her downstairs at the front desk."

We said good-bye, and I hung up, my thoughts spiraling, the questions reverberating around my brain. As if on autopilot, I quickly washed my face and brushed my teeth, then threw on the same clothes I'd worn the previous day, because they were still hanging on a chair back.

I dug in my purse and found a candy bar I'd bought in New York before we left, and handed it to Beau. "You get to have chocolate for breakfast. How great is that?"

Beau's face brightened as he looked up at me, a rare smile showing a missing lower front tooth. I rumpled his hair, making a note to myself to make sure that his lunch would be healthy. Kneeling in front of him, I said, "Beau, I need to go downstairs for a few moments to talk with somebody, but I need you to stay here by yourself. Is that all right?"

His smile faded and his thumb found its way to his mouth. Beau slowly nodded.

"Good." I wrote my cell phone number down in large numbers on the bedside notepad and tucked it next to the phone. "I'll have my phone on, so if you need anything I want you to call me, all right? You have to push the number nine first, so just punch in all the numbers on the phone just like I've written them." I waited for him to study the numbers and the paper before returning his attention to me. "I'll turn on some cartoons for you to watch, and I want you to sit on your bed and eat your candy bar until I get back. If somebody knocks on the door, do not answer it. I'll put a sign on the door so the cleaning people won't open it. But you stay put until I come back; do you understand? And I promise that I won't be gone long."

"Okay, Julie," he said, then returned to sucking hard on his thumb. I watched him sitting there in his SpongeBob pajamas, his mother's red hat pressed against his face. I didn't feel right about leaving him, but he'd never been a defiant child, even as a toddler. He'd always seemed content to listen to his mother. Besides, I convinced myself, the greater danger could be waiting for him downstairs.

Touching his cheek, I said, "Thanks for being a big boy. I promise you that things will get better." *Because they can't get any worse.* Standing, I tousled his hair again, then flipped on the television to Nickelodeon. Putting my purse on my shoulder and tucking the room key in the outside pocket, I kissed his forehead then placed the Do Not Disturb sign on the outside doorknob as I pulled it closed behind me.

My palms were sweaty as the elevator descended much more slowly than I remembered. It opened on the lobby floor and had almost closed again before I could make myself move forward.

I would have recognized Aimee Guidry even without knowing her name from the pictures Monica had made from her stories, her words the flesh and bones of the people who came to live in my head. Mrs. Guidry was what had once been called a handsome woman, with strong features and a wide forehead. I imagined she'd been beautiful when she was younger, her once red hair now faded to a muted yellow, her fair skin now covered with a web of fine wrinkles. But her corn-flower blue eyes were sharp and clear, the one hand visible sitting on top of her cane strong and capable, the cane the only nod toward her seventy-two years.

My tentative smile faded completely as the man standing next to Mrs. Guidry with his back toward me turned around. His face registered the same surprise I felt.

"You?" he said, his voice harsh.

I was unprepared with a response and stood there silently, wondering why I was hoping he wouldn't notice that I was wearing the same clothes he'd seen me in the day before.

Ignoring her grandson, Aimee Guidry held out her free hand. "You must be Julie Holt. I'm Aimee Guidry, and this is my grandson, Trey Guidry."

I took her hand and she squeezed gently, her skin like polished paper. Trey kept his hands at his sides, and I made no mention that I knew exactly who they were.

"I hope you don't mind my bringing someone else along, but I can't drive myself anymore, and Trey offered to bring me." She indicated a sofa and two chairs on the other end of the lobby by the front door. "Shall we?"

I nodded and allowed Mrs. Guidry, with her free hand tucked into the crook of Trey's elbow, to lead me to the seating area.

After Mrs. Guidry and Trey settled themselves on the couch, and I sat in one of the chairs, Mrs. Guidry leaned forward, preparing to speak, but Trey stilled her with a hand on her arm.

"Where did you get that painting? Is that why you were at our house yesterday?"

Mrs. Guidry, whose eyes were guarded but not unkind, interjected. "I was on my way back from the beauty parlor and I saw the painting in the store window. You can't imagine the surprise—"

Trey interrupted her. "Did you know the painting is stolen property?"

"What?" I made a move to stand, but Aimee held up her hand.

"Please wait." She frowned at her grandson. "I'm sorry. Trey's a lawyer, and I think he's too used to cross-examining hostile witnesses."

I settled back in my seat. "Look, I had no idea it was stolen. It was . . . given to me. By a good friend."

"By whom?" Trey sat on the edge of his seat, his hands on his thighs as if he were ready to spring.

I looked from a hopeful face to an angry one, knowing that what I was about to tell them would change them forever. I glanced toward the window that showed an outside that had turned a greenish gray, the wind blowing the hair of passersby. A storm was coming. I met their gazes again. "By Monica Guidry."

Aimee's hand clutched at Trey's. "You've seen her? Is she here?"

I shook my head. "No. I'm sorry. That's what I came to tell you yesterday. But I . . ." I couldn't continue. There was no easy way to admit to cowardice. Taking a deep breath, I said, "Monica died nearly three months ago. In New York."

Aimee let out a soft gasp as her hand went to her mouth. Trey reached for her, and she placed her face against his shoulder. I looked away, unable to witness the one thing I'd been denied all these years. "I'm sorry," I said, feeling so stupidly inadequate.

Trey's voice was thick when he spoke. "I'll need some proof. A death certificate. Something."

I nodded, then slid a business card from my purse. "This is the name of Monica's lawyer, who took care of everything. I'm sure he'll be able to get you what you need."

Aimee lifted her head, her eyes stricken. "We'll want to bring her body back, too. She needs to come home."

Trey snatched the card from my hand. "Grandmother, we don't know . . ."

She squeezed his hand, silencing him. "Thank you, Julie, for telling us."

I clasped my hands together. "But the painting. It wasn't stolen. Monica would never have taken something that didn't belong to her. And she left it to me, along with River Song."

Trey looked at me with annoyed surprise, but it was the small smile on Aimee's lips that I found more intriguing. I was about to tell them that they could verify my claims with Monica's lawyer, but stopped when I saw Trey's face go slack as he seemed to catch sight of something behind my shoulder.

I followed his gaze and spotted Beau in the middle of the lobby. He was barefoot and still wore his SpongeBob pajamas that were now smeared, along with his face, with melted chocolate. He clutched the ratty hat in his right hand, and as he realized that people were watching him, he slowly raised his thumb to his mouth, inadvertently making him look even more the orphan than he actually was.

"Beau," I said, covering the distance between us as quickly as I could. Ignoring the chocolate covering him, I lifted him into my arms. "Why did you come down here? I told you to stay in the room."

He gazed solemnly at me through thick lashes and with eyes that were disarmingly like his uncle's. "I got chocolate on me and I needed a washcloth but I couldn't reach it. So I went to find you so you could get it for me."

I closed my eyes, feeling nausea creep into my stomach, and squeezed him tighter. *Dear God.* How could I have been so stupid? "Oh, Beau. I'm glad you found me. But promise me that you'll never, never go anywhere without me again. Promise me."

He placed his palms on my cheeks, mashing the red hat against one of them. "I promise, Julie." He patted my cheeks as if trying to comfort me, and it almost made me laugh. Almost.

"Beau?"

We both turned to Trey, who'd moved to stand next to us. The boy and the man stared at each other with identical eyes, their hair almost the same shade of dark blond except that Trey's had gold streaks through his, as if he spent a lot of time outdoors.

Aimee stood and approached us. "This is Monica's boy, isn't it?" She reached up a trembling hand to touch him, but Beau buried his head in my neck.

I shifted the heavy child on my hip. "He's been through a lot lately. He's normally very outgoing."

Beau lifted his head and held out his hand, spreading all of his fingers. "I'm five," he said before sticking his head back into the crook of my neck.

The softness that had gathered around Trey's eyes and mouth as he'd studied Beau disappeared as soon as he turned back to me. "Let me guess. Monica gave Beau to you, too, along with the stolen painting and a house."

I closed my eyes, trying to keep my temper in check, if only for Beau, who'd been traumatized enough already. "Look, I didn't ask for any of it, and I'm not going to stand here and argue with you about whether what Monica did was right or wrong. Right now, I need to get Beau cleaned up and dressed, and try to figure out what to do next."

"Don't even think you're taking him out of our sight."

I didn't think I'd ever been angrier or more exhausted, or more lost. Beau stiffened in my arms, and I knew he could feel my tension. Taking a deep breath, I spoke quietly and with measured words. "I loved Monica like a sister, and I miss her every day. What I'm trying to do here is make sense of her last wishes and do the best I can. If you would stop being a lawyer for one minute, you might be able to see the situation I'm in, and that Beau is in, and give us a damned break."

Quiet clapping brought our attention to Aimee, who was trying her best to clap with her cane still clutched in one hand. "Brava, Julie. Finally someone who isn't intimidated by Trey. I'm thinking Monica made the right choice."

I resisted smiling back, still unsure who my allies were.

Aimee continued. "Please come back with us to the house so we can discuss all of this in a civilized manner." She touched my arm, her hand weightless. "Please. I loved Monica, and I've just learned that I'll never see her again." She looked at Beau. "But this is her son, and I want to get to know him. And I want him to know about his mother." Her blue eyes looked candidly at me. "Please come with us. There's so much we need to know."

Marveling once again at the inevitability that had been my life for so long, I nodded, my choices narrowed down to zero. "All right. Give me about an hour, and we'll be there. I know the address."

"Thank you." Aimee squeezed my arm, then dropped her hand.

I began walking toward the elevator. "We'll be as quick as we can."

I'd almost reached the elevator when Trey called out, "You're wrong about one thing, you know."

I turned and looked at him, my eyebrow raised in question.

"You don't own the beach house property. I have the deed and can show you."

I felt anger stir again in my chest. "What do you mean? Monica left me the keys via her lawyer, with instructions that I was to take ownership."

He shook his head. "Half of it belongs to me. Our grandfather gave it to Monica and me. To both of us."

Then why is it in ruins? I wanted to ask, but held back. Unlike him, I refused to rush to judgment, to assume things even when all evidence to the contrary seemed nonexistent.

Our eyes locked, and it seemed to me that he was goading me on, provoking me to ask the last question that still lingered, unspoken. Finally, after a long moment, I said, "Did you ever look for her?"

His eyes widened for a second, allowing me to see the same hurt and anger I saw in my own eyes every time I bothered to look in a mirror. "Every day. Not a single day has gone by since she left that I haven't searched for her."

I held his gaze for a moment longer before turning again toward the elevator, wondering what it was like to have finally found the one thing he'd been looking for. I stepped into the elevator and pushed the button for our floor, watching Monica's brother and grandmother slowly disappear as the doors shut between us.

CHAPTER 5

Storm warning: A warning of 1-minute sustained surface winds of . . . 55 mph . . . or greater, either predicted or occurring, not directly associated with tropical cyclones.
                                        —NATIONAL HURRICANE CENTER

I drove slowly, hoping my thoughts would catch up with me, and trying to remember something Monica had once told me—something about the Mississippi River having a memory of its old banks, before man tried to change her, and how every once in a while the great river tried to reclaim what was once hers.

I passed by sweeping front porches, turrets, and cast-iron balconies, all in various stages of either reconstruction or disrepair. The mixed scents of fresh wood and stagnant decay permeated the streets, a unique perfume for a city I couldn't easily define. New Orleans was a symbol of both Monica's home and her banishment, but as I drove again to the house on First Street, I could see it only as my own last chance.

It had taken me almost two hours of getting ready and procrastinating before I finally found myself parking the van once again on First Street. Trey was waiting for us in a rocking chair as we closed the garden gate and walked toward the porch. He stood, his face not completely hiding his surprise that we'd actually shown up. Slow fans turned above our heads, wafting the green and ripe smells of the garden toward us.

Trey saved his smile for Beau. "Hey, buddy. I'm Trey."

He looked at me as if waiting for my permission to say more.

I knelt in front of Beau. "He's your uncle Trey. Your mother's brother."

Beau looked confused, as I imagined anyone would look after being told for the first time that his mother even had a brother. The little boy glanced from one adult face to the other to make sure we weren't lying. Finally, he said, "Oh."

Keeping one hand in his pocket, Trey lifted his other toward the boy, hesitating just a moment before lightly tousling his hair. "Your mama loved her ice cream, and I'm betting you love it, too."

Beau dug his face into my leg, then nodded.

"Great. Because I've got some waiting for you in the kitchen. I thought you could go eat it in there while Julie and I have a little talk."

Remembering the candy bar Beau had eaten for breakfast, I said, "Actually, he needs lunch first. Something healthy."

"I can do that. But definitely ice cream, too." He winked at Beau and opened the tall, wood door, then stepped back, indicating for me and Beau to walk in ahead of him.

I was aware of polished wood floors, sparkling chandeliers, and glowing dark furniture. Halfway into the enormous foyer a grand staircase with a balcony landing rose on the right, a ten-foot gilded mirror echoing it on the opposite wall. A pair of Queen Anne chairs were ensconced in an alcove made from the curve of the stairs, and what appeared to be children's artwork was framed in elaborate gold frames on the wall inside the door, adding an unexpected warmth to the space, and doing nothing to detract from the grand paintings on the other walls. An assortment of various pottery pieces sat displayed on a hall table near the door.

Without thinking I stepped closer to get a better look, recognizing the almost iridescent glaze and impossibly thin walls of the small bowls and pitcher. "Are these George Ohr pieces?"

Trey stood next to me. "Yes. 'The Mad Potter of Biloxi.' You've heard of him?"

"Of course. He's well-known in the art world. Besides being an art history major, I worked at an auction house in New York. We had a few pieces come in from time to time. They're beautiful."

"They're not my taste, but Aimee and Monica loved his stuff and acquired these over the years."

A petite woman with completely gray hair, somewhere in her fifties, wearing a denim skirt and a T-shirt, emerged from a door in the rear of the foyer.

Trey introduced her. "This is Kathy Wolf. She takes care of my grandmother and the house. She also makes a mean pimento cheese sandwich and is very generous in her ice-cream scoops. I think she can set you up in the kitchen, Beau. How does that sound?"

"What's pimento cheese?" Beau and I asked in unison.

"Heaven on earth," Kathy answered as she held out her hand to Beau with a friendly smile.

After a reassuring nod from me, Beau allowed himself to be led to the door Kathy had come out of. I called after them, "The red hat—it's okay if he doesn't put it down, all right?"

Kathy nodded and gave me the thumbs-up sign as she led Beau through the door.

I turned to Trey. "The hat was Monica's. He hasn't let it out of his sight since she died. I'm not a child psychologist, but I think he needs it right now."

With a brief nod, he led me to a tall doorway near the bottom of the stairs and allowed me to precede him into the room. A beautiful arch framed a banquet seat and window on the left side of the room, a wood-manteled marble fireplace opposite. The tall ceiling was beamed, highlighting the floor-to-ceiling French doors that led into a side garden. Framed paintings lined the walls, and I had to restrain myself from studying each one in detail. But two over the fireplace made me pause. The children were about five or six in their portraits, each with identical sandy-colored hair and blue-green eyes full of mischief and matching half smiles.

"That's Monica and you, isn't it?"

Trey nodded, his face expressionless. "Mine was painted live, but Monica's had to be done from a photograph because she wouldn't sit still."

With a soft smile, I said, "Sounds like Monica. And the portrait of you could be Beau." Recalling the pictures in the foyer, I asked, "The artwork in the foyer—were those Monica's?"

"Yes. Aimee was always Monica's biggest fan. Even from the age of five, which is about when those paintings were done. Aimee wanted Monica to get used to having her art displayed."

I felt the hollowness again. I sat down on a cream-colored sofa that Trey indicated, wondering what he thought of the family resemblance between him and Beau, and wondering, too, if he were always so unreadable. "Where is Mrs. Guidry?"

He sat down on the sofa opposite but didn't sit back, reminding me of a lion ready to pounce. "She was exhausted after getting up so early, and then meeting Beau and hearing about Monica. I told her to lie down for a short while and that I would go get her when you arrived."

I looked back at him with a raised eyebrow. "I'm here now."

"I wanted to talk with you alone first. Clear up a few things." He raised an eyebrow that matched mine. "Don't worry. I don't bite."

I frowned, not really sure I believed him. I'd heard too many of Monica's stories of how her brother had a penchant for fistfights that got him kicked out of school more than once. And how he'd once dragged a boy to Monica's doorstep to get him to apologize to her for breaking up with her in a note left in her school locker. I felt my lip twitch at the memory, as I tried to reconcile that boy and protective brother with the stern and angry young lawyer sitting across from me. I couldn't. But I could understand why that boy from Monica's memory had changed. Searching for the missing took a toll on the ones doing the searching. I knew that from simply looking in a mirror.

The door opened, and Kathy appeared with a tray filled with a coffeepot, cups, teaspoons, cream, and sugar. I recognized the peculiar nutty smell from the coffee Monica had always made, the same coffee I had once spurned but now found myself craving.

"Thought you might want some coffee," Kathy said, placing the tray on the elegant low table that sat between the sofas. She straightened, her hands on her hips. "And that boy sure does like his pimento cheese. Let me know if you want the recipe. It was my grandma's, but recipes are meant for sharing."

"Thank you," I said.

It appeared that Kathy wasn't finished talking, but Trey was looking at her with two raised eyebrows.

"Well, then. I guess I'd better go see about Beau."

"Thank you, Kathy," Trey said as he lifted his cup to his lips and took a sip.

I cut the rich chicory coffee with cream and sugar before venturing a taste, recognizing the china as an old Haviland Limoges pattern. "Have you called Monica's lawyer yet?"

"Of course."

"So you know I'm telling the truth."

"About some things, yes." He drained his cup and set it down, the china clinking against the saucer. His fingers drummed on the tops of his legs before he stood. "How did you meet Monica?"

I told him the story I'd told Ray Von, about meeting Monica at the Abe Holt art show. "She'd been in New York for about five years by then and had started to make a name for herself."

"As Monica Armstrong." He said the name with a smirk. "I didn't know she'd changed her name until I spoke with her lawyer this afternoon."

"I didn't even know that wasn't her real name until . . . until after she got sick, and she told me."

"It made it easier for her to hide," he said softly.

"Why did she want to?" I held my coffee cup still as I waited for him to answer, the soft ticking of the clock on the mantel the only nod to time passing.

"I don't know," he said, his voice weary, as if he'd asked and answered that same question many times before, and I could almost believe that he was telling the truth.

"I need you to tell me how she died. Be as blunt as you need to be, and I'll decide how much to tell my grandmother. This has already been hard on her, and I want to spare her as much as I can."

I took another sip of coffee, the chicory aroma reminding me of Monica and the first time she'd watched me try it, and I'd wanted to spit it out. "It was her heart. A congenital heart defect she didn't discover until it was too late. She was on a transplant list. . . ." My voice trailed off as I realized I hadn't told him what he really wanted to know. "She died peacefully. In her sleep. But not alone. Monica and Beau lived with me the last year, because she couldn't pay her rent and she was so . . . weak. She needed help with Beau. I had a futon in the living room, and she and Beau had the bedroom. And one day I went in to wake her and . . ." I stopped, unable to continue. "I'm sorry." For what, I wasn't sure. Sorry that he'd lost his sister? Sorry that he'd finally found her, but found her too late? Or just sorry that it was me instead of Monica who'd made it back to New Orleans?

Carefully placing my cup on the tray, I said, "About the portrait. You said it was stolen."

"Yes. In a way it was. By Monica. It hung in the upstairs hallway for years. That's why when my grandmother saw it at Mayer and Ryan, she recognized it and called me."

"Are you saying Monica took it when she left?"

"It disappeared when she left, so it was an obvious conclusion. My grandfather, Aimee's husband, told us she must have taken it for security. As you're probably aware, it's very valuable. We'd all assumed that Monica had sold it years ago, although we couldn't find any trace of it afterward. And now we know why."

I frowned. "Not really. All we know is that she didn't sell it. And that she left it to me when she died." I looked up at Trey. "I figured that Monica left it to me for the same reason you assumed she took it. For security." I swallowed, deciding to be blunt. He was a lawyer, after all. "I need the money. For Beau." I took a deep breath, forcing myself to press on. "I've suddenly found myself unemployed and, frankly, broke. I need to know if the painting is mine to sell or not."

His blue-green eyes studied me. "What about Beau? Is he negotiable, too?"

I jerked to a stand, my knee knocking the corner of the coffee tray, making everything on it clink with indignation. "I am Beau's guardian. Not you. And I have to assume there's a reason Monica did that. I'd hoped I could allow him to get to know Monica's—his—family, while I tried to figure out what made her run so fast and so far away from you all. And until I figure that out, there's no way in hell I'm negotiating anything where Beau is concerned. If you want access to him, you'll have to go through me."

Outwardly, he appeared unruffled, but I noticed the tic in his jaw as he clenched his teeth, something his sister had done, too. "He has family. He has a home. Here, with us. And you"—he made a stabbing gesture in my direction—"left him alone in a hotel room." His eyes were hard.

His words stung, because I was still beating myself up about that, but I refused to lower my eyes. "Because Monica ran away from you. I had no idea what kind of people you were, and I was doing the best I could to protect Beau. Monica trusted me to be his guardian. Not you. And you all are strangers to him. Do not make this a battle where the only loser is Beau."

Trey hadn't moved the whole time I'd been speaking. It unnerved me, but I didn't sit back down.

Slowly, he stood, too, easily towering over my five feet, six inches. "And the beach house? Have you figured out what you're going to do with that? I'm half owner, remember."

I filled my lungs, imagining I could smell the water again, and see the broken oaks and phantom porch steps. "I'm hoping the lot might be worth something, because as I'm sure you know, there's nothing but sand, dirt, and an oak tree left."

His words were clipped. "I've seen it. More times than I care to think about. And there's a lot more left than just sand, dirt, and a tree, but I wouldn't expect you to understand that."

I listened to the way he formed his words, to the peculiar way he rounded his vowels, and it made me miss Monica all over again, reinforcing my anger. "It's been five years since Katrina, but nothing's been rebuilt on the lot. Did you think she wasn't coming back so it didn't matter if you rebuilt or not?"

The tic continued in Trey's jaw, and for a moment I didn't think he was going to answer, but I refused to lower my gaze. I'd grown accustomed over the years to asking difficult questions of people in authority. It was easy to do when you didn't have anything to lose.

"I was waiting for her to come back." He paused. "So we could rebuild together. It didn't seem right doing it without her."

My heart tightened a bit in my chest, understanding exactly what he meant, understanding that his reluctance to rebuild without his sister had everything to do with the same reason I never studied clouds anymore.

I cleared my throat. "If it's any consolation, I don't think Monica knew that the house was gone. I could never decide whether it was because she was an optimist or preferred to live in a fantasyland. We all saw the news coverage of the hurricane. Most of it was focused here, on New Orleans, but we noticed the Gulf Coast stories because of Biloxi and the house there. I guess we both assumed that since River Song was so old and had withstood other storms, it would have survived Katrina."

Trey crossed his arms over his chest, as if holding something in. "I'd go for the fantasyland. She held herself and others to impossible standards. Most of us couldn't live up to them."

As if anticipating my next question, he abruptly changed the subject.

"I'd like to buy out your half of the lot. And because I think Monica would want me to, I'll give you more than fair market value. As you can imagine, a lot with a house on it would be more valuable, but I'm aware of your situation and that you don't have time to wait for a house to be rebuilt."

I stared back at him, but his eyes were inscrutable. I thought of the desolation I'd seen on the coast, all the empty lots, the thinned trees, and tried to imagine rebuilding a house on a beach that had already betrayed it once. It would take an arrogance and a blind faith that I was pretty sure I didn't possess. Even the thought of all that still needed to be done exhausted me. And Trey was offering me a way out.

"You want to buy out my interest in the Biloxi house. At more than market value."

"Yes."

I looked away, ashamed at how much I wanted to say yes. But something held me back. Maybe it was the simple knowledge that Monica had loved the house and had wanted to one day bring her children there. Or maybe it was because the image of the white house on the beach had been a symbol of future happiness for both of us. Of days in the sun where the pressures of making ends meet, and sickness, and the endless searching would no longer exist.

Trey spoke. "Take a few days to think about it, but I think you'll realize it's your best option right now." He turned and walked toward the window, pulling aside a curtain to look out. "Beau's father—is he a part of the picture?"

I looked down, noticing a scuff on my sensible black pumps, the ones I'd bought for a job I no longer had. I shook my head. "He was a . . . temporary boyfriend." I forced myself to meet his eyes. "She didn't know his last name. By the time she realized she was pregnant, he was long gone. But she wanted the baby—badly, even though her doctor advised her against it."

"Because of her heart?"

I nodded, remembering.

He continued studying the street outside the window, but I could tell that his posture was a studied nonchalance, that his every word was planned, and that I needed to be very, very careful.

He continued. "I'm curious about something. Do you know the identity of the woman in the portrait?"

A cold pop of air shot down my spine as I shook my head. "No. My great-grandfather painted lots of portraits for private homes, many of them never seen in public. Looks like mid nineteen fifties, from the style of the hair and dress, but that's all I know." I narrowed my eyes. "Why?"

He turned to face me, his expression almost smug. "It's a portrait of my great-grandmother, Caroline Guidry. And it was painted by your great-grandfather, Abe Holt, in 1956. Odd coincidence, isn't it?"

The sound of rushing air seemed to envelop me as I stood facing Monica's brother, not comprehending what he was telling me. When I was small, Chelsea and I would stick our heads out of the open car windows and try to have a conversation with the wind whipping at our faces and filling our mouths. I felt that way now, unable to speak or breathe, suffocating by simply opening my lips. I sat down heavily on the sofa, trying to form words that would ask the right question. "I had no idea. . . ."

The door opened and Kathy Wolf walked in. "Beau's on his second helping of ice cream. I hope that's okay. He did eat carrot sticks with his sandwich, if that makes you feel any better. He just loves the praline chunks, and it's like he's never had them before."

I offered a weak smile. "Because he hasn't. Thank you, Kathy." My own stomach grumbled as I realized I hadn't eaten all day, and knew, too, that my stomach couldn't handle food right now anyway.

Kathy glanced at Trey. "Miss Aimee's arthritis is bothering her too much to come down, but she wants to speak with Julie."

Trey moved from the window. "I can take her right up."

Kathy shook her head. "No. She wants to see Julie alone. She suggested you spend time with Beau while they chat. She said it could be a while."

It looked for a moment like he would protest, but then he nodded. "Fine. I'll show Julie where to go and I'll meet you in the kitchen with Beau."

Kathy flashed a smile at both of us, then left, her sneakers silent on the hardwood floors.

"This way," Trey said, indicating the doorway. I stood, my legs feeling as if they belonged to somebody else, and headed out into the foyer. I glanced toward the kitchen door, wanting to reassure myself that Beau was all right.

"He's fine with Kathy," Trey said, as if reading my mind. "She's a registered nurse and can handle any emergency."

I nodded, reassured. "Just let him know that I'm upstairs, that I haven't left. He gets anxious sometimes."

Trey looked as if he wanted to say something, but instead pointed to the grand staircase. "Go up one flight of stairs and take a right. It will be the second door on the left. Just knock first and let her know you're there."

My nervousness made me giddy. "You're not afraid I'll steal the family silver?"

His lip twitched but he didn't smile. "It's insured."

I turned my back and began climbing the stairs, aware that he hadn't moved.

"How did you lose your job?"

I turned halfway and shrugged. "Beau needed me. I couldn't leave him with a babysitter after what he'd gone through. Unfortunately, my boss didn't agree." I didn't want to see his doubt or disdain, so I turned around and continued to climb until I reached the landing and the balcony that overlooked the foyer, a large stained-glass window covering most of the outside wall.

"Thank you," he said to my back.

My steps slowed.

"For what you did for Beau. But it's not going to change anything. My offer to buy out your share of the house still stands. You and I both know that you don't belong here. We're grateful that you've brought Beau back to his family, but he's not yours and he never will be."

Heat flooded my face as my throat closed and my eyes stung, and for a horrifying moment I thought I might cry. But I concentrated on taking each step, keeping my back straight and my chin up, and continued to the top without looking back once.

The door to Aimee Guidry's bedroom was slightly open. I tapped gently, then entered into a soft white room that glowed from the light of the floor-to-ceiling windows that lined two walls of the room. An arched alcove to the left of the door held the ornate rice poster bed and a small bedside table and armchair. Aimee Guidry, wearing the skirt and blouse she'd had on earlier but without her jacket, sat in her stockinged feet on top of the bedclothes, propped against large pillows, small reading glasses perched on her nose. Next to her on the bed sat a large wooden box with a hinged top, its lid gaping open like a mouth.

The older woman smiled as I approached the bed. "Please sit down," she said, indicating the overstuffed armchair, upholstered in a yellow-and-white toile fabric. Everything in the room was exquisite—from the fine antique furniture to the hand-painted walls and the elaborate ceiling medallion. Just like the woman reclining in the bed, it was beautiful, and comfortable, and elegant—all the things I would have wished for in my own bedroom had I ever thought about it—had I ever wanted anything as permanent as a house with my own bedroom.

I sat and clenched my hands in my lap, unsure of Aimee's reception, Trey's stinging words still fresh in my mind.

"I've asked for Kathy to bring up Beau as soon as we're finished, but I wanted us to have a long chat alone first."

Warily, I nodded. "I'll be happy to answer any questions about Monica. She always spoke fondly of you."

Aimee smiled sadly. "We will, we will. But first I wanted to talk about you."

I shifted uneasily in my chair. "All right. But there's not much to tell."

Aimee studied me over her glasses, making me feel like a bug under a microscope laid out for examination. "My grandson was very busy on his phone and computer while we waited for you and Beau to arrive. He found a number of newspaper articles from 1993, when you were twelve."

The central air whirred to life, lifting the corners of several photographs that were scattered on the bedclothes near the box. I stared at them, trying to find words to defend myself, but knowing that after years of trying to find them, they weren't there.

"How sad for you. You were so young, only twelve when your sister was taken. I imagine you blamed yourself."

I raised my eyes, hearing the understanding in Aimee's voice. "Of course I do. My mother asked me to be in charge and watch my little sister while she ran to the grocery store to get milk and eggs." I paused, then forced myself to continue. "It was my birthday, and she was making my birthday cake."

Aimee carefully took her glasses off and laid them on her lap. "And your family—where are they now?"

I put my hands on the arms of the chair, ready to leave. "I don't mean to be rude, but this is none of your business. We need to discuss Beau, and the portrait. The beach house. And none of what happened to my family has anything to do with it."

The older woman smiled, but a slight frown creased her forehead. "I disagree. Your past has everything to do with why you're here now."

I sat back, confused. "I don't see how."

"Allow an old woman her ramblings, if you will. Now tell me, where is your family?"

After a moment, I answered. "My mother died ten years ago from a brain aneurysm. My father is living in the Canadian wilderness with a succession of girlfriends, and my older brother, last time I talked to him some five years ago, was living in California and working as a waiter.

Now please tell me how any of that relates to Beau and everything else." I didn't bother to hide the hard edge in my voice.

Aimee didn't say anything. Instead, she reached over and picked up two photographs, then slid them over to me. "Do you know what this is?"

I picked them up to examine them, shifting them slightly to escape the reflection of the bright sunlight coming from the windows. The first photograph was of River Song exactly as Monica had painted it: the graceful columns, the front porch littered with rocking chairs of all sizes, the sandy front yard with the large oak. Even the tire swing hung on the same branch Monica had painted. Clustered on the front steps of the porch were six people, varying from about Beau's age to older teenagers. I recognized a tanned and happy younger version of Monica standing in the back of the group and leaning on a column, a small child perched on her hip.

Without taking my eyes from the photo, I said, "Monica painted the house for me, and told me so much about the summers and weekends she spent there that I almost feel as if I've been there, too." I paused for a moment, needing to swallow the thickness in my throat. "She had big dreams of returning to it one day with her children."

A soft smile filled Aimee's voice. "She loved that house. Loved to have her cousins and friends visit. It was her escape from the city, and school. From her parents fighting. She hated that. But the house and the beach were like a prayer to her. They soothed her soul like nothing else could."

I flipped the photograph behind the second one, and found myself lowering it onto my lap, not wanting to see this one in such close detail. It was the same house, minus the people, the roof, most of the second story. Tree limbs and garbage lay strewn over the lawn, an old car in pristine condition resting upside down by the oak tree as if somebody had placed it there as a joke.

I held the photograph up to Aimee. "Was this after Katrina?"

"No. That was August 1969. Hurricane Camille."

"Camille?"

"You're too young. Ever since Katrina, people tend to think of it as the only hurricane ever to hit the Gulf Coast. But Camille was a category-five hurricane, just like Katrina. Made a direct hit on Pass Christian, but New Orleans didn't have the catastrophic flooding that time. The Mississippi coast was as devastated back then as it was after Katrina."

I placed the photos on the bedspread near the box, eager to get them away from me. "Why are you showing these to me?"

"Trey offered to buy out your share of the property, didn't he?"

"Yes."

"And what did you say?"

I allowed my head to fall back against the seat. "I didn't have an answer for him, because I honestly don't know."

"And if you don't stay to rebuild, what would you do? What would Beau do?"

There was no incrimination in Aimee's voice, but I knew I had to tread carefully. I looked Aimee in the eye and told her the truth. "I have no idea. Despite Monica's vote of confidence in me by leaving Beau in my care, I have no job, no home, no family, really, to speak of. Not a winning situation." I tried to smile but felt my lips tremble.

"I've been sitting up here while Trey interrogated you downstairs, thinking very hard about this situation. First, I had to come to terms with not ever seeing Monica again." She closed her eyes briefly. "But my grief is made easier knowing about Beau. It's like he's here to give us all a second chance. Including you."

I started to protest, to tell her that I wasn't the kind of person who deserved second chances, but she held up her hand and continued. "You own half of a beachfront property, and have custody of a little boy who loves you and whom, I expect, you love back. I don't know you well at all, but I know that Monica was a good judge of character and always selective when choosing her friends. Which is why I think you should stay here and rebuild River Song. That would give you and

Beau enough time to grow accustomed to a place, to decide if it's where you want to stay."

"Me? Rebuild?" I shook my head. "First off, I don't know anything about construction or reconstruction. And second, have you been down there? Have you seen it? So many people haven't moved back or rebuilt, and I totally get it. Why invest all of that time and money when each hurricane season brings a new threat?"

Aimee regarded me with a steady blue gaze. "Why build skyscrapers in San Francisco that might be knocked down by an earthquake? Or why build farms in Kansas and Oklahoma that might get blown away by a tornado?" She snorted, and it seemed so uncharacteristic for the elegant old woman that I almost laughed. "Where did they want us to go, anyway? I figure if we're still breathing, then we're meant to keep going. So we rebuild. We start over. It's just what we do. I imagine she wanted that for Beau: a sense of belonging, of having a place to return to from wherever else he goes. A place he can call home because he feels it, and breathes it. Tastes it."

Aimee leaned forward, her cheeks pink. "You haven't had a place to call home in a very long time. Maybe if you did, you'd understand." Her shoulders lifted and I had a glimpse of the young woman Aimee Guidry had once been. Aimee tapped the pictures. "Who do you think restored River Song after Camille? I did. Because walking away wasn't an option I cared to consider."

I closed my eyes for a moment, trying to remember what Ray Von had said. Quietly I repeated, "'If you ain't dead, then you ain't done.'"

"Ah, you've met Ray Von." Aimee smiled softly, lost in secret thoughts.

I nodded. "Then why did Monica leave? If all of this meant so much to her, why would she leave it all behind her and never come back?"

"I don't know." Aimee's answer was tempered with the same weariness as Trey's answer to the same question, and I found myself wondering once again if I could believe it.

Aimee continued. "But I do know that regardless of her reasons for leaving, Monica would want Beau to come back, to experience a happy childhood at River Song, as she did."

I leaned my elbows on my knees, cupping my chin in my hands. "So maybe I should let Trey buy out my interest and rebuild it himself."

Aimee frowned as if she were talking to a recalcitrant child. "Why do you think Monica left you her portion of the house instead of Trey? It would have made sense to have Trey own the entire property. So leaving it to you was intentional. She might not have known how devastated the house was, but she must have guessed that it had sustained some damage. And knowing her brother as well as she did, she would have also guessed that he wouldn't do anything with it until she returned."

I shifted in my seat, unsure where this was leading. "So what are you saying?"

"I'm saying that I think that she wanted you to restore River Song to the way it used to be."

"But why me?"

Aimee's face softened as she regarded me. "Maybe because she thought that you had more to rebuild than just a house."

I sat up abruptly, angry but not sure at whom.

"Don't be angry, Julie. I'm grieving for my granddaughter and trying to accept and understand her wishes, which is hard to do when the recipient of her wishes is both a stranger and a reluctant participant. But for her sake, and Beau's, I'm going to try to convince you to stay and restore River Song." She leaned forward, her hands clasped tightly together in her lap, as if she were trying very hard to restrain her emotions. "Have you ever thought about what happens when you find your sister? Where will you bring her home to when you find her?"

I put my forehead in the heels of my hands, clenching my eyes shut. "I don't know. I've never thought about what comes next."

Aimee began to gather the things from the bedspread and place them in the box, leaving out the pictures of the house. "I don't want to state the obvious, Julie, but you've got a child to consider now. A child who needs a home. And a future. It's time that you started seriously considering what comes next."

I wanted to argue, but I knew Aimee was right. *When you find your sister.* Aimee had said that as if she believed it to be true, and I warmed to her. "I haven't been able to look ahead for a long time. It's always been about finding Chelsea. And I still believe that I will. Blind faith, I guess, but I can't stop hoping."

Aimee slid the photographs toward me. "Believe me. I know what blind faith is all about."

I rubbed my palms against my skirt again, still unsure of what I was supposed to do. I knew without a doubt that rebuilding River Song was out of the question. It was too far gone, too consuming, too . . . permanent. Everything I didn't need, and everything Beau did.

Aimee was watching me as if she could hear my thoughts. After taking a deep breath, I said, "I should go get Beau now."

As if she hadn't heard me, Aimee said, "Did Trey tell you who was in the portrait Monica left you?"

"Yes, he did. It surprised me, actually. Your mother-in-law, right? Made me question . . . a lot of things. Like Monica's finding me at an Abe Holt show. It makes me think our meeting wasn't entirely coincidental. But I can't figure out why." Uncomfortable, I stood. "I'll go get Beau."

Aimee's blue eyes were piercing as she regarded me. "When Monica went away, it wasn't the first time this family has had to deal with a disappearance."

The air-conditioning vent blew cold air on my face, making me shiver. "What do you mean?"

"Caroline Guidry, the woman in the portrait, disappeared, too. In 1956. Not long after that portrait was painted by your great-grandfather."

I forced myself to speak against the dryness in my mouth. "What happened to her?"

Aimee sat back against her pillows. "It's a long story."

I glanced at my watch, eager to leave. "I should go get Beau. We've been here a long time already."

"Where do you need to go? Beau is my great-grandson and you're his guardian. You're welcome to stay as long as you like. Besides, Trey is with Beau right now. And if there's anybody who needs the kind of attitude adjustment that only small children can give, that would be him."

I felt my mouth lift in a half smile. "Can you just tell me if they ever found her?" Goose bumps tickled my arms as I shivered again, my words reverberating in my head. *It makes me think our meeting wasn't entirely coincidental.*

Blue eyes regarded me quietly. "That would be jumping ahead. Besides, you need to know the whole story. It will give you insight into the kind of people who rebuild again and again, even in the face of another hurricane."

I sat down slowly, feeling the cool fabric beneath me again. "All right. But only for a short while. I'll need to get back to Beau."

Aimee closed her eyes again and began to speak.

CHAPTER 6

Not houses finely roofed or the stones of walls well builded,
nay nor canals and dockyards make the city, but men able to
use their opportunity.   —ALCAEUS

Aimee

SUMMER 1950

Even now, after all these years, when I smell the summer grass and
the thick odor of the muddy water of the Mississippi River, I think
of Gary and the summers when we were young. The summers when
the burdens of growing up had not yet found us. And I think of the first
time I ever fell in love.

I had been spending my summers in New Orleans, and eventually
Biloxi, too, all of my life. Always alone, without my father. My mother
died when I was three, and my father moved us up to Philadelphia and
away from New Orleans and all that reminded him of her. I think he
might have left me, too, for the same reason, except for the fact that I
was his flesh and blood as well as hers. I had inherited her deep red hair,
and I knew he was reminded of my mother every time he looked at me.
My father never returned to the city of his birth. Instead, he would send
me to my grandmother's old house in the Garden District every sum-

mer, as a sort of peace offering to his mother, who had never forgiven him for taking away her only grandchild.

Grandmother was a formidable woman, short and pencil-thin, with silver hair always tucked into a tight bun. I used to sneak up on her at odd hours of the day and night, hoping to see if there was ever a hair loose. I was always disappointed. She was stern, proper, aware of her status in New Orleans society, and always concerned that my Yankee upbringing would turn me into someone too uncouth to be a true Southern lady. In her way, she loved me—almost as much as I loved her old house and the city of my birth. And, later, our next-door neighbors.

The summer I was twelve I met the Guidrys. I already knew Mr. Guidry—he and Grandmother were friends, and he was our supper guest more nights than not. A tall, thin man with dark eyes and a sad smile, he sometimes talked about his wife and two sons. I asked Grandmother why they never came to dinner with him, and she told me they lived in Atlanta. She then shushed me and said it was something that wasn't discussed.

Mr. Guidry's house was another huge Victorian on First Street, but with a wraparound porch and two turrets. Painters on tall ladders would splash on a fresh coat of paint almost every summer, and the white wicker rockers on the porch would have new cushions, but the windows were always shrouded in darkness. I would stare at the black glass, and they would stare back at me like empty eyes. I wondered what had happened inside that house to make it so sad.

At the beginning of that summer, as Grandmother's car turned onto the tree-lined street, I knew something was different next door. The overgrown bushes that usually hid the house and garden from the street had been pulled out, allowing me to see the water fountain of the little boy peeing. Bright red hibiscus edged the wrought-iron fence like a hemstitch on one of Grandmother's napkins. As soon as the car stopped, I ran out to the sidewalk when I spotted Mr. Guidry backing out of his driveway in his Chevy Bel Air, the whitewalls of his tires gleaming in the bright sun.

I waved to him, making him stop the car. "Hello, Mr. Guidry. I'm here for my summer visit." I watched my distorted reflection disappear as he rolled down his window the rest of the way.

"Good morning, Aimee. It's good to see you."

I caught a strong odor of cologne. I took a step back and nodded toward his garden. "I like what you've done with your flowers."

"My wife did that. She's come with one of our two boys. Our oldest will be joining us as soon as his term's up at school." He smiled, but his eyes remained somber. "I've got to go to work now. I'll see you later, Aimee."

He rolled his window up and backed out onto First Street, his tires squealing on the asphalt as he turned his car toward Magazine Street.

Later I asked Grandmother why Mrs. Guidry had come back, but she ignored my question and said, "The past is best forgotten. We must make Mrs. Guidry feel welcome for Mr. Guidry's sake." Her lips turned white from the pressure of keeping them together as she slammed the drawer of the breakfront, knocking over all her carefully stacked silverware.

Grandmother was true to her word and invited Mrs. Guidry to a formal tea the following week. I sat on a scratchy yellow sofa in Grandmother's parlor, wearing a stiff, high-necked collar that irritated my neck and forced me to keep my head straight, eyes staring directly ahead. But she'd allowed me to wear my mother's pearls, so I felt very grown-up.

When Caroline Guidry entered the room, I could smell her musky perfume before I turned in my chair to see her. It was the scent I had smelled in Mr. Guidry's car, something oddly familiar. A smart, small hat perched on her dark head, and she wore a gray dress made of some kind of shiny, crinkly material with a big shawl collar and a huge bow at her tiny waist.

I think I stopped breathing. She was the most beautiful woman I had ever seen, including my mother. I felt a little guilty at the thought, but Mrs. Guidry smiled at me, erasing all thoughts from my head. She had black hair, and blue cat's eyes that seemed to miss nothing, and her acknowledging smile made me feel as if I'd just been chosen. For what, I wasn't sure, but I knew I wanted to be a part of it.

A boy about my age linked his arm with hers. As they walked into the room, I realized how frail he looked. His cheekbones jutted out from sunburned cheeks, and each step fell slow and purposeful, as if each one were counted. He stumbled, and his mother caught him. He angrily brushed her hand aside, and I caught a glimpse of his eyes—the wary eyes of a wild animal caught in a cage. Blue-gray eyes, fringed with black lashes and full of fire. I recognized something within him, and I smiled.

Grandmother stood and walked over to them. "Caroline, Garrick, allow me to present to you my granddaughter, Aimee Mercier."

Caroline Guidry smiled at me again with her cat's eyes, looking at me as if she already knew me. She took my fingertips and squeezed them. "Aren't you a precious thing? And the spitting image of your mother."

She smelled of cigarette smoke and heavy perfume. Shalimar. The same perfume my mother had worn. I knew that because of the old bottle on the dressing table in my father's room. The liquid had long since turned a golden orange, but I still smelled it on her clothes in my father's closet. I tilted my head to the side. "You knew my mother?"

She raised an elegant dark brow. "We were the best of friends." Her eyes darted away as she moved to the chair next to where my grandmother had been seated. She sat down and crossed her legs at the ankles, exposing her needlelike stiletto heels that I'm sure my grandmother didn't approve of.

I noticed then the brooch on the bodice of her dress in the shape of an alligator, its eyes red rubies and its scales flashing with enamel and jewels. Its tail ended in a sharp triangular point. "I like your pin, Mrs. Guidry."

Her gloved hand squeezed it briefly, as if she were touching a good-luck charm or something. "Thank you, dear. Your mother gave it to me, and I call it my signature piece. I love alligators, you see. They remind me of me, I suppose—often misunderstood." She glanced up at my grandmother, but my grandmother was focused on pouring tea into her prized Hungarian porcelain cups.

My mother. I wanted to ask Caroline Guidry more about it, and why my mother had given it to her, but the boy next to her bowed slightly in greeting, his face serious.

"How do you do?" I said, in a highly practiced tone that had been drilled into me the night before by Grandmother. In fact, it was so highly practiced that it came out with an English accent thick enough that the queen herself would have been proud.

The boy smirked, and I smirked back. Patting the chair next to me, I said, "Garrick can sit here."

As he sat, I slid my plate over to him. "Have a pastry." I wasn't saying it to be rude, but Grandmother was always banishing such things from my plate so I wouldn't get fat. And getting fat was something this boy sorely needed.

He picked it up and bit it, the white cream oozing out the back of the flaky crust, plopping onto his navy blue jacket. Surprised blue-gray eyes looked up at me.

It was more his expression than the blob of cream on his jacket that made me laugh, and I held my hand over my mouth so Grandmother wouldn't see. Still looking at me, Garrick scraped off the white blob with his finger, then promptly wiped it on the front of my lace dress.

I looked down at the smeared puff of cream and stared in surprise as it slowly slid down the front of my dress, then fell to my lap. I raised my eyes to his, and he smiled. I smiled back and laughed. Soon we were doubled over with laughter, giving each other shoves on the shoulder. Until I fell off the sofa.

Grandmother pinched my upper arms as she hoisted me up. Garrick stopped laughing. "Aimee! Aren't you a little old to be acting this way?"

I stood in front of her, my laughter silenced.

She leaned toward me and said very quietly, "Go clean yourself up. And when you return, I expect to see a mature young lady."

She released me quickly, and I felt the bruising on my arms.

Grandmother looked expectantly at Mrs. Guidry, who appeared to be attempting to hide a smile. A mask seemed to drop over her face, and she gave Garrick a stern look. "And, Garrick, I expect you to act like a young gentleman."

I slunk up the stairs, stealing a backward glance. Mrs. Guidry and Garrick were looking up at me. Mrs. Guidry winked, reminding me of a cat slowly waking up after a long sleep.

Gary and I were inseparable after that—spending all our afternoons together in the long New Orleans summer until I had to go back to school in Philadelphia. Most days we rode our bicycles down St. Charles Avenue—slowly, so Gary wouldn't get too worn-out—and through Audubon Park, crossing Magazine and the railroad tracks to the levee to see what we could find floating in the river. On days when the rain tore at the live oak trees on St. Charles, we climbed to the topmost corner of Grandmother's house to spook each other with ghost stories. We sat in the dark with a platter of pralines and Coca-Colas, brought up the steep, narrow stairs by Aunt Roseanne.

Aunt Roseanne had worked for Grandmother long before I was born and was as much a fixture at Grandmother's house as were the trademark leaded-glass windows. We called her Aunt Roseanne, although I never knew whose aunt she was. Her skin was as black as the eyes on my Raggedy Ann doll. Placing the tray between us with a scrutinizing gaze, she would warn us about conjuring ghosts. I wanted her to explain, to tell me how to conjure ghosts so I could talk to my mother again, to understand her death. But Aunt Roseanne would shake her head and cross herself and leave me with all of my unanswered questions.

On an afternoon a week before I was to leave, Gary came over to see if I wanted to race our bikes to the levee. We'd both received Schwinn Phantoms for our birthdays, his red and mine black, since Grandmother thought the red too flashy for a girl, and we'd ridden them everywhere all summer. She'd even given me permission to buy a pair of blue jeans, since she figured those were more decent than a skirt when riding a bicycle.

Reluctantly, I opened the door. In a failed attempt to make myself look like my favorite movie star, Rita Hayworth, I'd cut my own hair. It never occurred to me that naturally curly red hair wouldn't look quite the same as hers.

Gary stood in front of me in shocked silence, his mouth open, but speechless for the first time since I had met him, his eyes focused on my hair. I slammed the door in his face before he could think of something to say and walked away from it. He opened the door, his voice full of laughter. "Gee whiz, Aimee. I didn't mean to stare. You just look kinda . . . different."

My feelings were hurt. His mother's hair looked just like Rita Hayworth's except for the color, and I had wanted my hair to look like hers. But whereas hers fell in ink black waves around her face, mine resembled a clown's wig.

Unable to escape him in my own home, I ran past him and out the door. I grabbed my bike, jumped on it, and flew out into the street, pedaling as quickly as I could to get to the levee. Gary followed me in hot pursuit, coughing and laughing. I was glad to hear him cough. I hoped he'd choke to death.

I jumped the curb on my bike and rode over the sparse grass of the park area, clenching my teeth to prevent them from breaking. As I neared the steep rise, I leaped off my bike, letting it crash to the ground. Furiously, I stomped off in the direction of the river, climbing the incline of the levee until I reached the top.

A bloated cat lay on its side, its fur matted with mud, and flies creating a halo over it. Its cloudy feline eyes were open, staring sightlessly out into the summer day. I walked slowly toward it and bent over, my hands resting on my sweaty knees. Flies buzzed hungrily around its face, the open mouth stuck in a permanent cat smile.

Gary shuffled toward me, pushing his bike, his breathing labored. He stopped, attempting to pull in a deep breath. "Aimee . . ."

I could still hear the laughter in his voice, and an idea of revenge danced gleefully in my head. Without a second thought, I reached down and grabbed the cat by its two front paws. With a soft grunt, I hoisted it in the air and swung around, letting go as soon as I had made half an arc in the air with it. It pelted Gary in the stomach, and his eyes opened wide, oddly resembling the dead cat's.

Gary dropped his bike and staggered backward, his arms flailing like a windmill, a slimy smear staining the front of his blue-and-white-striped shirt. He teetered on the edge of the levee, his arms pumping wildly, then slid down the rocky slope toward the water. He lay on his back where he'd stopped, staring up at the sky—laughing.

"Shut up!"

He didn't. I hoisted his bike, scrambled down the rocks and chicken wire, then threw it into the water. Gary sat up, finally silenced.

"What in the hell did you do that for?" He pulled himself to his feet, swaying slightly, watching the handlebars slowly sink into the murky water, the rear wheel still visible.

All the anger had gone out of me, and I swallowed the knowledge of the awful thing I had just done. "Gary—I'm sorry. I'll make it up to you—somehow. I'll give you mine." The bike pitched forward, rear wheel somersaulting over the front as it headed toward deeper water. A large tree branch protruded from the water like an avenging hand, and grabbed the front wheel spokes, halting the bike's progression down the fast-moving river.

Gary stepped forward onto the large rocks, the water reaching his ankles.

"Don't, Gary! It's deep out there—and the current's real bad."

He glared at me. "I can swim. And it's not that far." He took another step forward, sinking down to his knees. I couldn't see his feet anymore.

"Please stop—no one can swim in that current."

He ignored my pleas and continued into the water. When it was up to his neck, he kicked out to swim to the bike.

The river immediately propelled him off course. As he was pushed past the bike, he shot out a hand and grabbed a part of the branch, its dark, slick skin sticking out from the brown water. His head disappeared under the surface, then reappeared with pieces of debris sticking in his hair from the polluted water. The racing water formed whitecaps around Gary and the bike. If he tried to fight the river and swim back to the levee, the river would win.

Footsteps pounded on the levee behind me, and I turned to see a boy of about seventeen running toward us. Relief made my knees sag, and I stumbled, barely catching myself before I joined Gary in the water. The older boy must have seen what had happened, because he brushed by me and went directly to the edge of the levee.

"Garrick! Hold tight! I'll get you out of there!"

The boy turned around, his arms at his sides, his hands opening and closing as he scanned the area for anything that could help pull Gary out of the water. Without a second thought, I unbuttoned my blouse, my sweaty fingers slipping on the plastic buttons. The older boy stared at me; then his eyes widened in understanding. I didn't even think to be embarrassed. I was a late bloomer, and my white cotton training bra was for encouragement purposes only.

Shrugging out of a button-down shirt, he took my blouse and tied the two articles of clothing together. Without pausing, he undid his belt and slipped out of his pants, adding them to make one long rope.

Anchoring his feet on the rocks, he pitched the impromptu lifeline into the water. I stood next to him on the slippery rocks, heedless of the water rushing into my shoes. I saw my blouse under the surface of the water, inching its way to Gary like a pale river snake. His pallid fingers clutched the branch, and his head had fallen back into the water to keep his mouth open. His eyes were closed, and the first tremors of panic hit me.

"Gary! Open your eyes! Now's not the time to take a nap!" My voice caught in midshout.

He cracked his eyes open, and he gave me a weak smile. I let out a deep breath.

The older boy spoke again. "Garrick, I want you to grab that blouse. But don't let go of the branch before you've got a good hold on the rope first, you hear?"

Gary nodded, his eyes only slits, a blue tinge around his mouth.

His hand reached out for the blouse and missed it, his arm splashing aimlessly in the water.

I shook all over, making my voice warble. "Gary. You need to push yourself up so you can see the blouse. Give it all you've got! I'll even let you hit me when you get out of there, okay? Just *try*."

His head popped out of the water enough for his shoulders to clear the surface for a brief moment. He spied the arm of the blouse, grabbed it with one hand, then let go of the branch. His head disappeared into the murky water, and I scrambled to my feet.

"Gary!" My stomach churned. I threw a sidelong glance at the boy next to me and decided I would rather die than further disgrace myself by throwing up.

Gary's head reappeared, and I garbled a silent Hail Mary before moving to the older boy's side to assist him in hauling Gary out. The two of us grunted in unison as we pulled. He was much heavier than he should have been. Gary was small and probably weighed only eighty pounds soaking wet with his shoes on. Then I noticed his other hand was gripping the bike.

I shouted, "Drop the bike, Gary—it'll be easier."

He shook his head and kicked his legs near the surface, but he continued to clutch the handlebar of the bike. Holding the improvised rope, we started backing up as Gary came closer to the side of the levee. The older boy turned to me; his eyes narrowed.

"Can you stand here and hang on to this? I'm going to get a bit closer."

I nodded, defying my body to fumble. My shoulders were pulled forward as he let go, causing my sneakered feet to skid on the slick rocks and chicken wire, but I held my ground. The boy began to pull the line in with Gary dangling on the end. I heard a shout of triumph as he grabbed Gary's shirt.

The older boy lifted Gary and the bike and half carried and half dragged them up the rocky slope to the top of the levee. He tossed the bike aside and laid Gary down where the dead cat had been. Gary's eyes were closed, and he was racked with uncontrollable coughs, gulping for air. I crawled over to him and rolled him onto his side. I sat back as dribbles of murky water eased out the corner of his mouth.

The older boy was busy trying to untie his sodden pants from the makeshift rope. He sat in his boxers and white shirt, his wet black hair forming a vee on his forehead. Through my half-closed eyes, he looked like pictures I'd seen of Bela Lugosi in the movie *Dracula*. I don't know if this was a natural reaction to shock, but staring at a vampire sitting on the levee in his underwear suddenly hit me as uproariously funny.

The first giggle came out like a bubble; then the rest spilled out. I couldn't breathe, so I lay back on the asphalt next to Gary, the sun baking my skin. The puddle of water forming around him seeped toward me and nudged me in the seat, saturating my blue jeans. Still laughing, I turned to face Gary. His eyes remained shut, but I could see the shadow of a grin on his lips.

"What in the hell are you laughing at? You could have killed my brother!"

The word "brother" soaked up my laughter like a sponge. I sat up, looking at the foreboding shadow hovering over me as the older boy stood. He had managed to pull on his wet pants and sweep his hair back off his forehead, obliterating all thoughts of bloodsuckers. I stared, dumbfounded. This was Gary's older brother, Wesley, who was due back today from his prep school up north. The same brother Gary spoke about with such awe, and who I was half convinced didn't exist, despite the fact that the Guidrys' house was full of pictures of him.

But the boy in front of me didn't resemble the one in the flat, one-dimensional photographs. Wesley in the flesh was truly something to look at. At only seventeen, he towered well over six feet, with broad shoulders and well-muscled legs. I could see a tuft of dark hair peeking out from the collar of his undershirt, and his voice was as deep as my daddy's. I blinked twice, thinking about how much he looked like the movie stars Aunt Roseanne was always talking about in *Life* magazine.

"Here." He thrust my sodden blouse toward me.

I grabbed it and scrambled to my feet, feeling the telltale prickles around my eyes. Grandmother always told me I looked like Frankenstein when I cried, and I wasn't about to let him see me like that. I swallowed deeply before speaking, turning around and thrusting my arms into the wet shirt. "What do you mean? He's the one who was stupid enough to jump in the river." I sent a worried glance at Gary. "Holy cow, Gary—how could you be so dumb?" I knelt down next to him.

Gary had managed to sit up and was hugging his knees. He put his forehead on them and said in a weak voice, "Honest, Wes, it's my fault. Please don't get her in trouble." He took a deep breath, grinning broadly. "Besides, I got my bike."

Wes looked at me, then back at Gary. "I still think we need to tell her parents." His eyes strayed to my flat chest. "She's not too old to get a good whipping, I wouldn't think."

Defiantly, I stuck out my chin. "You can't tell my parents. They don't live here. And I'm practically twelve."

Gary looked up. "That's right. She's staying with her grandmother—Mrs. Mercier from next door."

"Gary!" I shot him a dirty look.

He put his head back on his knees. "Sorry." His voice sounded muffled.

Wes looked back at me, bright blue eyes under dark brows. His wet eyelashes came to little points above his eyes, like a crown. A smile tweaked the corner of his mouth. "You sure don't look twelve." He shook his head, as if trying to clear an image. "All right. But you have to promise me you'll be more careful with him. He's, well, he's delicate."

"I am *not*!" Gary raised his head, and I was relieved to see bright spots of color on his cheeks. "I just get tired sometimes—it's not like I have the plague."

Wes squatted down on his haunches in front of Gary. "I didn't mean it that way. It's just that you tire easily—and your friends should know that." He shot a glance at me.

Wes hauled Gary to his feet. "Come on. I'll push your bike home for you."

Gary shoved Wes away. "I'm not a wimp." He stalked toward me, his wiry hair sticking up. As he neared, he drew back his arm and punched me hard in the shoulder.

I staggered backward. "Ouch! What did you do that for?" I touched my sore shoulder and wondered how I'd explain the bruise to Grandmother.

"Because I'm not a wimp." He rubbed his knuckles and gave me a small grin. "And besides, you told me I could."

Wes threw his head back and laughed. "She sure did."

I wanted to be peeved at Wes for not sticking up for me. He was older and knew all about how a gentleman isn't supposed to hit a lady. It didn't occur to me that perhaps he didn't see a lady when he looked at me, but instead saw a scrawny kid with a flat chest, long, skinny legs, and bright red hair that didn't know how to stay pulled back in a ponytail. But I couldn't be angry with him. My voice lodged in my throat. I could feel red heat creeping up my neck to my cheeks as I looked at him with his wet shirt plastered against his chest.

Ashamed at my thoughts, and even more perturbed that he might catch my blush, which I knew made me resemble an unfortunate radish with red hair, I stomped on ahead of them. I grabbed my bike and blurted out the most mature-sounding insult I could come up with. "I hope your balls fall off on your wedding night! Both of you!"

I hopped on my bike and pedaled as fast as I could until I could no longer hear their laughter.

Julie

A tapping on the door was followed by Kathy Wolf entering the room carrying a small tray with a glass of water and a small plastic cup with two white pills inside. "It's time to take your pills, Miss Aimee."

Aimee brushed her hand at Kathy. "I'm not a feeble old woman. I made the mistake of telling my doctor that my hip hurt, so now I'm supposed to take this medication. I don't like it. It makes me tired, and I don't think I'm ready to be spending afternoons in bed."

Kathy handed her the pills. "Miss Aimee, you have an appointment next week, so you can discuss your concerns. In the meantime, you need to take your pills."

I uncurled myself from my chair and watched as Kathy administered the medication, realizing that my cheeks hurt, as if I'd been smiling for a long time while I'd listened to Aimee speak.

As Kathy handed the glass of water to Aimee, she said, "Are you ready for Beau now? I think Trey wore him out pretty good playing chase outside."

"I wish I'd seen that," said Aimee as she placed the glass back on the tray, echoing my thoughts. "Yes, please send Beau on up."

With a smile, Kathy left, and I found myself still lost in a hot summer's day from sixty years ago. "So if Caroline Guidry was your mother-in-law, which son did you marry—Wes or Gary?"

Aimee's eyes seemed darker, as if they, too, were still seeing people and events from long ago. When she spoke she didn't answer my question, and it didn't occur to me until later to wonder whether it was intentional.

"After that first summer, most of the summers I spent with the Guidrys were spent in Biloxi." She looked down at her hands, spread now on her lap, her only jewelry a plain gold band on her left hand. "I think people love a place because of the people they encounter there. I love New Orleans, mostly because my mother did, and now because it's home. But I loved River Song for the same reason Monica did. Because it made us feel happy." She paused for a moment. "And safe."

I leaned forward. "Why did you and Monica need to feel safe?"

There was a tapping on the door again, and Beau ran in, launching himself at me. I hugged him to me, smelling his little-boy scent of sweat and baby shampoo. I looked up in alarm when I realized that he didn't have the red hat. Before I could say anything, Trey stepped into the bed alcove, holding the hat aloft.

"Don't worry; I've got it. He gave it to me so he could stick both hands in the fountain."

I tried to remain calm. "You let him get near the fountain?"

He looked at me with disdain. "And I've managed to keep both the hat and the boy safe. I guess that means I'm not completely inept."

"Look what Uncle Trey gave me!" Beau stepped impatiently from my embrace and, with his lower lip jutting out, looked down at his chest, where a necklace filled with gold, green, and purple metallic-looking beads sparkled. At the end of it lay a plastic medallion with the likeness of a Roman god holding a glass of wine, and grapes winding their way along the edges of the circle. Printed on the bottom were the words KREWE OF BACCHUS 1987.

"That's very nice, Beau. Did you say thank-you?"

Beau nodded. "Yes. And he said that every time I shared my candy with him, I could have another."

I looked up at Trey.

He shrugged. "Kathy won't tell me where she keeps the candy stash, so I had to resort to nefarious methods to get what I wanted."

His words were said lightly, but I felt the back of my neck prickle.

I stood and took Beau's hand. "Beau, this is your great-grandmother. She and your mom were very special to each other."

Aimee patted the side of her bed. "Come sit, sweetheart, and we'll have a little chat. And you can call me Miss Aimee like everyone else."

For a moment it looked as if Beau would hesitate. I waited, my hand on Beau's shoulder, until he walked forward, then voluntarily climbed up the small steps by the side of the tall bed. Trey handed him his hat.

I watched as Aimee placed her hand on Beau's, her face glowing as if she were recognizing someone she hadn't seen in a long time.

"What's your favorite color, Beau?" Aimee asked, her voice catching.

Without hesitating, he said, "Red," around his thumb that had managed to creep into his mouth.

Trey touched my elbow, making me turn. He crossed his arms and spoke slowly. "Did she convince you to sell to me?"

"Hardly." I closed my eyes for a moment, recalling what Aimee had said to me. *Maybe because she thought that you had more to rebuild than just a house.* I took a deep breath. "She thinks that Monica would want me to rebuild River Song. For Beau. And I can't believe I'm saying this, but I think she might be right."

Trey's eyes hardened. "I'm Monica's brother. I'm more than capable of rebuilding the house as her legacy for Beau. I can't think of any reason either one of them thinks that you're more capable than I would be."

I met his gaze. "Maybe because I've been dealing with the unknown for longer than you, but I find that it's less important sometimes to know why. And maybe to try to focus on moving forward instead."

"I see how well that's worked for you so far. You've been so focused on finding your sister that it appears to me that you let the rest of your life slide."

Flashes of light exploded in my head, the searing anger nearly blinding me. He had no idea what it had been like, what it was like to be the only one still looking. I knew I didn't want to rebuild River Song, knew I had no interest or experience, knew I wasn't the kind of person to knowingly tempt fate and build on shifting sands near open water. *Maybe because she thought that you had more to rebuild than just a house.*

"Julie?"

I turned my attention back to Beau.

"Miss Aimee says we're done for now, but tomorrow she's going to let me play in the fountain and let the statue pee on me."

I steadied my breathing, finding it easier to calm down if I turned my back on Trey as he left the room, his anger heating the air. "That sounds like fun." I forced a smile. "Although we might not be here tomorrow—"

"I was just thinking," Aimee interrupted, "that maybe you and Beau should stay here with me. It's been years since this house has seen children, and I want to spend as much time with Beau as I can, to make up for the first five years of his life."

"I don't think . . ."

Aimee held up her hand. "You don't have to decide right now. Think about it tonight at the hotel and let me know tomorrow. I figure you'll need someplace for Beau to stay once you get moving on River Song."

I frowned. "I didn't . . ."

"You didn't have to. I could tell from Trey's face. Please be patient with him, Julie. He's suffered a terrible blow. He and Monica were as close as twins."

I lowered my head, trying to stifle my anger so Aimee couldn't see it.

Beau leaned his head against my hip and began to suck his thumb again.

"I'll call you tomorrow with an answer. And to discuss the portrait." I took Beau's hand and led him to the door, the red hat pressed between us. "Miss Aimee? You never answered my question. About why you and Monica needed a place to feel safe."

The old woman's blue eyes darkened. "I guess you'll have to come back to hear the rest of the story."

"Will it tell me why Monica left?"

Aimee lifted her shoulders in a delicate shrug. "Maybe. I'm hoping you'll have the missing pieces so we can put them together."

"But what if I don't come back?"

Aimee turned her head on the pillow and closed her eyes, a soft smile haunting her lips. "You will."

I watched her for a long moment before turning away and leaving the room, closing the door quietly behind me.

CHAPTER 7

Fujiwhara effect: The tendency of two nearby tropical cyclones to rotate cyclonically about each other.

—National Hurricane Center

Julie

It was barely dawn two days later when I pulled up to my familiar spot at the curb on First Street and gently lifted a sleepy Beau from the backseat. Trey met us at the garden gate, holding it open with one hand and clutching a steaming cup of coffee with the other. The fountain burbled in the garden, and Beau lifted his head to stare at the peeing statue of the little boy with interest. "Don't get any ideas," I warned as I headed up the front steps to the open door.

Aimee was waiting inside dressed in jeans, white Keds, a long-sleeved checkered shirt, and a wide-brimmed straw hat. She opened her arms to Beau and when I set him down, he ran to her. "Remember what you promised about getting ice cream, Miss Aimee."

"I remember," she said before turning to me. "We're going to do some gardening today. I like to get out there before the sun gets too strong. Xavier should be here shortly."

"Xavier?" I asked.

"Yes, Ray Von's son. I thought she might have mentioned him. He's been working for the Guidrys since Hurricane Camille, which makes him older than dirt, I suppose." She tousled Beau's hair. "He's a magician when it comes to flowers and landscaping, and as long as he says he's too young to retire, he has a place here."

I remembered the man with the scarred face and the single green eye and suppressed a shudder.

Aimee continued. "I figure we'll wear each other out by the time Kathy arrives at eleven thirty; then we'll have some lunch and take a nice long nap so he's good and rested by the time you and Trey return from your visit to Biloxi. I had Kathy set up a room for Beau—right next to yours and across the hall from me." She winked at Beau. "You told me yesterday you liked LEGOs, so your uncle and Kathy spent a lot of time racing around town to make sure your room would be to your liking."

Beau grinned back as I sent a sidelong glance at Trey, trying to imagine him racing around to linen and toy stores to make a motherless five-year-old boy happy.

Aimee faced me again. "I know your coming here is a leap of faith on your part. And I'm thankful."

"Not completely." I blushed. I liked Aimee, and not just because of what Monica had told me. I liked her because of the way she accepted Beau without question. The way she accepted me. But the matter of why Monica had left hung between us like a sleeping tiger, safe until awakened. "I called my lawyer, who assured me that my guardianship of Beau is legally binding. It can be challenged in a court of law, which would take time. And if such a thing should occur, I would have custody until and unless a decision was made to overturn Monica's will." I looked away, unable to meet Aimee's eyes. "He also did a little background check and told me he didn't think you were a flight risk."

"No, I don't imagine I am."

I looked up to see a small smile tweaking the corner of the older woman's mouth.

"You brought your luggage?"

"Yes. It's in the van. I'll go get it."

Trey handed me his coffee mug. "Hold that, and I'll go get the luggage. Is your van unlocked?"

"Yes. There's not much in there—you'll probably be able to get it all in one trip."

He looked at me, his eyes flat. "Don't leave your car unlocked. Even for a minute. Just like in New York." He looked at the mug in my hand. "There's more coffee and mugs in the kitchen. Help yourself."

He opened and closed the door quickly, allowing in warm air that fanned my hot cheeks. Cradling the mug, I turned to Aimee. "I insist on paying you rent—I have some money left in savings, and I'll have more once the painting is sold." I paused for a moment. "Are you sure you don't have any objections to that? If Monica took it without your permission, then she couldn't legally will it to me, because it still belongs to you."

I watched as Beau moved to the hall table, where several George Ohr pieces were displayed. He kept his hands clasped behind his back, just like I'd shown him on his frequent visits with Monica to the auction house, as he carefully studied a small pitcher.

"Monica must have wanted you to have it, Julie, because she left it to you. And it would make me happy to know that her wishes are being carried out."

"But it's a portrait of your mother-in-law, Trey's great-grandmother. Surely you want to keep it in the family."

Aimee waved a manicured hand dismissively. "My husband never liked it, hated it when I hung it in the house. And his father before him had it hidden away in the attic. I can't say there's any sentiment toward it. I knew Caroline, of course, but she was always an enigma to me." Her eyes narrowed slightly. "She wasn't . . . accepted everywhere. Had a lot of cosmopolitan tastes and ideas for a Southern woman in the fifties. Conformity didn't appeal to her, and back then conformity was everything." She began walking toward the kitchen, her voice calm. "I think that's why Monica took the portrait—knowing it had monetary value but not sentimental value."

I followed her into the bright kitchen with white beadboard cabinets, gleaming stainless-steel appliances, and black granite countertops. "Then if it sells, I'll pay you room and board until I can figure out a more permanent situation for Beau and me. He's a young five, so he won't start kindergarten until next fall. I'd like to think that would give us enough time to get everything sorted out."

We heard Trey enter with our baggage and then head for the stairs. Attempting levity, I called out, "The LEGO duffel and backpack are Beau's; the brown suitcase is mine."

He paused for a moment. "Go lock up your car now so it doesn't get stolen. We'll take my truck."

"Is he always so friendly?" I asked as I poured myself a cup of coffee after Aimee declined.

"Only when he's sad or threatened, and I think he's both right now," Aimee said as she led us back to the foyer.

I frowned, then moved to Beau, who was standing too close to a shallow bowl, its metallic glow like that of a pearl, reflecting a rainbow of light and color. "When we spoke yesterday, Trey told me that he wanted us to drive to Biloxi today 'to get the ball rolling,' and that we had a ten-o'clock appointment with a builder. But do you know exactly where he's planning on taking me? I figure if I don't come back with him, you'll know what to tell the police."

Aimee's eyes sparkled. "Old friends of ours, the Kenneys, own a construction company in Biloxi—Kenney-Moise Homebuilders, Inc. It's the same family who helped me restore River Song after Camille, actually, although it's the son and daughter-in-law of the family now and not the father. Trey will want to discuss building plans and insurance money and time frames and that sort of thing. And I'm thinking he's expecting you to be discouraged over the whole scope of the project."

"And in that he'd be right," I said, leading Beau away from the table.

"But I'm bringing one of Monica's small paintings of River Song and a couple of photographs to guide the design. I don't think she'd want it changed, and I'm hoping Trey thinks the same thing."

Trey came down the stairs. "We should be back around suppertime, and if not I'll call you." He kissed Aimee on the cheek, then rumpled Beau's hair. "Don't have too much fun without me now, you hear?"

Beau giggled and Aimee smiled. "We'll try."

I knelt in front of Beau. "You have my cell phone number memorized now, right? Call me for anything, okay?" I hugged and kissed him before making my way to the front door. Before I made it outside, I turned back to Aimee. "Are you ever going to tell me which brother you married?"

"I imagine so. We'll have another chat when you get back. There's so much I have to tell you."

I nodded. "All right. I'll see you then." I followed Trey out the door, and as I shut it behind me, I thought I heard Aimee say something else. It wasn't until I was climbing into the passenger seat of Trey's pickup truck that I realized what it was. *There's so much you need to know.*

When I was ten years old and Chelsea about eight, our parents took us, and our older brother, to Cape May, New Jersey, to see the ocean for the first time. I had stood barefoot in the sand, feeling the uncomfortable grit between my toes, each digit curling up to escape. The surf crashed onto the beach, causing me to back away, unsure and afraid. But Chelsea had raced forward, her face tilted toward the sun, and then thrown herself into the water. She'd emerged with her hair plastered to her skin, with stories of how quiet and still it was beneath the waves, how dark, reminding her of a secret world where all past wrongs were forgotten and all that was old was new again. But all I could think was how big the ocean was, and that it seemed that if I went far enough I'd fall off the edge. And how very, very cold it had felt on my feet as I'd tried to escape it.

The hour-and-a-half drive to Biloxi was silent except for Trey's constant flipping of the radio stations, alternating between classic rock, country, and talk radio. It seemed less to do with his listening tastes and more to do with his reluctance to speak with me.

I spent the time staring out my open window, appreciating warmth in September and scenery that I hadn't completely taken in on my previous trip, because I'd been behind the steering wheel.

We crossed over Lake Pontchartrain, a name I wanted to know how to pronounce but had made up my mind not to ask Trey, and then we were passing through swamps and pine forests as the interstate followed the line of the coast. At one point, on an isolated stretch of highway to which I could see no beginning or end, something long and narrow lay up ahead by the roadside that reflected the sunlight. As we neared I squinted, trying to get a better look at what lay on the side of the road, thinking for a moment it was a large deer.

I craned my neck as we passed it, startled to see the long snout and ridged back of an alligator, a smear of blood on the pale and partially exposed underside. Trey didn't even turn his head.

"Was that alligator roadkill?"

Trey nodded, taking a sip from the coffee he'd stopped to get at a McDonald's drive-through. "We get that from time to time."

I sat back, my head pressed against the seat back. "Up north, we only have deer and the occasional dog or cat on the side of the road."

The side of his face crinkled. "Yeah, well, things are a little different down here."

My chest squeezed as I remembered Monica saying the same thing.

We passed signs for towns with familiar-sounding names: Waveland, Long Beach, Bay St. Louis. I wasn't sure why they were familiar to me but figured Monica had mentioned them, or I'd heard them on post-Katrina television coverage. But when I read them, I wanted to say them out loud, to let the names roll from my tongue like a favorite recipe long savored and eagerly anticipated. Instead, I remained silent, aware of Trey's brooding presence in the seat beside me, and of how very out-of-place I felt amid the alligators and strange place names.

I allowed my eyelids to drift closed, my body lulled by the rhythm of the tires against the road. When I awoke, I was unaware how long I'd slept or why Trey and I weren't supposed to be speaking. But I did remember what I'd been dreaming about, and it was still so vivid upon waking that when I looked out the truck window, I expected to see the house, its white columns reflecting the sunlight so that it was nearly blinding.

"Why was the house called River Song?" I asked, closing my eyes to shield them from the dream light.

He didn't answer right away. Finally, he said, "Monica named it. Thought that it needed one, I guess. The house had survived since the eighteen forties without a name, but that didn't sit right with Monica. And it wasn't all that grand a house, either, or one that you would think required a name. Just a typical raised cottage built more for comfort than show."

"That's what she loved about it," I said, forgetting for a moment whom I was talking to.

Trey looked at me, his eyes questioning. "Yeah. That she did." He focused on the road ahead when he spoke again. "She told you a lot about herself and her family, I guess. Lots of personal stuff."

I shifted in my seat. "Yes. She did. And I told her a lot about me and my family. We both led pretty isolated lives. I guess that's what drew us together initially. But we always seemed to understand which things we could share, and which things we didn't discuss."

He was silent for a long moment. "Did she ever tell you why she left?"

We sped by a highway sign indicating the East Beach Boulevard exit. I shook my head. "No. I asked her—many times. She never wanted to talk about it." I stared hard at the side of Trey's face. "I know the two of you were close. And that Aimee and Monica were more like mother and daughter, and that Aimee practically raised the two of you. I can't believe that neither one of you would know why Monica would just pack up one day and leave without explanation."

"Me, neither," he said quietly. Without looking at me, he said, "It's interesting, though. Because I also find it hard to believe that somebody she knew well enough to trust with her own son, she didn't trust enough with the truth."

I felt the familiar anger begin to burn again in my throat like bile, but I held it back. "I guess that makes us even, then, doesn't it?"

He took a sip of his coffee as if he hadn't heard me. When he finally spoke again, it was about the house. "The Pascagoula River, not too far from here, is called the Singing River. That's where the name came from."

"That's beautiful. But why is it called that?"

"Because near dusk in late summer and early fall, it makes the sound of a swarm of bees. Nobody's been able to come up with a scientific explanation, so people think the legend's true. I know Monica did."

"The legend?"

He turned on his signal and merged into the far lane, preparing to exit the interstate. "They say that the Pascagoula Indian tribe chose to drown themselves by walking into the river rather than be killed or enslaved by their mortal enemies, the Biloxis. They chanted as they walked to their deaths, men, women, and children, and it's that chant that people claim to hear."

"And Monica believed that?"

"She said she did. When Ray Von told her the story, it made her cry for days. It was only after Aimee allowed her to name the house in their honor that she stopped. But that was Monica. Couldn't tolerate injustice or dishonesty in any form. Guess we had our parents to thank for that."

"Because of their divorce."

He glanced at me briefly. "Yeah, and all that stuff that came before it. They never held anything back, even with Monica in the room. I reacted by punching out the first guy who looked at me the wrong way.

Monica reacted by . . . well, by becoming a real good kid. Honest and fair. It was as if she felt that if she was good, they wouldn't scream at each other so much."

I rested my head on the seat and closed my eyes for a moment, remembering my own family, and how each member reacted so differently when confronted with the same calamity. "She was still like that. In New York. Even when she couldn't make her rent, she never passed a panhandler without giving him something."

He pushed the "off" button on the radio, then waited a moment before speaking, as if each word had to be measured and weighed first. "Did you ever share with Monica about your sister?"

I felt as if a stone had rolled over on my heart, seeing for the first time the man next to me not just as an adversary, but as someone who'd known a missing girl, and searched for her, not knowing for years where she'd gone.

"Yes. I did. A lot at first."

A tic started in his jaw. "And yet you couldn't persuade her to call us?"

The heaviness inside was pushed aside as I turned on him. "Of course I did. That's why we stopped talking about it. There was nothing I could say or do that would convince her otherwise." I was embarrassed to feel tears pressing against the back of my eyelids, and I turned my head to the side, watching as tall pine trees slid past us. But as angry as I was, I could hear the desolation in his voice, the complete loss and lack of understanding, and for the first time I began to believe that maybe Trey really hadn't known why.

"I'm sorry," he said, his voice quiet.

Too close to tears, I just nodded.

We exited the interstate and made our way onto Beach Boulevard, the divided four-lane highway that ran parallel to the beach. On my trip before I'd been too nervous and exhausted to notice much more than street names and the address for a house that I hadn't yet known no longer existed. I didn't remember seeing the white sand or the gleaming water, or the stately homes that defiantly faced the shore—homes that were sandwiched between empty lots with steps leading to nowhere.

I turned to Trey. "Are we going to the home site first? We still have over an hour before our appointment with the builders."

"Eventually. I just figured you needed to see more of Biloxi to really appreciate what you're getting into."

I stared at the side of his face, the determined set of his jaw reminding me so much of Monica and Beau. Once they'd made up their minds, there was very little hope of dissuading them. But I was from New England, and I knew a thing or two about stubbornness that even mules hadn't yet discovered—something Detective Kobylt had told me more than once.

"If you think that showing me hurricane damage is going to change my mind, you're wrong. I've already determined that rebuilding in a hurricane zone is shortsighted and somewhat egotistical at best. I'm doing this for Monica. She had dreams of bringing her children here one day, and she was unable to fulfill those dreams. So she entrusted them to me, for whatever reason. When it's done, I'll go away. I don't think she ever meant the house to be mine, but for me to hold it for Beau. But I figure you can do that, too."

His jaw hardened slightly as he pulled the truck to a stop. "'Shortsighted and somewhat egotistical'?" He jerked his seat belt off. "I can't believe that I have waited all of this time to rebuild River Song with my sister, and I'm rewarded for my patience with having to deal with somebody who doesn't understand what it's like to live here. Or what it is to be a part of a place that has survived far worse than people like you who want us"—he swept his arm, encompassing the boats out in the sound, the cars, the oaks, the lighthouse, the houses—"to go away. Let me tell you—we've been fishing, building, producing, growing, living here for hundreds of years. And I'm not going to let somebody like you, somebody without roots, without a home, without any understanding of what it's like to have either, tell me that I'm being 'shortsighted and somewhat egotistical.'" He opened his door and slammed it shut behind him.

I scrambled out after him, feeling ambushed. "Look, I'm sorry. I didn't mean to insult you. I realize I'm an outsider, and I suppose that makes me a bit insensitive. I promise I'll keep my feelings to myself while we attempt to work together on this project. I'll do my best to try to think as Monica would have and leave my thoughts out of it."

"What about Beau? You'll just walk away when the house is finished?"

"I don't . . . no. I could never do that. Could I raise him by myself? I don't know. I need you to accept that we're all in a holding pattern right now, with no clear answers. I can't tell you that leaving Beau with his family instead of his staying with me is the right choice. Not until I know you better. But even then, Beau will always be a part of my life." I took a deep breath, tasting salt, and feeling the truth of my words. It was the first clear thought I'd had in months.

He didn't say anything, but folded his arms across his chest and stared out over the open water as gulls screeched above us searching the water and sand below. We stood in a "U"-shaped parking lot that jutted out onto a nearly deserted beach. I knew that even though the early fall temperatures were relatively warm, the water would not be. Behind us, in the median between the divided highway, stood the Biloxi Lighthouse. I recognized it from the pictures Monica had shown me: the photographs of a laughing Monica as a young girl with her brother and cousins.

"Monica loved this lighthouse. She said that on her trips to the coast, as soon as she saw it she knew she was home. I can't believe it survived Katrina." I looked over my shoulder, remembering what Ray Von had told me about not speaking the name out loud, wondering who else might have heard.

"It survived Katrina. And Camille. And all storms since it was built in the mid–eighteen hundreds. It leans now because of the thirty-foot storm surge after Katrina, but it's still standing." He slid on a pair of sunglasses, twin lighthouses visible in the lenses. "They just finished a major restoration, so I imagine it can withstand more hurricanes. And an oil spill."

I looked at him sharply. "I guess you guys down here didn't need that on top of everything else."

"No, we sure didn't."

He pointed to a construction site across the street. "That's the new history center. A house that was built in the eighteen fifties used to stand there."

"Before Katrina."

He nodded. "All that was left was eight stained-glass windows they found intact in the middle of a pile of rubble. It's amazing what survived and what didn't. No rhyme or reason, it seems."

A strong breeze pushed at me, making me pull my sweater close to my neck. I looked away, toward the water, seeing a faint and distant stretch of land. "What's out there?"

"Ship Island. Actually West Ship Island. It used to be one big connected island until Camille in 'sixty-nine cut it in half so that we now have East and West. Katrina pretty much took out what was left of East Ship. There's an old fort on the end of the island, and you can take charter boats out there to see it. It was one of my favorite things to do as a boy."

I studied Trey, trying to picture him as a boy like Beau, excited to get on a boat to see a fort, but couldn't. Nor could I imagine the kind of a storm that could rip an island in half. "Do we have time to take a walk?"

He shrugged. "Why not?"

I stared at him for a moment, wanting so much to like him, to remember the kind of brother he'd been to Monica, how all of Monica's stories and good memories revolved around him.

He slid out of his topsiders as I took off my ballet flats, then followed his lead as he stepped over the short barrier at the edge of the asphalt and onto the sand of the beach. I stood still for a moment, remembering the long-ago day when I'd stood on the beach in Cape May with Chelsea. But the surf here was gentler, the water browner, the sand whiter. It was familiar but not the same, like biting into chocolate ice cream to find out that it tasted like strawberry instead.

"What's wrong?" Trey had stopped to look back at me, his face wearing an unexpected grin under his sunglasses.

"Nothing. It's just that . . . the sand. It's so white. And fine—almost like salt."

Nodding, he turned and began walking west down the beach. "Yeah, it's kind of a specialty here. Like alligator roadkill." I could hear the smile in his words.

I caught up with him, and we walked for a short distance, past a closed Jet Ski and beach umbrella shack, keeping away from the surf on the wide beach and staying near Beach Boulevard. I kept my head down, looking for shells, occasionally stopping to pick one up and slip it into the pocket of my sweater. Always collecting things. Monica had said that to me so many times that I had stopped hearing it. Or wondering why I felt compelled to gather objects in small collections.

I stopped for a moment, brushing off the fine sand from my hands. "Can you build sand castles with this stuff?"

He cocked an eyebrow above his sunglasses. "Absolutely." He took a couple of steps. "Maybe Beau can show you someday."

I looked at him to see if he was offering an olive branch, then stopped, noticing some kind of a sculpture up on the median of the road. "What is that?" I asked, pointing.

He followed my gaze, then began walking toward the road. "It's a Katrina tree. Come here; I'll show you."

I quickened my steps to catch up, then quickly wiped off the sand from my feet before putting my shoes back on when we reached the road. We waited for a car to pass before crossing to the median, where I found myself standing beneath what appeared to be a pod of dolphins carved from raw wood, now stained and sealed in brown.

Trey stood next to me and looked up at the sculpture, his face expressionless. "This used to be one of the hundreds of oaks that lined

Beach Boulevard before the hurricane. A lot of them died because the storm surge brought in the salt water and killed them. And the ones that survived were stripped down to the wood. Eventually, the leaves grew back on the live ones, but the dead ones were too painful to look at." He slid off his sunglasses and tucked them into the collar of his shirt. "A guy from Florida came up and decided to transform the dead trees into different sculptures. And I know at least one other artist has joined in and transformed a bunch of the dead trees. There're over a dozen of them—mostly on Beach Boulevard."

I examined the sculpture more closely, the graceful arch of the backs of the dolphins as they swam through invisible waves, reaching for sky. The pod was split in a low vee, each leg a string of connected dolphins, the ones on the tips balanced on the wooden nose of the dolphin behind them. The sculpture exuded an odd mixture of fragility and strength, like a spiderweb spun from steel. "And this isn't too painful to look at?"

He faced me, his eyes cold. "What do you mean?"

I closed my mouth, unsure. I didn't understand the need to cling to remnants of a painful memory, considering them an unnecessary detour. Like my father, who would sit in Chelsea's bedroom for hours, just crying. It was my mother, and then me after she'd died, who'd pressed on in the search, knowing that our family could be complete again only once we'd found her.

"I would think that people would want the trees cut down, and new ones planted. Or to build a tall wall or . . . something. Maybe plant the trees on the empty lots instead of rebuilding houses that are liable to be blown away again. Anything, really, that would help people solve the problem instead of re-creating it."

He looked at me as if I'd just suddenly spoken in fluent Mandarin with no hope of translation. "Why are you here, Julie? What do you want?"

I stared back at him, trying to think of a way to explain how I'd eradicated the word "want" from my vocabulary long ago and replaced it with "need." It made life so much easier that way, blowing away all the unnecessary and distracting clutter from a life of purpose, much like I imagined a storm sweeping away anything not strong enough to withstand the struggle.

"Nothing," I managed. "I'm here to do what Monica wanted, because she can't. And that's all." I glanced at the dolphins again, at their almost-smiles and their bodies straining forward toward . . . what? Looking down at my watch, I said, "We'd better get back to the truck."

Turning my back on Trey and the dead oak tree, I trudged down the side of the road toward the lighthouse, dropping the seashells I'd collected one by one, until my pockets were empty.

CHAPTER 8

He who, having lost one ideal, refuses to give his heart and
soul to another and nobler, is like a man who declines to build
a house on rock because the wind and rain ruined his house on
the sand.   —CONSTANCE NADEN

Julie

The ride back to New Orleans in the dark was more silent than
the trip to Biloxi. Not even the radio interrupted Trey's stewing
anger over our conversation about the oak trees, or my own uncertainties. As we hurtled through the night, past swamps and deep forests, I
pictured all the slithering reptiles outside my window, and not one of
them scared me as much as the thought of rebuilding Monica's house.
I just wasn't sure what frightened me more: failing in my attempt to
fulfill somebody else's dream, or discovering that my detour could be
more permanent than I expected.

My phone rang around seven thirty. It was Nancy Mayer from
Mayer and Ryan to let me know that she'd had a generous offer from an
anonymous buyer to purchase the portrait. I accepted the offer without
much thought, eager to prove to Trey that I could contribute to Beau's
and my living expenses. But I also wanted him to sweat a little longer,

so I kept the details of my conversation to myself, letting him guess and waiting for him to ask. He didn't.

As we approached the city I stared out my window into the dark, watching as its twinkling lights drew near. New Orleans wore night like a carnival mask, hiding her imperfections under the forgiving and sporadic arcs of light. She was still much of a stranger to me, and I looked forward to getting to know her for myself and not from Monica's stories or pictures from the evening news.

I was starving, and I was sure Trey was, too, since we hadn't eaten since a brief lunch with the people from Kenney-Moise. But Trey and I seemed to be in a contest as to who could be more pissed off with the other, and both of us remained silent and hungry until we pulled onto First Street. This proved nothing more than that New England dog-gedness had found its match in Southern-bred stubbornness.

The front door opened, and Aimee stood waiting while Beau, dressed in his LEGO pajamas, threw himself at me, nearly toppling me from the bottom step, where I'd braced myself. "Hey, buddy. I missed you, too." I picked him up, and as he rested his head on my shoulder I smelled soap and baby shampoo.

"Kathy gave him a bath, seeing as he was wearing most of the garden—what wasn't washed off in the fountain, of course. I hope that's all right."

I walked up the rest of the steps. "Of course. Thank you."

She stepped back to allow us in. "Beau said he needed you to read to him before bedtime, so I let him stay up until you got back." Her gaze took in Trey's closed expression. "From my last phone conversation with Trey, I take it that neither one of you has eaten. I had Kathy make two plates and put them in the warmer in case you wanted something."

"Thank you, Aimee. Let me put Beau to bed first, and I'll be right down."

To my surprise, Beau hugged Aimee and kissed her cheek loudly before racing toward the stairs. As if in afterthought, he paused on the balcony and turned around again. "Good night, Uncle Trey."

Trey grinned, transforming his face. "Good night, Beau. I'll see you tomorrow."

I listened to the patter of Beau's feet against hardwood as he ran up the rest of the stairs; then I followed, my stomach rumbling loudly.

When I returned, the foyer was empty but the swinging kitchen door had been propped open. I entered, surprised to find Aimee alone, a glass of white wine in front of her and an untouched glass on the kitchen table across from her. A foil-wrapped plate sat next to it, along with silverware and a cloth napkin.

"Where's Trey?" I asked as I pulled out my chair and sat down.

Aimee didn't answer right away and I sensed her disapproval. "He took his plate to his study. Said he needed to catch up on some work, since he missed a whole day today."

I took off the foil, my stomach grumbling even more loudly when I smelled the fried chicken, sweet corn, and mashed potatoes swimming in gravy. "Where does Trey work? I know he went to Tulane under-grad, but that's all Monica told me."

"He went to Tulane law and then worked for my husband's firm for a while after law school, but then formed his own practice with two other partners."

I nodded, my mouth too full of chicken for me to respond right away. Finally, I asked, "How is he going to find the time to restore the house in Biloxi and work?"

"Trey has always been good about getting things done. Especially when he's motivated. He'll find a way to get it done as quickly as possible, if it means that you'll be leaving when it's done."

I quirked an eyebrow.

"I'm just telling you what he told me. I'm taking it that things didn't go well in Biloxi today."

I took a bite of potato and washed it down with a sip of wine. "Actually, the talk with the builders went very well. I brought a painting that Monica had done of River Song, and they said that it would take a lot of the guesswork out of starting from scratch. Plus, they still had the plans from when it was rebuilt after Camille, and Trey was able to fill in any missing pieces, so they've got a great place to start. I just find it very hard to work with somebody who doesn't want me there, and I have to admit that I didn't make it easy for him. I made the mistake of telling him that people who rebuild in hurricane zones are 'egotistical and shortsighted.'" I grimaced at the memory. "He didn't appreciate my opinion."

Aimee sat back in her chair, her hands cradling the bottom of her glass in her lap, her expression unreadable. "No, I don't imagine he would have."

When she didn't say anything else, I added, "They're saying they could have it all done in seven to nine months, depending on the weather and other factors that we can't control. Trey wants to use new hurricane-resistant materials, and there aren't a lot of suppliers, so we might be at the mercy of their time line."

A sharp tap on the back door leading out into the yard startled me, but Aimee was already rising from her chair. "That's just Xavier stopping by for his check."

I stood, too, and faced the door.

Aimee grabbed an envelope from the counter before opening the door. Xavier stood outside and out of sight at first, and I felt myself relaxing. And then Aimee invited him into the kitchen, and I could see his face in the yellow glow of the chandelier, his scars seeming to undulate in the uneven light from the overhead fixture.

"Julie Holt, this is Xavier Williams. You met his mother, Ray Von, already."

I forced myself to move forward and even held out my hand, which he ignored. Slowly, I lowered it to my side. "It's nice to meet you." He carried with him the scent of the garden: of the moist earth and green, growing things. I hadn't expected that.

He remained silent, his one good eye beneath a gray, grizzled eyebrow focused on me.

Aimee continued. "She was a good friend of Monica's. And Julie's the one who brought Beau to us."

Xavier nodded as he neatly folded the envelope Aimee had given him into compact rectangles before shoving it in his back pocket. "Thank you, Miss Aimee. I'll be back next week and start getting your garden ready for fall."

His voice surprised me, too. It was light and melodic, his diction as precise as his mother's. With a quick good-bye, he slipped outside the back door and disappeared soundlessly into the yard.

I gathered my nearly empty plate, then rinsed it in the sink before placing it into the dishwasher.

"Looks can be deceiving, Julie." I faced Aimee as she poured more wine into both of our glasses. "He was burned as a young boy, and as a result people have shunned him all of his life. It's made him painfully shy, but he's a good person."

Feeling chastised, I sat down at the table. "I know. I'm sorry. You'd think after living in the city for so long nothing would shock me." I picked up my glass and took a sip of wine. "Monica said that his mother, Ray Von, used to work for you?"

"Eventually. She worked for my mother-in-law before Caroline was married. Caroline's the one who educated her, taught her how to speak like she'd gone to an English boarding school. In nineteen fifty, the Duke and Duchess of Windsor came to New Orleans for Mardi Gras and Caroline thought she'd be in town to be presented to them. I was told that she and Ray Von spent months practicing their accents for that, and that Ray Von never stopped practicing. Unfortunately, Caroline didn't make it back to New Orleans until later that summer and missed that Mardi Gras season completely."

"What a shame, after all that work. Why did she miss it?"

Aimee's eyes avoided mine. "Her husband didn't think she was ready to mix with society yet. Caroline had had some kind of a . . . breakdown, I guess you'd call it today. That's why she moved to Atlanta with the boys. Her parents were there and the best doctors." She smiled. "But she was back in New Orleans that summer."

I drained my glass. "You said that you and Monica loved River Song, because it made you feel safe. Why did you need to feel safe?"

Her eyes settled on me. "Are you ready to hear more of the story?"

I nodded and watched as she emptied the bottle into our glasses.

Aimee

SUMMER 1950

Cigarette smoke invaded the early-morning air as I stepped onto my grandmother's front porch. It seemed to sit on the thick humidity, lingering in the trees and bushes. I walked next door on the cracked sidewalk past our stiff and formal gardens to the Guidry house. Pushing open the gate, I saw what my grandmother called the "garish display of color." Climbing hydrangea drooped haphazardly off of trellises, while large clay pots exhibited their gaudy offerings of forget-me-nots and verbena in the shade of the fountain. The bronze little boy peed happily in the burbling fountain. A lime green gecko crept up the side of the newly patched cement of the shallow basin, lifting his head and examining his surroundings. I let the gate close, the iron clanging in the hushed atmosphere of the front garden. Startled, the gecko scurried into one of the clay pots.

"Good morning, Aimee."

Mrs. Guidry sat at a small wrought-iron table on the porch. She blew smoke out through her nose, and I watched it expand and evaporate as it reached the ceiling. I wondered what Grandmother would say about that, seeing as how I'd had to listen again and again to her lectures regarding the evils of smoking and how only a certain class of women would even consider doing it.

"Good morning, Mrs. Guidry," I said as I climbed the steps. Her eyes were red rimmed and puffy, with dark circles marring the delicate skin under them, her beauty hibernating under stale makeup. She took a long drag from a cigarette and closed her eyes. I caught a whiff of alcohol clinging to her silk robe, and her hand shook as she took another puff. Her alligator brooch was pinned to the collar of the robe, which didn't surprise me. I don't think I'd ever seen her without it.

Mrs. Guidry had changed in the short time since I had met her at the beginning of the summer. The pink bloom of her skin had faded, her posture drooping slightly, like one of those delicate flowers left out in the hot sun too long. But she was still beautiful to me.

She opened her eyes to slits and looked at me, offering a gentle smile. The only time I ever saw her smile was either at me or at one of her boys. "Sit down, Aimee. Let's have us some girl chat."

I had never seen her like this. She was always well-groomed and burning with vibrant energy. But this morning she was wilted, frayed around the edges. I sat gingerly on the edge of a cushioned chair opposite her, the fabric moist on my bare legs from the pressing humidity. Although I'd had a tongue-lashing from my grandmother and a gentle scolding from Mr. Guidry regarding what I'd done to Gary on the levee, Mrs. Guidry had yet to say anything to me, and I wondered if she'd been waiting for an opportunity like this to get me alone. I swallowed thickly, and waited.

She continued to regard me through half-open eyes. "Seeing as how you are without a mother, I was hoping I might give you a little bit of motherly advice."

Curious, I slid back in my chair, feeling the damp chill of the wrought iron on my bare arms. She leaned forward and stabbed out her cigarette in the crystal ashtray. Her eyes were dark, muddy pools, without focus. She seemed to stare through me, seeing something I couldn't. Leaning over, she took my hand. I flinched at the iciness of her touch.

She picked up my hand and turned it over slowly. Gary had told me that his mother liked to tell people's fortunes by looking at their palms, and I felt a tremor of excitement as she examined my upturned hand. A long red fingernail, something else I knew my grandmother wouldn't approve of, traced the lines of my palm as Mrs. Guidry silently studied my pale skin. Finally, she gave my hand a squeeze and placed it on my lap.

Sitting back, she reached for her gold cigarette case.

I couldn't hold back my curiosity. "Did you see anything?" My voice sounded hesitant.

She tapped the end of a cigarette against the closed case. She looked at me without smiling. "Yes, I did." A matching gold lighter appeared from the pocket of her robe. Her long, elegant fingers flicked it and held it to the end of the cigarette. She took a deep drag and leaned her head against the back of the chair.

"You have beautiful hands, Aimee. Delicate, but strong. Like your mother's. Like you. You'll need to be strong." Her voice dropped to a whisper as she lifted her head to look at me. "Do you sing, Aimee? Your mother had the most beautiful voice. She could have been something if she hadn't married and had you."

I remembered my mother's singing. She sang in the garden, and in the kitchen, and to me. It had been the unnatural silence of the house after her death that I think eventually unnerved my father enough to make us move away. Even now, when I fall asleep, I imagine I can still hear her singing. But I'd never thought that her being married to my father and being my mother had been a sacrifice. I blinked at Mrs. Guidry, not understanding.

Suddenly, she sat up, crushed the cigarette in the ashtray, and leaned toward me to grab each wrist. "Be careful with your heart. You will have a choice to make, but you are destined to love only once. Choose wisely." She squeezed my wrists, causing numbness in my fingers, but the vehemence in her eyes wouldn't let me pull away.

"Be happy, Aimee. Without happiness in your heart, you have nothing." Her eyes were wide and bright, tears pooling at the bottom but not yet spilling over.

I leaned forward. Nobody ever spoke about my mother, as if she'd never existed. As if my memory of the coppery smell of blood and my mother's cold skin were a nightmare from which I'd never completely awakened. "Tell me about her, Mrs. Guidry. Tell me about my mother."

The front door opened and Mr. Guidry strode out onto the porch. Mrs. Guidry released my arms abruptly, shrinking back in her chair.

Nodding in my direction, Mr. Guidry leaned over his wife. His voice was soft, but I could tell he was angry. "What are you doing out here? You're not even dressed."

Her chin dropped to her chest.

He turned to me. "I'm sorry, Aimee. Has she said anything to upset you? She gets confused sometimes and says things that . . . don't make any sense."

I shook my head, desperate to leave.

"She needs to rest. She had a bad night." He took her by both elbows and lifted her from the chair. She seemed to droop in his grasp, her head bowed and the dark hair falling over her face. He guided her inside the house without a backward glance.

I continued to sit on the porch, rubbing my wrists. A movement at the door caught my attention, and I saw a woman in her early thirties staring at me with open curiosity. Her skin was the color of café au lait, creamy and smooth, her green eyes brilliant against her darker skin. From her expression, it appeared she knew who I was. I was sure I had never seen her before. I stood to leave but heard a deep voice coming from inside.

"Aimee." Wes appeared where the woman had been. I was embarrassed by the scene I had just witnessed and tried to escape from the porch.

"Don't go." He touched my elbow and led me off the front porch toward the fountain. His wet hair was combed off his forehead and he smelled of soap. We stopped behind the statue, and I suddenly remembered that he had seen me in only my unmentionables and jeans. I felt the blood rush to my cheeks, so I turned my head, only to find myself staring directly at the peeing part of the little statue.

Sensing my discomfort, he touched my elbow again and led me out the front gate. Instead of turning right to go to my house, we turned left, our pace leisurely.

"I'm sorry you had to see my mother that way. She's . . . ill. We were hoping she was well enough to return to New Orleans, but I suppose we were just being optimistic. She was in a home for delicate women up in Atlanta—that's where our grandparents live. But she kept wanting to come back to New Orleans. There's something about this place. . . ."

We stepped carefully over the cracks in the sidewalk where large roots from towering oaks protruded from between the flagstones like arms from underground monsters. I waited for him to continue, but he changed the subject. "I hope she didn't say anything to scare you."

I shook my head. "No, not really. She did read my palm, but I wouldn't call it scary."

"Really? What did she say?"

I stopped, trying to remember all of her words. "She said I would have a choice to make, but that I would only fall in love once, and to choose wisely."

"That's odd."

We faced each other, and he looked directly into my eyes. His were darker than Gary's, deeper. I felt myself blushing, and I silently cursed this affliction of mine.

"Why are you blushing?"

I could feel my face turning at least two shades darker. I studied my feet, not really sure how to answer.

He touched my chin and brought my face back up. "Don't be embarrassed. The ability to blush is an admirable trait—I certainly don't see it very often. You get that red when you're angry, too, you know."

His hand dropped, and I grinned. "It's a good thing, then, that I don't get angry very often. Wouldn't want my head to explode or anything."

He laughed and shook his head. Turning around, he gestured for me to follow him back to his house. "Nope—wouldn't want that to happen to such a pretty head." His words were teasing, but I found myself straining to hear more in his voice.

Gary stepped out from my grandmother's front gate. He wore white Converse sneakers and rolled-up blue jeans, his starched plaid shirttails hanging out the back. "Aimee! I thought we were supposed to go for a bike ride."

"Hang on; I'm coming."

Wes sent me a sidelong grin as I walked back with him. Then I remembered something he had said. I pulled on his sleeve. "Why is what your mother told me odd?"

He looked down at me, his blue eyes bright in the morning sun glow. "Because she told me the exact same thing."

Before I could respond, he waved to Gary, then walked across his front garden and into the house.

My attention returned to Gary, who was leaning over with his hands on his knees, taking deep breaths. "Shit, I can barely breathe in this humidity."

"Do you kiss your mama with that dirty mouth?"

He gave me a crooked grin. "Where do you think I learned it?" He stood up straight. "Instead of a bike ride, wanna go to McKenzie's? I've been dying to have one of their éclairs."

"Sure." I followed him down the sidewalk toward Prytania, where Greek Revival mansions mingled with gingerbread Victorians. I stopped, feeling the hairs on the back of my neck stand at attention, and looked behind me. I saw Aunt Roseanne on our porch, stiff broom in hand.

She waved to me and shouted, "You be back by eleven, you hear? Your grandmama wants to take you shopping."

I waved back, still feeling the prickly sensation at the base of my skull. Before I turned around, I looked at the Guidrys' house in time to see a curtain close in an upstairs window, the lace sheers swinging slightly. I turned and ran to catch up to Gary. Grabbing his hand, I pulled him across to the other side of the street.

"What's the matter?" Gary gripped my hand tightly, his eyes anxiously searching mine.

I shrugged, not sure how to explain what had just happened. "I just got spooked, that's all."

He continued to hold my hand until we reached the bakery. He held the door open, and I stepped in ahead of him. The sweet smell of baking bread hit me full force, immediately making me hungry. I sat down in a wrought-iron chair and slid up to the table while Gary placed our order at the counter. I stared at the shelves on the side of the store crammed with cookies, ladyfingers, brownies, macaroons, and Belgian slices. My gaze traveled along the wall to the refrigerated cases where the clerk was plucking up pastries for Gary with a giant tweezer. I saw the famous McKenzie Doberge cakes under the glare of fluorescents, and thought of Aunt Roseanne, who sometimes hid one in the kitchen for me out of Grandmother's sight. I could almost taste the thin layers of cake tucked between additional layers of pudding. I licked my lips, then turned to look out the window.

Gary returned to the table, his tray laden with creamy confections. Feeling self-conscious, I smoothed down my napkin over my thighs.

"Life isn't fair," I said as I took a sip of my Coca-Cola.

"Whaddaya mean?" Gary asked with his mouth full, a blot of cream perched on the corner of his lips.

"You eat like a horse, but you're so skinny. I'll probably get fat just by watching you eat."

He paused in his chewing. "I sure hope not. I don't think your blue jeans could get any tighter."

I opened my mouth to make some retort about how I wasn't fat nor my blue jeans tight—like my grandmother would allow that—when the glass door swung open, the bell ringing loudly in the quiet room. The same woman I had seen behind the screen door at the Guidrys' walked in.

Gary turned to see what I was looking at. He gave the woman a wary smile as she walked up to our table, and I became aware of other people turning to watch. She walked as if she owned the place, and it wouldn't have surprised me at all if she'd sat at our table.

"Garrick, you know you're not supposed to be eating that stuff." Her words were precise and measured, allowing no room for any kind of accent, as if she'd rehearsed them over and over again until she got them right. "And you forgot your medicine." She slid a small vial of pills across the table to him.

The pink stain on Gary's neck spilled over his jawbones and spread up to his forehead until even the tips of his ears were afflicted. He grabbed the pills and shoved them into his shirt pocket. "I'll take them when I get home."

The woman reached over and took the vial out of his pocket. "No, your heart needs them now." She opened the lid and two pills clattered onto the tabletop.

I stared at the woman in surprise. "His heart?"

I found myself looking into a pair of pale green eyes. "His heart is fine now, because he's taking his pills. But those doctors over at Ochsner know this young man quite well."

Without looking up, he picked up his pills and put them both in his mouth. Then he leaned back in his chair, his arms folded across his skinny chest, and shoved the last bite of an éclair into his mouth.

The woman turned to me. "You must be Mrs. Mercier's granddaughter. The girl who made Garrick go into the river." Her cool eyes appraised me, and I felt she found me lacking.

Gary tilted his head in her direction. "This is Ray Von Williams. She helps Mama get through her days."

Ray Von crossed her arms over her chest and looked at Gary. "And him, too, when he's smart enough to let me."

Gary resumed his attack on the pastries, but the scowl still sat on his face. He barely glanced at me.

Ray Von returned to me. "If you need any love potions or some such you just let me know. When you grow into your looks you'll be needing potions to keep all them boys away—two in particular I can think of."

I felt the blood rush to my face and looked at Gary for relief. His face was conveniently averted as he began digging in his pocket for money. "You and your ghosts and voodoo stuff, Ray Von. If my father ever found out about any of your mumbo jumbo, he'd fire you in a minute."

Ray Von gave him a regal stare. "You know as well as I do, Mr. Garrick, that that will never happen." She picked up the vial of pills and put it back in her purse. "And don't forget to take your pills next time. I don't have the time or energy to go chasing you all over New Orleans." Her tall, lean form left the bakery, and heads turned to watch.

I looked back at Gary, who was slapping change on the table. "Who is she really, Gary?"

He slid his chair back and stood. "She's been with Mama's family since she was born. Ray Von's mother was their cook, and she just sort of grew up being around my mother. Considering Ray Von's the only person who can handle Mama, she's pretty much the boss."

"Like a companion?" I asked, recalling the occupation of one of the heroines in the novels Aunt Roseanne liked to read. I hadn't known that such a thing existed in the real world.

"Something like that."

He held the door open for me, and I stepped out onto the wide side-walk. Ray Von was nowhere in sight. "Where'd she go?"

Gary glanced both ways on Prytania and across the street to First Street. "I don't know. Ray Von's always doing stuff like that. Don't let her worry you. She's always looking out for us. And she takes good care of my mother."

We started down the sidewalk, the summer heat slowing our pace. As we reached the intersection of Prytania and First, I swung an arm out and knocked him in the shoulder. "Why didn't you tell me about your heart? It's not like I would tell anybody if you didn't want me to." It had suddenly occurred to me why he wore a T-shirt when we went swimming. He told me it was because he burned easily, but I now had a suspicion he was hiding something.

His jaws clenched, and he kept his gaze straight ahead. He walked as he talked, not once looking at me. "I don't want anyone thinking I'm a wimp or anything. I see how people treat my mother, and I don't want them to look at me that way."

I tugged on his arm. "Your brother said she'd been in a home for delicate women. What's wrong with her?"

He stopped so abruptly, I almost ran into him. Sweat beaded on his forehead, and he angrily wiped it away with his forearm. "Besides my father, you mean? God knows—she's got lots of problems. But he's the reason for every single one of them."

He stared at me as if he knew he had already said too much. "I gotta go. I'll see you later." Gary pushed open the black iron gate leading into his front garden, then let it slam behind him before rushing up the path and into the house.

The little boy in the fountain continued with his business, the only sound in the still garden. I was about to turn when a movement at the corner of my eye caught my attention. Tilting my head back, I saw a face in a third-story window. I was sure it was a boy—a few years older than me—with light brown skin. One eye was closed, the other one staring right at me. Something about his skin and closed eye didn't look quite right. His hands were pressed against the panes, as if to form another barrier between him and me. Slowly, he backed away, out of my sight, until the window again appeared as an empty eye on the front of the house.

Despite the heat and heavy humidity, goose bumps prickled my arms. Without turning my back on the house, I inched my way to the gate, then walked away as quickly as I could to the safety of Grandmother's house.

CHAPTER 9

Center: Generally speaking, the vertical axis of a tropical cyclone, usually defined by the location of minimum wind or minimum pressure. —National Hurricane Center

Julie

I looked down into my empty wineglass, wondering how long it had been since my last sip. "Is that why you needed a place to feel safe?"

Aimee looked at me, and her eyes were tired. "Because of Xavier?" She shook her head, then stood. "No. It was because of how my mother died, and why nobody ever spoke of it or her again."

I stood, too. I felt light-headed from the wine, and it loosened my usual reserve. "How did your mother die?"

She paused for a moment, leaning heavily on the table. "It's a long story, and it's too late to go into it now. Another time, all right?" Without waiting for me to answer, she placed her wineglass in the sink and headed toward the kitchen door, holding it open for me.

"Your room is ready—it's the blue room right next to Beau's, and there's a connecting bathroom in case he gets up and calls for you. You'll probably want to leave the doors open. There're clean towels behind the doors, and I put a night-light in there, too. Please let me know if there's anything else you need."

"You've been more than generous, Miss Aimee. Thank you. But there is one thing." I hesitated just for a moment, not wanting to ask her for anything else. "Do you have a computer I could use? I need to access the Internet."

Her eyes softened, as if she knew the reason, and I felt like a child with her hand caught in the cookie jar. "Trey has one in his office that I'm sure he wouldn't mind you using. It's the door next to the kitchen by the stairs. If the door's closed, just knock. Otherwise, you're welcome to go in."

We said good night, and I stood in the foyer watching until she was safely up the stairs. The door to the study was open, but I tapped anyway, not wanting Trey to find another reason to dislike me. It was a man's study, with dark wood paneling and red plaid fabric on the windows, with a small couch tucked between the windows. A partner's desk was positioned near the middle of the room, a flat-panel monitor monopolizing a back corner of it. A wastebasket sat by the desk, and I recognized the wadded foil from our dinner sitting on top.

Two walls were lined with crammed bookshelves that went up to the ceiling. Curious, I moved closer to get a better look at them. Most were law books of various vintages. Several had bindings that were shredded at the top, the binding threads exposed through the leather, the gold lettering on the spines nearly vanished. Others had barely a spine crease, either because they were new or maybe just never opened.

There was very little fiction, and most of it the oddly placed Nelson DeMille or Stuart Woods thriller, but there was also a surprising collection of art books. I counted at least five on the potter George Ohr, and at least as many about William and Ellsworth Woodward and Newcomb pottery. They were like old friends to me, and I itched to be able to take them off the shelves and read them. I decided to borrow one to take upstairs to read when I was finished on the computer.

I was about to head toward the desk when a slender volume in a red dust jacket caught my attention. It was placed on a high shelf, just about out of my reach, and stuck between two larger books so that it was almost hidden, and would have been except for the color of the jacket. And the fact that I recognized the book.

A short wooden ladder sat in the corner, and I pulled it over, and even then barely managed to dislodge the book from the shelf. It stuck slightly to the wood and created a puff of dust as I pulled it down, making me sneeze. *Abe Holt: The Man and the Artist.* I owned the book, and had since its first printing in 1999. I wouldn't have been surprised to find the book on these shelves, considering the subject matter of the other books, except that this was my great-grandfather, and the artist of the portrait Monica had given to me.

I stepped off the ladder with the book and placed it on a small table by the door to bring up with me when I went upstairs. I stared at it for a long moment, a feeling of déjà vu enveloping me, before turning away from it and moving to the desk.

I sat down and jiggled the mouse to get the computer out of sleep mode, then stopped when I saw the computer desktop background, my eyes suddenly blurry. It was a photograph of two sun-bleached blond children at a beach, building a sand castle. A young boy, unmistakably Trey, about ten years old, appeared to be digging a moat, his tongue tucked between his teeth as he concentrated on his task. But eight-year-old Monica, wearing a red bathing suit with a ruffled peplum, was tucking small shells into a lacelike pattern along the edges of the para-pet of the castle and doorway arch. The shadow of the photographer loomed over the sand castle and children as Monica looked at the cam-era with a mixture of surprise and concentration. I sat back in the chair and looked at her face, and the innocence of childhood that was long gone by the time I'd met her. I remembered Aimee's words, something about childhood summers before the burdens of growing up had found them. Looking at the picture on the computer screen, I knew exactly what she meant.

"That's Biloxi Beach about 1990."

I startled and jerked around in the chair. Trey stood behind me, holding a short glass with gold liquid and an ice cube in it and looking at the monitor.

"I'm sorry," I stammered. "I'll get up if you need to use the computer. Aimee said I could use it if you weren't in here."

I stood to leave, but he held me back with his hand. "You're fine. I was just coming in to shut it off." He pointed at the picture. "That's so Monica. She could never just build a castle. She always had to make it a work of art. And then she'd cry for a day after the tide washed it away." His words almost sounded critical, but the picture was on his computer screen, where he could see it every day.

I looked back at the screen. "Who's taking the picture?"

"Aimee. She's the only one who took pictures of us as children."

I studied Monica's face again, wishing I had one more chance to talk with her. Without turning around, I asked, "Where were your parents?"

I felt him shrug. "Who knows? They rarely came to River Song. I think that they and Aimee had a mutual agreement about that."

Facing him, I asked, "Where are your parents now?" I knew they were still alive—Monica had told me that much—but she hadn't mentioned them with any frequency or affection.

His voice sounded nonchalant, but there was a current of hurt there, too: the same current I recognized in Monica's voice as she'd told me her stories. "Our mother is on husband number four and living in Costa Rica. Our father is around somewhere. He's a real estate developer, so you can imagine the kind of hit he took from Katrina. You can normally find him at Tipitina's or Miss Mae's—the first has great music; the second has cheap beer. Or any other establishment that serves alcohol that's close enough for him to stumble home to his apartment on Magazine." He took a drink from his glass and ice clicked against the side.

He indicated the computer. "Is there anything I can help you navigate to?"

"I can't find your Internet Explorer icon. After that, I can manage on my own."

It looked for a moment as if he would say something. Instead, he leaned over and clicked the mouse on the far left corner and then went to the bookmarks tab and a folder called "Monica." The tabs inside the folder were listed alphabetically, and he scrolled down until he reached one labeled "FBI." He straightened but remained silent.

I swallowed. Then I raised my hand and hit the backspace button to view all the other bookmarks in the folder, state agencies and other sites for missing persons, many of them the same ones I used in my search for Chelsea. *Every day. Not a single day has gone by since she left that I haven't searched for her.* I remembered what Trey had said, and, staring at the evidence in front of me, I finally believed it to be true. I couldn't look at him, afraid he might see that I had ever doubted him.

After clearing my throat, I said, "I try to go through these sites on a regular basis, so that if anybody is found, or goes missing in the same geographical area, or even bears a physical resemblance to Chelsea, I can let the detective in charge of her case know about it."

"It's hard to look at them all, isn't it?"

I nodded.

"How long has it been?" he asked.

"Seventeen years. She and Monica would have been the same age. The police did an age-progression picture of Chelsea a few years ago to show what she'd look like now. But I still see her the way she looked when she was ten."

Ice clinked in his glass again. "Seventeen years. That's a very long time."

I didn't answer, knowing there was no way to quantify time spent in searching as if it were nothing more than measuring rainfall in a cup.

The ice clinked again; then he said, "Just turn off the computer when you're done, and any lights. I'm in the carriage house out back if you need me, but try not to open any of the outside doors, because I'm setting the alarm behind me." He began to walk toward the door.

"Trey?"

He stopped.

"How did Aimee's mother die?"

He tilted his head, and it reminded me of Beau when he was contemplating something new and incomprehensible to him. "Why do you want to know?"

"Because she mentioned it tonight, how nobody wanted to talk about her mother or how she died. But when I asked her, she said it was a long story. I thought maybe you'd know."

"She was killed. Murdered. In their house a few blocks over on Coliseum."

I stared at him, hoping I'd misunderstood. "Murdered?"

Trey shrugged. "They never found out who did it. Or why. They said it was a random robbery. Her husband was having dinner with clients and came home to find his daughter screaming in the dark house and his wife dead. He had an ironclad alibi, so he was never considered a suspect. But the only thing taken was her wedding ring. Nothing else in the house was touched. This was in 1941, so there was little more than fingerprinting used, and the case was never solved."

"How did she die?"

He paused, his lips thinning. "Stabbed—multiple times. Wasn't a knife, they're pretty sure, but they were never able to find the murder weapon."

I cringed, unable to reconcile the sweet and gentle Aimee with such a brutal memory. "Aimee must have been a toddler then. How awful to lose her mother so young."

He took a deep breath. "She was there when her mother was killed. She would go to sleep in her parents' bed most nights, and her mother must have crawled in beside her when she went to bed. Aimee was most likely sleeping when the murder occurred. She was too young to remember seeing anything, but I imagine something like that doesn't really ever go away."

I felt sick to my stomach and wished I had known about her mother's death before I'd asked Aimee why she needed a place to go to feel safe. And then I remembered something else she'd said to me. "Trey, would the murder of your great-grandmother have anything to do with Monica needing a place to go and feel safe? It's one of the reasons why Aimee said Monica loved River Song so much—because it was like a sanctuary to her."

"I can't imagine how they'd be connected. River Song was a great place to escape from our parents' acrimonious relationship, but that's the only reason I could think Monica would need a sanctuary. Besides, the murder happened long before Monica was born. She knew about it because Aimee told us when we were kids, and she overheard me making a wish that my mother would go away permanently. She was trying to tell us why we shouldn't take our mother for granted." He leaned against the doorway and crossed his arms. "Why all this interest in my family?"

I glanced down at the worn rug under my feet. "Monica told me so much about all of you that it was as if I knew you. And then yesterday Aimee said something about sharing our stories, how maybe now we could put all the pieces together. I was trying to figure out what she meant."

I looked up and saw that he'd stepped closer, his height towering over me. I wondered if he used the same technique to intimidate witnesses. "I'm curious about something, Julie. My sister had in her possession a painting of our paternal great-grandmother painted by your great-grandfather, and yet you claim that she never mentioned it to you. Don't you find that odd?"

He was watching me closely, studying my body language. I stood. "Of course I find it odd. She knew Abe Holt was my great-grandfather, and we even met at an Abe Holt exhibit. Yet she never mentioned it to me."

He kept his gaze on me, unmoving. "It seems deliberate to me. Like she wanted to meet you, because you were related to him but didn't want you to know."

I swallowed, wondering if he could hear it in the quiet room. But I couldn't think of anything to say, because I'd been wondering the same thing, over and over, and had come no closer to an answer than when I'd first seen the portrait.

Trey stared at me for a long moment before stepping back. "Good night, Julie."

My mind churned with all of the unknowns, wishing I knew which questions to ask, but knowing they'd only lead to more unanswerable ones. I heard his footsteps in the hallway before I remembered to respond. "Good night, Trey."

I turned back to the computer and began searching the familiar links, the endless faces and descriptions of the missing, the circumstances behind each baffling disappearance. But I was distracted tonight by the image of a young Aimee sitting in the dark with the body of her dead mother and of a painting of a woman with blue cat eyes and an alligator brooch that sparkled in the light.

The next few weeks passed in a blur as Beau and I settled into our new temporary home. Our rooms were furnished with expensive antiques and art—with the addition of LEGO-print fabrics in Beau's room— and at first I was too worried about damaging anything to be truly comfortable.

But when Aimee caught me straightening pillows in the living room and telling Beau to take his milk and plate of cookies to the kitchen, she told me that the house wasn't a museum and needed the occasional cookie crumb or spilled milk to make it a home. We were more relaxed after that, and I found myself loosening up enough to allow myself to be comfortable, but not enough to want to stay long enough to grow roots.

The book about my great-grandfather stayed on my nightstand, unread. I'd think about it only at night, when I was too tired to do much of anything besides crawl beneath the covers and fall asleep. I spent the days with Beau, and sometimes Aimee would join us, exploring the city of his mother's birth. We rode the streetcars on St. Charles and Carrollton avenues and ate lunch several times at the Camellia Grill—Monica's favorite restaurant, according to Aimee. We rode borrowed bikes in Audubon Park and then picnicked under the shade of an ancient oak tree. We took long, leisurely walks through the Garden District, then went to the library on St. Charles and checked out children's books on the city's history and the origins of LEGOs. I wanted to give Beau the freedom to be a child again, away from sickness and uncertainty.

I'd gone downtown to sign the sales agreement at Mayer and Ryan and opened up a checking account at Whitney Bank to deposit the proceeds. It gave me a sense of pride when I was able to write a check to cover my portion of the retainer for the builders. I brought Beau with me and then afterward took him to the Audubon Aquarium of the Americas to spend the afternoon. We saw penguins and sharks and sea lions, but when I noticed that Beau seemed more focused on the other children with mothers and fathers, I decided it was time to go.

I didn't see much of Trey. Aimee said that besides certain social obligations, he was also preparing for a big case and would spend a lot of time at his office on Canal Street downtown. I didn't ask her what those "social obligations" were, but it made me question again his ability to focus on something as important as rebuilding River Song. Especially when he believed his partner in the rebuilding effort wasn't wholeheartedly committed to the effort.

My suspicions were confirmed when Steve Kenney called to say the blueprints were ready, and Trey said he was too busy to make the trip to Biloxi to see them. Feeling like a martyr, I buckled Beau into the backseat of the van and headed down the now familiar highway, no longer needing my GPS to guide me.

I'd decided earlier that while I was in Biloxi I'd stop by and see Ray Von again. I kept thinking about my conversation with Trey about the portrait and my family connection to it, and how Monica had kept it a secret. Ray Von said Monica had sent a note along with the portrait, and I knew that, for my own peace of mind, I needed to read it, to see if there might be any message in there meant for me. Some kind of explanation.

Aimee had given me Ray Von's phone number as well as a bag of late tomatoes that Xavier had picked from her garden. I dialed the number from my cell phone several times, but nobody answered. I was halfway down Beach Boulevard traveling west before I decided to just stop by her house to see if she was there. I made a U-turn and pointed the van in the direction of Bellman Street.

Now that I was more familiar with where I was heading, I paid more attention to the scenery. The blue sky allowed for few clouds and the sun beat down on the van, making me warm despite the cooler weather. I'd yet to see it rain, and I'd started to wonder if it ever did, and then I passed another dead tree and remembered. Of course it did. I slowed to study the tree carved into a flock of pelicans, their necks craned upward to the sky, straining toward the unseen. It reminded me of the dolphin tree, and I thought about what it was they were reaching for. I drove slowly the rest of the way to Ray Von's, the image of the bird tree making me restless as I wondered what it was about the Katrina trees that I found so unsettling.

It was a cool day, and I lowered the windows of the van before getting out. The black cat was perched on the front step, regarding me with half-closed eyes as if I weren't important enough to warrant his full attention. As I climbed out of the van, I noticed a white Land Rover with Mississippi plates parked on the street, its right tires parked in the sparse and sandy grass of Ray Von's front yard. It didn't seem to be the kind of vehicle Ray Von would drive, assuming a woman in her nineties would be driving at all.

I took Beau out of the backseat and climbed the front steps before knocking on the door. I heard the phone ringing inside and counted as it rang ten times before stopping. I knocked one more time, knowing it was futile.

I remembered all of the herbs and dried flowers hanging from the ceiling of her kitchen and thought that she couldn't hear the phone or my knocks if she was working in a garden in the back of the house. Taking Beau's hand, I walked through tall grass at the side of the house toward the back. I stopped in surprise, Beau bumping into me. As I'd thought, there was a garden with neat, tidy rows of small plants interspersed with stripes of rocks to make a path between each row. In the middle of one of the paths a woman and a little girl, with matching blond heads and wearing identical pink polka-dotted gardening gloves and capri-length jeans, knelt in front of a squat, bushy plant. They both looked up at us, and we spent a long moment staring at one another in mutual surprise.

I broke the silence. "I'm looking for Ray Von Williams."

The woman smiled as she stood, pulling the girl up with her. "She's not here. I took her to her Bible study meeting, and I said I'd tidy up her garden until it was time to pick her up." She walked toward me and stuck out her hand. "I don't believe we've met. I'm Carol Sue Thibodeaux. And this"—she pulled the little girl forward—"is Charlotte Thibodeaux, although we call her Charlie after her daddy." She indicated Beau with her chin. "She just turned five in August, and I'm thinking she's about the same age as your little boy." Her words drawled like syrup, a true Southern accent, I suspected, and completely different from those I'd heard in New Orleans.

Beau had stuck his face in my side, sucking his thumb with the red hat bunched between us, but with his head turned so he could see. Charlie stared at Beau with open curiosity, the thumb in particular, and I put a protective arm around him. "This is Beau, and he did just turn five at the end of July."

The woman continued to smile at me, waiting. "Oh, and I'm Julie Holt." I stepped forward and held out my hand. She slipped off her gardening glove and shook my hand in a firm clasp.

Charlie now stood in front of Beau. "How come you still suck your thumb?"

Beau's eyes found mine, and he seemed so lost standing there facing down a girl who was a whole head shorter than he was. I wanted to pick him up to let him know it was okay, that I understood that he found comfort in it, and that he missed his mother and probably always would.

Before I could move, Charlie said, "Mama said that my teeth would start sticking out like a rabbit and that I'd better stop before that happens, so I go to sleep every night with a sock on my hand." She glanced at her mother, then lowered her voice before continuing. "But when there's a thunderstorm I take it off and suck my thumb because it makes me feel better."

She smiled at Beau, revealing small, square, and perfectly straight baby teeth, and Beau smiled back, making my heart squeeze.

Carol Sue looked at me, and I noticed that we were about the same age, but her brown eyes seemed to be those of a much older person, as if they'd seen more of life than they were supposed to. And I wondered, too, if she was thinking the same thing about me.

"So how do you know Ray Von?" she asked. "Are you a member of the Ladies Auxiliary? I don't think I've seen you at any of the meetings."

"Oh, no. Actually, it's a long story. I've only met her once. And I don't really know her. But I know of her through a mutual friend, Monica Guidry."

Carol Sue's face paled slightly. "Oh, you're that Julie. Trey mentioned you'd come here from New York." Her eyes shifted to Beau, and she moved to kneel in front of him. "You're Monica's little boy?" She looked closely at him. "Yes, of course you are. How could I miss it? You look just like your uncle Trey, don't you?"

"You knew Monica?" I asked.

Touching Beau's cheek, she nodded, then stood. "I've known the Guidrys all of my life. I'm from Biloxi, and we always hung out together during the summer. My parents' house was two doors down from River Song."

I remembered all the empty lots. Slowly, I asked, "Is it still there?"

She shook her head. "No. I have a new place, though, a few blocks inland. Mama and Daddy have been living with me ever since Katrina, which has been great, actually, helping out with Charlie."

"I'm sure," I said, watching as Charlie pulled Beau over to a corner of the garden before squatting to look at something in the dirt. I tried to sound as if I commiserated with her, but I couldn't help but wonder what all she needed help with.

"So you were friends with Monica?" I was hungry for information and was trying to remember whether Carol Sue was one of the many names Monica had mentioned.

"Not exactly. Trey and I are the same age, so Monica just sort of tagged along a lot. Trey and I were in undergrad together at Tulane. We even dated for a while. Until I met Charles." She crossed her arms over her chest and grabbed her elbows as something flittered across her face that made me wary. "Trey and Charles were roommates at the Sigma Chi house, so I suppose it was fate." She gave an uneasy laugh. "Guess there were no hard feelings, since Trey and Charles remained good friends and even started their own law practice together."

"No, I suppose not," I said, feeling like I was missing something.

"Trey says that you're rebuilding River Song."

"Yes." I couldn't help but think about what else he'd probably told her. "It was Monica's dream to have her children come to River Song. I thought it was the right thing to do."

She studied me with somber brown eyes. "That's pretty generous of you."

My choices suddenly felt very selfish, and I wondered if she'd meant that to happen. "Actually, I'm not completely sure that it's the right thing to do, but I seem to have run out of options. I don't know if Trey told you, but I'm Beau's guardian. Trey and I both need time to figure things out, and rebuilding River Song is giving us that time. I haven't really thought beyond that yet."

Carol Sue was looking beyond my shoulder. "Charlie, don't do that, honey. You're getting your shirt all dirty."

The little girl had dumped something in Beau's equally dirty hands and was now wiping hers on her shirt.

Returning her attention to me, she said, "Trey's actually told me a good deal about your situation and how he offered to buy out your half of River Song. And I have to say that what he told me made me like you before I met you. It's not often that Trey doesn't get his way." She gave me a half smile. "As far as I know, besides you, there were only three people in this world who could say no to Trey and get away with it and that would be Aimee Guidry, Charles, and Monica. It's an exclusive club, but a necessary one. Trey shouldn't be allowed to rule the world, even though he seems set on trying to save it."

I smiled back, relaxing a little. "So you and Charles are still good friends with Trey?"

I remembered what I'd first thought when I'd noticed her eyes, how it seemed they'd already seen too much of life, and what passed behind them now made me realize I'd touched something raw in this woman I hardly knew but somehow seemed connected with.

"Charles passed away five years ago." She said the words quickly, either to get them over with or because she'd had five years of practice saying them.

"I'm sorry," I said, my eyes shifting to Charlie as I made a simple calculation. "Then . . ."

Lowering her voice so the children wouldn't overhear, she said, "Charlie never met her daddy. She was born in Hattiesburg, where we evacuated with my parents during the storm."

I stared at her, wondering how a person should respond to that. "I'm sorry," I stammered.

She bent to retrieve two garden trowels, then faced me. "Thank you. But we're doing all right. I've got my parents and my friends and we're doing fine."

I should have let it go at that, but despite my New England upbringing, my years in New York wouldn't let me hold back the obvious question. "Your husband didn't evacuate with you?"

Using the back of her gardening glove, she began to brush dirt off of the trowels. "We had a house in uptown New Orleans—on Broadway. I evacuated early, because I was so near my due date, but Charles stayed a few extra days to make sure the house was boarded up, furniture moved to the upper floor and attic, things like that that I couldn't help him with."

She took a deep breath, and I could tell she was pushing away the emotion to be able to tell me all the facts that led to the point where her life was forever and irrevocably changed. If I'd been raised a proper Southerner, I probably would have made her stop.

Carol Sue continued. "Part of the reason Trey and Charles started their own firm was that they wanted to donate a set number of hours for pro bono work. Charles had been working hard on a foreclosure case for a ninety-year-old client in the Ninth Ward. The old man lived there with his handicapped granddaughter and her four children and was refusing to evacuate. Charles went down there with our SUV the day before the hurricane hit, after the mayor issued an immediate evacuation order, ready to evacuate them himself."

"But they wouldn't go?" I asked, my throat dry.

Carol Sue shook her head. "They wouldn't leave. They said the house was the only thing they had, and they weren't going to leave it behind. And they wouldn't let Charles take the children. He called me to say that he was going to stay a little longer to see if he could convince them to leave, and then he'd come to Hattiesburg whether they were with him or not." She looked at me and her eyes were bleak. "I'd started having my pains, and I told him to hurry." She bit her lip. "He called me one more time to tell me his cell battery was low but that he was about to leave, because he wanted to be here to see his baby being born. That was the last time I heard from him." Her hands twisted the gloves, smearing dirt and mud. "I wasn't worried at first, because the news was that Katrina had missed New Orleans."

"I don't understand. Katrina was the big disaster for New Orleans."

"That's what most people think. Katrina actually made landfall here on the gulf in Waveland, just a few miles down the beach from here. But in New Orleans it was the surge from Lake Pontchartrain afterward that overwhelmed the levees, and the city flooded. We had a storm surge here, but we're twelve feet above sea level, so there was a place for the water to go. But New Orleans is a bowl below sea level, and it just kept on filling and filling."

Her voice had gone very soft.

I touched her arm. "You don't need to tell me any more."

She gave me a grateful smile. "So I lost my husband, and Trey lost his best friend and business partner. And I don't think anything's been the same for us ever since."

I looked around the garden, the sun feeling warm on my back. "So why are you here? I would think you'd want to be as far away from a hurricane zone as possible."

She looked at me as if I'd just suggested streaking down the beach. It took her a moment to answer. "Because this is home." She waited to see if the words registered with me, but I just looked back at her, not understanding at all.

After a deep breath, she looked up at a tall oak tree beyond the garden, its leaves still green against the early October sky, the limbs now thick with foliage. "Because the water recedes, and the sun comes out, and the trees grow back. Because"—she spread her hands, indicated the garden and the tree and, I imagined, the entire peninsula of Biloxi—"because we've learned that great tragedy gives us opportunities for great kindness. It's like a needed reminder that the human spirit is alive and well despite all evidence to the contrary." She lowered her hands to her sides. "I figured I wasn't dead, so I must not be done."

"I've been hearing that a lot lately." My mouth twisted into an uneven grin.

Carol Sue smiled at me, the sun turning her hair gold, and I realized how beautiful she must have once been, how beautiful she still was if you didn't look too closely into her eyes. "I don't know your story yet, Julie, but I'm just so glad you're rebuilding River Song. We need that.

All of us." She swept her arm out again, and this time I was pretty sure she was talking about all of Biloxi.

"I'm still not so sure, but thanks for your vote of confidence." I looked at my watch. "I have to go. I need to pick up the blueprints for River Song and then head back to New Orleans. It's been great meeting you. I hope I get to see you again."

"Same here." She indicated Beau and Charlie, who were now playing a makeshift game of hopscotch. "And it looks like the children have found a friend. We'll need to get them together soon, although I'm sure I'll be seeing a lot of you while River Song is being built. Where will you be staying?"

I looked at her, my mind drawing a blank. It was the first time that I'd thought about the logistics of supervising the construction of a house. I guess I'd imagined living in New Orleans for the duration, but I suddenly realized the impracticality of it. I shook my head. "To be honest, I hadn't even thought about it. I guess I'll need to get a place here during the week, especially since it looks like Trey stays pretty busy in New Orleans and somebody should be here. I'll bring Beau back to New Orleans to spend time with Aimee during the weekends." I rubbed my hands over my face. Planning for the future wasn't something I was used to. "I suppose I should think about getting a job, too."

She walked to the back door, where her purse sat on the step, then dug into it until she pulled out a card. Handing it to me, she said, "This is all of my contact info. I'm a licensed Realtor, so I have a lot of connections. I'm sure I can set you up in a rental. Don't know about a job, though. What did you do before you came here?"

"I was an executive assistant for the director of an auction house. I have a BA in art history, and it was a great foot-in-the-door position. Didn't really think about where it might lead, but I liked it."

"And now you're here."

"And now I'm here."

She nodded, her eyes narrowed as she scrutinized me. "You've heard about the Ohr-O'Keefe Museum of Art, I'm sure."

"No, actually, I haven't. Where is it?"

"Here in Biloxi. George Ohr's from here, you know. The museum was near completion when Katrina hit. They built it to withstand one-hundred-and-fifty-mile-per-hour hurricane winds, but they didn't think to protect it from casino barges—which is what demolished it during the storm surge. So they had to raise the money all over again, and it's set to open in November. Five years late, but better late than never. I'm sure they're looking for people, and Mama has been really involved in the fund-raising. She might be able to point you in the right direction."

She took out another card from her purse and flipped it over. "Give me your cell number so I can reach you."

I gave her the number and she jotted it down. "Charlie, we have to go pick up Ray Von now. Say good-bye to Beau." She turned to me. "Do you want me to tell Ray Von that you stopped by?"

"If you wouldn't mind. And I've got a bag of tomatoes from her son, Xavier; if you can give them to her I'd appreciate it. Please tell her that I'll call her later. I just need to ask her about something."

Carol Sue laughed. "Good luck with that. She rarely answers her phone. Figures if she wanted to talk with somebody she'd go talk to them. So of course she doesn't have a cell phone, either. Which is why one of us in the Ladies Auxiliary stops by once a day to check on her or to take her where she needs to be. Her son sends money so that she always has something to buy her groceries, but you can never call her to set up a time. She's just always ready when you show up."

I raised my eyebrows. "Well, I guess I'll just stop by another time. Looks like I'm going to be here on a fairly regular basis." I waved her business card. "I'll be in touch about a rental property. And thank you. You've been more than helpful."

She shrugged. "It's just what we do." She glanced over at Beau and Charlie, who were hugging each other good-bye.

We headed to our vehicles, and after I handed her the bag of tomatoes, we waved good-bye and headed in opposite directions. I stopped

by the offices of Kenney-Moise Homebuilders on Reynoir Street to
pick up the blueprints. Steve and Julia Kenney offered to show them to
me on one of the large tables in the back room, but I declined. I wanted
to look at the blueprints the first time with Trey, to see them through
his eyes, and Monica's eyes, to make sure that every detail was right.

It was around four thirty by the time we headed to the van, the
early autumn sun already beginning its descent. I drove the van to
the interstate, in a hurry to get back to New Orleans, remembering
Aimee's promise to tell me more of her story. As the water of the bay
slipped beneath us, I thought of the pelicans carved from a dead tree,
their necks stretched as if trying to see the sky. And I wondered why
they reminded me of a woman who'd lost so much but who could tend
to someone else's garden, and who could remember that storm waters
recede and leaves grow again on empty trees.

CHAPTER 10

Too low they build, who build beneath the stars.

—EDWARD YOUNG

Aimee

1954

For the remainder of my adolescence, I spent the yellow-hued Philadelphia autumns pining for the sultry air of the Crescent City and the creaking floors and salt breezes of River Song. All through the biting winters and chilly springs, I anticipated my summer trip down south, to a world so completely foreign to my own that it could have been another planet.

I checked the mailbox every day after school to see if I had a letter from Gary. We wrote often—he more than I, really. Sometimes it was just a two-line joke. Other times it would be about school and his unfulfilled wishes to try out for the baseball team. A few times he wrote about his mother, and how my grandmother was the only neighbor who still spoke to her, and how that was probably only because of the friendship she maintained with Gary's father. Mrs. Guidry had taken to dressing in the new "beatnik" style (according to Gary) and inviting black musicians and artists into her home for big parties, even seating them at her own dining table, which caused a lot of scandal. Gary's father would be conspicuously absent during these events, and for that Gary called his father the biggest coward. Gary made a point to stay downstairs as long as his mother allowed, the music and laughter going on long after he'd gone to bed.

Gary mentioned Wes a lot, and how Wes was now at Tulane, and his plans to eventually go to law school there. He even wrote about the lizards and flowers in his garden. But, aside from the cowardice, he rarely mentioned his father.

He always rode with Grandmother to pick me up at the airport, and when he was finally allowed to drive, he surprised me by showing up by himself. He told me about girls, and I made up stories about boys. I went to an all-girls Catholic school, where there were very few opportunities to mix with boys, but I hated for our conversations about the opposite sex to be solely one-sided.

I asked him once about the boy I had seen in the attic window. Gary gave me a strange look, then, with a dismissive smirk, told me I was either crazy or I must have seen a ghost. Chastised, I dropped the subject and forgot all about it—until much later.

I didn't see a lot of Wes during my visits. He seemed to want to spend as much time away from home as possible and spent most of his school holidays with friends and their families. I didn't blame him. The atmosphere in the Guidry household was claustrophobic. Mrs. Guidry spent days on end in her room, shouting at people from behind her closed door. Ray Von was the only person allowed to see her, bringing her trays of food and Mrs. Guidry's flask. And it was Ray Von who cleaned her up and made her come out of her room, beautiful and vibrant once more, the glittering alligator brooch at her breast. Whenever I saw it, it always made me think of my mother and what Mrs. Guidry had said about alligators the first time I'd complimented her on the brooch. *They remind me of me, I suppose—often misunderstood.*

Mr. Guidry spent a lot of his time at his law offices on Poydras, but

I always knew when he came home. Their shouting could be heard all the way inside my grandmother's house. Gary ate more dinners at our house than his own. Wes just stayed away altogether. Even during the school year, according to Gary, Wes lived on Tulane's campus, just a few miles away.

The summer of my sixteenth year, Wes surprised us all by coming home for the last three weeks of vacation. He'd been in Boston all summer, working in a law firm where a friend's father practiced. He spent most weekends on Cape Cod, and sent postcards to Gary every week that he would reluctantly share with me, and only after he blackmailed me into bringing over contraband food.

I was lounging on a chaise in the side yard, trying to get my skin to do more than just burn. Grandmother was playing bridge at a friend's house, or she never would have allowed it. I don't know if she were more offended by suntans or two-piece bathing suits, but either way I was sinning grievously. She called girls with tanned skin who showed their bellies "fast," a name I almost wish I deserved.

My brand-new transistor radio was set to WNOE, and I was singing along with Patti Page about a doggie in the window when the iron gate creaked. Startled, I looked up from my *Seventeen* magazine, quickly throwing a towel over it in case it was my grandmother, who insisted I read literature or history books to keep my mind exercised during school breaks.

My sunglasses had slipped in sweat to the bottom of my nose, and I pushed them back up in time to see Wes walking toward me.

"Hi, Aimee." He stood directly next to me, blocking the sun. Feeling suddenly self-conscious, I sat up and crossed my arms in front of me and tried to sound nonchalant.

"Hi, Wes. I didn't know you were coming home."

"I didn't know it myself until two days ago. It was sort of last-minute." He wore cream-colored slacks with penny loafers and a blue plaid shirt he'd left untucked. Despite the casual clothes and going to a Southern school, he looked very much the Ivy Leaguer. He sat down on my spare towel in the grass, his long legs stretched out in front of him and crossed at the ankles. His blue eyes stood out in his tanned face, and his feet moved back and forth in constant motion. This nervous energy reminded me so much of his brother. But whereas Gary's incessant movements seemed more like a nervous habit, Wes's were restrained energy.

He reached for the radio, where the song had disintegrated into static. "Why aren't you listening to the news? Little Mo might be winning at Wimbledon right now."

I shrugged, trying to pretend I knew what he was talking about. "I like listening to music. And this is the only place I can listen to it, since Grandmother won't let me play my radio inside the house."

"Hope you don't mind me interrupting your sunbathing session, but I saw you from an upstairs window and wanted some company. Nobody's home. Thought a one-person welcoming committee would be better than an empty house." He smiled up at me, and I felt the familiar tightening in my throat.

Besides Gary and my father, I had never been in such close proximity with a member of the opposite sex. I felt the blush creep up from my neck and pushed the glasses back on my nose as a distraction. "Welcome home, then. Gary will be thrilled you're back."

"Really? From his letters, I thought Gary was happy not having to share your company."

"Huh?"

He brought his knees up and wrapped his arms around his legs. "You and Gary—you're an item, aren't you?"

"What? You mean like girlfriend-boyfriend? Not quite! I mean, we're friends and all—but that's it." I hoped I had gotten sunburned, because I really needed something to hide the hideous red I was sure my face had become.

He held up his hand and laughed. "Sorry, Aimee. I didn't mean to make you feel uncomfortable. It's just that from Gary's letters, I thought that you two were jacketed."

I stood, speechless and beyond embarrassed. He stood, too, facing me, his face suddenly serious.

"Put your towel on, Aimee." He reached behind me and grabbed my towel from the chaise longue and held it out to me.

"Why? I don't need it—it's hot out. And what did you mean about Gary and me?"

"Put your towel on. Really." He threw it over my shoulder so that it hung down the front of me, covering my pale yellow bathing suit.

The constrained look on his face forced me to comply. I hung it over my shoulders, clutching it together in front of me. "Why am I doing this?"

He cleared his throat. "Your top . . ." He paused, as if waiting for me to finish his sentence.

"Yes?"

"I think you need to fix the strap."

I opened the towel slightly and looked down to find that the strap that tied behind my neck had come lose and had flopped down to my waist, exposing my entire chest. I must have opened my mouth to say something, but could not seem to make my lips form words. I tightened the towel around my shoulders, and then, with as much dignity as I could muster, I strode into the house without looking back.

With no desire to relive my mortification, I planned to avoid him for the rest of my summer vacation and was thrilled to be invited again to River Song in Biloxi. Until I found out Wes would be going, too. As only a sixteen-year-old could think such a thing was possible, I made up my mind I wouldn't even look in Wes's direction for the entire three weeks we'd be there.

I had accompanied Gary and his parents to River Song every summer since we were twelve. We would always make sure we were there the last week in July to celebrate Gary's birthday. He made a big deal of his birthday being before mine. I was a December baby and was envious of Gary celebrating his birthday at the beach—but I never let him forget that I was seven months older.

I loved River Song. It seemed to cast a spell over anyone who slept under its roof; even Mr. and Mrs. Guidry weren't immune, and their moods shifted to quiet amiability as soon as we left the outskirts of New Orleans. I was never sure if for them, though, it was merely their escape from the city, and not their destination, that allowed them to lay their animosities aside. It was as if something hovered in the air over their house on First Street, poisoning them.

River Song had been in the Guidry family for three generations, a stubborn wood-frame two-story. It had withstood the Gulf Coast hurricane of 1947, although it had lost its roof and most of its top story. Clinging tenaciously to the shifting sand of its foundation, it weathered the storm, to be rebuilt and used by future Guidrys. It became my home away from home, and I looked forward each summer to our visit, where I could escape for several weeks from Grandmother's scrutiny.

For this trip, we took two cars: Gary, me in the middle, and Ray Von in the back of Mr. Guidry's Cadillac—Mr. and Mrs. Guidry in the front seat. Both of them stared straight ahead, never talking to each other, but sometimes I would catch a glance as it passed between them, and I would know that whatever poisoned cloud hovered over them in New Orleans had been lifted.

Wes drove his own car, a brand-new Oldsmobile 98 Fiesta convertible coupe with blond ornament in the passenger side. Lacy Boudreaux was a Sacred Heart girl—a neat little package with her stiletto heels and perfect nose. She was petite, perky, and infinitely annoying in her very short shorts and bared midriff. I hated her on sight. I hated her even more when Wes rested his arm casually over the back of her seat as they sped alongside our car onto Highway 90, her pink silk chiffon scarf trailing in the wind behind her. Ray Von caught me staring at them out the window and gave me a knowing look. I turned my attention to Gary and forced myself to ignore the flash of the blue-and-white Oldsmobile for the rest of the trip.

I loved the drive on U.S. 90 along the beach through Bay St. Louis,

Pass Christian, and Gulfport, the water reminding me of what I had to look forward to in the weeks ahead. People called it the Route 66 of the South, and although I'd never seen Route 66, I'd seen pictures in magazines and figured that the string of restaurants, hotels, and brightly colored lit signs certainly made it seem so. As we passed under the huge arch and overpass of the Sun 'n' Sand Hotel Court in Gulfport, I knew we were near and turned to Gary with a big smile, surprised to find him looking at me instead of the scenery.

In previous summers, Gary and I had slept on cots on the second-floor sleeping porch, with its pitched ceiling and acoustical anomaly that allowed a person to whisper something in one corner and have it be heard loud and clear on the other side—a real boon for children who were supposed to be sleeping. Somehow I knew things were different this summer. Perhaps it was the obvious physical signs of maturity. Or maybe it was the way Wes was looking at Lacy. But it was decided that Lacy and I would share one of the two upstairs bedrooms, and Gary and Wes would share the one across the hall.

Lacy immediately grabbed the bed closest to the windows and dumped her suitcase on top to stake her claim. She shimmied out of her shorts and blouse and stood in her two-piece bathing suit, rifling through her suitcase until she found what she was looking for. One of Wes's Tulane fraternity shirts slid over her head before she pulled her long blond hair into a high ponytail. The shirt fell almost to her knees, making her seem more petite and adorable than usual. I hated her even more.

"I'm going to catch some sun. I'll see you." Hefting a beach bag over her shoulder, she left the room in a flurry of swinging blond hair.

Slowly, I dressed in my one-piece bathing suit—something my grandmother had insisted on—and caught sight of myself in the full-length mirror behind the closet door. Unlike Lacy's tawny skin, mine was pale white, with patches of peeling sunburn. I was all legs and arms, my saving glory my newly acquired bust. My snow-colored skin glared under the severe black of my suit. I slid one of my father's old undershirts over my head, promising myself I would not remove it if Lacy were anywhere near me.

The door burst open and Gary stood in his dark green bathing suit, his skin almost as white as mine, and wearing a white T-shirt, holding a bag of potato chips and a rolled-up beach towel. "Come on, Aimee. Aren't you ready yet?"

"Gary! You're supposed to knock. What if I had been naked?" I flipped my hair behind my shoulders with a grunt of disgust and threw my baby oil and comb in my beach bag. I looked up, expecting to see Gary smirking at me. Instead, his face had gone an unnatural shade of pink and his jaw hung open like a fish on a line. I suddenly remembered my conversation with Wes about Gary. Knowing I needed to wipe all such thoughts from his head, I took my beach bag off the bed and tossed it at him.

"Think fast!" I called, watching him fumble with it in the air.

"I'm not carrying your bag," he said, tossing it back to me.

"Suit yourself." I broke into a run and sprinted down the stairs, calling over my shoulder, "I get the chaise longue!"

I'd reached the pier before I realized he wasn't behind me. Thinking he was playing a trick, I cautiously tiptoed back to the front door to peer through the screen. Heavy dread settled on me as I saw Gary sitting on the bottom step, his head between his knees and Ray Von beside him. I threw my bag down and raced inside.

"Gary! Are you all right?"

He looked up, his face the color of flour. "I'm fine."

Ray Von slowly shook her head. "You didn't take your pills today, did you, Garrick?"

Gary dipped his head, not acknowledging her question.

Looking directly at her, I asked, "Will he be okay?"

"He needs to rest right now and stay out of the sun. You go on." She squeezed his arms, trying to lift him to his feet.

Gary shrugged out of her grasp and stood. "I'm fine—I'm going to the pier with Aimee." His knees buckled, and he slid down onto the step again. I lunged for him, grabbing his head before it hit the wall of the stairwell.

Ray Von looked at me with calming eyes. "Go get Mr. Guidry. I need him to help me carry Garrick to his room." I hesitated, not wanting to leave Gary. "Go ahead, girl. He'll be all right. I can help him. Go get Mr. Guidry."

I raced back up the stairs past them until I reached the closed door of the Guidrys' bedroom. Without thinking, I threw the door open. Mr. and Mrs. Guidry's naked bodies tumbled to a paralyzed stop on the bed. Their skin shone with slick sweat, the sheets and bedspread pooled on the floor. Mr. Guidry covered most of his wife, but I could hear her sobbing like a mewling kitten.

"Leave, Aimee."

I hardly recognized Mr. Guidry's voice. This wasn't the same quiet man I had known. This man had hardened, somehow, like a thick layer on pudding that had been sitting out too long. Too stunned to be embarrassed, I blurted, "Gary's sick and Ray Von needs your help."

I swung the door shut with a thud, letting go of the doorknob as if it would scald my hand. Then I ran down the kitchen stairs and waited there until I heard Mr. Guidry head down the front stairs; then I dashed through the door before I saw anybody else.

Lacy and Wes were nowhere in sight, so I walked to the end of the pier and sat down. My feet dangled over the edge, the chipped pink toenail polish glowing in the fading sunlight. I sat for a long time, watching the sun bleed into the Mississippi Sound, and thinking of ways to avoid Mr. and Mrs. Guidry for the rest of my life. Why had she been crying? What had he done to hurt her? And somewhere, under all the teenage angst, lay my biggest worry—Gary. I saw his pasty face and felt real fear for the second time in my life.

A board creaked behind me, startling the thoughts from my head. Wes, tall and tanned, approached from the other end of the pier. I toyed briefly with the idea of plunging into the water and swimming to shore, but I didn't want to call any more attention to myself.

"Hi, Aimee."

I averted my head, resting my chin on my raised knee as the warmth flooded my cheeks.

"Mind if I join you?"

I shook my head without looking at him as he stretched out beside me. We sat for a while in silence, listening to the soft drone of a distant motorboat. A woman in a two-piece and a bathing cap skied behind the boat, trailing white water tracks. After a while she let go of the rope, softly sinking into the water.

"I hope you haven't been avoiding me, Aimee. I didn't mean to embarrass you. I just thought you'd rather hear it from me than the mailman."

I kept my chin on my knees, not looking at him. "I don't want to talk about it, if you don't mind." I was thankful for the fading sun hiding the shades of red on my face.

"Sure. But you can stop pretending I have the plague now, okay?"

I lifted my head. "I didn't think you'd noticed. Lacy seems to keep you pretty busy."

He frowned, his brow line forming a deep vee, then threw a stick into the water, where it landed with a soft plop. "She certainly tries to."

Not wanting to continue a conversation about Lacy, I changed the subject to the one person who was occupying the other half of my thoughts. "Wes, how sick is Gary?"

He took a deep breath before answering. "He could be very sick—but we seem to have it under control." His gaze flickered over my face as if to judge whether I was qualified to hear the rest. Wes continued. "Garrick was born with a bad heart. As long as he takes care of himself and takes his medicine, he can lead a pretty normal life, although it might not be as long as we'd all like."

I waved away a swarm of gnats flitting about my face. "Oh." I didn't know what else to say.

Wes rose suddenly and offered his hand. Pulling me up, he said, "It's getting dark and they'll be waiting on us for supper." He let go of my hand when I stood, then walked with me toward the house.

Wes stopped in front of the door. "I've got to get something from my car—you go on in." He paused for a moment before adding, "I'm glad you're here. You're different, Aimee. Like a bright light. I'm glad Gary has you." I turned my face to tell him that Gary didn't have me, and as I did he leaned over to kiss me on the cheek. Instead, our lips touched for longer than an accidental kiss should have been. He pulled away, his eyes avoiding mine, then headed for the driveway.

My hand went to my lips, feeling the lingering moisture from his kiss. I heard a movement and turned to see Gary through the screen door, his face illuminated by the outside light. His eyes were narrowed as he looked past me and in the direction Wes had gone. His gaze traveled back to me, and I recognized the look on his face as the one he wore when he was out of breath and struggling for air.

"Gary . . ."

It was too late. My voice evaporated into the dusk air as he turned and disappeared inside.

Julie

I crept down the stairs, admiring the way the streetlights outside bled through the stained-glass window on the landing, pooling jewel-colored light on the stairwell. When I reached the bottom step I noticed that the hall table lamp was on, as was a light in Trey's study.

It was almost one o'clock in the morning, and as I walked to the door I hoped that the lights had been left on by accident, since I was dressed in only my long New York Yankees T-shirt that hit me a little higher than midthigh.

I poked my head around the doorframe and saw to my relief that the desk was empty and the computer already turned off. I stepped inside, then froze. Trey stood on the far side of the room, where he'd pulled out a table to lay out River Song's blueprints. Both hands were braced on the table as he studied the prints in front of him.

For the first time since I'd met him, he wasn't immaculately dressed in pressed pants and a button-down shirt. Instead, he wore work boots, paint-splattered cargo shorts, and a dark green T-shirt covered in what looked like sawdust.

I started to back out of the room.

"You can come in." Trey didn't turn around to look at me.

"I'm not really dressed for company."

This time he did turn around, and I saw that his shirt had TULANE emblazoned in light blue letters across the front, and that his hair was matted with sweat and more sawdust. He held out his arms, his lips quirked up in one corner as he took in the shirt and bare legs. "Neither am I." He turned back to the table. "I was wondering what you thought about the house plans."

I walked toward the table, so surprised about his soliciting my opinion that I didn't think to ask him why he was dressed that way at one o'clock in the morning, or to be embarrassed that I was wearing a T-shirt and barely anything else. I stopped next to him and looked down at Monica's memories rendered in blue and white. The notepad that I'd placed next to the prints was filled with notes and comments I had jotted down when I'd studied them, and I noticed that the list had been continued in an unfamiliar, masculine handwriting. "I didn't think you were all that interested in them."

He sent me a sidelong glance. "Why would you think that?"

"Well, you were too busy to go to Biloxi and look at them with the builder, and Aimee told me that you're tied up all week and that I have to go back to the builder by myself with any of our changes."

He pursed his lips. "I have other commitments that occupy my time. I'm sorry. Rebuilding River Song wasn't exactly on my agenda right now. Things should open up in a couple of months."

"A couple of months?" I faced him, not trying to hide the annoyance in my voice.

"Yeah, a couple of months." His words were clipped. "Unless you're planning on working a bulldozer, there's not a lot you and I can do at this point, anyway."

I crossed my arms, prepared to argue, before I realized that he was probably right. Instead, I turned my attention to the house plans, remembering why I'd been unable to sleep and had come downstairs in the first place. "Can I move this?" I asked as I lifted the first page showing the front elevation of the house.

Trey nodded, then stepped back.

I flipped through the large sheets until I found the one showing the back of the house and what had once been the sleeping porch. Something Aimee had said tugged on my memory, as I recalled stories Monica had related about summer nights spent with her cousins, brother, and friends on the sleeping porch listening to the tree frogs and crickets, their whispered confidences shared only with the high rafters and cedar walls.

I placed the page on top of the others and spread them with my hands. "I want to make sure the builders know how to re-create that acoustical anomaly Monica told me about. Even Aimee remembers it and must have deliberately rebuilt it after Camille to duplicate the effect. Do you know what I'm talking about?"

When he didn't say anything, I faced him and found that he was smiling with both sides of his mouth in the first real smile I'd seen since we'd met. "Of course," he said, still grinning.

Uncomfortable, I asked, "What's so funny?"

He shook his head, his smile dimming only slightly. "Nothing, really. I'm just . . . oh, I don't know. I guess I'm just happy to know that Monica remembered that. That she cherished it enough to share it with somebody who'd never been there, but who remembers that it was important enough to my sister to make sure it's re-created in the house for her son."

I blushed. "You really have Monica to thank for that. It was her ability to create such strong visuals with her stories that is responsible for my being here. It's not like I just jumped in a van with a five-year-old boy seeking an adventure."

Still smiling, he turned back to the prints. "Whatever. I still appreciate it." He leaned closer to examine something on the sketch of the back porch roof. "I spoke with Carol Sue today. She said she suggested that you apply for a job at the George Ohr museum."

I wondered how often they spoke, and what else she might have said, and then chastised myself for even caring. "I think it's a good idea. I'd like to put as much of the money from the sale of the painting as I can into a savings account for Beau. If I get a job, I can try to live off of my paycheck. And if I'm working in Biloxi, I'll be near River Song to keep an eye on things."

He looked up at me, amusement still in his eyes, but turned back to the table without saying anything.

Uncomfortable, I cleared my throat. "I'm sorry about your friend Charles. It's hard losing a friend."

Trey straightened, his eyes darkening as he regarded me, reminding me of how Monica's eyes betrayed her emotions, too. "Yes," he said. "It is."

"And a sister," I added, although I wasn't sure why.

He nodded. "It seems we have a lot in common."

I gave a weak laugh, trying to dispel the tension in the room. "Yeah, and none of it good."

He raised an eyebrow and I had the impression that he might actually smile again. He didn't. "When are you heading back to Biloxi?"

"Probably in the next couple of days. I figured we'd need a few days to look at the plans to make sure that we've thought of everything before I bring them back. Why?"

"Aimee's only been back once since Katrina, and she'd like to see Ray Von. I was hoping you'd be willing to take her."

"Of course. I actually wanted to see Ray Von, too."

He raised both eyebrows. "I didn't realize you two knew each other."

"I wouldn't go that far. Monica sent the portrait of your great-grandmother to Ray Von for safekeeping. She included a note to Ray Von telling her that I would come to retrieve it at some point. I was hoping that she'd kept the note, that there might be something written that wouldn't make sense to Ray Von but might to me."

"Good idea," he said. "Let me know if you find anything."

I hesitated to disturb the odd little truce we seemed to have forged over our conversation over the blueprints, but I knew I had to be frank. "You do realize that I'm trying to determine why Monica left. You might not like what I find."

His expression was inscrutable, and I wondered if they taught that at law school. "The answers we seek aren't always the answers we want, are they? But knowing the truth is what helps us sleep at night."

I thought of my search for Chelsea, and his for Monica, and knew he was right. I just couldn't acknowledge it. I wanted only one outcome and I'd never really stopped to consider an alternate truth. I turned back to the table, seeing Trey's notes again. Reading aloud, I said, " 'Two ceiling fans and not three on sleeping porch. Beamed ceiling in den. Front walkway to beach is brick.' " They were small changes, but they were in keeping with the old River Song, and it touched me that he'd remembered the details as well as Monica had, and I wondered if that offered him the same comfort it gave me.

Changing the subject, Trey said, "On your way to Biloxi, would you mind taking Aimee to see my grandfather? I usually take her a couple times a week but I've been swamped."

I looked at him in surprise. "Your grandfather is still alive? I thought . . ." I stopped myself, realizing that Aimee had never told me otherwise.

"Yes, he's alive, but he's been in a nursing home for almost ten years now. He had a stroke that paralyzed his right side and left him without the ability to speak. He has some dementia, too."

"I'm sorry. I'd be happy to take her." I looked at him, my eyes narrowed. "Which brother did she marry, Wes or Gary?"

He turned his back to me and began stacking the pages of the blueprints so that their edges met. "I think she wants to tell you." A smile had crept back into his words.

"Seriously? I'm fascinated by her story, but I'm only getting little snippets at a time. I'm dying to know. I could just start digging on the Internet and get the answer myself."

He reached for the pull cord on a floor lamp by the table and yanked it, throwing the house plans into shadow. "You could. But you won't." Trey stood still as he waited for me to answer.

"Why do you say that?"

"Because you're good at waiting for answers. Because you're not sure whether the answer you're going to get is the one you want to hear, so you wait just a little longer."

A flash of anger burned behind my eyes, but I didn't say anything, because I was afraid that what he said was true.

Quietly, he asked, "Who paid for Monica's burial?"

"I did."

"Funerals aren't cheap."

"She deserved to have a decent burial, and a marker. I didn't think to ask her family, because I knew she hadn't been in contact for a decade." I remembered scraping together the money, selling my small collection of sixteenth-century sterling snuffboxes that I'd started when I first went to work for the auction house. They were beautiful pieces, and I'd loved them, but they were as easily sold as I had purchased them, admired but not desperately wanted.

He nodded, his face in shadow. "I've started the bureaucratic paperwork to bring her body home. I hope you'll be here for the funeral."

I started to ask him why he thought I might not be, but stopped. I'd been honest with him about my opinion of people who built houses in a flaky climate, and I supposed that was his way of being honest with me about his opinion of people who had no home, or roots, at all.

"I hope so," I replied, seeing again the sawdust and paint splatters, the work boots. His eyebrows shot up as he noticed my perusal, and I waited a moment for him to offer an explanation. He must have been waiting for me to ask him about it, because neither one of us said anything. I wanted to roll my eyes at the two of us, but turned to leave instead. "Good night, Trey."

"Good night, Julie." His words definitely carried a smile in them, but I ducked my head and left the room before he could see me smile back.

CHAPTER 11

It is easier to pull down than to build up. —LATIN PROVERB

I awoke several days later to the sun streaming through the slats in my blinds. I looked at my bedside clock, alarmed to see that it was past nine. I'd told Aimee the night before that I'd drive us both to Biloxi and knew she must be waiting for me. She was an early riser, preferring to visit her garden before the noon sun became too warm.

Grabbing clothes from my dresser and closet, I threw them on the bathroom counter, then moved to close the adjoining bathroom door so I wouldn't awaken Beau. I peeked into his room, past the LEGO castle that he and Trey were in the process of building in the middle of the room, my gaze pausing when I saw the empty bed.

I thought for a moment that he must be with Aimee or Kathy, and that I should go ahead and shower and dress, but years of guilt wouldn't allow me to go anywhere until I knew where he was. I threw on a pair of sweats, then ran downstairs, calling Beau's name as I walked from room to room, my steps quickening as I found only an empty house.

When I reached the kitchen, I stopped short, a familiar nausea creeping into my throat. Monica's red hat, inseparable from Beau since the day of her funeral, sat in the middle of the kitchen table, nestled between the ceramic salt and pepper shakers shaped like giant red beans. I picked it up, wanting it to feel warm, to know that Beau was near, but there was nothing there in the red, pilled knit to remind me of Beau.

I jerked around, looking for the phone to call 911, realizing even as I did so how irrational I was being. My gaze settled on the back door leading into the garden, and my heart slowed slightly. Of course. He'd be in the garden with Aimee.

I practically flew through the door and into the garden, feeling as if I'd suddenly time-traveled to another world—or at least into another season. It was almost November, yet colors shouted from hedges and pots, and a miniature topiary of small animals paraded around a brass sundial sunk into the brick walkway.

I opened my mouth to shout Beau's name again, but stopped when I saw a flash of movement near a small toolshed nearly hidden by the heavy limbs of a giant magnolia tree. Beau and Xavier were squatting down together, examining different gardening tools laid out in a neat row on the brick walkway in front of the shed. Xavier's straw hat covered most of his face, but I could still see the tight and mottled scarring on his jaw and neck. Beau was speaking animatedly to him as if he saw no scars at all.

"Beau!" I called, rushing to his side. "I was worried about you when I didn't find you in your bed. You know you're not supposed to go anywhere without me."

They both stood, Xavier facing me while Beau hugged me. "Xavier's gonna help me make a LEGO tooprary. Isn't that cool?"

"Yes," I said, my voice weak with relief. "That's very cool. But where're Miss Aimee and Kathy?"

Xavier spoke, the tenor pitch of his voice surprising me again. "Miss Aimee took her morning walk with Kathy and asked me to watch Beau." His green eye remained blank, but I sensed a rebuke in his voice. "This is Miss Aimee's grandbaby. I won't let anything happen to him."

I made myself smile. "Yes, you're right. I know that. It's just . . . well, I get a little nervous when I don't know where he is, that's all." With all the emotional strength that I could muster, I kissed the top of

Beau's head and took a step back. "Thanks, Xavier. If you don't mind keeping an eye on him for just a little longer, I'm going to go shower and dress so I'm ready to take Miss Aimee to Biloxi when she gets back from her walk. Is that all right?"

He didn't return my smile, but continued to stare back at me with his odd, light green eye. "I'll take good care of him, just like I take good care of Miss Aimee. And I won't let anybody hurt her—or this baby boy, because he's Miss Monica's boy."

The skin on the back of my neck tightened, and I looked closely at him to see whether his face conveyed the thinly veiled threat I thought I'd detected in his words. Instead, he just stared back at me, his expression inscrutable.

"Thank you," I said again, watching as they bent down to select tools before I raced back into the house to take my shower as quickly as I could.

Clouds had begun to gather by the time Aimee, Beau, and I left for Biloxi. After a brief stop at the nursing home in Metairie where Beau and I waited downstairs in a reception room, I pointed the van toward the interstate. The house plans for River Song were rolled up in the backseat next to Beau, but the notes and my résumé—at Aimee's request—were in the front seat so she could look at them while I drove.

She laughed, and I looked over at her, wondering what she could find amusing in either document. "What's so funny?" I asked.

She quoted, "'The second, ninth, and twelfth steps creak when stepped on.'" She looked at me over the top of her reading glasses. "That's something old houses do naturally, you know. From years of people stepping on them."

"I know. But I was hoping that the builder could re-create some of that, so that it doesn't seem so new."

She continued to look at me.

"What?"

"You and Trey are so much alike. That's probably why Monica took to you so quickly."

I raised my eyebrows. "I know he's your grandson, and I don't mean to offend, but I find him officious, overbearing, and suspicious to a fault. How is that like me?"

Aimee threw her head back and laughed. "All very true—and add 'observant' to your list of traits. But he's also loyal, compassionate, and generous with friends and strangers alike. The two of you are just so busy pretending you're none of the above that you don't see it in yourselves or each other."

I bit my bottom lip. "And I don't think either one of us is overly loyal, compassionate, or generous. We'll just have to agree to disagree on this one, okay?"

"That's fine, dear," she said as she returned to the list. "'Two ceiling fans and not three. Three over three windowpanes in the front windows. Living room ceiling tall enough for twelve-foot Christmas tree.'" She rested her head on the back of the seat and laughed softly. "The two of you are going to enormous lengths to make sure the house is Monica's house the way she loved it. Yet Trey has neither the time nor the interest, and you think people rebuilding their houses in a hurricane zone are 'shortsighted and somewhat egotistical.'"

I blushed. "I'm sorry. I didn't mean that about you."

"Yes, you did. But that's all right. I don't take it personally, and you're certainly not the only person in the country who thinks that. I just prefer to think that I'm a restorer of humanity."

I squinted at the haze, trying hard to think of rebuilding River Song as anything more than rebuilding a house. "What do you mean?"

"After a hurricane, when everything is in such disarray, you look up at the sky and see that everything's clear up there, the sky's blue, and the birds are stretching out their wings and rebuilding their nests. And it's up to those who can bear to look down again who are left with the responsibility of restoring life down here. If you could see the destruction of a hurricane you'd understand why so many prefer not to look down."

I focused on the road in front of me, and I think a part of me understood. I'd lived through a different kind of devastation, and watched as each member of my family, except for my mother and me, refused to look anywhere else except at the wreckage. But I couldn't help but believe that looking down again also meant accepting your vulnerabilities.

We pulled off the interstate and made our way to Ray Von's. I knew I wouldn't find Carol Sue there, as she was visiting her sister in Vicksburg, but we'd made plans to meet the following week to look at apartments and get the children together again.

The same cat I'd seen on my previous two visits sat in his usual perch on the front steps, meowing at us as we approached, before running away. Beau was back to clutching his red hat and clung to it with one hand and my jeans with the other. I climbed the three steps to the door and knocked. I could hear the television set inside, so I knew she was there, but I didn't hear shuffling steps until after I knocked the second time.

The door opened slowly and Ray Von's face appeared, taking in me and then Beau before finally settling on Aimee. She held a tissue to her nose, then sniffed. "I'm feeling poorly today, or I'd invite you in."

Aimee climbed up the three steps to the door. "We won't intrude, then. Just wanted to let you know that Xavier is doing well. He and Beau are getting along, and Xavier's teaching him everything he knows about gardening." She handed Ray Von the sack that we'd brought. "It's late in the season, but Xavier thought you'd like them."

What might have been a smile crossed Ray Von's face as she took the bag. "Thank you, Miss Aimee. I appreciate you looking after my boy."

Aimee reached up and squeezed Ray Von's hand. "You know that it's the least I can do."

A glance that I couldn't decipher passed between them before Ray Von turned to Beau. "You being a good boy, Mr. Beau, and listening to your grandmama?"

Beau hesitated for a moment, then nodded, sucking hard on his thumb.

"You look just like your mama. I hope you listen better than she did."

I cleared my throat. "Ray Von—remember how you said that Monica sent you a note with the painting? Do you still have it?"

She studied me for a long moment. "I think I threw it away. But I told you before, all it said was that you would be coming for the package. That's it."

I nodded, disappointed. "Well, if you do find it, could you please let me know? I'd like to see it, just in case you might have missed something."

Ray Von's lips pressed together tightly. "I'll do that." She stepped back from the door. "Thanks for stopping by," she said before closing the door gently in our faces.

I led Aimee and Beau back to the van and waited for everyone to get settled, staring at the freshly painted house with new windows and mowed grass. As I put the van into gear, I asked, "How was Ray Von able to afford to rebuild her house and keep it so well maintained?"

Aimee smiled without looking at me. "I call it part of her 'retirement' package. She worked for the Guidrys for so long that making sure she's taken care of in her old age is a responsibility that I take very seriously. We owe Ray Von so much that can never be repaid."

I was about to ask her what she meant when Aimee leaned forward and pointed at a street. "Let's make a little detour. There's something I want to show you."

Following her directions, I took a right on Beach Boulevard then another quick right, finding street parking where Aimee indicated. I locked the van door, then allowed Aimee to slip her hand into the crook of my arm while I held on to Beau with my other hand and walked a block back toward the beach.

We stopped across the street from where the Hard Rock Café's bright orange-and-brown oversize guitar sat like a misplaced toy. The water of the sound under heavy clouds was now the color of slate, as if the waves had swallowed all the shadows.

"When I was a girl, there wasn't a sandy beach like you see now. It was just a seawall with steps leading down into the water. Gary, Wes, and I would sit on the steps and go crabbing."

"Crabbing?" Beau looked up at her, his neatly combed hair now swirled by the wind, and I wondered if he remembered his mother telling him about crabbing with her brother and cousins, and how Trey would chase her down the beach with the largest one he could find.

Aimee put her arm around Beau. "It's an acquired taste that I'm sure you'll get used to. I'm hoping that this oil spill will be cleaned up in time so that I can show you how. I was the best, you know. Had 'the touch.' Always caught more than the boys." She smiled to herself, and I imagined her picturing a Biloxi between hurricanes and before oil spills. But all I could see in front of me was the empty beach and the water heavy with shadows, as deceptive as a lounging leopard.

We turned and passed under a large archway with the word "Biloxi" spelled out in lit capital letters above two rock pillars, and entered a large town green. Directly across from us was what appeared to be a monument with a flagpole in the center, the flag waving wildly in the storm-scented air. "It's going to rain, Miss Aimee. Do you want to go back to the car?"

She shook her head. "Not yet." She led me forward on a brick path, Beau racing on ahead toward the monument. Large oaks, most with patches of missing bark, stunted limbs, and uneven growth, dotted the green like wounded guardians. When we got closer to the memorial I could see a curved cement wall with a mosaic wave in the center of it rolling from one end to the other. At the far end sat a taller wall of black granite, columns of names marching in block letters under the word KATRINA and the date August 29, 2005. A glass case filled with small objects protruded from the marble wall, its base filled with empty oyster shells.

"What is this?" I asked, leaning forward to study the sun-bleached artifacts: a broken china plate, a ceramic angel, a trophy, a police badge, an American flag folded neatly as if unaware of its position over a pile of rubble.

"That's debris found after the hurricane. And see the slab of white granite on top of the black granite?" She pointed to the black wall. "It's twelve feet high, which was the height of the water here on the Town Green during the storm."

I looked around, mentally extending a line over everything I could see: the palm trees, the bruised oaks, the grass, the buildings, the cars. The people. All of that water. All of that destruction. I felt heavy with the thought of it, felt the weight of the water pushing me under.

"Why did you bring me here?" I asked, my words scattered by the wind.

"Before River Song is rebuilt, I wanted you to understand a little more about the people who live here in Biloxi. This memorial was dedicated to the citizens here, to remind everybody of a horrible tragedy. We have the names of the dead written on the wall, and cherished belongings in a glass case." She wrapped her arms around her chest, the wind turning cold. "I wanted you to understand that moving on doesn't mean forgetting."

My eyes stung and I turned away, noticing another Katrina tree nearby on the green. It had a large and sturdy trunk, with a green loggerhead turtle climbing down one side of it, a yellow-and-green fish swimming up one limb. A magnificent blue marlin erupted from the trunk into the air, its mouth open as it strained up toward the sky, poised forever on the brink of reaching what it sought.

I stared at it for a long time, wanting to understand something that continued to elude me. I noticed again the bruised oaks nearby, and their gallant attempts to flourish as if their scars didn't exist. "Why did some of the oaks die and some survive?"

Aimee gave me an elegant one-shoulder shrug. "Why do some people stay after a hurricane and why do some never come back?" She looked at me, her eyes measuring. "Why do some people continue to search for the missing, and others give up? I don't know. But I think sometimes a person has to be forced underwater to see if they're going to drown or swim."

I looked away, uncomfortable with her scrutiny. "It's going to rain soon. We should go." I called to Beau, who was trying to climb on the base of the flagpole, as Aimee placed her hand in the crook of my arm and we began to walk back toward the arch.

We'd almost reached the car when she spoke again. "I haven't thanked you for seeing to Monica's burial, and for taking care of her when she was sick. Those are things for which I'll never be able to repay you. So please don't mention paying me for rent or board or anything else. I'm already in your debt."

I wanted to protest, to say that Monica would have done the same for me, but Aimee placed her hand on my arm. "Don't say anything. Just agree, because I don't want to hear about it again." Her eyes were moist and she blinked them quickly. "You have a generous heart, Julie. But don't forget to save some of it for yourself."

I opened the passenger side of the van for Aimee, then helped Beau in, wanting to disagree, to say that circumstances had shaped all of my choices, and that I'd done nothing but follow the only path I could see. But I remained quiet as I started the van, following Aimee's directions to the museum office, to drop off my résumé in person, then to Reynoir Street to take the blueprints and discuss the next steps in River Song's resurrection.

Steve Kenney smiled when he saw some of our notations, but agreed they were all doable and that he would have the revised plans ready by the end of the week. When he asked which number he should call, I gave him mine, remembering what Aimee had told me about how rebuilding River Song wasn't fitting into Trey's agenda.

As we climbed back into the van one last time before heading back to New Orleans, Aimee said, "Let's go by River Song. I think I can stand to see it again now."

We headed down Beach Boulevard, past the now familiar empty lots, the fresh-painted houses, the boarded-up houses, the spray-painted boards in front of sandy grass and cement-slab foundations. Aimee lowered her window and the three of us looked at the vacant lot, the oak in front waving its leaves in the wind as if shaking with great expectation.

Aimee let go a heavy sigh. "So many memories here." Her knuckles were white where they rested on the door. "Most of them good." She pointed to the oak. "There used to be a shoofly there built around the tree. That's one of those raised porches with steps. It would keep the bugs off you, and it was big enough to dance on. It's been gone since before Monica's time, but she always wanted to rebuild it. Now maybe we can." She was silent, studying the empty lot.

I remembered what Aimee had said about her visit here with the Guidrys and wondered if that was what she was thinking about, too. "Why was Mrs. Guidry crying, Aimee, when you walked in on them? Did you ever find out?"

She shook her head. "Not really. There were rumors . . . Well, I suppose there are always rumors about people in society who don't conform. But I think a part of me didn't want to know. I had enough drama in my life without digging too much into theirs." She continued to look out at the bare lot, but I imagined she was seeing a white house with tall columns and rocking chairs, and two young men waiting inside. Eventually, she sat back in her seat, ending the discussion. "Let's go home now."

By the time we turned back down Beach Boulevard toward the interstate, the sky had shifted from gray to black, a subtle transference of power. I noticed Aimee's hands clenched in her lap, and I lifted my foot a little off the gas pedal. "I'll drive slowly, if that's what you're worried about," I reassured her.

She shook her head, keeping her eyes on the road ahead. "It's not the storm I'm afraid of. I just don't like the dark. I haven't since I was a little girl." She paused and I waited for her to tell me why, watching as the palms along the beach bent and swayed at the wind's whim.

Aimee continued. "It's not so bad anymore, but on days like this, when I dredge up old memories, it comes back to me."

I remembered what Trey had told me about her mother's death, and I couldn't ask Aimee why the dark held a hidden terror for her, believing that I already knew.

Feeling we both needed a change in the conversation, I asked, "Miss Aimee, are you ever going to tell me which brother you married?"

A wan smile softened her face. "We haven't gotten to that part yet, have we? We will, I promise." Her smile broadened. "We have an hour and a half in the car right now. But first you tell me a little more about your life in New York with Monica. About her work. And then I'll tell you a little more about mine."

"It's a deal," I said, as the first fat fists of rain hit the windshield, and the sky began to weep.

~∞~

CHAPTER 12

Storm surge: An abnormal rise in sea level accompanying a hurricane or other intense storm, and whose height is the difference between the observed level of the sea surface and the level that would have occurred in the absence of the cyclone.
—NATIONAL HURRICANE CENTER

Aimee

FALL 1955

My fingers scraped along the inside of the mailbox to retrieve the single letter in the back. I didn't recognize the handwriting, but my heart hiccuped when I saw the New Orleans postmark.

> *Dear Aimee,*
>
> *I hope you don't mind me writing you. I'm finding a rare free moment this afternoon and my thoughts have turned to you. I suppose it's because I spent the day with Gary yesterday and we talked mostly of you. I probably shouldn't be spoiling the surprise, but Gary is planning on asking you down here next February for the Mystick Krewe of Comus Ball. Invitations are very hard to come by, but my father has a business*

connection. Not that you need an added incentive to come. It would mean the world to Gary—to us—to have you here, so please say yes.

Gary showed me your senior picture. Wow! I hardly recognized you. (I guess I didn't word that the way I wanted to!) You'll certainly be the belle of the ball (I can see you blushing as you read this, by the way—it's your most endearing trait).

I suppose we'll be seeing a lot more of you in the next four years— Gary told me you'd been accepted at Newcomb College. Congratulations! I hope you'll allow me to take you to Commander's for lunch to celebrate your accomplishment.

All right—I think I've procrastinated enough. Back to work. I actually love the research and writing (which is good if I want to be a lawyer), but there are too many distractions living in an apartment with three other law students. I guess I'll head for the library.

Warm regards,
Wes

P.S. Please tell Gary yes—I don't think I could stand to see his disappointment.

I stared at the scrawled signature, my palms sweaty. I kept reading a single sentence over and over—*I hope you'll allow me to take you to Commander's for lunch.* Absently, I wondered if he included Lacy as one of his distractions.

This marked the beginning of a correspondence between Wes and me. As our pens scrawled across paper, Wes and I became equals with no age or family barriers. On paper, I was as safe to him as a confessional. I kept all of his letters in a shoe box under my bed, tied together with a pink hair ribbon, and would read and reread them until the folds began to tear.

I didn't question the reasons he continued writing to me, afraid that his letters meant much more to me than he'd intended. For the same reason, I didn't ask whether Gary was aware of it. But I couldn't help but hope that his memories of the girl from the levee, as he frequently called me, had changed and that he considered me a woman now—a woman who shared not only a love of his home city, but also a deep loneliness invisible on the outside, but a beacon to those who shared a similar absence.

Dear Aimee,

I was pleasantly surprised to receive your letter—it really brightened my day. I'm thrilled you're coming for Mardi Gras. And as a further incentive to keep you here, I've enclosed a Mardi Gras King Cake from McKenzie's. Be careful when you bite into it, because I've instructed the bakery to put a tiny plastic baby in each section. If you're not aware, the person who gets the baby has to buy the King Cake for the follow-ing year and throw a party. Looks like you're stuck with us, Aimee.

That letter had grease spots and green confectioner's sugar all over it from the King Cake, and I would smile every time I read the letter, re-membering the sixteen babies I had pulled from the cake. I kept them, too, nestled in among the letters.

I'm sorry if you think I'm out to sabotage your figure with King Cake. From what I remember of you in a bathing suit last summer, your figure is doing just fine. I don't think I'll see the need to "harpoon you on the beach," whatever that's supposed to mean.

Thanks for all of your comments on my rants about law school. Just knowing you're there to listen is a tremendous help to my mental health. What did I ever do before you?

He never mentioned Lacy, but I knew from Gary's letters that they were still dating. But his omission let me daydream. And in his letters, I held his undivided attention.

Did I ever tell you that your handwriting resembles a spiderweb after a good rain? You should be a doctor—it's really that bad! Actually, I think it's just another fascinating facet of your personality. I imagine it gives your grandmother fits, but I love it.

Thanks for asking about my mother. She stays the same, drinking and smoking—and no longer tries to hide it. I think it's progress, but Gary thinks our father has just given up. According to our father (and your grandmother), she dresses too outrageously and seeks the company of those she shouldn't. I love my mother, as does Gary, and I know she loves us back, but she is unreachable to us. It wasn't always this way. I sometimes wish we'd never returned to New Orleans, but how can I say that if it would mean we would have never met you?

Ray Von stays by Mother's side—and thank goodness for that. My father stays at the office as much as possible, leaving Mother to her own devices. God only knows what she'd be doing without Ray Von to curb her behavior.

I know my parents love each other—but it's not the kind of healthy love there should be between a man and a woman. I sometimes get the feeling that they each know something about the other that nobody else does, sort of like insurance so one will never leave the other. There's something unhealthy there, Aimee, but they won't allow me to get close enough to really see it. I'm not sure I want to.

I, too, took the opportunity to use our letters as a confessional, and began to reach out to him about my nightmares: nightmares from childhood that had suddenly resumed after a long hiatus. I never remembered anything about them when I awoke, only that in the dream I'd awakened from a heavy sleep in a darkened room, the coppery taste of blood on my tongue, the horrible and certain knowledge that I wasn't alone. Fear would settle on my skin like a sheet, and I'd awaken almost choking on the pungent smell of sweat and something so familiar yet nameless, its identity as fleeting as my mother's kiss.

The nightmares brought back memories of my mother, the few I had of her, and I began to question what I knew of her, and what I remembered of her death—questions my father wouldn't answer, and ones I could not. My memory of the night my mother died was like a black box, shut tightly and locked, the key hidden.

I don't know if I ever told you, but I remember your mother. I was a little boy—we were still living with my father then. She came over to bring us some tomatoes she had grown in her garden. She was beautiful. And that glorious red hair—just like yours, Aimee. But most of all I can recall her voice. It was sweet and high-pitched and it made everybody smile. We would sit in the pew behind your parents at Holy Name on Sundays and listen to her sing. My mother stopped coming to Mass with us because of it.

I think it bothered her a great deal that your mother was perfect in all the ways that she was not. I suspect that is one of her reasons she has embraced nonconformity now, feeling that if she couldn't fit in anywhere, she might as well emphasize her differences.

I'm not an expert on these sorts of things, but I have to believe that your nightmares are due to the fact that nobody knows who killed your mother, or why. Or why you were spared. It must be unsettling and unnerving, and I suspect the uncertainty is manifesting itself in your dreams.

If it would help you in any way, I will look into the police reports from the night your mother died, to see if there was anything that might have been overlooked, or should be reinvestigated. I have connections in the legal system and in the police department. I'll ask my father, too, since he was a good friend of your parents' and stayed by your father's side during the investigation and afterward.

In a different way I, too, know the loss of a mother. Perhaps it's this thing we have in common that seems to pull us together. I have never shared so much of myself with anyone, Aimee. I feel almost silly knowing that we have never spoken in person to such depths, but instead have relegated all our thoughts to paper. I hope we can continue this face-to-face when we see each other again.

On a much lighter note, Gary wrecked his car again. He's okay,
but I don't think his car is going to make it. My father's furious. Re-
member how you once told us you hoped our balls would fall off on our
wedding nights? I don't think Gary's will make it that far.

As February approached, I began to prepare for my trip down to
New Orleans. I didn't think much about Gary. All I could think of
was seeing Wes again. I had seen him the previous summer, but I knew
I had changed a great deal in the intervening months. My father had
taken to making comments about how he was going to have to beat
the boys away with a stick. Not that there was much of a chance of that
happening, since I rarely met boys my age. I couldn't wait to see Wes's
expression when he saw me again.

Standing in my hat and gloves with my baggage at the New Orleans
Moisant Field airport, I craned my neck searching for a familiar face.
Grandmother was on her yearly European cruise, so I would be stay-
ing with the Guidrys. She'd been appalled at the idea, but for once my
father intervened and worked it out with his mother and Mr. and Mrs.
Guidry.

I assumed Gary would be picking me up. I folded my garment bag
carefully over my arm, not wanting to crush, wrinkle, or obscure in
any way the simple beauty of my ball gown. My father had surprised
me by taking me to New York to shop and hadn't even blinked twice
at the price tag.

"Aimee."

I started at the deep, familiar voice. Wes stepped in front of me and
easily lifted my suitcase from the ground beside me.

"Welcome back." Wes leaned down and kissed me on the cheek,
then stood back as if to get a good look. I felt the heat rise to my cheeks
as he examined me. The awkwardness floated between us as we both
recalled the intimate thoughts of our letters.

He finally broke the silence. "It's a good thing you're blushing or I would have had to check the ID tag on your suitcase to make sure it was you!"

His blue eyes flashed, and I couldn't help but smile back at him.

"Hi, Wes." He wore a suit and a hat, and for a moment I thought that we both looked like children playing adults. I glanced behind his broad shoulders. "Where's Gary?"

A small flicker passed behind his eyes. "He stayed up all last night studying for a trigonometry test. He was exhausted."

I felt a pang of guilt for being glad of his absence.

"Believe me—he wanted to come. Ray Von practically had to tie him to his bed." He maneuvered us toward the exit of the large, hangarlike structure. "I know I promised you lunch at Commander's."

I felt a flush of pleasure. "I thought you would have forgotten all about that."

"Of course not. But you're going to have to take a rain check. Gary is too eager to see you to wait."

I tried to hide my disappointment—and my guilt. I'd hardly thought of Gary at all since getting onto the plane. I smiled. "Sure. I don't mind."

He reached to take my overnight bag, pausing for a moment to look down into my face, his own serious. "I've enjoyed your letters very much, you know."

"Oh," I said, his words taking me by surprise. I patted my hair into place beneath my hat, then followed him out into the parking lot. We headed toward the sea of cars and approached a red-and-white Corvette convertible. When he stopped in front of it, I asked, "What happened to your Oldsmobile?" I carefully placed my garment bag on top of the other bag in the trunk.

He shrugged. "Lacy wasn't crazy about it. She really wanted me to have a Corvette." His voice sounded flat, just like a lawyer who had practiced hiding his emotions from his speech.

"Well, *I* loved your Oldsmobile."

He gave me a sidelong glance before donning his sunglasses and putting the car into reverse. I laid my head back on the seat, letting the sun seep into my skin, my hand on my hat so it wouldn't fly away. I'd seen a yellow chiffon scarf in the glove box when Wes had retrieved his sunglasses, but I knew to whom it belonged and wasn't going to ask to borrow it, even if it meant destroying my new and favorite hat.

The weather was unseasonably warm, hovering in the low seventies. It had been a long winter in Philadelphia, and my body screamed for the sultry warmth of New Orleans.

As we sped down the highway, the rushing wind prohibited conversation. I clung to my hat and spent the time surreptitiously examining Wes and comparing him to his brother. Gary had sent me his senior picture, and I remarked to my father how little he had changed since I had first seen him.

With my head against the backrest, I admired Wes's strong profile and was struck again by the similarities between him and Gary. They shared the same straight, slender nose, the nostrils forming perfect ovals. The narrow foreheads and prominent cheekbones marked them as related, despite their differences in builds. Whereas Wes had blossomed into full manhood, Gary's cheeks and nose still held a roundness to them. Perhaps it was owing to Gary's slightness, but even at seventeen, he still looked like a prepubescent boy.

We listened to the prattle of the deejays on WNOE the rest of the way home, not speaking. He parked the car in the driveway and slowly pulled the key from the ignition. Neither one of us moved.

"Wes." My voice cracked and I swallowed.

He turned to me and removed his sunglasses, and I saw the red marks they left under his eyes.

"Ask me out to lunch again, okay?"

His cheeks creased in a smile. Wes opened his mouth to say something when the front door flew open and Gary appeared on the threshold. His face was pale, and he gave me a wan smile as he sauntered down the front steps, his mother close behind him dressed in skintight pencil pants and a midriff-baring blouse tied above the waist, her ever-present alligator brooch pinned above her right breast. A cigarette in a holder trailed smoke behind her.

I stepped out of the car, and Mrs. Guidry enveloped me in a perfumed hug, then kissed me on both cheeks, European style. A hint of alcohol teased the air surrounding her, not completely masked by the Shalimar perfume she still wore. "Aimee! We're so thrilled you could be here. I don't think Gary's slept a wink in two weeks!"

"Mama!" Gary protested, his hands shoved deeply into his pockets, his eyes not quite meeting mine. He had grown in the months since the previous summer, and he stood almost as tall as his brother. They towered over me, wearing identical grins.

"Hi, Gary," I said, grinning back at him and unsure whether I should hug him. We had been greeting each other after long absences for years, and I remembered him giving me a little punch on the shoulder when we had said good-bye only six months before. But this time was somehow different. We had left childhood somewhere behind us, perhaps on the levee above the muddy river. The bridge into adulthood had been crossed, and we stood warily facing each other, looking for whatever remained of our childhood friend.

He leaned toward me, arms outstretched, and hugged me. I hugged him back and could feel how his back and shoulders had broadened. He squeezed me tighter and then I felt the old familiar snap of my bra strap.

"Gary!" I shoved him away, laughing, and he laughed with me, a bright glint in his eyes. This was my Gary, and I recognized him.

Wes retreated to his car to retrieve my suitcase, Gary close behind. As soon as Wes lifted the suitcase, Gary wrested it from his hand. "I can carry that."

He stretched his arm to take my garment bag from Wes, but Wes held it out of his reach. "I got it, Gary."

Gary lunged for it, grabbing the side of it and pulling at the thin cover. "No, I can do it."

I stared at them in horror as they played tug-of-war with my dress. I wedged myself between them. "May I please have my dress before you two ruin it?"

A small yellow MG convertible pulling up in the driveway interrupted us. I recognized Lacy immediately, with her crown of blond hair covered with a pale pink scarf, white sunglasses sparkling in the sun. A long-boned hand waved from behind the steering wheel, a gold bracelet glinting on her wrist. She looked like Grace Kelly, and my stomach made a sick lurch.

Gary used the opportunity to grab my garment bag. I didn't dare offer to take the suitcase, even though he struggled to lift it. Firm muscles showed on his arms, but I could see the effort it took for him to take a deep breath of air as he lumbered to the front steps. He teetered a bit on the top one, but managed to propel himself forward and through the doorway.

I paused a moment before going in and turned to see Lacy greeting Wes. Her small, curvy body molded to his as she stood on her toes to kiss him, long scarlet fingernails visible in his dark hair. Turning away, I spotted Ray Von in the foyer, staring at me and shaking her head.

An arm went around my shoulders and I looked up into Mrs. Guidry's face. Bright red lipstick was smeared on her lips and sat on her teeth, her eyes unnaturally bright, bringing to mind a zombie in those horror movies Gary and I liked to watch, like the real person inside had long since gone, leaving only a shell behind.

She gave me a squeeze and guided me inside. "This is going to be so much fun, Aimee. You must show me your dress—and I insist on helping you get ready before the ball tomorrow night. I don't have a daughter, so I hope you don't mind indulging me." She seemed to be reading from a script, her words saying the right thing but meaning nothing to her.

Gary stopped at the foot of the stairs. "Mama is having her portrait painted in her ball gown by an artist from up north. He came down here just to paint her; isn't that swell?"

Mrs. Guidry smiled at Gary. "He's a very modern painter—let's just say that Mr. Guidry isn't a fan—but I love his style, and I'm flattered that he'd come all this way to paint me. I'm unveiling it after the ball." She squeezed me again. "I'm so excited to have a daughter here."

She continued to chat about her preparations and past balls, her speech rambling and her words tumbling together like runaway cars at an amusement park ride. Gary had told me that she hadn't attended a Mardi Gras ball in years, his father not thinking she was ready, but something this year was different. I welcomed her chattering as I tried to sort through my feelings.

The door shut as Lacy and Wes followed us in, her arm draped possessively through the crook of his elbow. Her sunglasses rested saucily on top of her gold head and she gave me a wide smile. "Hello, again. It's Annie, isn't it?"

I shook my head, making a conscious effort not to stoop my shoulders so I wouldn't look like such a giant next to her compact petiteness.

Wes shot me an apologetic grin as Mrs. Guidry spoke up, her cigarette dropping ash on the hardwood floor. "No, Lacy—it's Aimee. And I must say she's grown up to be as pretty as her name, don't you think?"

A loud crash from behind us shifted the attention from me, and we all turned. Fronds from a large green fern lay heaped on the marble tiles of the foyer, dirt-encrusted roots splayed out amid the crumbled remnants of its former home. Terra-cotta bits and pieces lay scattered across the floor and around the shoes of a caramel-skinned boy.

My gaze traveled up a pair of skinny legs, past knobbly knees and cutoff shorts, raked past an almost nonexistent neck to the face. I tried not to flinch. Half of the boy's face drooped and sagged in bunches of skin, as if someone had gathered it together before it was dry and allowed it to set. The closed left eye slouched into the cheek area, the lids melded together. It wasn't until I saw the right side of his face that I realized he was a boy just a few years older than me. A bright green eye stared out at me from his wrecked face.

"Xavier!"

When he turned his head at Ray Von's voice, I shuddered at the small knot of skin where an ear had once been.

Ray Von knelt and started picking up the pieces of the broken planter. "Are you all right?"

He nodded, his gaze fixed on me while Ray Von continued picking up chunks of terra cotta. "Help me clean this up before somebody gets cut."

The boy bent down and picked up a large section of the pot and began scooping up the broken pieces and putting them inside the shell. A jagged tear in Xavier's thumb began gushing blood and dripping rapidly onto the floor, unnoticed by him as he continued to pick up pottery pieces while spreading the blood around in a grotesque pattern.

I swallowed, wondering why he'd been staring at me and why nobody else seemed to care that he was bleeding. "You've cut yourself." I reached into my pocketbook and pulled out several tissues and handed them to him.

He took them from me, his expression passive, and allowed Ray Von to wrap his hand and lead him from the room.

Mrs. Guidry watched them, her body completely rigid, her faced blanched, and for a moment she appeared to be terrified. And then she looked at me with her vacant eyes and smiled. "Watch where you step, Aimee. I promised your father that I'd return you to him as good as new." She excused herself and went toward the kitchen.

Gary leaned toward me. "That's Ray Von's son. He's come to live with us. He looks scary, but he's nice. Comes and stays with Ray Von during breaks sometimes and we do stuff together."

I looked at Gary, my eyebrows raised in an unspoken question. As before, Gary knew what I was asking without my having spoken. "His father burned him when he was a baby." He squeezed my arm. "Don't worry—his father's long dead. Xavier's been at a boarding school in Ocean Springs, but he got too old to stay there. My dad said he could come here."

Mrs. Guidry returned and placed a dish towel over the mess on the floor. "I don't think anybody wants to look at that." Her eyes furtively darted toward the front parlor, finally resting on the liquor cabinet. A nervous smile twitched her lips. "Come on, Aimee. Let me get you all settled in your room, and we'll have a nice drink together before lunch."

She breezed past us to the wide stairs, her slender hands holding the dark mahogany banister. Gary and I followed with my bags, and I was glad to be away from the smeared bloodstains and the young man whose scars didn't appear to be all on the outside.

Later that night, as I settled into my large four-poster bed, I listened to the night sounds of an old house as wind gusted against the windowpanes. Somewhere, a loose eave whistled into the darkness, creating an unnatural moan. I plumped up the pillows behind me and grabbed a romance novel, not yet quite ready to close my eyes and submit myself to sleep.

Then I heard it—a *thump-thump* coming from under my bed. Every hair on my body stood at attention, my mouth drying. I curled into a tight ball in the middle of the bed, waiting for something to grab at any exposed appendage. Almost imperceptibly, the yellow damask bedspread began to slide from the end of the bed and slowly disappear over the edge.

"Help." My voice was hardly louder than a whisper. The wind and moaning of the eaves seemed to intensify, almost drowning out the thumping from under the bed.

I sat up straighter, unwilling to have any contact with the bed. I hunched over my legs, trying to decipher the sound I was hearing. I tilted my head, trying to imagine why I was hearing laughter. Smothered laughter.

I leaned over the edge of the bed and saw a decidedly large, albeit human foot peeking out from under the dust ruffle. Before I could drop a table lamp on it, Gary burst forth from under my bed, his face contorted from the effort of trying to hold in his laughter.

"What are you doing?" I screamed.

He lifted himself off the floor and sat down on the edge of the bed, shaking his head in an effort to control himself.

"You think it's funny trying to scare me to death?" I was struggling to stay angry with him. "And where in the hell were you when I was changing clothes?" He lifted his arm to protect himself as I slammed my pillow over his head. I sat like an Indian chief in the middle of my bed, arms and legs crossed, staring him down. "Aren't you a little old to be playing tricks?"

As his darkened eyes contemplated me, his laughing sputtered, then died. His gaze slowly traveled down my neck to the low neckline of my white baby-doll pajamas. I crossed my arms higher on my chest, realizing the fabric was only a shade thicker than transparent.

He licked his lips. "I, um, guess I should go now." His gaze seemed reluctant to leave my chest.

"Yes. You probably should."

Still, he sat at the edge of my bed, within an arm's length of me. He raised his eyes to my face, then leaned toward me. I didn't move.

A knocking on the door made him shoot off the bed, stumbling over my slippers in his haste. He catapulted himself at the door and threw it open.

"What is all that noise?" Ray Von poked her head around the door.

Gary scratched the back of his head. "Just Aimee being immature. I'm going to bed now. Night, Aimee." He disappeared into the darkness without looking back at me.

Ray Von entered my room, her eyes like black shadows in the dim light of my bedside lamp. She approached the window and undid the tiebacks on the draperies, letting the thick yellow fabric fall together.

"That boy shouldn't be in your room, you know."

I scooted back against the headboard. "He wasn't invited."

"Hmmm." She shook her head and moved to the other window. She eyed the night-light I had plugged into the wall outlet. "You still scared of the dark, Miss Aimee?"

I gave her a dismissive wave, not letting on that I was still, in fact, terrified of the dark. That when the lights went off, I was a little girl again, feeling the hot stickiness of blood on my hands, and smelling sweat that wasn't my own. "No, of course not. Just habit, I guess. I bring my night-light with me wherever I go."

A flicker of light warbled in the air in front of her, and she shot out her hand and captured it in her fist. "It's a lightning bug. Isn't that strange?" Her voice lowered to a grumbling whisper. "All that mosquito spraying just about killed all them lightning bugs." She clucked her tongue. "This one must be here for a reason."

She walked over to the side of the bed and picked up my empty drinking glass. "Lightning bugs bring death to a house." She indicated the glass. "You keep him in here till he dies so he can take the death with him."

Flattening her hand against the open end of the glass, she then slammed it upside down onto the nightstand.

Putting her chin down to her chest, she said, "Don't let him out, now, you hear?" She narrowed her eyes at me, then left the room, the latch clicking slowly as she shut the door.

I stared at the hapless insect, its body tapping against the sides of the glass, its abdomen glowing brightly. I reached over and lifted the little prison, allowing its captive to escape. I flipped off the lamp and lay still, listening to the howling wind and following the blinking of the bug until I fell asleep.

CHAPTER 13

The weather-cock on the church spire, though made of iron,
would soon be broken by the storm-wind if it . . . did not
understand the noble art of turning to every wind.

—HEINRICH HEINE

Julie

I sat on a stone bench by the garden fountain, watching as Beau played
with the flotilla of wooden sailboats his uncle had given him. Their
bonding had been sudden and surprising, at least for me. Or maybe
because they were both male it was natural for them to find common
ground in toys that snapped together, or had wheels and moving parts.

Beau's red hat sat next to me on the bench, not too far from him, but
not with him. I took this to mean that his dependency on it was less-
ening, and hopefully his grief, too. I suddenly wished for a completed
River Song, so that newer and happier memories could begin to fill the
empty space carved by his mother's absence.

"Vroom, vroom," Beau said as he pushed the sailboats around in
the water. He looked so intent and happy that I didn't have the heart
to tell him that sailboats didn't have motors. Recalling the lines of
docked boats at the marina in Biloxi, I figured he'd have to learn more

about watercraft eventually, but for now I'd let his imagination over-rule reality.

I looked down in my lap at the Abe Holt book I'd borrowed from Trey's study, finally having found a few moments to go through it. I opened the front cover and flipped to the opening pages, noticing again the copyright date of January 1999. The year before Monica ran away. I flipped to the title page and found myself staring at long, elegant script written in black ink. *Merry Christmas, Monica. From one art lover to an-other, with love from Grandmother Aimee.*

I looked at the signature for a long moment, wondering why Aimee hadn't mentioned the book. But it had been given to Monica so long ago that she'd probably forgotten it. Or maybe even assumed that Mon-ica had taken it with her. Still, I wondered what had precipitated the purchase and the gifting of it.

As I absently strummed my finger along the edge of the closed pages, my fingernail caught on something. Lifting the book, I noticed a tiny extra space between two pages somewhere in the middle. I slid my thumb to the edge of the page to open it at the break, rewarding myself with a paper cut.

I sucked on the cut as a small breeze rustled the white rectangular receipt that had been used to mark the page. The purple lettering had faded so I could barely make out the name of the store—something with "art and supplies" in it—and the year was definitely 1999.

Lifting the receipt from the book, I examined the page to see if I could determine what it had been marking, my heart seeming to beat a little faster as I recognized the black-and-white photograph on the bot-tom right of the left-hand page. It was the portrait of Caroline Guidry, with her cat eyes and provocative stare, the sparkling eyes of the alliga-tor brooch nearly dominating the picture.

Squinting, I brought the book closer to my face so I could read the caption. *Portrait of unknown woman, oil on canvas. New Orleans, 1956. Private collection.*

Unknown woman? I sat up, still sucking on my thumb, just in time to see Trey emerge from the backyard at the rear of the property. He was wearing the same outfit I'd seen him in the last time, but without the sweat-matted hair, and his white socks appeared brighter. The work boots, Tulane T-shirt, and torn shorts were still paint-splattered but otherwise appeared clean. He stopped when he spotted me, apparently as surprised to see me as I was to see him.

"Uncle Trey!" Beau lifted his hand from the water and waved wildly, liberally sprinkling me and the book.

"Careful, sweetie," I said, using the sleeve of my cotton sweater to wipe off the page.

Trey approached and stood next to me, looking down at the book. "Sorry," I said. "I borrowed this from your study, planning to return it without any damage."

He leaned forward to lift the cover to see what it was, then lowered it again. "That was in my study?"

I nodded. "I didn't think you'd mind."

"I don't mind. It's just that I don't think I've ever seen it before."

"There's an inscription on the front dated 1999, from Aimee wishing Monica a Merry Christmas."

Trey frowned. "She would have been seventeen. A year before she disappeared."

"Yeah, I thought the same thing. Do you think they're related in some way?"

He sat down next to me, and I smelled soap and laundry detergent. "I have no idea. Have you found anything in the book?"

"Just this." I opened the book to the page showing the portrait of Caroline Guidry. "But look here." I tapped the caption. "It says 'unknown woman.' Any idea why it would say that?"

He shook his head. "No clue. As far as I know, the identity of the woman in the portrait has always been known." He pointed at the photograph. "This is an old picture—you can tell by the graininess of the photo, and it's in black-and-white. I would guess that it was taken for publicity shortly after it was painted. Probably even by the artist himself for his portfolio. Maybe my family didn't give permission to print her name. Society was very different back then. Southern women were not supposed to call attention to themselves."

"It was painted in 1956, the year Caroline disappeared. Maybe that's why the family hid her identity. Because of the scandal."

"Maybe," he said, tapping his fingers on his knee. "We can ask Aimee, see if she knows."

We? I nodded, still staring at the photograph of the portrait, an insistent thought knocking at the back of my brain. "Does Aimee have the alligator pin?"

"Not that I know of. In fact, I don't think I've ever seen it. Why do you ask?"

I shrugged. "From what Aimee's said, the brooch was Caroline's signature piece, and she was never seen without it. Even on her house-coat. I was wondering if it was with her when she disappeared."

He didn't say anything, and when I turned to look at him, his eyes registered surprise. "That's some detective work, Julie. Maybe you missed your calling."

I closed the book. "I've hung out with detectives since I was twelve, so I guess it's only natural that I would start thinking like one."

He continued to drum his fingers on his knees. "Find anything lately on the Internet to send to your detective friend?"

I shook my head. "Not since I've been here. I've actually only gone to look twice—the second time this morning. I've been so preoccupied with other things—like Beau, and River Song. And Aimee. I love listening to her stories. Still, I need to get focused again, so I don't miss a lead."

He stared at me for a long moment. "Or maybe you need to determine what's the real distraction."

"What do you mean?"

"Well, is your new life here distracting you from searching for your sister, or is your search distracting you from living a life?"

I stood abruptly, lifting the book with me. Staring down at him, I said, "You don't know the first thing about me. And what would you know about having a life? You work all the time, and you still live with your grandmother."

It looked for a moment like he might actually smile, but his eyes remained serious. "You should come with me this morning."

"To your office? Why?"

This time he did smile. "It's Saturday, Julie. Although I have worked on Saturdays before, I'm not actually going to work."

I looked down at what he was wearing, knowing he wouldn't volunteer the answer if I didn't ask the question. "Then where are you going?"

"To help out with building a house in the Lower Ninth Ward. I volunteer with the Make It Right Foundation—a team of architects, businesses, and just regular people trying to get residents to move back."

I knew the neighborhood from news footage showing the worst of the flooding following Katrina. "But isn't that whole area below sea level?"

I saw the tic begin in his jaw. "Yes. And a lot of families have lived there for generations and want to move back but have no homes to move back to. MIR is trying to fill that gap. New Orleans can't come back without its people."

We looked at each other as if we were speaking the same language but with accents that made our words indecipherable to each other.

"But the neighborhood is still below sea level," I repeated.

As if speaking to a small child, Trey answered me in slow, measured words. "The levee system is being fixed. And we're building sustainable, storm-resistant houses that are being built with raised first floors. It's a fixable situation."

"And why would you want me to come?"

He stood, too. "Oh, never mind. I guess I thought you might learn something."

I wanted to ask him if he hoped my participation would teach me the ropes of rebuilding a house, or if he thought the experience would leave me too discouraged at the thought of building something so permanent.

Instead, I asked, "What got you involved in the project?"

Without hesitation, he said, "Xavier."

"Xavier?"

"Yeah, Xavier." He used a fingernail to flick away a blob of green paint on his forearm that had eluded the soap and water. "A few days before Katrina, we evacuated Aimee and Ray Von inland to Jackson. Just like Charles, I didn't want the house to remain empty for too long, too much of a target, you know? So I came back, doing some last-minute boarding up and moving furniture. But when it came time to leave, I couldn't get Xavier to go. He said he wasn't going to let anything happen to Miss Aimee's house on his watch."

I remembered what Xavier had told me about how he wouldn't let anything happen to Miss Aimee, like he was her great protector. "Why is he so attached to her?"

He shrugged. "I guess because she showed him kindness at a time in his life when nobody else did. My grandmother has always had a knack for harboring lost souls."

I refused to take his words personally and instead allowed him to continue.

"So I stayed with Xavier. I can't say I'll ever do anything as stupid again, but I'm glad I did it. We lost a few trees and part of the roof, but we—along with a pair of my hunting rifles—kept the looters away from our house and our neighbors' houses. And then, when it became clear that the Garden District had been mostly spared, I left Xavier here to guard the house and headed downtown to see what I could do there. Found a spot on a friend's pontoon boat and helped pull people out of flooded houses."

We watched as Beau, still making motor noises, lifted two of the boats high in the air and dropped them into the fountain, splashing his face and shirt with cold water. He laughed and then did it again, and I didn't say anything about sailboats or motors, or about getting wet when it was chilly outside. And I couldn't decide whether that made me the best guardian in the world or the worst.

I turned back to Trey, recalling something Carol Sue had told me. "'Great tragedy gives us opportunities for great kindness.'"

He looked at me oddly. "Yeah, something like that."

He turned and strode quickly over to Beau, reaching behind the little boy before scooping him up and twirling him in a circle, much to Beau's shouted delight. Regardless of Trey's lukewarm attitude toward me and his uncertainty about my presence here, I could feel nothing but relief that he'd never once doubted that Beau belonged.

Putting Beau down, he tousled his hair. "Okay, bud, I'll be back for dinner, and afterward we can finish our LEGO castle, all right?"

"All right!" Beau shouted, jumping up and trying to reach Trey's hair as if to tousle his, too.

Trey turned to leave, then paused. "By the way, Julie, I had a house in the Venetian Isles neighborhood in New Orleans East. Lovely spot on the water but outside the levee's protection. It's no longer there. And Aimee didn't want to live alone anymore. That's why I live with my grandmother."

"Oh," I said, feeling properly chastised but not wanting to show it.

He waited a moment as if to see if I would say anything else, then lifted his hand in a wave and let himself out of the gate.

I sat on the bench for a long time after Trey had gone, watching Beau splash in the fountain until he finally moved the ships to the muddy grass. I thought absently that I'd have to give him another bath before lunch, but didn't care. He was having fun, and his hat remained by my side, forgotten, at least for now.

My cell phone sat in my hands, my thumbnail tapping the blank screen as I ruminated over my conversation with Trey and about what he'd said about distractions. He knew what it was like to search for a missing loved one. Why couldn't he understand that my need to focus on finding my sister had to be my priority? That my father and brother had long since given up, and that my mother had died without ever knowing? I couldn't abandon Chelsea now. I'd already done it once.

I quickly hit the memory-dial button and waited.

"Detective Kobylt here."

"Hi, Detective. It's Julie Holt."

"Hello, Julie. How are you?" For one of the few times I'd spoken to him, his voice was unrushed. "I'm fine, thank you. And you?"

"I'm doing well." He paused. "Just found out that my oldest daughter is going to have a baby. My wife and I are real excited. It'll be our first grandchild."

I sat there, staring at my phone, wondering how I hadn't known that he had children, and that at least one of them was probably married, and that he could be excited over the prospect of becoming a grandfather. Belatedly, I added, "Congratulations, Detective."

"Thank you." He cleared his throat. "So what can I do for you, Julie? I don't recall getting any e-mails from you."

"I actually haven't been online in a while until this morning and thought I'd call instead. Just to touch base."

"Did you see anything?"

"Just one thing—and it's a long shot, which is why I didn't immediately e-mail you. But the girl Hilary McMahon, the one who disappeared in Hartford after cheerleading practice, I thought you should take a look at her case. In her school photo, she looks a lot like Chelsea."

"I'm already on it. I saw it, too, and put a call into the detective in charge. I'll let you know if anything comes up."

I smiled into the phone. "Thanks. Hey, has anyone ever told you that you're pretty good at your job?"

His words carried a smile. "A couple of times."

"Detective Kobylt?"

"Yes, Julie?"

"How many children do you have?"

He paused briefly before answering. "Four. Two girls and two boys. Why do you ask?"

"I just . . . well, I guess I just always imagined you sitting at your desk, solving crimes. I never thought of you as somebody with a family and another life."

He laughed, and a phone rang in the background. "Yeah, well, I couldn't do this job if I didn't have another life, you know? We all need something to soften the sharp edges. To give us balance. Otherwise, I think we'd find ourselves stumbling around in the dark like lost souls."

"Yeah, well, I'd better let you go. Thanks for talking with me. And congratulations on becoming a grandfather."

"Thanks, Julie. Take care."

The line went dead, and I looked at my cell phone for a long time before turning it off and sticking it back in my pocket.

I held my hand out to Beau. "Come on, Beau. I told Miss Aimee we'd take her to lunch, and you need a bath first."

He gathered the sailboats in his arms while I picked up the Abe Holt book and red hat and retreated into the house, thinking about lost souls and wondering what had happened to the alligator brooch with the glittering ruby eyes.

CHAPTER 14

Eyewall: An organized band or ring of cumulonimbus clouds that surround the eye . . . of a tropical cyclone.
—NATIONAL HURRICANE CENTER

Aimee

FEBRUARY 1956

The scream tumbled me from my bed. I stood barefoot on the wood floor, trailing bedclothes and shivering. I blinked, then used my night-light as a point of reference in the darkened room. Disoriented and still half-asleep, I stumbled to the table, knocking over my glass, and turned on the lamp. I stayed there, hunched over, wondering what to do. The scream had come from close by, and it was undoubtedly female.

A shout followed by the sound of splintered glass moved me out of my inertia. I ran to the door and opened it to stare into the darkened hallway. Light trickled through the transom window over the master bedroom, the leaded glass creating murky shadows on the walls and floor but leaving the corners in total blackness. The boys' rooms were in another area of the house, and I hesitated, wondering if I should get one of them first.

Angry words crashed through the master bedroom door like bullets. My curiosity overriding my good sense, I closed my bedroom door behind me and moved closer.

Mrs. Guidry's voice bordered on hysteria. "No! No! No! I won't have it, you hear? I won't have it!" Footsteps approached the door. I backed into a shadow as the steps receded.

"You must see reason, Caroline." Mr. Guidry's voice was low and gravelly, barely audible. "We don't have any choices, do we? You've made certain of that. This is the only way—even you must see that."

Another explosion of glass shattered the stillness of the house. I held my breath, waiting for the door to open, or a person to shout, or footsteps on the stairs. But there was nothing. I let the air out of my lungs bit by bit.

Then heavy footsteps crossed the room, followed by the distinctive sound of a hand slapping flesh, followed by female sobs. Almost incoherent now, with her words slurring through her sobs, she said, "I can't do this! He is dangerous to both of us; don't you see?"

Mr. Guidry's voice was so low I could barely hear it, but I sensed the threatening tone just the same. "I've already explained it to you. He needs to be here, and I won't change my mind. I can't."

"I will not stand for it, do you hear? I will not stand for it. Either he leaves, or I will. And then I'll tell everything to anyone who will listen. And maybe then I can finally be free." I almost didn't recognize Mrs. Guidry's voice. It carried depth and power in it and a dark tone I had never heard from her before.

High heels tapped against the wood floor, and then a door slammed. I took another step backward and bumped into something soft and fleshy. My skin tightened over my skull as the smell of body sweat assaulted my nose. I turned abruptly and recognized the warped landscape of Xavier's face. The filtered light from the transom skipped over most of the scars but could not hide the clumped skin that melted his left eye shut. A scream caught in my throat as he put a damp palm over

my mouth. I tasted salt as I looked into his eye and saw no malice—
only sadness. I relaxed in his grip.

A drawer slammed shut behind the closed bedroom door, the brass
handles vibrating like fear. Bedsprings squeaked and then a heavy sigh
escaped through the door before all was quiet again. Slowly, Xavier removed his hand. A drop of moisture hit my forearm, and I realized that
he was crying. The Guidrys must have been discussing him.

I put my hand on his arm. "Don't worry, Xavier. Things will work
out." I didn't know if they would or not, but he looked so devastated I
had to say something.

He ducked his head and stared into the blackness around our feet.
"No, miss," he whispered. "She's too afraid to let me stay any longer."
I felt a shudder go through him before he stepped away from my grasp
and disappeared down the hallway, as silent as a ghost. I felt my way
to my bedroom and closed the door behind me, wishing I'd asked him
what Mrs. Guidry was so afraid of.

I rose early the following morning, the bright sun sneaking from
behind the venetian blinds and coloring the room with a golden tint.
I showered and dressed, then followed the aroma of batter sizzling in
the kitchen. I smiled when I saw Gary wearing a bright red apron.
Humming to himself, he cradled a bowl of batter close to his chest
as he stirred.

A wide smile split his face. "Good morning, Miss Mercier. What
would you like for breakfast? Beignets, beignets, or beignets?"

I pretended to consider my options. "How about a beignet?"

He looked up toward the ceiling, as if considering. "I'll see if I can
accommodate you."

Gary continued stirring the batter as I slid into a seat at the kitchen
table by the window. The wrought-iron table and chairs mimicked the
ones outside in the garden. It was almost hard to tell that one wasn't

actually sitting in the garden, because of the vast number of plants suspended from the twelve-foot kitchen ceiling.

A small spider spun on its thread, propelling itself down from the fronds of a fern. It stopped, suspended momentarily in midair. The gossamer thread shimmered briefly in the sun as the spider continued its descent and landed on the table in front of me.

"Don't touch it." A brown hand reached from behind me and scooped it up. I turned and saw Xavier, his eye calmly regarding me. Cradling the spider in one hand, he set my plate and silverware in front of me with the other. His large hands seemed incongruous against the delicate china and silver, but he put each piece down without a sound. I waited for him to say something about the night before, but he silently finished his chore, his face impassive. He poured the chicory coffee without a drip and left the room.

I thought about telling Gary about the events of the previous night, but talked myself out of it. His relationship with his father was already precarious, his mother's emotional state uncertain. I didn't understand anything that had transpired between Mr. and Mrs. Guidry and knew that involving Gary could only complicate an already difficult situation. In retrospect, I was selfish, too, not wanting any ugliness to encroach on a weekend I'd been anticipating for months. So I ignored my uneasiness in much the same way I never thought too hard about the origins of my fear of the dark, knowing that there were some things that should never be seen in the bright light of day.

Gary approached with a platter full of powdered-sugar beignets. I scooped one up with a serving fork and dumped it on my plate. Without a word, Gary stood by my chair and flicked another one onto my plate, where it landed in a puff of powder. "Don't be shy, Aimee. I know you love these."

And I certainly did. From my first trip to Café Du Monde in the French Quarter I had loved the little French doughnuts: hot, fluffy, caloric confections covered in powdered sugar. It had always been Gary's special treat to make them for me when I came to visit.

I picked one up, held it to my face, and blew on it. A sugar cloud puffed its way to Gary's face, dusting his navy blue shirt.

"Thanks, Aimee," he said, smiling, the loosened powder flaking off his lips. He stood and returned to the fryer next to the stove. I closed my eyes, listening to the sizzle of the doughnuts and smelling the wonderful aroma. I knew I would never be able to hear that sound or smell that scent without thinking of Gary. A quote came to mind and I said it out loud. "'Smells are surer than sounds or sights. To make the heart-strings crack.'"

Gary turned his attention back to me, powder still clinging to his face. "What?"

"It's Kipling."

He shook his head. "I don't think I've ever Kippled before—but I'd like to try it."

He gave me an evil leer, and I waved my hand at him before turning back to my breakfast. My teeth sank into the soft mushiness of my doughnut as I stared out into the garden and spotted Xavier walking down the flagstone walkway leading to the front of the house. He stooped and opened his large hand and held it open, his thick fingers splayed wide. I pictured the tiny spider disembarking from its prison, rejoicing in its freedom to once again spin webs among the oleander.

The front door slammed, and I turned to see Wes pausing in the kitchen doorway. My mouth went dry. He was wearing a white tennis shirt and shorts, the shirt plastered to his chest with drying sweat. I took a deep sip of coffee, then let my cup clatter in its saucer. I didn't even notice the scalding liquid as I forced it down.

"Good morning, Aimee. I was hoping I might catch you for a little chat sometime before you leave." He leaned against the doorframe, a crooked smile lighting his face. I had never seen him look quite so appealing, and it took me a moment to register what he might want to talk about with me. His last letter had said that he'd gained access to my mother's case file, and I hoped he'd have some news for me.

"Hi, Wes. Anytime. Besides the ball, I really don't have any plans." I picked up a beignet to give my hands something to do.

A glass mixing bowl clanked in the sink. Gary wore a frown as he contemplated his brother. "Actually, I have lots of plans that will be keeping Aimee pretty busy." He gave an exaggerated sniff. "You stink. Shouldn't you go take a shower?"

Wes's answer was interrupted by another door slam. "Hello, everyone." An elegant hand snaked around Wes's midriff as Lacy peered out from behind him. Her long blond hair was pulled back in a ponytail, and all she wore was a short tennis skirt and formfitting top. Even with no makeup and covered in sweat, she was stunning. I dropped the beignet back on my plate.

"Where's the fire, Wes? I'd barely turned off the car and you were gone."

A look of irritation passed across his face. "I was just thinking—I guess I forgot to wait." He unhooked himself from Lacy's embrace. "I'm going to take a shower."

Lacy eyed me with my plate of beignets and then turned to follow him out of the room without saying another word.

With no more appetite, I turned my head toward the window again. Mrs. Guidry stood in front of Xavier now, her posture one of surprise, as if their paths had crossed accidentally, and I thought again how frightened she looked. She wore the same dress she had worn the previous day, but now it was fractured with wrinkles. She swayed on her feet, her usually coiffed hair in wild tangles. She brought her hands up to her face as if she were crying, and I watched as Xavier turned to go without saying a word, his face expressionless. Mrs. Guidry stumbled on the path as she made her way to the front lawn.

I bolted out of my chair and practically fell into the arms of Mr. Guidry. I don't know how long he had been standing behind me, but from the look on his face it was apparent he had seen the whole thing.

His words were quiet, meant for only me to hear. "Don't be involving yourself in things that don't have anything to do with you, Aimee. You hear?"

I excused myself, then ran out of the kitchen to the back garden.

Mrs. Guidry was gone, but Xavier sat on a garden bench, his shoulders slumped, his head hanging down. I sat next to him and watched as he stiffened.

"Are you okay?" It sounded stupid even to me, but I couldn't think of anything else to say.

He didn't answer for a long time. Finally, he lifted his head. He wiped his face with the bottom of his shirt and said, "You're a nice lady, Miss Aimee. Just like your mama. You don't belong here." He looked for a moment as if he were going to say something else but instead stood. As he walked away, his steps were slow but purposeful, as if he had come to some sort of decision.

A dragonfly flitted toward me, its wings a rainbow of iridescence. I followed it until my gaze paused at the kitchen window, where Mr. Guidry still stood staring out. He looked past me, his eyes hard and his vision turned inward.

Tuesday morning dawned hazy and overcast, but nothing could dampen my excitement about the Comus ball that night. I hadn't seen much of Wes except at the dinner table, with Lacy hanging all over him. I was eager to ask him what he'd found out about my mother, but it was hard to talk to him with so many people around. He would catch my eye from across the table and give me a smile, but all attempts at conversation were quickly quelled by Lacy's incessant chatter about her gown or some other item of extreme importance.

Gary and I went for a long walk along the levee, passing by the spot where I had thrown his bike in the river six years before. I asked him about Xavier and whether or not he knew what the disagreement between him and Mrs. Guidry might have been about. He only shrugged and continued walking, his hands in his pockets as he kicked stray rocks off the path.

Midafternoon, I took a nap and then had a long soak in the bathtub. Mrs. Guidry insisted I use her bathroom to get ready and gave me all sorts of exotic oils, lotions, and scents to pamper myself with. I thought I could almost see the cloud of perfume that surrounded me as I stepped from the bath and wrapped myself into one of Mrs. Guidry's silky robes.

After a tap on the door, Mrs. Guidry entered to begin fixing my hair. She had changed her clothes since that morning, and her hair was now piled high on her head in an elegant chignon. She no longer resembled the weeping woman I'd seen in the garden, and I felt relieved that whatever had transpired between Mr. and Mrs. Guidry and Xavier had apparently passed. I sat down in the little chair in front of her vanity while she stood behind me. "You look beautiful, Aimee. And I'm going to make sure you are the most stunning woman there tonight, just like your mama would have done. Probably not as well as her, but I'll do my best." Softly, she added, "She'd expect me to."

Her red lips widened into a smile, and I saw she had a dimple on her right cheek. I had never noticed it before—probably because I don't think I saw her smile very much. She was so different when her vibrant personality wasn't drowned in Scotch. I wanted her to be this way all the time.

She didn't say anything else but ran her slender fingers through my hair, adjusting wayward strands. Her touch comforted me. I didn't remember my own mother's touch—a fact that seemed to separate me from other girls. I was always looking for a surrogate mother, and at times I thought I had found her in Mrs. Guidry. But I couldn't quite reconcile the woman who was gently stroking my hair with the same woman who drank to excess and screamed at her husband.

As eager as I was to learn more of my mother's unsolved murder, it seemed even more urgent to me to find out what she'd been like when she was alive. I met Mrs. Guidry's eyes in the mirror. "Do you think my mother would like my dress?"

Her hands stilled in my hair and a shadow passed behind her eyes. They'd been friends, and it comforted me to know that she missed my mother, too.

"Your mother had exquisite taste, Aimee, and you have inherited that from her." Her hand rested on the ever-present alligator brooch. "She gave this to me; did you know that? She knew of my passion for alligators, and when she saw it at a jeweler's in New York, she knew I had to have it."

"You told me that before, when we first met. I'm glad you still wear it."

Her lopsided smile was reflected in the mirror, distorting her face. Softly, she added, "Your mother would love your gown not just for its beauty, but because you chose it." Something in her tone made me look up, trying to read her face to understand why her words sounded like she was making an apology.

She finished with my hair and makeup, then sent for Ray Von to help me dress so Mrs. Guidry could finish with her own preparations. I stood in front of the cheval mirror in my room, my deep green gown held in front of me, as the door opened and Ray Von stepped in. She paused at the threshold before slowly shaking her head.

"Oooooh, lordy, Miss Aimee. You're asking for trouble looking like that. I surely don't want to be around when those two boys start fighting over you."

I dropped the dress and turned to face her, my hands on my hips in mock indignation, secretly pleased. "So you think I should wear a potato sack to the ball?"

She crossed her arms and closed the door with her back. "No. I don't think it will matter. Seems to me it doesn't matter what you wear— they've already made up their minds about you."

I turned back to the mirror and studied my reflection. Mrs. Guidry had worked wonders with the makeup. My blue eyes were darker, my brows finely arched with the help of a pencil. My lips seemed downright pouty in the shade Mrs. Guidry had chosen. She had given me the lipstick to tuck into my purse to retouch as the night wore on. She had winked at me when she had said it, and I hadn't quite understood her meaning until now. I blushed at the thought, not quite ready to contemplate which brother might be responsible for wiping the lipstick off of my mouth.

Ray Von helped me into the strapless dress. I hadn't remembered so much bosom pushing out of the top when I had bought it. Ray Von grabbed the bodice under my arms and, with both hands, gave a tug to bring it higher.

The raw silk of the gown rustled as I walked to my suitcase and pulled out my jewelry case. My father had given me my mother's pearls and earrings to wear, and I had a brief flash of my mother wearing them as she leaned over my bed to kiss me good night. I thought I could smell her perfume and closed my eyes briefly to hold the image of her.

Ray Von helped me with the necklace clasp and opera-length gloves before I stood once again in front of the mirror. There was no trace of the girl I had been just a few hours before. In her place stood a grown-up woman who vaguely resembled me.

As I descended the stairs, Mr. and Mrs. Guidry and the two boys were already waiting in the foyer. Their attention was focused outside the open front door and they didn't hear me come down. Mrs. Guidry saw me, and for a brief moment before she smiled, I thought I saw a flash of panic cross her face.

"Aimee. You look divine!" She crossed the foyer with both arms outstretched as all heads turned in my direction. Wes and Gary turned and started walking toward me at the same time, almost colliding with each other. Wes stopped, allowing Gary to come to my side.

Gary leaned close to my ear. "You're beautiful, Aimee. I don't think I'll be snapping your bra tonight."

Emboldened by his look of admiration, I quipped, "Good. Because I'm not wearing one."

He pretended to stagger, as if weak at the knees, and I laughed, noticing how very handsome he looked in his tuxedo.

Gary placed my wrap over my shoulders, then held out his arm, and I took it with my gloved hand, allowing him to escort me to the door. He paused as we passed Wes, as if to show me off.

Wes cleared his throat. "You look wonderful tonight, Aimee. I'm sure I'll have to help Gary in fighting off all those other guys."

Gary jerked on my arm, propelling me toward the door. "I'm sure you'll be busy enough with your own date."

I turned to say something to Mrs. Guidry, but my gaze was caught by the two figures on the stairway behind us. Ray Von and Xavier stood so close as to be almost touching each other, portraying a united front.

I gave a small wave, since I couldn't think of anything to say that wouldn't sound trite. I caught Xavier's glance, but he quickly looked down at his shoes. Without a word, I turned and stepped out into the humid, glorious night.

Julie

I replaced my meat- and cheese-laden muffuletta sandwich on my plate and took a sip of my Diet Coke. We sat at Café Maspero in the French Quarter, our table only a short barrier away from the bustling sidewalk outside. I wiped ketchup off of Beau's chin as I looked around at the former slave market and pirate hangout, the bare tiles and stone arches adding to my feeling of currently existing in the past more than the present after listening to Aimee's story.

"Did you ever get a chance to talk with Wes about your mother?"

"Not until much later. My mother's death had occurred so many years before, and Wes had more pressing concerns, as you can imagine." She took a sip from her water glass. "Not that there was anything, really. The case was pretty cut-and-dried—no witnesses, no evidence. Alibis for all family members. No distinguishable murder weapon, even. It was difficult for the police when the case was new. They weren't too happy when Wes brought it up again, but they did allow him to see the files."

"Did he find anything?"

Her eyes slid down to her plate, shutting me out. "Not that he ever told me. Only that it was a robbery, and the only thing taken was her wedding ring."

It was apparent that Aimee had no more interest in pursuing our line of discussion. Changing the subject, I asked, "The painting Caroline Guidry spoke about that she was going to reveal after that ball—that's the portrait, isn't it?"

Aimee nodded, delicately wiping her mouth with a paper napkin. "It was. Except she didn't get a chance to reveal it that night, unfortunately."

"Why?" A horse-drawn carriage full of tourists rumbled outside on the street, so close I imagined I could hear the buzz of the persistent flies around the horse's head.

"Because she never came home." She darted a look at Beau, who was busy drawing ketchup figures on his plate with the end of a french fry. "Why don't I share that story another time? I'm not sure it's meant for young ears."

I nodded in agreement and recalled my earlier conversation with Trey. "Who has her alligator brooch now? I asked Trey, and he says he's never seen it."

Aimee looked at me, appearing confused for a moment. "You know, I've never once thought about that pin or wondered what happened to it. She definitely wore it on her evening gown that night, because I remember seeing it."

I pictured the photograph of the portrait in the book. "She's wearing it in the portrait with her ball gown, so that's what I assumed." I took another sip of my drink. "Do you remember giving Monica a book about Abe Holt for Christmas in 1999?"

"Yes, actually. I do. It was the last Christmas she was with us."

"Do you remember if she asked for it, or was it just something that you saw that you thought she might enjoy?"

Aimee nodded, her eyes closed. "She was taking an art history class at school, and had asked for a book about a modernist painter. Abe Holt wasn't as well-known as some of the others, but I thought she'd enjoy the fact that we owned one of his paintings. I don't know how that book ended up in the study. The rest of her books and personal things were boxed up and stored in the attic shortly after she left."

Thoughtful, I took a sip of my iced tea. "I hope you don't mind my asking, but why so soon? Didn't you think she'd return?"

She looked down at her hands. "On the day Monica left, my husband had his first stroke and needed round-the-clock care. Since Monica's room was next to mine, we figured that would be the easiest thing for everyone to move him there. We all expected it to be temporary." Her eyes met mine. "He stayed in the room for a year until we realized he'd be better off in a nursing home."

"I'm sorry," I said. "Are Monica's things still in the attic?"

"Yes, although I'm sure they have water damage. You'll have to ask Trey—he took care of the roof repair and everything else after Katrina. He'll know if anything was salvageable and if her things are still up there."

"Thank you, I will." I picked up Beau's plate and handed it to the server, then asked for the check. After placing the cash on the table, I stood. "Did you miss Caroline after she left?"

It took a long time for Aimee to answer. "It's hard to miss someone you never really knew."

Something in her tone troubled me, but I didn't have a chance to think why as I retrieved my purse from the floor, then helped Beau from his chair.

Walking to the exit, Aimee took Beau's hand. "I think it's time for Beau's first visit to Café Du Monde."

"Great idea, Miss Aimee. I'll just make sure that you're the one babysitting when he hits that sugar high." I stopped and watched them walk ahead of me. *It's hard to miss someone you never really knew.* Her words haunted me, not because of what she'd said, but because when she'd looked at me and spoken, I was fairly sure she hadn't been talking about Caroline Guidry.

Slinging my purse over my shoulder, I hurried to catch up, wondering who else in Aimee Guidry's life had become a stranger.

~❧~

CHAPTER 15

Come, for the House of Hope is built on sand; bring wine, for the fabric of life is as weak as the wind. —Häfiz

Julie

Autumn on the Gulf Coast arrives late and lingers through what I used to think of as the winter months. Like everything else I'd seen so far on the coast, fall was vibrant, sudden, and indefinable: bright, falling leaves nestled amid the perpetual greens of live oaks and palm trees. Although I missed the extended period of russets, ambers, and gold of my New England falls, I savored a temperature that seemed reluctant to dip much below sixty degrees for any extended length of time.

With some luck, and no doubt vouched for by both Carol Sue's mother and Aimee, I received a job offer as docent at Ohr museum, scheduled to start early November following their grand opening on the eighth. I was to have an abbreviated training period due to my past work history and education, for which I was grateful, since it would allow me more time to acclimate Beau to his new routine. Carol Sue had agreed to watch Beau on the three days a week I worked— Thursday through Saturday—and as excited as Beau was at the idea, I wasn't convinced that he was ready to leave me for any length of time. At Aimee's insistence, we'd return to New Orleans for the rest of the week, so she could spend time with Beau and I could meet with Trey.

I didn't see much of Aimee in the early part of the fall, due to her heavy involvement in the Garden District's Christmas home and garden tour, and I was eager for her to continue her story about Caroline Guidry. When I'd first arrived in New Orleans, Aimee had said something about combining our stories to maybe put the pieces together regarding Monica's disappearance. And the more I listened to her stories, the more I was beginning to believe that she was right.

I'd hoped that Trey would be able to tell me where Monica's things had been moved to following Katrina, but all he could say was that most of it had been so damaged with mildew that it had to be thrown away. But he recalled one box that he'd managed to save and thought he might have stored it with what remained of his possessions from his house in New Orleans East in a storage facility in Metairie. He promised me he'd go look as soon as he found time. I wasn't holding my breath.

The bulldozers had begun their excavation of the lot, preparing to rebuild River Song following new hurricane-zone building codes. Although I knew the changes would mean a significant savings in insurance premiums as well as peace of mind during storms, I found it difficult to make any alterations. I'd finally acquiesced to a significant change in design and looked on with some trepidation as pilings, driven deep into the sand, were constructed to raise the foundation of the new house. I only hoped that Monica would understand.

On my frequent trips to Biloxi, I stopped by to measure progress on the site, texting pictures and any remarks from the builders to Trey, whose reply was usually a simple, "Okay."

The only time I'd received anything more was after my report of how I'd run onto the building site, waving my hands, when a bulldozer got too close to the oak tree. I'd argued with the operator, unmoving from my spot between the bulldozer and the tree, until he'd radioed in for backup. After calmly explaining that the tree was even more important than the house and needed to be treated gently, I left, reassured that no harm would come to Monica's tree.

Trey's response that time had been a texted, "Good job."

A week before I was to start work, Carol Sue took me on a house-hunting tour in Biloxi. We'd left Charlie and Beau with Carol Sue's parents at Miramar Park, a local playground, with plans to meet them back there by lunchtime.

As I settled myself into her Land Rover, I watched as Beau ran after Charlie, his red hat safely in the hand of Carol Sue's mother. I felt Carol Sue's hand on my arm.

"He'll be fine. My parents have more than thirty years of experience."

I laughed. "I'm sorry. I guess I'd better get used to it, huh?"

She smiled and started the engine. "I know I said I had a bunch of houses to show you, but I think our search might be over after this first one. It's a two-bedroom, two-bath bungalow in a nice neighborhood, just a few blocks from the ocean and a quick drive to the museum. It's been completely rebuilt and you'd be the first to live in it. Best of all, I know the owner is desperate and is more than willing to make it a month-to-month lease."

We pulled onto White Avenue, a street of tall oaks and crushed-shell driveways, with modest homes that wore fresh paint and new roofs. I liked the street because at the intersection with Beach Boulevard, next to the large fountain in the median, a Katrina tree had been carved into a large owl, its gaze steady and wise. I thought Beau and I could use its wisdom on a daily basis by sharing the same street.

"Best of all," Carol Sue said as her tires crunched over the driveway, "it's dirt cheap. The owner has two more just like this one in Ocean Springs, and I know she'd like to break even on her investment."

I stared at the simple beige siding and sparse landscaping and felt no strong urge to call it home. It didn't matter. I didn't want or need a home, just a place for Beau and me to live. Like everything else in my life, it would be temporary.

"I like it," I said as I stepped out of the car.

"Great. The backyard is a decent size, too, and definitely big enough to put in a swing set for Beau if you're so inclined."

I followed her to the front door, where she unlocked a lockbox and then stepped back to allow me inside. There was brown paper making paths over the hardwood, and the whole house smelled of fresh paint and new carpet. The doors were plywood, and the fixtures in the bathrooms and kitchen were builder's grade, but the rooms were large, the light bright, and the convenience and price were unbeatable. "I'll take it," I said.

Carol Sue looked at me with surprise. "I was just joking about this being the only place you needed to see, Julie. I'll be happy to show you the other houses I have lined up."

"No, really, I'll take it. Show me where to sign."

"All right, if that's really what you want. I'll take you to my office and we can sign the papers there. I'll be happy to help you decorate, too. Nothing fancy, since it's a rental, but you're allowed to put color on the wall, as long as it's not something crazy, and hang drapes or blinds on the windows."

"It's really fine the way it is."

She looked at me oddly. "Didn't you live in New York for a while? And work at an auction house?"

"Yes. Why?"

"Because I would have thought you would have picked up some kind of a sense of style or love of color and fabrics along the way. I figure you must have been working all the time to have missed that."

"Aren't you supposed to finish that with 'bless your heart' to soften the insult?"

Carol Sue threw back her head and laughed. "I'm sorry. I didn't really mean it the way it came out. I think being a single mom and in charge for so long has made me just a little too outspoken. What I meant to say was that Trey said you're very focused, and I guess he wasn't kidding."

"Did he mean that in a good way or a bad way?"

"Neither, really. He meant that in a Trey way."

She didn't elaborate, as if I should understand. A fly buzzed around us before striking its hard body into the window over the kitchen sink. I moved to see into the backyard with its simple concrete-slab patio and overgrown grass. A tree with pointed leaves and clusters of large, oblong nuts dominated a corner of the yard. "What kind of tree is that?"

Carol Sue moved to stand next to me. "A pecan tree. October's harvest time, and it looks like you're going to have lots of nuts."

"What am I supposed to do with them?"

She regarded me with raised eyebrows. "Have you never had pecan pie?"

"Not that I know of."

She gave me an exaggerated roll of her eyes. "Well, then, I'll have to fix that. I'll make you a pie and use pecans from your tree, as long as you shell them first. We'll have to work fast, since I don't think you're allowed to live in the state of Mississippi if you've never had pecan pie." She winked, then returned to the kitchen island and retrieved her purse.

I continued staring out at the tree, wondering how it had survived the storm, or if it was a new tree, pollinated at the whim of the wind, and thinking about what Trey had said about me. "Aimee said that Trey and I have a lot in common. I don't see it, though. He appears to be completely emotionless—unless he's with Beau. I haven't even seen him grieve for Monica. All of his energies seem to be focused on getting me to leave and building somebody else's house."

I turned and saw her lips curve in a half smile. "I'm one of the very few who've seen Trey Guidry cry, and Monica's death hit him hard. He's dealing with it by throwing himself into his work. And I can't say that's any different from devoting your entire life to searching for someone who's been missing for seventeen years."

I turned around to face her, my mouth open in surprise. "He told you that?"

"Not in so many words. Just sort of my own conclusion when he told me about your sister." Turning away from me, she began slowly stacking sales sheets into a neat pile in the corner of the counter. I watched as she squared her thin shoulders and spoke again. "They didn't find Charles for two weeks, and I remembered thinking that as long as they didn't find him, he was still alive." Her hands stilled. "So I know what it is to hope and pray so hard that you're sure God will answer your prayer just so you'll stop asking." She turned her head halfway and smiled, but her eyes were damp. "It was only two weeks, but I remember what that was like."

She tapped the papers down on the counter with a snap. "Well, if you're sure this is the house, let's go down to the office and sign these papers."

With a professional smile, she led me outside, locking the key in the lockbox behind us.

We drove the short distance to the downtown area in silence as I stared out the window to get my bearings in my new neighborhood.

As she parked in a small lot behind her building, Carol Sue said, "Trey mentioned that you were looking for a box of Monica's things that had been stored in the First Street house before Katrina. He remembered that he gave me a few boxes, but he doesn't know if they're from the First Street house or his in New Orleans East. I ran out of room at my house, so I stored them here at the office. You're welcome to look through them while you're here, if you like."

"Are you serious? I've been wondering how to ask Trey about Monica's boxes again without seeming like a nag, and you're telling me you might have had them all along?"

"Yes, well, Trey's not the big communicator. Come on; let's go see what I've got."

We walked through the parking lot to the back door of the two-story brick building that housed the realty office. We passed through a narrow hallway with a door to a restroom on the right and a water-cooler opposite, and into a larger room with four cubicles set around the perimeter. Two of them were empty, while at another an older woman was on the phone and waved at Carol Sue as we walked by. I could tell which one was Carol Sue's from the photographs of Charlie placed on the desk and shelves. And the conspicuously absent photos of her late husband.

She placed her purse on her desk, then tossed an empty Styrofoam cup into the garbage. "Let me make sure we have everything we need and start making photocopies. While I'm doing that, I'll show you to the storeroom, where I put the boxes."

I followed her back into the hallway and headed this time toward the front of the building, where a large window dominated the space, the company's name and phone number plastered on it. She opened a door right outside the reception area, flipped on a light, and stepped back. "All of the business records for the realty business are marked. Trey's have his last name written in red marker—my idea, of course, so that they wouldn't get mixed in with the rest. It shouldn't be too hard to find them. Come on back to my cube when you're done and I should have everything ready for you."

"Thanks," I said, staring into the room of stacked boxes lit only by the single bulb in the ceiling as her heels clicked back down the hallway.

As Carol Sue had said, it didn't take me long to find Trey's boxes. They were stacked separately from the rest, behind the door. I had to remove three heavy company boxes from on top of them, but then had easy access.

The boxes were sealed with only a single strip of packing tape going along the opening at the top, as if whoever had sealed them had thought it a temporary measure. There were three boxes, identical, with only the name Guidry written across the top and side that I could see. I slid the first one off of the stack, dislodging dust as it hit the floor.

I was able to peel off the tape easily, then opened the box to peer inside. Leaning back to allow in the feeble light, I spied a folded Tulane sweatshirt on top. Moving it aside, I found a nearly deflated football, a small Green Wave flag, a plastic cup filled with Mardi Gras beads, a framed photograph of a yellow Labrador, and a baseball trophy. Tucked into the bottom of the box was a stack of photographs.

Feeling like a trespasser, I leaned forward, hesitant to touch anything. The photograph on top was of a much younger Aimee with Trey and Monica on a Christmas morning, an enormous and lit Christmas tree behind them. They were around twelve and ten, and Monica's hair was long and blond and didn't look like she'd brushed it yet. Her mouth was open and her eyes focused on the present in front of her, what looked like an artist's palette.

I imagined Trey preparing to evacuate his house, choosing what was most valuable to him, and ending up with the contents of this box. The sentimentality of the items surprised me, and I found my attitude toward Trey Guidry shifting slightly.

The next box yielded similar items—a tennis racket, two framed Tulane diplomas for undergrad and law school, more Mardi Gras beads, a Jax beer sign, and, stuck inside another plastic tumbler with the Greek letters SAE on them, two tickets for the Mississippi Coast Coliseum dated June 11, 1998. I almost laughed when I saw that the tickets were from a Backstreet Boys concert. If I hadn't known that the band had been one of Monica's all-time favorites, I would have planned to bring it up with Trey as often as I could just to torture him.

I slid the second box off the bottom one and peeled the tape off quickly, eager to see if I'd found Monica's things. I wasn't sure what I hoped to find, but if there were anything that Monica had left behind her when she left that might offer a clue as to the reason she ran away, this was the only place I knew to look.

For the third time, I opened a box and peered inside. This time I found stuffed animals and dried flower corsages, their petals crushed and broken, sprinkled over the other contents like seasoning. I spotted several framed school art department awards and ribbons, along with a dog leash and a rhinestone tiara. There was more, but I knew that I'd found the box I needed, so I quickly resealed it and stacked Trey's boxes back behind the door. I shut off the light, hoisted the box, and made my way back to Carol Sue's cubicle.

As I walked into the brightly lit space, I stopped, my arms straining to hold the heavy box. Standing in the cubicle with Carol Sue was a tall, dark man in a business suit. He was standing very close to her, but she didn't seem to mind, as her hands were placed flat on his chest and her cheeks were pink as she looked up at him.

Feeling as if the box were going to drop from my hands, I quickly turned to a nearby desk and let it fall, the noise causing both Carol Sue and her companion to look up in alarm and step back.

"Julie," she said, her voice flustered. "I didn't hear you come in."

"Sorry," I said, not moving any closer. "I didn't mean to interrupt."

Tucking her hair behind her ears, she walked toward me, her eyes bright. "I'd like you to meet my friend Walker King. His dental office is right down the street, and he came to see if I had lunch plans, but I told him that we were meeting Charlie and Beau and my parents at the park as soon as we were through here."

I looked at her to see if she realized she was babbling, then turned to Dr. King with my hand extended. He shook it in a firm grasp. "Nice to meet you, Doctor. I'm Julie Holt."

"Likewise, Julie. And please call me Walker." His manner was relaxed, and his straightforward smile made him easy to like. "I know you two ladies have business to attend to, so I'll leave you to it. A rain check, Carol Sue?"

"Sure," she said, a deep dimple showing in her cheek, and for the first time since I'd met her, the shadows seemed to have been lifted from her eyes.

With a smile and a wave, he left the office. Carol Sue picked up a stack of papers from her desk. "Follow me to the conference room and we'll get everything in order. I can collect a cashier's check from you for the deposit later this week. You'll have until the first of the month, so you have plenty of time."

I nodded and followed her into the conference room, oddly feeling as if I'd been betrayed and having no idea why.

After storing Monica's box in the back of Carol Sue's SUV, we settled into the front seat and buckled our seat belts. She sat with the key in the ignition for a long moment; then, staring out the windshield and not looking at me, she said, "It's been five years, Julie. That's a long time."

"I didn't say anything."

"You didn't have to." She started the ignition. "Charles will always be my first love, and the father of my child. And if I'd been given a choice, I'd be married to him for the rest of my life, and we'd be raising a bunch of kids together. But I wasn't, so here I am."

She put the car into drive and made her way out of the parking lot. We were silent as she drove the short distance down Beach Boulevard. I could see the water, as calm and placid as the eye of a child, instilling in me a false serenity. A lone shrimp boat moved out into the sound, and I wondered if it, too, felt the silent pull of the water, like a lullaby urging sleep, despite the always-lurking threat of a storm.

"Do you take Charlie to the beach?" I asked, unable to look away from the water.

"I didn't for a long time, but she kept asking, and I eventually gave in. I'd loved the water and the beach my whole life. There's something about it, like a cocoon, almost, in the way it reminds me of home. Besides, it's hard to hate something for so long. I had to let it go or the hate would have taken over and stolen all of my good memories." She gave me a hard stare. "You're not familiar with water, are you?"

I shook my head. "I've never lived near water and went to the beach only once when I was growing up."

She smiled softly. "You need to have Trey take you to Deer Island. It's one of the islands between the Mississippi Sound and the Gulf. It's his favorite place on earth—and Monica's, too. It's the real Gulf Coast, not the cheap tourist shops or the casinos, or even the beach. It's the real deal. You'll understand when you see it."

Carol Sue stopped the car near the park and we got out. "We're a little early, but I'm sure my parents could use a break by now."

We walked slowly to the bench, where Carol Sue's mother, Mrs. Wimberly, sat reading a book, the bench next to her piled with the children's coats and sweaters that they'd started the cooler morning with.

"Hi, Mama." Carol Sue bent to give her mother a kiss on the cheek. "Glad to see the children haven't tied you up and built a bonfire."

Mrs. Wimberly smiled. "Hello, girls. And the children have been lovely. They do play so nicely together, and they've made a few new friends, too."

I cupped my hand on my forehead to block out the bright sunlight, staring at the vividly colored slides and the red play fire engine, looking for Beau's shock of sandy blond hair. "Where are they?" I asked, beginning to walk slowly toward the swings.

Mrs. Wimberly looked up, staring across the playground. "They were with my husband just a second ago." Her voice trailed away as we all spotted Mr. Wimberly by himself, leaning against the fence and talking to a young father. Charlie stood by his side, her hand tucked into his. But Beau was nowhere to be seen.

The sun suddenly seemed brighter, the laughter of children louder, and my own voice, unfamiliar to me, began shrieking Beau's name. I heard my name being called, but I couldn't tell where it was coming from. I turned my head past the sliding pole, the loop ladder and balance beam, and an entire wall of steering wheels. All the things children loved. All the things that made them vulnerable.

I could tell that a lot of faces were turned toward me now, the swings stilling, the parents gathering their children to their sides. I heard my name called again and it was Carol Sue standing by a giant orange play web where children had begun to dismount. But one child remained where he was at the top, oblivious to everything as he hung upside down by his knees, swinging back and forth and laughing with his blond hair catching the sun.

I stumbled, the rush of relief flooding through me nearly making me nauseous. I made it to Carol Sue, and she put her arm around me as I collapsed on a bench, sagging into her. "He's okay, Julie. No need to worry; he's fine." She patted me on the back as a mother would a child, hugging me tightly, and all I could do was breathe. "Let it go," she whispered in my ear.

I hugged her back, knowing how much she understood, yet knowing I could never be that brave. "I can't," I said softly.

She hugged me tighter. "Let it go," she said again, as if I hadn't spoken at all.

It was dark when we returned to New Orleans. I carried a sleeping Beau up to his room and put him to bed, then retrieved Monica's box from the back of the van before returning to the house. I assumed Aimee was at yet another Christmas tour-of-homes meeting, and I'd long since given up trying to keep track of Trey's comings and goings.

Thinking of the large table Trey had set up in his study for the house plans, I went there and set the box on it, then began to unpack everything. I laid out the frames and ribbons, the stuffed animals, baby doll, and Rubik's Cube. I pulled out a vinyl photo album with what appeared to be water damage on the corners, the pages all glued together. I left it alone, afraid to ruin any of the pictures inside. The corsages were too brittle, so I left them where they were. But in the corner of the box in the bottom, beneath a hand-knitted scarf with the needles still sticking in it, was a dark red leather-bound journal. In the top right in thick black ink and in fancy calligraphy, someone had inscribed the initials MMG. Monica Mercier Guidry.

I lifted it out carefully and stood holding it for a full minute before I could talk myself into opening the front cover. Inside, in her unmistakably girlish handwriting, Monica had written, *The Life and Times of Monica Guidry, 1992.* I let out a held breath, all of my expectations slowly dissipating. Monica had been ten years old in 1992, and

I couldn't imagine her having anything monumental to write about besides prepubescent crushes and the never-ending quest for a true best friend.

I flipped to the first page, dated January 1, 1992, and read the two-line entry. *Trey gave this journal to me for Christmas, so I guess I should write in it. But I think I want to draw in it instead.* Below the writing was a pencil sketch of a young Trey. It just showed him from his neck up, but it was unmistakably him. But as I looked closer, I realized that there was something I didn't recognize in the eyes of the Trey I knew, something innocent and mischievous, as if he were in the middle of devising a prank when the ten-year-old Monica decided to capture him in lead and paper. Where did that boy go? I was left wondering if he'd fled in the aftermath of Katrina, as if his innocence had been one more loss, or if he'd gone when Monica had left ten years ago.

I turned the pages slowly, drawn in by the sketches of New Orleans landmarks—Saint Louis Cathedral, close-ups of wrought-iron fences, street vendors, and Café Du Monde. Interspersed with these were sketches of River Song and its environs, of Trey fishing on a pier and in a kayak with another boy, of multiple pairs of feet and flip-flops in the sand, and many sketches of Aimee with an older man sitting in beach chairs on a dock, walking hand in hand in the sand, working side by side in the garden as if it were Gary or Wes. There was none of her parents, and I remembered what Trey and Aimee had told me, about how Monica and Trey had been mostly raised by Aimee, and it made me think of how unforgiving Monica must have been to cut her parents out of her life so completely. And what they must have done to make her that way.

My favorite was a self-portrait of Monica in a hammock on the porch at River Song, with only her face and bare feet visible above the netting. I made a mental note to make sure we had a hammock ready to hang as soon as the house was completed.

"I remember giving that to Monica for Christmas."

I turned around to see Trey standing behind me, holding his suit jacket with one hand and a briefcase in his other. His tie hung loose around his neck, his cuffs were rolled up, and he had dark smudges under his eyes—eyes that no longer resembled those of the boy in Monica's sketches.

He placed his jacket and briefcase on the desk and I handed the journal to him. "She was really talented, wasn't she?" I said, watching as he opened the front cover and his lawyer face softened.

"Yes, she was," he said, leaning back against the desk and beginning to thumb through the sketches.

I turned back to the box. "I got this from Carol Sue today. She wanted me to tell you that she still has two of your boxes refugeeing in the storeroom at her office. Her boss has been hinting that it's time to remove them."

He nodded without looking at me. "Yeah, she's probably right. Now that we have the roof fixed here, there should be room in the attic."

I continued lifting out Monica's childhood memorabilia from the box and placing them on the table much like I imagined an archaeologist would lay out ancient bones. I was surprised at how little there was, considering it all represented the first eighteen years of her life, and then remembered that some of her things had been destroyed in the attic during Katrina. I would make sure that I preserved what remained for Beau, along with the few belongings she'd had in New York, for much the same reason I still had Chelsea's hairbrush, packed up and brought along with me whenever I moved.

Smoothing back the hair of the baby doll, I said, "I had a phone call from Steve Kenney today regarding the roof straps for River Song. He's found a new supplier—better product for a little more money. I told him that he needed to speak with you. I'm happy to consult on the aesthetics, but I'm going to let you handle the technical details, since you have some experience in that department. I hope that's all right."

When he didn't respond, I turned to face him. He was still holding Monica's journal in one hand, but in the other was a folded sheet of paper that looked as if it had been stuck somewhere in the middle of the journal pages. His eyes met mine and something in them made me feel a cold flash of fear. "What's wrong?"

As if I hadn't spoken, he asked, "Was your mother's maiden name Sarah Pearson?"

An icy cold hand seemed to settle around my neck. "Yes, why?"

"And your father's name William Holt?"

"Yes," I said as I stepped closer to him, the word coming out like a hiss. "How did you know that?"

Without answering, he handed me the sheet of paper. I recognized Monica's handwriting, neat and concise, similar to that in the journal but more mature and more like I'd known it. At the top in black marker she'd written in block letters, *ABE HOLT'S FAMILY TREE.*

It started with his generation, with the names of his two wives branching beneath them, the first wife childless, the second wife with three boxes under her name showing her two surviving sons and one daughter who died in infancy. My eyes scanned to the next line, where the eldest son, Jeremiah Holt—my grandfather—had two sons, William and John. I closed my eyes for a second and took a breath, then looked again to the next line. William married Sarah Pearson in 1975 and had three children, William Lloyd Holt Jr., Julie Grace, and Chelsea Marie.

My hand trembled as I held the paper, then raised my eyes to meet Trey's. "What does this mean?" I asked, afraid that I might already know the answer.

"I'm not sure," he said. "But I think it's pretty clear that Monica already knew who you were long before she met you in New York."

I shook my head, wanting to believe that Monica's surprise in finding out who I was when we met at the art show was genuine. But then my gaze slid back to the paper and to my name in bold, black letters, and I finally understood how very wrong I was.

CHAPTER 16

And ye, who have met with Adversity's blast,
And been bow'd to the earth by its fury;
To whom the Twelve Months, that have recently pass'd,
Were as harsh as a prejudiced jury,—
Still, fill to the Future! and join in our chime,
The regrets of remembrance to cozen,
And having obtained a New Trial of Time,
Shout in hopes of a kindlier dozen!

— THOMAS HOOD

Aimee

1956

As we stood outside in the brisk evening air, the sounds of Mardi Gras in the city echoed into the Garden District, making me shiver with excitement. The Zulu and Rex parades had already come and gone in the morning, and the culmination of the entire Mardi Gras festivities would end tonight with the torch-led Comus parade, followed by the Comus and Rex balls at the enormous Municipal Auditorium on the edge of the French Quarter.

Rex, lord of misrule, would pay homage to Comus, god of mirth and revelry, as tableaux, dancing, and merrymaking would take us to midnight, when the city's church bells rang in the forty days of Lent: forty days of penitence and sacrifice. Looking around at the Guidrys as we waited, I couldn't help but wonder what sins they would seek atonement for, and what they were willing to give up.

The theme for this year's Comus Ball was "Our Early Contemporaries," but I was distracted from my attempts to translate what that meant by Mrs. Guidry. She seemed nervous and distracted, her fingers fluttering like uncertain moths as she hovered around me, avoiding her husband's steely gaze, and stealing sips from the small silver flask in her purse.

Mr. Guidry had hired a car and driver for the evening, large enough to hold only Mr. and Mrs. Guidry, Lacy, and me. Wes and Gary followed in Wes's Corvette. Because Mardi Gras fell on Valentine's Day, Mr. Guidry had surprised us all and given his wife a bouquet of two dozen roses. She'd smiled at him, her eyes distant, then taken one and placed it in her elegant updo, its radiance vivid against the darkness of her hair, making her appear even more exotic than usual. His smile was frosty as he regarded his wife, no doubt wondering what the other ballgoers would think.

I stared out the car window, taking in the sights of a city at play. Earlier that day Gary had taken me for a streetcar ride and a walk through New Orleans to get my first taste of the city during Carnival, as the natives referred to it. The city hummed with excitement, the streets and many of its citizens decked out in green, yellow, and purple. People thronged the avenues in the French Quarter, the thrumming of the crowds melding with the brassy sounds of jazz. The city itself was on display in an odd juxtaposition of elegance and decadence. Street vendors selling voodoo powder and cheap trinkets fronted old buildings with lacy wrought-iron balconies. The spicy aromas of jambalaya and gumbo from restaurant kitchens mingled with the smells of sweat and stale alcohol. I was at once attracted and repelled by it all, reminding me of having to kiss the scar-pocked cheek of an old and favorite uncle.

The glitter of dresses caught my eye as I was helped from the car by Mr. Guidry. I felt something slip around my neck, and I turned to see Wes grinning at me. Looking down, I saw a strand of Mardi Gras beads in iridescent pink glowing against the green fabric of my gown. I clutched it as he leaned to speak in my ear so as to be heard above the din of the crowd. "For your first Mardi Gras, Aimee. May it be everything you expect it to be—and more." I could smell a faint scent of cologne and felt the smoothness of his skin as his jaw brushed my face. He kissed my cheek, then straightened. I felt a tug on my arm as Gary turned me to face him. His hands were crammed with strands of long white beads and he shoved them over my head before I could say anything. I looked down at the mass of beads on my chest and caught sight of the single pink one, shimmering against all the plain white.

Wes and Gary waved and nodded to friends and acquaintances, and introductions were made as we moved through the crowd to the Guidrys' table. I looked up where balconies of well-dressed people sat, pointing and making great shows of admiration at the crowds below. When I asked Gary who they were, he explained that they were spectators, invited to the ball not to dance but just to look. I thought it an odd custom, but relegated it to my mental list of things found only in New Orleans.

Lacy and I were invited to the "call-out" room, where girls who had been selected for dances by members of the Krewe of Comus congregated before being claimed for their dances. I felt like Cinderella dancing with my masked and costumed prince, his identity unknown to me. Nobody seemed to notice or care that I was still a few months underage, as elegantly dressed waitstaff kept wineglasses in front of me. I don't remember whether I ever completely finished a single one, but by midnight I was certainly feeling the flush of intoxication.

Gary and Wes took turns dancing with their mother, Lacy, and me. Gary led me effortlessly in a two-step, his feet never missing a beat, his natural sense of rhythm carrying us through the song. He seemed more out of breath than usual, and I insisted he sit and rest for the next few songs. Surprisingly, he didn't protest—even when Wes appeared for the next waltz.

His hand dropped to my waist as our fingers entwined, my free hand resting on his shoulder. "I'm glad you came, Aimee."

"Me, too," I murmured, lost in the smell of him, a distant part of me wishing that I could recall Gary's scent.

"Are you having a good time with Gary?"

"Oh, yes—very much. He's a good friend." I moved my hand lower until it rested on his chest. I could feel the strong beat of his heart beneath my gloved palm.

"Is that all he is to you, a good friend?"

I stared into his deep blue eyes. "Yes—a very, very good friend." Without thinking, I blurted, "What about you and Lacy? Are you going to marry her?"

He looked away for a moment. "No, I don't think so."

I looked up at him. "Don't you love her?"

His hand on my back pulled me closer. "I thought I did. At least through the eyes of a naive teenager, I did. Before I learned that love wears many faces." His gaze traveled to where his parents danced, their bodies close, but their faces turned away from each other.

Wes looked down at me. "It took all the letters you sent me to make me finally realize how blind I've been. I know now that I need more than a pretty face or witty conversation. I need strength of character, a gentleness in the soul. A shared understanding."

I felt a knot in my throat. "Then why are you still seeing Lacy?"

He rested his jaw against the side of my cheek and I sighed. "Because she loves me unconditionally. I've never had that before—certainly not from my parents. It's addictive." He closed his eyes, then rested his forehead against mine. "Remember once, in one of your letters, you told me you had always wanted a brother or sister. Somebody who would follow you around and probably annoy you but would always be there. A consistent relationship, you called it. That's sort of what Lacy is. I don't need to work at the relationship, but it's always there, waiting for me." He sighed again, and I could feel the heat of his skin next to mine. "But I know I'm not being fair to Lacy. I need to end it." He kissed my forehead, and I closed my eyes so I wouldn't have to know whether Gary had seen us.

The music died and suddenly Lacy was at his side, dragging him into the next dance. I walked back to the table a little unsteadily and asked a passing waiter for coffee. Tuxedo jackets hung on the backs of chairs, discarded as soon as the men had sat down. Gary was still in his chair, his head resting on the back of it, his eyes closed.

I put my hand on his arm and watched his eyes flutter open. He didn't even attempt to stand up. "Are you all right, Gary?"

A reassuring grin spread across his face as he looked at me from the corner of his eye. "Sure—I'm okay. Sit down." His arm fanned about in the direction of the chair next to his. I sat down and watched his eyelids close again.

Mr. and Mrs. Guidry were standing near the dance floor and speaking with another couple. His hand was on her back, and they appeared just like any other couple, except for the way she kept stepping away to avoid his touch. I noticed her alligator brooch, remembering how she told me that my mother had given it to her, and it warmed me somehow.

I looked back to the dance floor, where Wes and Lacy swayed to the music, their bodies nearly touching as the band played "Cry Me a River." The gold in her dress picked up the overhead lights, making it twinkle like a thousand fireflies. Wes bent to whisper something in her ear, and they stopped dancing. Her head jerked back as her hands slid down his arms and clutched at them tightly. I could see her clawlike grip as she pulled on the fabric of his starched shirt. He was trying to steer her off the floor, but she remained where she was, holding on to something more than just a shirt.

I turned my head, not wanting to see any more. I didn't like Lacy, but I still couldn't watch her devastation. I looked at Gary, who seemed paler, and I suddenly felt sick. If Wes and I were to pursue a relationship, what would it mean to Gary? Could he be happy with just my friendship? And could I face either of them, knowing that I was responsible for a rift between the brothers?

Reaching over, I placed my hand on his. "Gary, do you need to go home? You're looking like the underside of a catfish right now."

His left cheek lifted in a lopsided grin before he shook his head. I looked to see if I could find his parents to get a second opinion and had half risen from my chair but stopped. Mr. and Mrs. Guidry were standing away from the crowd, and from their earnest expressions I could see that whatever they were discussing wasn't a whispering matter. Abruptly, Mrs. Guidry turned away, weaving slightly as she passed members of the New Orleans society whose opinion she'd long since stopped caring about.

Mr. Guidry's gaze followed his wife's movements until he left, too, walking away in another direction. I looked back at the dance floor, but Wes and Lacy had also disappeared.

Gary and I spent the rest of the evening alone, not dancing with each other or anybody else. We had sporadic visits from some of his friends, who stopped by briefly, but then moved on. Gary remained seated, his head either resting on his arms on the table or on the back of his chair. He kept insisting he didn't need to leave, and I strained my neck for sight of Wes or his parents to help me bring Gary home. We talked about the coming school year, when we would both be freshmen at Tulane—Gary in pre-med and me at Newcomb College. He kept referring to us as a couple—how "we" would do this or that. I didn't say anything.

Despite the loud din of the music and merrymaking, Gary fell asleep with his head on his hands. I stepped outside to see whether I could find any other member of the Guidry family, then returned at midnight as the two kings greeted each other and toasted the revelers. Gary stirred and opened his eyes, but kept his head on the table.

Mr. Guidry emerged through the throng of people near the royal court. He approached without smiling. "Where are Wes and Lacy?"

I shook my head. "I don't know. I haven't seen them for a while."

"Have you seen my wife? I expected her back here by now."

Gary and I looked at each other. "No—we've seen no one for quite some time."

Mr. Guidry picked up his jacket from the back of a chair and, to my surprise, put it on. His shirt was drenched with sweat and his dark hair clung to his forehead. He gave a cursory glance around the room before letting his gaze rest on Gary. "We need to get you home," he said, his voice tight and controlled as he moved to help Gary out of his chair.

Gary resisted, pulling his arm away. "What about Mother? We can't leave her here. I'm going to wait for her."

A dark look passed between them as Gary leaned heavily on the table. "Look at you," Mr. Guidry hissed. "You should be at home in bed." More gently, he added, "Your mother will understand. I'll leave the car and driver here for her and tell our friends that we've gone so they can let her know. We'll take a taxi."

Again, Gary resisted. I grabbed his arm. "Gary, come on. I'll go with you. Your mother's here with her friends, and the car will be waiting for her when it's time to leave. Please come—for me?"

His blue-gray eyes regarded me quietly. Finally, he nodded and allowed me to lead him outside.

Loud knocking on my bedroom door woke me up the following morning. I stared at my bedside clock—nine twenty. Without waiting for an answer, Gary walked in wearing only pajama bottoms. His trim torso was tight with sinewy muscles, his skin lightly tanned. A puckered scar ran between his breasts, white against his tan. I realized it was the first time he had ever allowed me to see him with his shirt off. His face was pale, his eyes panicked.

"What is it, Gary? What's wrong?"

"It's Mother. She never came home."

I sat up straight in the bed, rubbing my eyes and trying to think. "Are you sure? It's Ash Wednesday. Maybe she went to Mass."

He shook his head. "My father said she didn't come home at all, and I've been calling her friends all morning. Nobody has seen her since last night."

Dread settled heavily in my stomach. "Has anyone called the police?"

He gave his head an angry shake. "No. My father wants to wait, but I'm worried." He looked at me, his eyes pleading. "Can you see if you can talk some sense into him?"

My head still foggy, I rubbed my eyes again. "Come on." I slid out of bed and put on my robe. I opened the door and didn't smell the usual aroma of percolating coffee.

"How did you know she wasn't here?"

"When I saw my father this morning I asked him what time my mother had come in last night." As if anticipating my next question, he added, "And Wes's bed hasn't been slept in, either."

My stomach clenched, but I tried not to read anything into his words.

We walked over to the Guidrys' bedroom door. The transom over the door was still dark, so I knew the curtains hadn't yet been opened. I had lifted my hand to knock when the door was flung open. Mr. Guidry stood in the doorway wearing a dark blue bathrobe, his hair in disarray and dark smudges under his eyes.

"What is it?" he said, his voice low and gravelly.

Gary started to speak but I silenced him with a hand on his arm. "We're both worried about Mrs. Guidry."

Mr. Guidry took a step forward, then stopped. As if controlling every single word, he said, "As I told Gary, Mrs. Guidry has not come home from the party last night. I would prefer not to call the police and draw everyone's attention to my wife's behavior. I can only hope this time she's thinking about her family and acting more discreet."

"How dare you?" Gary lunged for his father, his long fingers grabbing at Mr. Guidry's throat.

I reached for Gary and winced as I felt my nails scrape against his bare back. He had knocked his father to the ground and they were now grappling with each other. Gary drew back his fist and punched his father in the jaw.

I ran to the staircase and shouted, "Help! Ray Von! Xavier! Come quick!" Only the silence of the house answered me.

Gary was now pummeling his father. Blood streamed from Mr. Guidry's nose. I was thankful Gary was the only one throwing any punches; Mr. Guidry was simply raising his arms to shield his face from Gary's flying fists. But the effort was having its effect on Gary. His energy flagged as the blows came slower and with less force. I could see him trying to breathe deeply, his chest almost concave, but he couldn't seem to pull in enough oxygen.

"Stop it!" I screamed, pulling a weakened Gary off his father. "You're killing yourself." Gary fell into me as I sat down with a thud, his head cradled in my lap. His father stood, swaying slightly, and wiped his face with the tie to his robe as red blobs of blood dripped on the Oriental carpet runner.

I looked up at him, my voice surprisingly steady. "Get Ray Von. Gary needs help."

Without a word, he stumbled to the staircase and went downstairs.

"Gary, why did you do that? Look at you—you shouldn't have done that." I was crying now, staring at his pale face. I picked up one of his hands and started crying harder when I saw the bloodied knuckles. "Aw, Gary. Your beautiful hands—you might not be able to play the piano anymore."

He squeezed my hand. "You're . . . babbling, Aimee. Please . . . shut . . . up." He closed his eyes briefly, trying to draw in a deep breath. "And I haven't . . . played . . . the piano . . . since I was thirteen." He closed his eyes again, the effort from talking and breathing seeming to overwhelm him.

I laughed and cried at the same time, relieved to hear Gary's voice but shedding tears for the irreparable damage done to my adopted family.

∼∽

Mrs. Guidry didn't come home at all that day. Nor the next. Wes had also disappeared, but only Gary and I seemed concerned. Even Ray Von remained indifferent, seeming aloof when we asked her if she knew where they were, or even if they might be together. By the third day, Gary called the police.

A uniformed officer showed up to interview us, followed shortly by a stocky man in a filthy raincoat. He introduced himself as Lieutenant Houlihan, a detective with the New Orleans Police Department. The lieutenant asked questions, writing everything down in a stained and faded leather notebook. Gary sat through his interview in the parlor, his back to his father, still not having completely recovered his strength from their earlier encounter. He answered all the questions slowly, going over every detail of the previous Tuesday.

"Any reason you can think of why your mother or brother would run away?" As Lieutenant Houlihan spoke, the stocky policeman surveyed the parlor with its dark paneling and expensive antiques.

Gary glanced back at his father and paused, his jaw tightening. Slowly, he shook his head. "They would never leave me here alone. They just wouldn't."

I could see the pointed look the detective gave to Mr. Guidry, noting Gary's definition of "alone."

Mr. Guidry spoke in clipped tones, his manner dismissive. I could see Gary clenching his fists, so I grabbed one and held it tightly. The detective looked at the officer with raised eyebrows and continued taking notes.

I cleared my throat. "Have you spoken to Wes's girlfriend, Lacy Boudreaux? They were together at the Comus Ball."

Detective Houlihan nodded. "Yes. She says Wes took her home

early and then planned on returning home himself. Witnesses corroborate her story." He turned to Gary's father. "When did you last see your wife, Mr. Guidry?"

He rubbed his palm over his face, as if to wipe off a memory. "It was before midnight. I went to go chat with some friends—the Claibornes—and Caroline excused herself to go to the ladies' room. I didn't see her again after that."

I looked away, knowing what he was saying wasn't what I had seen. But it was partly true, and they had walked off in opposite directions. I remained silent, not wanting to incriminate Mr. Guidry on a minor matter, and believing I had nothing new to add.

The scratch of the detective's pen echoed in the silent room, accompanied only by the gum-smacking of the officer.

"Miss Mercier, did you see anything? Anything at all that you think might be of interest?"

I had been staring at the policeman, amazed that a person could make that much noise with a single piece of gum. I jerked my head back to the interrogator. "No. Nothing."

The detective stepped closer to Mr. Guidry, his eyes narrowed. "Looks like you've been in a fight."

Mr. Guidry crossed his arms across his chest. "It has nothing to do with my wife or Wes, if that's what you're getting at." He paused for a moment, his lips in a grim line, his eyes avoiding Gary. "My son and I had a disagreement. That's all."

The detective looked over at Gary, his gaze taking in Gary's raw knuckles splayed over his knees like spiders in a web. Gary didn't say anything, just stared at the carpet examining the intricate fleur-de-lis pattern.

The detective scribbled something down on his notepad, then shoved it into his pocket. He grappled in his coat for something and said, "All right, then. If you think of anything else, or either one of them shows up, give us a call." He pulled out three business cards, all as disheveled as the coat they had come from, and handed them to us. I looked down at the name. Lieutenant Pierre Houlihan.

Mr. Guidry stood and began escorting them to the door. "Thank you, Lieutenant. I'm sure my wife will show up soon. Between you and me, her behavior isn't a surprise. She's long scoffed at polite society. I thought all of that was behind her, which is why I consented to attend the ball. I guess I thought wrong. As for Wes, I have a feeling he's still having a good time with friends somewhere and has no idea that his mother is missing. If you find him before I do, please tell him to call me as soon as possible. Good night, gentlemen."

Mr. Guidry opened the door wide, making it clear the interview was over. The two men left, their heels clicking on the wet walkway. As the door shut behind them, I recalled that I hadn't seen Xavier since Sunday, either. And the thought of Xavier brought to mind the scene we had witnessed in the darkened hallway. I wondered if that were the sort of thing the lieutenant was talking about when he said if I thought of anything else. I looked over at Mr. Guidry's stormy face as he quickly poured himself a double Scotch and let my thumb run over the embossed print on the front of the card. Then my glance strayed to Gary, his face in his hands, the back of his neck exposed. The skin was white, raw, untouched by the sun, and I remembered how his mother would rub him there to calm him down after an attack. I saw the little boy still in Gary, and I felt a tightening in my chest. I folded the card in half and shoved it into my pocket, unwilling to be the one to raise one more demon in this household.

CHAPTER 17

Explosive deepening: A decrease in the minimum sea-level pressure of a tropical cyclone of 2.5 mb/hr for at least twelve hours or 5 mb/hr for at least six hours.

—NATIONAL HURRICANE CENTER

Julie

Aimee and I sat on the stone bench in the garden, bundled up against a sudden cool spell that had descended on New Orleans and taken away the sun, replacing it with heavy gray clouds. Beau stood nearby, watching as Xavier used large shears to cut branches from the row of crape myrtles that lined the side fence. I had learned their names, along with half a dozen other plants in the garden, from Beau, who'd become Xavier's avid student.

Aimee sat with her hand clutching the neck of her coat, preventing any cool air from getting inside. Turning to her, I asked, "So what happened to Mrs. Guidry and Wes? Were they together?"

Her eyes seemed confused for a moment, as if she were trying to place me or remember why I was there. Shaking her head, she said, "No, they weren't together." She lowered her arm and lifted the cuff of her coat to look at her watch. "I think we've run out of time. I have a meeting for the home and garden tour in half an hour, and Trey is going to drive me. I suppose I'd better go inside and put some lipstick on." She smiled, then stood, leaning heavily on her cane. I'd seen her with her cane many times, but until now it had never seemed to me as if she might actually need it. "We'll have to continue later."

I stood, too, offering my arm to help her up the steps to the front door, trying to hide my impatience to hear more of her story. But I realized, too, how the recounting of her past must be a lot like watching a movie where you knew what would happen, but didn't want to look. She seemed hesitant to push forward with her story, but I thought I understood why.

To my surprise, she took my arm, allowing me to lead the way. As we walked slowly up the path, I said, "We found a box of Monica's things that had been stored in the attic before Katrina."

She leaned heavily against my arm. "Did you find anything?"

"We're not sure. Folded inside a sketchbook we found a piece of paper with her handwriting. It was a drawing of my family tree, starting with Abe Holt, my great-grandfather."

She stopped and looked at me, her blue eyes clear behind her glasses. "Why do you think she would have that?"

"Trey and I couldn't figure it out. Trey thought that maybe she was such a huge fan of Abe Holt's that she wanted to know if any of his descendants were artists, too. But then why would she have never mentioned it to me?" A cold breeze blew at our backs, pushing us forward.

"I don't know. Maybe we never will." She paused for a moment as she reached the top step. "If you see Trey, please tell him I'll be right out."

I walked back to the bench slowly, something small but insistent tugging at my brain. Pushing it aside, I turned my attention back to Beau and Xavier. Beau was focused on collecting leaves from the ground as Xavier continued down the row of crape myrtles, their once leaf- and flower-filled branches now reduced to stunted limbs. They were in contrast to the rest of the still-lush garden, like a stark reminder of the approaching long sleep of winter.

"It makes them grow better in the spring," Xavier said without turning around, and I realized that I must have been staring for some time. "Sometimes you got to put up with a whole bunch of ugly so you can appreciate a little bit of beautiful."

"Oh, thanks. I was wondering." I watched as his arms, still as strong and muscular as a young man's, continued to clip off thick branches. "Did your mother teach you that?"

He didn't turn around, but I saw the side of his face crease in a smile. "Yeah. Sure did."

I watched as Beau bent to pick up a single leaf, pressing it delicately into his other hand, where he held more leaves. Monica's red hat hung from the back of his elastic waistband, forgotten for now. As I turned back to Xavier, a sudden thought occurred to me. "Do you remember Miss Aimee's mother?"

I imagined I saw his neck muscles tighten. He lowered the shears and faced me. "Yes, I remember her. Not too much, though. I was only nine when she got killed. But she sure was pretty—a lot like Miss Aimee when she was younger. And kind, too. She'd bring me one of those Doberge cakes from McKenzie's for me on my birthday, and would treat me like I didn't have this scar on my face." He glanced up at me, and I felt ashamed knowing that I'd made assumptions about his appearance.

"So you were living here with Ray Von when Mrs. Mercier was killed?"

He lifted the large shears and pinched a thick branch and I watched as he yanked it harder than appeared necessary, shaking loose dozens of spent leaves. "For a time. Mama and I lived in the carriage house where Mr. Trey lives now. But Mr. Guidry said I needed schooling and sent me away not too long after Mrs. Mercier was killed."

I recalled the scene in the hallway that Aimee had recounted to me, how she'd found Xavier in the hallway, crying. "What do you remember about Mrs. Guidry?"

His movements became jerky as he attacked the tree, the popping sound made by each severed limb loud in the silent garden. A bird twittered from somewhere behind me as a squirrel skittered under the toolshed. I looked back at Xavier as I realized that he'd stopped.

He turned toward me. As if he hadn't heard my question, he said, "People disappear all the time. Some get found, and some don't. And some it's just better that they stay gone."

I thought of Chelsea and all the other faces of the missing I'd found on the Internet since my search for my sister had started, and I wanted to shout at him, tell him that everyone deserved to be found.

As if reading my mind, he said, "And there's those like Miss Monica, who stay gone no matter how much their families want them back. And waiting for them to come back's just as useful as sitting in your house and waiting for a hurricane to go someplace else."

My fingers pressed into my knees, my fingertips turning white. "Did your mother tell you that, too?"

When he didn't respond, I looked up at him. His face was void of all expression, his words matter-of-fact. "No, ma'am. I learned that one all by myself." He hoisted the shears again and began to hack away at the remaining crape myrtles.

Trey's truck pulled up to the curb in front of the house. He wore a rumpled shirt with rolled-up cuffs, no tie, suit pants, and dark shoes. It struck me how much more comfortably he seemed to wear his T-shirts and construction boots.

He came through the gate and stood next to me. "Looking good, Xavier. This weekend I'll help you clean out the shed and paint it. We're not supposed to have any rain."

Xavier stopped clipping. Turning slowly, he said, "I might be old but I'm not feeble. I can do it myself without anybody's help. Don't like anybody messing with my things."

"It's a big job, Xavier. I don't mind helping."

"I know that. But I can do it myself."

"All right. Just let me know if you change your mind."

Beau ran to me, his hands gently cradling the leaves he'd carefully selected. "Julie, I made another collection for you." Very slowly, he laid out each leaf on my lap, each brilliantly colored edge fitted neatly into its neighbor like an autumn puzzle. It was so unexpected and creative, and reminded me so much of something his mother would have done, that I leaned down and kissed his lowered head. He looked up at me with his mother's eyes and smiled. "Why'd you do that for?"

"Because you're great," I said without thinking. "And because you remembered that I like to collect things and spent a lot of time gathering leaves you thought I'd like. It's like a birthday present even though it's not my birthday."

Trey crossed his arms. "I didn't take you for a collector. Thought you were a 'less is more' kind of person."

I stared down at the pattern of foliage on my lap, at the delicate veins bisecting the leaves like a road map leading to nowhere in particular. "I guess I inherited it from my mother. She was what we called a weekend warrior—heading out to all the estate sales and coming back with teaspoons, or thimbles, or old hats for her various collections. I still have them in a storage unit in New Jersey."

Unused to sharing anything personal, I felt myself blushing. I wanted to tell him that I continued collecting things after my mother's death not just because they reminded me of her, but because they were something permanent in a transitory life filled with temporary possessions that held no meaning. But when I looked up and met his eyes, I could tell that he already knew that about me. Just as through the planning of River Song I had learned that permanence, home, and family were as essential to him as breathing.

Beau giggled, and my attention was drawn to the movement of one of the leaves. A fat worm slithered from underneath a crimson leaf in the shape of a teardrop, and I tried very hard not to cringe.

"Look, Julie—a worm!"

"I know," I said, trying to sound enthusiastic. "Why don't you pick him up and stick him under a tree?"

Beau shook his head. "Uh-uh. I don't want to touch him."

I looked at Xavier, but his back was still toward us as he worked on the last of the crape myrtles. Reluctantly, I eyed Trey, who held up his hands. "Don't look at me. I don't like them either."

I frowned at him as I recalled the stories Monica had told me about how as a child he loved to chase her with anything he found crawling on six legs. "All right then," I said to Beau. "Why don't you go find me a stick, and I'll pick him up with that?"

Beau ran off and quickly found a stick about five inches long. I would have rather had more space between my hand and the worm, but it had begun to creep toward me. Swallowing heavily, I stuck the stick under the body of the worm and lifted it, then had to wait patiently as it dangled five inches from my hand as Beau carefully regathered the leaves from my lap.

After depositing the worm in its new home, I stood and brushed off my hands as Xavier turned, revealing what I swore was a smile. "They're not pretty to look at, but a garden can't grow without them." His smile faded quickly, as if he were recalling other necessary evils.

The front door opened and Aimee stepped outside. Trey said, "I've got to drive Miss Aimee to her meeting. Beau, you and me at the Creole Creamery for ice cream when I get back, right?"

"Right," Beau shouted, high-fiving his uncle.

I crossed my arms, and Trey looked at me. "You're welcome to come, too, if you like."

"Thanks," I said. "But I really just want Beau to eat something healthy first, all right?"

"Sure." He shook his head. "You're just like Monica, you know. She was always a health nut. Must have been the first person in New Orleans to eat tofu."

I smiled, remembering the girl who'd been so careful with what she fed her body but had died young anyway. I took a breath and spoke before I was even sure what I was going to say. "Definitely come get me when you get back. I haven't had ice cream in a long time."

"Will do." With a wave, he headed toward his grandmother, too late for me to tell him that I'd figured out what had been troubling me about my conversation with Aimee.

I waved back, then retrieved my leaf collection from Beau. Then I watched as Trey escorted his grandmother to her car while I wondered why she hadn't been surprised when I told her that Monica had drawn my family tree the year before she disappeared.

Aimee

FEBRUARY 1956

The last day of my stay in New Orleans seemed almost normal except for the eerie quietness of the house. I stood in the kitchen and noticed that the coffee hadn't yet been made and dishes from the previous evening were still in the sink. It was the beginning of Lent, and I usually gave up coffee, but now it seemed like such a frivolous thing. Perhaps if I gave up Wes instead, Mrs. Guidry would come back and everything would be back the way things had always been.

I closed my eyes. *Wes, where are you?* When I opened my eyes again, my gaze rested on the key rack on the wall with the keys to Mrs. Guidry's Cadillac, the red leather case highlighted against the pale cream wall. I remembered something Wes had written to me in one of his letters, something about how he would escape to River Song when he needed time to think.

Before I could talk myself out of it, I took the keys off the hook, then scribbled a note to Gary telling him I had taken his mother's car and would be gone for most of the day and not to worry. Then I stuck it under the salt and pepper shakers on the table. Without a second thought I grabbed my purse and let myself out the back door, closing it quietly behind me.

I blared the radio as I headed down the highway to Biloxi, not wanting to think about what I would say if I found Wes or his mother. I hoped the relief of finding them would make easy words flow to my lips.

The city disappeared behind me as the highway became a lone ribbon through tall trees. Bugs exploded on the windshield, speckling the glass like polka dots. Seeking the windshield wiper, I fiddled with the unfamiliar knobs and dials in the car. The hum of the tires changed as I ran onto the shoulder and jerked back onto the road.

River Song reflected the dim morning sun, the tall oak in the yard creating a large splotch of shadow across the front. The car rumbled over the rutted crushed-shell drive, and I lurched back and forth on the seat. A gull shrieked over the water as I stepped out onto the sandy soil and slammed the car door. I leaned against it and listened to the cicadas whir in the trees behind the house. My heart fell when I realized Wes's car was nowhere to be seen.

Slowly walking up the front path, I looked up at the windows, hoping to see a face or some sign of occupancy. Closed shutters and dusty screens stared back at me. I reached inside the flowerpot on the front step, the plant itself long dead, with tired, brittle stems, and pulled the door key from the dirt. A dark shadow passed over the door, and I turned to see a large cloud as it crept over the sun. The distant horizon lay dark and fuzzy, the waves near the beach already whipped to a frenzy. A storm was coming.

The hinges squeaked as I pushed the door open and stepped inside. The screen door banged behind me, making me jump. I laughed nervously and moved into the large front room. Rugs had been rolled up for the season and pushed against the walls, curtains flipped over rods in an attempt to keep off accumulated dust. Dust sheets lay over most of the furniture except for the couch. The house was different without the sounds of voices, like an empty oyster shell whose occupant was long since gone. My footsteps echoed on the bare wood floors as I walked into the room.

A floral sheet lay in a crumpled heap under the coffee table, the table itself covered with beer bottles. I walked over, lifted one up, and turned it over. Warm beer slid into my hand, dripped through my fingers, and landed on the side of an overturned bottle. I sneezed in acknowledgment of the dust motes flitting through the shaft of light from the open door.

A floor creaked upstairs, and I froze, a bottle in my hand. "Wes? Mrs. Guidry?"

A hard wind blew rain across the porch and through the screen door, sprinkling the floor mat with water. The floor creaked again.

"Hello?" I walked back into the foyer and stared at the stairwell, the first three steps visible until the fourth step disappeared around a corner. "Wes?"

A shadow crept up the wall of the stairwell as footsteps descended. I held the empty beer bottle in front of me as I backed up to the screen door, my other hand reaching for the knob. A tall figure emerged around the corner. The beer bottle slid through my fingers, breaking as it hit the wood floor.

"Hello, Aimee." Wes stood on the bottom step, barefoot and shirtless. A dark shadow of beard covered his cheeks and chin in a strangely appealing way. His eyes were sunken inside dark rings, his hair wet and slicked back as if he had just showered.

"Where's your car?" I asked, suddenly struck stupid.

"I couldn't find it—I think it might have been stolen. A friend dropped me off."

He started to smile but faltered halfway. Stumbling over the last step, he walked toward me. I flinched as I recognized the look in his eyes—I had seen it in his mother's eyes many times. He reached for me, and I allowed myself to be enfolded in his arms.

We stood like that for a long time, listening to the wind and rain hit the house. Splinters of water from the screen door splashed my bare legs, but I didn't move. Wes started to shake, and I realized he was crying. I put my arms around him and led him to the sofa.

We sat, and he pulled away from me, hiding his face and rubbing his eyes with the heels of his hands. "God, Aimee. I don't want you to see me like this. But there's no one . . ."

I touched his shoulder, knowing there was nothing I could say.

A loud thunder roll shook the panes in the windows as Wes looked at me. His eyes were dark and dangerous, the space between us volatile. He leaned toward me and pressed his lips against mine. My kissing experience was severely limited to a few brazen boys from the neighboring boys' school. Kissing them had been like kissing my pillow, except that my pillow was more pliable. But Wes was different. His lips were soft as he nudged mine open. He tasted them, nibbling on the lower one and moving leisurely to the top one. Slowly, he moved over me, pushing me down onto the couch. I smelled soap and the musty cushions, but all I could think of was the unnerving weight of his body pressing me into the couch and his warm lips on mine, tasting of mint toothpaste and salty tears.

My skin seemed to shrink tight over my bones, bringing every nerve ending to the surface. I was swimming underwater with no need for air. His lips moved to my eyes, then cheeks, then neck, his warm breath causing an eruption of goose bumps down the length of my body. The rain outside became more forceful, driving itself against the house.

Another roll of thunder crashed above us, but I hardly heard it. Wes did and he stopped. He raised himself up on his hands and looked down at me, as if really seeing me for the first time. He pulled himself off of me and sat down, his head in his hands. "Oh, God, Aimee. I'm sorry. I'm so sorry. I . . . I didn't mean to do that."

I got up on my knees and moved next to him, my hands on his arm. "Don't be, Wes. I'm not sorry."

He looked at me, his eyes hooded. "No—but you would be if . . ." He stopped. "There's too much between us right now—things that need to be resolved before we complicate our lives even more."

I breathed in deeply, feeling my skin tighten over my ribs. "Is this about your mother?"

He let out a sigh and sat back on the couch, reaching for me. I rested in the cradle of his arm, feeling the beat of his heart under my hand as he spoke. "Yes. It has everything to do with Mother."

I sat up to look into his face. He wouldn't look at me. "Where is she, Wes? Is she all right?"

Wes pulled me back to him and I felt his chest rise and fall. "No . . . I mean, I don't know." He slipped out from behind me and stood up and moved to the door, his hands pressed against the screen. "She's gone, Aimee. She won't be back."

I rose and stood next to him, but he still wouldn't face me. The hair on the back of my neck rose. "What do you mean, Wes? Where did she go?"

Droplets of rainwater sprinkled his skin, but he didn't blink as they continued to blow on him. His jaw clenched. "She . . . I saw her get into a car with another man. She went willingly."

The prickling sensation continued up the base of my skull. Something was wrong. Terribly wrong. I touched his arm and he looked at me, but his eyes were dark with hidden secrets. "Did you try to stop her?"

Wes shook his head almost imperceptibly, his voice very soft. "No. She wanted to leave, and I wouldn't have been able to stop her even if I wanted to."

My breath stuck in my throat, and there was nothing more to say. He led me back to the couch and pulled me into his embrace while we listened to the storm rage, the two of us an island in the middle of it all. Eventually, I got up to close the front door and turn on a light to chase the darkness out of the corners. I flipped the switch but nothing happened.

"The electricity and phones always go out during a storm—and usually for a couple of days. Nobody's ever in much of a hurry down here to get it fixed."

I walked over to the phone and picked it up to hear only silence. When I sat down again, his hands immediately touched me. "We need to tell your father, Wes—and Gary. He's worried sick. We've even called in the police."

He laid his head back against the couch and covered his eyes. "I figured as much. I've been such a coward, hiding out down here. I guess I was trying to spare Gary this." He lowered his hands and looked at me. "Finding out that Mother has left us will just about kill him."

I held his face in my hands and kissed his lips softly. I seemed to pull courage from the air, the storm, the old tree outside. Taking a deep breath, I said, "I love you, Wes. I have since that first moment I saw you on the levee. I won't let you do this by yourself."

His eyes darkened, and he kissed me again before putting me away from him. He jumped up and ran his hands over his stubble. I had never seen him so agitated. Even when his mother was on one of her binges, Wes was always so cool and in control. He turned to face me, his expression finally calm.

Reluctantly, I sat up. His voice held a new energy. "You need to get back to New Orleans before they realize you've been here. I don't want you involved in the police investigation—it will be bad enough with me, my father, and Gary involved. But I want you out of it. Leave now, and I will follow you later this evening or tomorrow morning. I'll find a ride somehow. Don't tell anybody you've been here."

"Can't we do this together—wouldn't it be easier for you if I were by your side when you went to the police?"

He shook his head, his mouth clenched tight. "No—it will be easier for me if I know you're not involved. And easier for Gary, too. You and me . . . we'll have to wait a while, okay?" His mouth tilted up at the corner in an effort to smile as he lifted his hand and smoothed the hair off my face. "We'll get through this. We all will—you'll see. Just go back to New Orleans as if you've never been here and spoken to me. I'll call you after I leave the police station."

The light at the windows brightened and I realized the storm had subsided, leaving only dripping eaves and sodden sand. Wes walked me out the back door and we strolled toward the side of the house with his arm around me. He seemed shocked for a moment to see his mother's car, then realized that I'd driven it. He opened the car door and I slid in. Leaning in the window, he kissed me. I smiled at him and put the car in reverse. He stood in the drive watching me as I pulled out onto the road, still standing, watching, until I could no longer see him in my rearview mirror.

I saw Lacy's car as I approached the house on First Street. I was parking Mrs. Guidry's car behind it as she came running down the front steps, blond hair flying. "Where have you been?" she screamed at me as I stepped out of the car. Too shocked to answer, I stood mute.

She approached and grabbed each of my arms and shook me. "Where have you been?" she shouted again, close enough for me to feel her hot breath on my face. She clenched her teeth. "Were you with Wes?"

Angry now, I shrugged her hands off of me. "It's none of your business, Lacy. Why are you here?"

She crossed her arms across her chest. "Mr. Guidry called me. Gary's in the hospital—he's had a heart attack."

I felt the air leave my lungs. "What? How is that possible? He's only seventeen, for God's sake!"

"He's at Ochsner and he's been asking for you. Mr. Guidry called me to see if I could find you."

"Oh, Lord," I said, my mind spinning, wondering what to do next. I sat down heavily on the bottom step. "I need to tell Wes. . . ."

"No. You need to get to the hospital. I'll tell Wes."

I looked up at her, noting the perfect precision of her bones, the clearness of her eyes. "You can't. . . . The phones aren't working."

She leaned down close to me and spoke quietly. "Then tell me where he is and I'll go get him."

I smelled her perfume, musky and exotic. "He's at River Song."

A look of triumph passed over her face. "I'll get him. You go to the hospital—Gary needs you."

Numbly, I nodded and watched her get behind the wheel of her car. I walked to the Cadillac, my legs rubbery, and tried to stick the key in the ignition, missing it twice. Too stunned to cry, I backed the car out of the driveway. As I gave it gas, a movement from the garden caught my eye. I turned my head in time to see a face peering from behind the fence amid the frost-pinched elephant ears, the one good eye staring at me. The face slid from sight as I raced down the street, seeing Gary's smile and feeling Wes's kiss.

CHAPTER 18

Live so that you tempt not the sea relentless
Neither press too close on the shore forbidding . . .
Thus in stormy days be of heart courageous
And when waves are calm, and the danger over,
Wise man, trim your sails when a gale too prosp'rous
Swells out the canvas.

—HORACE

Julie

The week before Thanksgiving and, I soon learned, the week before fishing season ended, I stood on the beach in front of River Song, its walls now outlined in two-by-fours, its roof still a hollowed shell allowing in the sunlight that settled onto the new raised foundation like a blessing. The old oak in the front yard, proudly wearing all of its scars, sat patiently as yet another house rose from the sandy earth. I found myself wondering if it ever got tired of watching people trying to build on an unforgiving landscape.

I looked up as a strong breeze lifted my hair and caused the oak's leaves to slap at the wind like a thousand hands clapping in approval. The wind pushed at me, forcing me to view the house again, its framed steel-enforced support columns no longer resembling the warm arms of Monica's description, but seeming instead to be more like defiant shields.

Tilting my head, I continued to regard the house, wondering how, with all of our meticulous planning, it looked so different to me—but not so much in the wood and cement and structure. It was almost as if the house no longer represented a promise delivered, or even the short-sighted folly I'd accused Trey of building. But what had remained the same was the spirit of the place, present here since even before Aimee had known it: a spirit of survival that had nothing to do with the building at all. I placed my hand on the scarred bark of the tree as if I could mend it, then drew my hand away, somehow knowing that I wasn't there to make the scars disappear.

Taking a sip from my fast-food coffee, I turned and watched Aimee stroll down the deserted beach with her cane as Beau ran, dipped, and swayed, mimicking the skimmers out on the sound searching for their breakfast. He had changed so much in the three months since we'd arrived. The clinginess and babyish behavior were slowly dissipating, and he seemed to grow more and more into boyhood each day. I knew Aimee's love and attention accounted for a lot of it, but so did Trey's influence. Still, I couldn't help but see the lost little boy he'd been after his mother's death, and I found it very difficult to let go of our mutual need for each other, or to fully relax whenever he was out of my sight.

A doglike bark brought my attention to the water, where a black skimmer cruised low over the waves sleek and fast like the fish it hunted. On our frequent inspections of the building site, Trey had begun to teach me the names of the shore birds, and how to recognize them. Some, like the great blue heron, were yearlong Gulf Coast residents. Others, like the orange-billed royal tern, were winter visitors, seeking the warmer waters and air of the gulf. They were all exotic and beautiful to me, and it thrilled me to see them regardless of how I tried to hide it from Trey.

Footsteps approached and I turned to see Trey, bundled in a flannel jacket, standing next to me nursing his own coffee. "They said that the oil spill would keep a lot of the birds away." He took a sip from his cup. "They said the same thing about Katrina, too. Guess they were wrong." My eyes met his and I saw the challenge in them.

We began to walk slowly down the beach toward Aimee and Beau. Trey continued. "I was at the Back Bay yesterday and saw two white ibises. You ever seen one?"

I shook my head.

"Beautiful birds, and they're here year-round. They have the distinction of never having been on an endangered species list."

I glanced up at him, squinting into the sun, knowing that he wouldn't tell me any more unless I asked. "Why?"

After a dramatic pause, he said, "When an old habitat is washed away by a storm, or gets coated in oil, they find another one that's just as good." He took another sip of his coffee. "Guess they figured it was worth the trouble to stay here, and a heck of a lot easier than packing up and moving to California."

Shading my eyes with my flattened hand, I looked at him, wondering if he expected me to laugh, but saw that his face was serious.

As if summoned, a pair of black skimmers swooped close to shore, barking loudly as they chased the waves onto the beach as if to prove to unbelievers that returning home was more than just instinct but a necessity of survival.

We faced the water and stared out at the blur of Ship Island in the distance, the waves lapping near our feet. Two shrimp boats slowly made their way out toward the gulf, dark blobs on the horizon and in the corners of my memory. This was Monica's favorite time of day while in Biloxi, a time alone with the water and the birds and the fish, a room of her own where her parents' fighting could never reach her. I took a deep breath of the crisp, salty air, the newness of it that seemed full of possibilities, and thought I understood a little bit more of why she had loved this place so much.

"Do you swim?"

I looked up at Trey, bringing me back to the present. "No."

He raised his eyebrows as he took another sip of coffee. "It's too cold now, but when the water warms up, we'll have to fix that. Same with Beau. Monica's son should know how to swim." I found myself nodding, unsure where the fear had gone. Maybe because I was sure I wouldn't be here long enough to immerse myself into warm waters, my bare feet stepping out into the unknown.

"Look," Trey said, pointing down the beach.

My gaze followed and I watched as a tall snowy egret, its plumed head waving regally as it moved, walked down a dilapidated dock as if the broken and splintered wood were a red carpet. Beau stopped to watch, keeping very still, as Trey had taught him. He looked at Aimee and put his finger to his lips, making me want to laugh out loud.

The bird stopped and stared at Beau as if in mutual admiration, then looked around at its environment like a king surveying his domain. Then, with a quick snap of its long and elegant wings, it shot into the cerulean sky.

But my focus was on Beau, whose head remained tilted back, facing the sky, until long after the bird disappeared. His cheeks were pinkened, his mouth open in joy, and his arms stretched wide as if to encompass the birds, the sand, the water, the people. The house. I no longer felt the cool wind slide up my sleeves or tease my hair. I saw only Monica's dream, and for the first time since I'd brought Beau on the long trip from New York, I began to believe that maybe I really had done the right thing.

A horn beeped from the road behind us and we turned to see Walker King in a silver pickup truck hauling a boat on a trailer pull into the driveway in front of River Song. Before Walker had opened his door, Charlie Thibodeaux flew out of the passenger side and ran to the edge of the road, waving wildly at Beau. She waited until Walker caught up to her and took her hand, and then, after checking both ways, crossed the road, pausing in the median to check again before crossing to the beach.

Charlie and Beau raced toward each other, then hugged like they hadn't seen each other in years instead of the day before. Walker sauntered over to us with a smile. "Carol Sue says they're already talking about getting married. I suggested that we should encourage them to take it slower, and wait until they're at least out of kindergarten."

Walker and Trey shook hands. Walker leaned down and surprised me by kissing Aimee on both cheeks. "Good to see you, Miss Aimee."

"You too, Walker. You taking good care of our Carol Sue and Charlie?"

"Yes, ma'am. As much as they let me."

"And how's your mama and daddy?"

"Just fine, Miss Aimee. Thank you for asking. Mama goes on and on about your garden clippings. Says you are solely responsible for restoring half the gardens in Biloxi ruined by Katrina. She's even finally admitting that her garden now might even be nicer than the one she had five years ago."

I turned to look at the boat behind the truck, feeling the first twinges of trepidation. "Are the four of you really going to fit on that?"

Walker tried to look offended. "That boat has reeled in more fish than you've probably ever eaten in your entire life. I know it's nothing fancy—just some seats and a motor, and a place for our fishing poles. Cooler for the fish we catch is already stored under one of the seats."

I frowned. "What about life jackets?"

"They're in the bed of the truck. I've got four—and two of them are made for children. They're not in the boat because I insist that everybody has one on before we get near the water."

Trying to smile, I said, "I'm sorry, it's just—"

He stopped me. "No need to apologize. I understand completely. Trey and I will take real good care of these children. I promise. And I promise that they'll have a great time, too."

"I know," I said, nodding and trying to convince myself.

"What's been biting this season?" Trey asked.

"Oh, a bunch of speckled trout, some cobia and redfish. And Bucky

Elmore caught a twenty-four-pound tripletail near Gulfport Harbor. Hope there's something left for us, seeing as how the season closes next week."

We walked back to the house, Beau's hand in mine, his other holding Charlie's, while he kept up a constant chatter about how he was going in a boat and how Uncle Trey was going to show him how to set up a plastic jig to catch trout. I had no idea what he was talking about, and could only hope that whatever it was wasn't dangerous.

We strapped the children into the back of the double-cab truck, and right before Trey got in, he gently squeezed my arm. "He'll be fine, Julie. Monica loved fishing, and was never shy about announcing to the world that she always caught bigger fish than me. I'm sure Beau would love to do the same thing. I've already told him that I would bark like a skimmer if he caught a bigger fish than me. That might be worth seeing."

I stepped back as he climbed into the truck, feeling slightly better. "Yeah. It sure would," I said, as I tried not to smile at the mental image of Trey Guidry barking like a bird.

Aimee and I waved as they pulled away, reconfirming the time we would meet them back at Carol Sue's for an anticipated fish dinner.

As the truck disappeared from sight, I saw that Aimee was holding Monica's red hat. "Oh, no! Beau forgot the hat." I started digging in my purse for the keys to my van, but stopped when Aimee rested her hand on my arm.

"I think he'll be all right without it." Her smile was warm, her touch firm.

I looked back at where the truck had long since disappeared, seeing Beau's happy face as he'd waved good-bye. Still, I couldn't yet forget the pale and sad boy who would wake up each morning asking for his mother long after I'd told him that she was gone.

"I hope so."

She nodded without speaking, her gaze focused on the house rising from ground. "This," she said, indicating the framed walls and roof, "is a good thing. For a long time I didn't think it would happen. Trey swore that he wouldn't rebuild it without Monica." Her eyes were troubled as they met mine. "And I was afraid that meant it would never be rebuilt."

She began to walk toward the house, where temporary wooden steps had replaced the old cement ones. "Call it a grandmother's intuition, but I knew Monica wasn't coming back. I hadn't always felt that way, but last year I began to feel that she was gone from us forever. I tried to tell Trey, but he insisted that until he knew for sure, he wasn't rebuilding."

Gulls shrieked behind us as they dipped over the sun-drenched water, searching for something only they could see, reminding me of the Katrina tree. Aimee hugged her arms to her chest, but I didn't think it was from the cold. "I don't know," she said. "It seems to me that if everybody lived with the philosophy of certain knowledge before proceeding, this part of the world would never have been settled." A soft smile touched her lips as she looked up to the skeleton roof as if seeking an answer. "After all, what're a few storms, pestilence, and wars? I think the uncertainties build character."

I opened my mouth to argue before realizing that I didn't know how. Instead, I touched her elbow. "Come around to the back. They've framed the sleeping porch on the second floor."

Carefully, I led her across plywood walkways to the backyard. I pointed up toward the back of the building. "Does it look like you remember?"

"Not yet. But from what I see of the ceiling, it looks like they're doing it right so far."

I smiled, pleased. "Steve Kenney has forbidden me from looking at it one more time until he's finished with the drywall. I've had him change it at least twice and Trey once. It's important that it's the same, I think. I want Beau and any other child who lives here to believe this house has always been here."

Her smile faded but she didn't look away.

"What's wrong?"

She faced me. "Nothing, Julie. You and Trey are doing a wonderful job. It's just . . . memories. There are so many here. Like ghosts."

I listened to the distant murmur of water and the cries of invisible birds and believed that she was right. "Come on. Let's see if Ray Von is home and then run your errands before we head on over to Carol Sue's."

As I drove the short distance to Ray Von's house, I sorted through all of the unanswered questions Aimee's stories had raised, questions avoided so far due to our busy schedules. But I was a guest in her house, at least part of the week, and felt the need to tread carefully.

"How do you know Dr. King's family?" I asked.

"Oh, his parents and I go way back. They're originally from Biloxi, but Mr. King worked for one of the big oil companies in New Orleans for a long time. When he retired, they moved back down to Biloxi. Walker had a nice dental practice in New Orleans East, but lost it and his house in Katrina. Decided to come back here to be near his parents, which just thrilled them. I suppose he figured that if he had to start over, he might as well start over in Biloxi. Mabel, Walker's mother, belonged to the Garden District Gardening Society, which is how I know her."

"I wonder why he didn't move away from the area completely. It must be hard to rebuild a dental practice with all new patients."

"I suppose he figured this was home." She didn't say anything else, as if she believed her answer had explained everything.

Changing the subject, I said, "You haven't told me about Gary. Was he okay after his heart attack?"

She continued to stare out the window and I thought she hadn't heard me. But then I saw her hands clenched in her lap and knew she had. "For a while, yes. He was upset when I ended up not attending Newcomb College as planned."

"Why did you change your mind?"

She turned to face me. "Because Wes married Lacy."

"But I thought . . ." I couldn't finish.

"Wes told me that he couldn't hurt Gary by being with me."

There was a moment of silence while I tried to sort through everything. "That was the only reason Wes gave you? And that was enough?"

She shook her head. "It wasn't enough, of course. And I suppose the reason didn't matter to me. The end result was the same." She waved her hand in the air as if brushing away a fly. "Anyway, it was too painful for me to stay in New Orleans, so I attended Bryn Mawr in Philadelphia instead."

"And you married Gary."

A soft smiled played on her lips. "Yes. Eventually."

"Did Wes and Lacy have any children?"

"Trey and Monica's father, Wesley John Guidry the Second. But we called him Johnny from the moment he was born." A smile illuminated her face. "He was such a sweet boy, and I couldn't help but love him even though he was Lacy's son."

"But Monica and Trey call you Grandmother."

She nodded. "Let's just say that Lacy wasn't the maternal type. I practically raised Johnny, and then he went and married someone just like his mother. So I raised Trey and Monica, too. But I didn't mind. I'd been an only child, and I wasn't able to have children of my own. They were my family, and I built a home around them, and that's all that mattered."

I pulled onto Ray Von's street, but drove slowly, not wanting our conversation to end. "But you came back to New Orleans eventually. Why?"

"I missed it. Philadelphia was never home to me. And I missed Gary." She smiled to herself, recalling a distant memory.

"What is it?" I prompted.

"He gave me a ring from a Cracker Jack box before I left, and gave it to me as an engagement ring. I wore it all through college. And the Mardi Gras beads Wes had given me." She pressed her hand against her chest and closed her eyes. "We don't always get to choose where our hearts call home."

I slowed the car as we approached Ray Von's house. "And Xavier? You said he sort of disappeared at the same time as Wes and Mrs. Guidry after the Comus Ball. Did he come back?"

Aimee kept her gaze focused in front of her. "Ray Von said he'd gone for good, but I didn't believe her. I kept on thinking I'd seen him in crowds on the street or leaving a building where I'd just been. Like he was watching me. But Ray Von said I must have been imagining it. Maybe I wanted to believe that somebody was looking out for me." She turned to me in the car and spoke softly. "You understand, don't you? Only those without mothers understand how truly alone we are."

I stopped the car at the curb behind a navy blue Lincoln. Ray Von stood at the passenger door, preparing to get in. A middle-aged woman, who I assumed to be another member of the Ladies Auxiliary, sat behind the wheel and waved as I got out of my car and approached.

"Hello, Ray Von. I was hoping we'd catch you at home. Are you on your way out?"

"Yes." She watched as Aimee opened her door and pulled herself up on the doorframe. "Sorry I can't stay to chat."

"Have you had a chance to look for the note yet?"

I watched as she furrowed her eyebrows as if trying to recall what I was talking about. "I haven't found it yet. But like I said before, there's nothing in it besides what I already told you."

Aimee stood by the side of the car, not moving but steadily watching Ray Von. "Xavier's doing well, Ray Von. Got the garden all ready for winter."

Ray Von's expression didn't change, but her eyes seemed to shift to a darker green. "Did you tell her yet?"

Almost imperceptibly, Aimee shook her head.

"Tell me yet about what?" I asked.

Ray Von lifted her chin. "I'm only saying this because of Monica. Because of how much she wanted to know the truth."

"The truth about what?" I asked, my voice rising with frustration.

Aimee shook her head again, but Ray Von ignored her. "Have you told her yet about the man Caroline Guidry left with that night?"

I jerked my head around to face Aimee, whose skin had suddenly paled.

"I've got to go," Ray Von said as she slid into the waiting Lincoln.

I walked around the car and helped Aimee into her seat before closing the door. In silence I buckled my seat belt and started the car. "What did she mean, Miss Aimee? Did Wes know the man his mother left with?"

After a moment, she nodded. "I didn't tell you because of Monica. I didn't want you to think badly of her. She was always so sensitive to any perceived slight, to any wrong. I didn't want you to know . . ." She stopped and took a deep breath before speaking again. "I didn't want you to know that Monica might have had her own reasons for finding you in New York."

A cold drop of dread slid down my neck. "What was his name?" I asked, believing I already knew.

Quietly, she answered. "Abe Holt."

CHAPTER 19

And your ancient ruins shall be rebuilt; you shall raise up the foundations of many generations; you shall be called the repairer of the breach, the restorer of streets to dwell in.

—ISAIAH 58:12

Julie

In those early months Beau and I spent on the Gulf Coast I learned to look at life as a series of befores and afters. For me, the line of demarcation was the day Chelsea disappeared and I lost my childhood. In the months I spent as a docent in the museum and as a new resident of Biloxi, I learned that in the Gulf Coast the line between before and after became Camille in 1969 that demolished the coast, toppled houses and businesses alike, killing one hundred and thirty-two people. In 2005, the line became Hurricane Katrina. It took the lives of nearly two thousand people, one hundred and seventy on the Gulf Coast, and created more havoc than could be seen in the flattened houses and flooded stadiums, or in news footage of stray dogs and orange paint on doors.

But, as I was beginning to learn, that was only on the outside, the only part the rest of the world bothered to see. As I watched new businesses open, and houses rebuilt, or even a ruin bulldozed, I was allowed to peek beneath that devastated surface to see a resilience and determination I knew I didn't possess.

Hurricane season ended in November, and although it wasn't officially acknowledged, I imagined I heard a collective sigh of relief. I'd started my job at the museum, and even though I did little more than lead tours of schoolchildren and give people directions to the bathroom, I was content with this temporary stop in my life. The museum itself, designed by Frank Gehry, was an architectural marvel and was built, in the architect's words, as a place that would dance among the trees. The three buildings that made up the first phase of the campus were created with soaring walls and tall metal pods nestled between ancient oaks. Looking at them from a distance, where it was hard to distinguish them as buildings, I believed that he'd fulfilled his promise.

Trey and I fell into a workable relationship—I was the eyes of the project, texting photos of the site and any details up close for his inspection. On the days I was in Biloxi, I would visit the building site and bring snacks and ice water for the workers. It was a good excuse to linger longer than necessary as I checked to make sure that Monica's house was as she'd remembered it.

For his part, Trey was on the phone to the builder on a nearly daily basis discussing elevations, shipment of Hardie siding, and whether or not resistance to one-hundred-and-fifty-mile-per-hour winds would be enough.

As if by unspoken agreement, we met in his office on Sunday and Wednesday evenings—since I worked in Biloxi Thursday through Sunday—comparing notes and making lists. Any alterations from the original house plans were met with strong objections from me, but I was usually overruled with assurances from Trey that all changes were for safety and durability.

A grudging respect began to grow between the two of us as our initial mutual distrust dissipated. Instead of viewing the other as an

adversary, we started to see instead a willing partner in our bid to fulfill the dream of a girl we had both loved and lost. We never spoke of
this connection, but it was there as the walls were raised and ceilings
drywalled on River Song, hovering over everything we touched and
oversaw, as present as a ghost.

My relationship with Aimee changed, too. I wasn't angry that she'd
withheld the information about Mrs. Guidry and my great-grandfather.
I even understood that she'd done it to protect my memory of Monica.
I was enjoying listening to Aimee's stories about her growing up with
Gary and Wes, and of Monica's first eighteen years. But I had a lingering doubt that she was telling me everything, leaving me to wonder if
we'd ever be able to put any pieces together if she kept so many behind
her back.

Despite the uncertainties, I'd gotten in the habit of searching the
Internet for Abe Holt as often as I searched the missing persons sites,
hoping to find some mention of Caroline Guidry, much as I imagined
Monica must have done after she'd somehow managed to find out the
identity of the person with whom Caroline had left the ball. It was
surprising, yet inevitable, to find my name, and those of other family
members, but not one mentioning Caroline, or even suggesting a mis-
tress or lover or any woman associated with Abe Holt except for his first
wife and my great-grandmother.

I was at an impasse, no closer to finding out why Monica had left
or why she'd befriended me, and River Song with its new walls and
steel roof straps still an empty shell. If it hadn't been for Beau's gradual
return to boyhood, I would almost say that this detour had been a co-
lossal waste of time. To justify my time spent, I expanded my Internet
search for Chelsea into international sites, and subscribed to several online newspapers from major cities throughout the country, just in case
Detective Kobylt had missed something.

On a sunny Sunday afternoon at the end of January, Trey showed
up after work to pick me up to bring Beau and me back to New Orleans. The van had a leaky head gasket and would be in the repair shop

until Trey returned us to Biloxi on Wednesday evening. He was smiling, which made me immediately suspicious. My curiosity was further aroused when I saw that not only was Beau not in the truck, but that Trey had also stowed a kayak in the truck bed.

"Where's Beau?" I asked as I tossed my purse on the floor of the passenger seat and then climbed in.

"He and Charlie wanted to go see a movie, so Carol Sue took them as a treat for being so good today—which I took to mean less rolling in the dirt than usual. I figured now would be as good a time as any to show you the real Biloxi."

"Why would you figure that?"

"Because last week you mentioned how it seemed the new condos and casinos outnumbered houses now. Which makes me think you haven't seen much beyond your street, River Song, Carol Sue's house, and the Ohr museum."

I didn't answer him, mostly because he was right. "I just hope that your tour doesn't include that kayak."

"Of course it does. You really need to experience the water, but since it's too cold right now to swim, the next-best thing would be to get you in a boat."

I glanced through the truck's window toward the endless water of the sound, interrupted by the barrier islands before heading into the great Gulf of Mexico and the unknown. It scared me, made me think of all that I didn't know, of all the possibilities I couldn't face. "That thing in the back of your truck is not exactly a 'boat.' Besides, I need to get back to New Orleans."

Not that I'd expected him to, but he didn't stop the truck. "Why? Got a hot date?"

"Maybe." It was hard to keep a straight face. I stared out the windshield seeing the winding ribbon of sand and the undulating water beside the road, wondering what lurked beneath the waves.

"You've got about two hours to kill before Beau's done, so you might as well enjoy yourself."

I looked down at my skirt and blouse, and saw another escape route. "I'm not really dressed to go kayaking."

He glanced at the rear seat. "Carol Sue said you'd say that. You're about the same size, so she threw some things in a bag for you. We'll stop off at McDonald's and you can change in the restroom."

Resigned, I let out a deep breath, an odd thread of excitement twisting through my fear. "Great," I said. "You've thought of everything." I forced myself to unclench my jaw, remembering the times Beau had gone out in a boat with Trey, and how he was already talking about learning how to water-ski. And he was only five years old. I suddenly felt very, very old.

We had almost driven past it before I realized we were about to pass another Katrina tree. I watched for them now, as they'd become for me more than just the landscape of this strange new place, but more like a kind of touchstone. They were damaged, yet ethereal and compelling, and I felt the need to learn from them, to understand their secrets.

The truck seemed to move in slow motion as we passed the tree. The bottom of its trunk was short and slim like a human wrist, its limbs the open fingers of a hand, each digit a different seabird with neck stretched long, wings back, diving for something I couldn't see. I turned my head as we passed by it, wondering what it was about the reclaimed tree that made my heart hurt and my fingers tingle. I shifted in my seat, ignoring the water so close to the truck, and said, "I guess I can stand anything for two hours."

I heard the grin in his voice as he spoke. "Don't let your enthusiasm get the best of you, Julie."

I smiled, too, but turned my face to the window to hide it.

After a quick pit stop for me to change clothes, Trey parked the truck and I helped him carry the kayak to the end of a dock near the marina. He handed me a bright orange life vest and put one on himself, showing me how to tighten the straps and then checking mine to make sure I'd done it right.

I watched his fingers, long and lean like Monica's, and wondered if he, too, had the heart of an artist, but one hidden behind his stern law-yer persona. I lifted my head and found myself studying the shade of his hair, still sun-bleached, although we were presumably in the middle of winter. His cheeks and chin showed blond stubble; his skin was lightly tanned. He looked up, his greenish blue eyes widening as he caught me staring. Stepping back, he appraised me from head to toe. "Neon orange suits you. You should wear it more often."

"Thanks," I said.

Effortlessly, he lowered himself into the kayak, then asked me to hand him the oars. Still standing on the dock, I said, "Why don't I watch you from here?"

"Coward," he said with a smile. "Now get in the boat."

He showed me how and held the boat steady against the dock as I found myself a secure seated position in front of him, his jeans-clad legs on either side of me. Small waves lapped at the side of the kayak, heavy with the scent of salt and plants and fish I couldn't see.

"You do know how to swim, right?"

I shook my head. "No. We didn't live close to the ocean, and we didn't belong to the community pool. It was always something my father said we should do. But both of my parents worked and . . ." I stopped, the memories of my family always like a bruise I didn't want to touch.

As if understanding, Trey changed the subject. "I don't have lights on the kayak, so we've got to be back before sunset, but that should give us plenty of time to get out there and back."

I shielded my eyes with my flattened hand. "Where exactly is 'there'?"

"Deer Island." He pointed to a nearby mass of land, close enough that I could see the trees. "It's only about a quarter of a mile away. There used to be a bunch of houses and docks on the island, but Ca-mille did a massive redecoration. Now it's owned by the state as a kind of nature preserve. Kids used to swim from Biloxi across the sound to the island. Don't know if they still do."

"Did you?" I asked, remembering the wild boy of Monica's stories, the boy who'd make a zip line out of anything he could find to propel him as quickly as possible into the water.

A mischievous grin lit his face. "Maybe. As long as Aimee wasn't watching. She'd tan my hide for sure if she caught me, but I know that she used to do the same thing, with Wes and Gary egging her on."

I pictured Aimee as a young girl with flaming red hair and long limbs, and could see it all so clearly. I threw back my head and laughed, but stopped abruptly when I caught Trey looking at me.

"What's wrong?" I asked.

Picking up his oar, he shook his head. "Nothing. It's just that I don't think I've ever heard you laugh like that before."

I sobered quickly and picked up my own oar. "I've never rowed a kayak, so you're going to have to take it slowly and explain what I'm supposed to do." I looked over the edge of the boat. "How deep is this water, anyway?"

"Deep enough," he said as he dug his oar into the water and we slid away from the dock. "Just do exactly what I do with my oars. To go left, use the right oar; to go right, use the left. And to go straight, do a series of both."

"Sounds pretty easy," I said, concentrating on pushing my oar through the water.

"I'll ask you how easy it was when we get there," he said behind me, and I heard the grin in his voice again.

We rowed in silence as I focused on the rowing, my arm muscles unaccustomed to any kind of a workout. I could only hope that I'd be able to raise them over my head the next day, or unbutton my blouse without too much pain.

The water's surface rippled gently, like feathers on a bird, for which I was grateful, and I tried not to think too hard about what might be swimming beneath our small boat. The distance wasn't that far, but by the time we reached the shallow water near the shore of Deer Island, I felt like I'd been rowing for days.

Trey beached the kayak and I climbed out onto the sand, managing to keep Carol Sue's sneakers mostly dry. Trey followed me and pulled the kayak out of the surf. I stood, suddenly emerged in a different world: a place of stillness and quiet that I hadn't visited since the day I'd watched clouds with my sister and she disappeared from my life. I turned my back toward the mainland, where the towering condos and casinos dominated the landscape, and faced instead the tall pines and verdant foliage.

"Where are the deer?" I asked, moving ahead, wanting to capture the stillness, to envelop myself in the green quiet.

Trey's footsteps followed behind me. "Haven't been deer on Deer Island for a few hundred years at least. They called it that when the Choctaw lived here and the deer would swim across the sound to get away from their hunters."

I continued to move forward, eager to make civilization disappear behind me, Trey following. "It's so silent."

"Because it's winter. It's my favorite time here. Monica's, too. We'd come here around this time and play cowboys and Indians, or just sit on logs and watch. No tourists or fishing charters. Just this." He raised his arms, indicating the tiny bird tracks in the sand, the tall pines, the weathered gray driftwood log with bark hewn from water and wind, beautiful now because of its journey.

Trey continued. "You need to come back in the spring. There's a blue heron rookery on the other side of the island, and a colony of brown pelicans, too. Not too far from here, on the eastern side, is the trunk of a dead oak tree with an osprey nest in the fork of the two branches. I've been coming here for a long time, and the ospreys are here every year."

I leaned against the trunk of a pine and closed my eyes, imagining the calls of hundreds of birds, the flapping of so many wings. But the space around me was hushed and I could hear myself breathe, feel the soft, cool air brush at my cheeks. I looked up through the pine branches and saw the glow of pink in the sky, the echo of sun in its last hours of day. Something fluttered to my right, and I watched as a blue heron, startled by our presence, shot out into the rosy-tinted sky, reminding me of the birds in the Katrina tree, their long, sculpted necks stretched in endless searching.

Slowly, I came out of the thicket and onto the sandy shore again, where sea grasses stood tall and swayed with the rhythm of the waves. I turned and walked eastward, keeping my gaze focused away from shore and signs of civilization, unsure of where I was heading. Trey followed but didn't speak. Without turning, I said, "Can you walk all the way around?"

"Not without getting your feet wet. And the winds and waves get pretty brutal on the gulf side. Not to mention the critters you might run into. There's a bayou right in the middle of the island. Beautiful to go see if you're prepared."

"Critters?"

"Yeah. Alligators, cottonmouths, that kind of thing. I'm pretty sure they hibernate during the winter months. Still, the bayou is its own little ecosystem and something you should see. Like I said, you need to be prepared first."

I watched as a crab scuffled sideways through sand ridges, making its way to the thicker brush to hide. "What was this place like after Katrina?"

"Brown. Lots of dead pines, no wildlife whatsoever. A large trench had been cut through the middle—and recently filled thanks to a fourteen-million-dollar restoration project."

I recalled the blue heron and the osprey nest and listened to the waves lap at the shore. "But they all came back."

"Yeah, they did. Even after the oil spill. There might be fewer numbers of blue crabs and other kinds of fish, but they'll come back. It's not like the gulf has never faced a hurricane or spill before."

Facing him, I said, "Makes me think of Monica, and how she always said she would come back."

He regarded me, his face unreadable. "She must have been wait-

ing for something. And I can't help but think that Aimee knows
more than she thinks she does." He paused. "I'm glad you're here
to talk with Aimee. I know that hearing about Monica before she
got sick has been really good for Aimee. And you've managed to
uncover more than I was able to in the ten years I spent searching for
my sister."

I raised my eyebrows, surprised that he'd concede that much. It
also made me feel like I had an ally. "Thank you," I said. "There's one
thing that's been bugging me, that I'm wondering if you'd be able to
help with."

"I can try. What is it?" He leaned down and picked up a shell,
then used his thumbs to dig out the wet sand encrusted in its scal-
loped palm.

"The last time I spoke with Aimee, she told me that Wes had looked
into her mother's case file and hadn't been able to find anything. I'm
pretty sure that none of it is related to Monica or my great-grandfather,
but it's just one more unanswered question. If you know anybody in
the NOPD, I was wondering if maybe you could take a look. There
might be some saved evidence that modern techniques can do something with. I don't know. I guess it's a place to start."

Pulling back his arm, he threw the shell as far as he could into the
water, where it landed with a soft plop. "Sure. No harm in that, I guess.
I know that Aimee would appreciate it."

He picked up another shell and I continued to walk, following bird
tracks until they disappeared near what looked like yellow-flowered
heather. It was strange to see color in winter, the brightness of the yellow almost garish against the neutrals of the sand and shells. My gaze
traveled to the shallow water near the shore, where stumps of trees
protruded like tombstones.

I pointed. "What are those?"

"Old dock pilings. Or pine trees. Hurricanes and erosion keep
fighting with the forest for ownership. I never stop wondering who's
going to give up first."

I watched him, noticing how the shade of blue left in the sky matched the blue part of his eyes. "What about you, Trey? Have you ever wanted to throw in the towel? Leave? After you lost River Song, and your house, and your best friend, didn't you feel like you'd had enough?"

He kicked a large piece of driftwood before sitting down on it. "I did at first. I remember coming down here right after Katrina. You can't imagine what it looked like. And there I was, stomping around what was left of River Song, trying to see whether there was anything I could salvage and feeling pretty sorry for myself. And then I saw one of our neighbors, Mrs. Anderson, and she was crying as she sifted through the rubble of her house. When I asked her if there was anything I could do, she told me about her daughter, who had died the year before, and all she wanted to find was a picture of her, because she didn't have one. They'd all been in that house. And a funny thing happened. I just didn't feel sorry for myself anymore." He stood, tossing the shell back in the sand where it had come from. "Somebody has to be left standing to put the pieces back together."

The sun had begun to sink, and the air was cooler on my skin. I rubbed my hands over my arms, hearing old voices I never expected to revisit. "My mom said that, too. After Chelsea was taken. My dad couldn't cope, and my brother just sort of checked out. She said she had to stick it out for as long as it took until Chelsea came home so we could all be a family together again. That's all she really wanted."

Trey's eyes met mine. "Then she died, and you took over. And you're still waiting for Chelsea to come home, so you can put your family back together."

His voice was matter-of-fact, his words seeming to have been spoken about somebody else. "Pretty much. And now I'm here."

We continued to regard each other before Trey looked away. "Come on," he said. "It'll be dark soon."

I nodded and followed him back the way we'd come. As we moved toward the kayak, something thick and heavy splashed in the gray-smudged water ahead of us. I looked up just in time to see a dorsal fin vanish below the surface. I stopped, my heart beating fast. "Was that a shark?"

I could tell that Trey was trying not to smile. "No. That would be a dolphin."

I'd never seen a dolphin outside of an aquarium, remembering Chelsea and me with our noses pressed against the glass, thinking the dolphins were grinning just for us, and wishing we could swim so we could jump inside and touch their smooth, gray bodies.

"Are there lots of them in the gulf?" I asked, walking carefully to the edge of the surf, staring at the place where I'd seen the fin.

"Quite a few. It's always good fishing for them here, even in the winter."

I stayed still, as if by not moving I could force the dolphin to break the surface again. Then, about fifteen feet from where I'd first spotted him, the dolphin emerged from the water, close enough that I could see his eye and the perpetual grin, his skin gleaming and wet, reflecting the endless pink sky before sliding beneath the waves one last time.

I pressed my hand over my mouth, still not moving, and wondered why I wanted to laugh and cry at the same time. I looked at Trey and recognized that I'd been wrong about something: about how I had once thought how much he and Monica resembled each other. But now I realized that when looking into Monica's eyes, I'd seen only what was lost to her. Trey's eyes were still full of all that had been lost and yet regained, all that was old but new again. His eyes were full of the hope and possibilities that were missing in Monica long before I knew her.

I spoke quietly, as if to the air, and the water, and the dolphin swimming in the darkened depths where I couldn't find him. "If I'd known this place, I would have brought her back."

Trey touched my arm. "I know." He began to lead me to the kayak. "Come on, Julie. The sun's beginning to set."

Trey helped me into the kayak and then launched us into the sound. I dug in with my oar, all the time looking for the telltale ripples on the surface of the pink-tinted water. "I would have brought her back," I said again to no one but the empty sky and silent waves and all that swam below unseen.

CHAPTER 20

Flowers never emit so sweet and strong a fragrance as before a storm. —JEAN PAUL RICHTER

Aimee

1960

I stayed away from New Orleans for four years, missing her peculiar scent, the accents of her people, and the heavy air that always made my hair twist and tighten. I missed the water, too, and wondered if my lethargy was mostly because of that: because I'd grown used to a place surrounded by water and its always present threat that seemed to lend the city its desperate joie de vivre.

I met new people, started new hobbies, but I could never forget. Wes stayed in my dreams, never far from me. And in the mornings I would push him aside and throw myself into my studies, safe again until nightfall.

Gary wrote and called every week. He was a biology major at Tulane, hoping to one day go to medical school, but he still found time to call. I listened to his soft accent and gentle laughter and I wanted to be there with him again. I wanted to race our bikes on the levee and tell ghost stories in my grandmother's tall attic turret. But we had left our childhood behind, and the burdens of growing up had found us. There was no turning back.

Wes wrote a few times, but I returned his letters unopened. And when the wedding invitation arrived, and, a year later, one for a baby shower for Lacy, I threw them away.

I stayed with my father in Philadelphia each summer and Christmas, working at Wanamaker's downtown as a shopgirl in the china, crystal, and silver department to earn spending money and to distract me from my thoughts that were never far away from New Orleans and Wes and Gary. But it was Ray Von who eventually lured me back.

A few weeks before graduating from Bryn Mawr with a degree in English, I received a letter with a New Orleans postmark with unfamiliar, yet distinctly feminine, writing on the front. For one brief moment, I thought it might be from Mrs. Guidry, and I quickly ripped into the letter. There was no salutation, just a single paragraph.

I love Gary like he was my own son and that's the only reason I'm writing you. His heart is not strong and he will not live to be an old man. He misses you so much it makes him sick, but he would never tell you so I am. Come back to him. Love comes in many shades— just don't throw it away because it's not red-hot. Sometimes all that is needed are glowing embers to start the fire. Ray Von Williams

I was worried, wondering what had prompted her to send me the letter, knowing that if Gary had been sick he would never tell me. Ray Von liked being in charge of her own domain without interference in either her duties or sphere of influence. For her to summon me back into her orbit meant something very serious.

I held on to the letter for a week, the paper soft and wrinkled from being read so many times. And then I received a letter from Mr. Guidry, on his business stationery, asking me to help him throw a graduation party for Gary, and it suddenly seemed to me that the universe had conspired against me to bring me back to a place I loved as much as I hated.

After my decision to return to New Orleans, things moved very quickly for me, much as I imagined the sucking pull of a storm surge gathered everything in its wake. I graduated, packed up my few possessions, and even procured a job in an antiques gallery on Conti Street in the Quarter. My grandmother sounded welcoming and even excited when I spoke with her on the phone, and plans were made for me to return to the city of my birth.

I made the long drive by myself in the red Chevy Corvair my father had bought for me for graduation. I arrived in the middle of the afternoon, having spent the night in a motel near Chattanooga, Tennessee. My grandmother was out, so I had time to examine my surroundings, including the bedroom I'd had since I was a little girl. It hadn't been changed at all. Then I began moving my suitcases and boxes from the trunk and backseat in the sweltering heat, having already waved away any help from Aunt Roseanne, who seemed to be suffering from the heat even more than I was. I had just come down to close the trunk after delivering my last load upstairs when I heard my name.

"Aimee?"

The front gate clanged and I turned in surprise, wiping at the perspiration on my forehead with the back of my hand. "Gary! You said you and your friends were spending the week after finals at River Song."

He gave me a reproachful look. "Like I would allow you to come back without a welcoming committee."

I stared at him, a grin tugging at my cheeks. He had grown in the past four years—and now seemed to have caught up to Wes's height and stood well over six feet. He'd also gained a much-needed twenty or so pounds, and it filled out his frame nicely. His hair was tousled, as if he had just climbed out of bed and thrown on his clothes. It was what separated him from his brother's always meticulous appearance, and I realized that it was one of the things that I loved about Gary.

I ran to him and threw myself into his outstretched arms, feeling them tighten around me as he swung me in a circle, and I was glad my grandmother wasn't home to see.

He kissed my neck and then pretended to gag. "Yuck! You're all sweaty. Couldn't you take a shower first before coming to see me?"

Our arms still encircled each other, and my face hurt from the wide grin. "It's so good to see you, Gary. It's been a long time." My hands slid down to his shoulders and biceps and squeezed. "You've gotten so big!"

He cocked an eyebrow. "Why, thank you, ma'am." His blue-gray eyes bored into mine, and I knew his feelings for me had not changed.

I gave him a playful punch in the shoulder. "You haven't changed a bit, Gary. Good."

He placed his hands on either side of my head and kissed me, his lips soft and lingering. We stared at each other in surprise, not sure what to say next.

A throat clearing turned our attention back to the gate. "Sorry to interrupt. Gary was supposed to be helping me move, and he disappeared." Wes smiled, his eyes dark. "Welcome home, Aimee."

Gary kept his arm draped over my shoulder. "I guess your balls really did fall off on your wedding night, Wes."

Wes raised his eyebrows. "What?"

Gary looked at me, and I grinned back at him, remembering my prepubescent insult on the levee the first time I had met Wes.

Gary hooked his thumb in the direction of their house, where a brand-new Dodge Pioneer station wagon sat in the driveway. "Come on, Wes—you're not even twenty-seven, and you're driving a station wagon. I'm just assuming you'd have to be pretty ball-less to let her talk you into something like that."

Wes gritted his teeth but kept smiling. "Sometimes it's easier to give in without an argument. The sooner you realize that, the happier you'll be."

Recalling what Wes had said, I asked, "Are you moving in with your dad?"

"Yeah—Lacy and I decided the apartment's really too small for a family of three. Dad invited us. I think he's a little lonely here without Mother. And Lacy's happy to have Ray Von here to help."

I tried not to cringe outwardly as Wes spoke Lacy's name. His wife. I forced a smile. "I'm sure Ray Von will enjoy having a young person in the house again."

Gary kissed the top of my head. "I'll come by and see you later. Got to help my big brother." Gary left my side and walked by Wes. As he passed, Wes cuffed him on the side of the head. "That's for calling me ball-less."

Gary shot a fist out and caught Wes on the arm. They faced each other with identical expressions of affection mixed with antagonism. I excused myself in an attempt to break the tension, noting how much of the little boy was still left in both men.

I cursed aloud when I saw the blue light flashing on the inside dashboard of the car behind me on St. Charles Avenue. I wondered how long it had been following me—it was hard to see out the rear window with balloons and flowers filling the backseat.

"You are so stupid," I said to the young woman in the mirror as I waited for the officer to get out of his car and approach. I had been saying that to her for weeks as I had thrown myself into settling in, my new job, and preparations for Gary's party. I'd been completely naive, believing that four years had changed my feelings for Wes, or would have prepared me for living next door to him, his wife, and his two-and-a-half-year-old son, Johnny.

I started at a tapping on my window. I opened it and looked at the man, wondering where I had seen him before. He wasn't wearing a uniform but held out a badge, and I recognized the name, Pierre Houlihan. He had been the detective in charge of the interrogation at the Guidrys' house after Mrs. Guidry disappeared.

"I wasn't speeding," I said.

"I know. That's not why I pulled you over."

I looked at my watch. Hardly enough time as it was to get everything ready for tonight. All that was left of my patience evaporated.

"Look, Detective. Would you mind just going ahead and giving me a ticket for whatever it is I'm guilty of? I really need to get going."

He tucked his almost nonexistent chin into his ample neck. "Do you think you're guilty of something, Miss Mercier?"

Panic seized me at the mention of my name. "You know who I am?"

He regarded me with light brown eyes. "Yes, I do."

I slowly reached over and flipped off my radio, my heart pumping faster. "Why were you following me?"

Lieutenant Houlihan opened my car door and asked me to step out. He stood back from the car and put his hands up, palms toward me, in a gesture of peace. We were near the intersection of St. Charles and Jackson and I prayed nobody I knew would see me. I had never known anybody to be asked to step outside of their car.

"Miss Mercier, I'm not here to intimidate you. I just wanted to talk to you alone—away from your friends and family. Just you and me in a little heart-to-heart." He regarded me steadily, and his eyes under his black fedora weren't unkind. "I didn't get a chance to talk to you again before you left, and I've been waiting a long time for you to return."

"Lieutenant Houlihan, if I had anything I wanted to say to you, I would have called. I still have your card. Somewhere."

He gave me a crooked grin. "Somewhere. Right." He paused and lit a cigarette, his movements casual but precise. "So, tell me. Where do you think Mrs. Guidry is?"

I crossed my arms in front of me, suddenly feeling cold despite the heat. "All I know is what everybody else knows. She ran off with another man." I looked away, not able to meet his eyes, and hoped he didn't notice. Wes had told me that she'd left with the artist who'd painted the portrait of her, but that his father didn't want anyone to know, as if that were somehow more of an embarrassment than her running off with a complete stranger. Maybe as far as society gossip was concerned, the unknown was always far more romantic than the facts.

Detective Houlihan took a long drag on his cigarette, studying the red car filled with balloons. "Can you think of any reason why Wes might lie to you—or to us—about his mother's whereabouts?"

His gaze turned back to me, cold and calculating this time. I rubbed my hands up and down my arms. "Of course not! Why would he lie about such a thing? He loved his mother. He would give anything to have her back."

Shrewd eyes stared into mine. "Anything?"

"He loved his mother," I said again. "Why are you asking all these questions? Why would you think Wes would lie?"

Lieutenant Houlihan flicked cigarette ash on the pavement. "It's what I do, Miss Mercier. Since Mrs. Guidry isn't here to tell me where she is, it's my job to find out and make sure that's where she wants to be." He looked at me closely.

I didn't flinch under his scrutiny. He stuck the cigarette into the corner of his mouth. "What about Mr. Guidry? Did he love his wife?"

I remembered Wes's parents, their odd relationship, and how I'd seen them in bed together at River Song. "Yes—he loved her. In a way."

He cocked an eyebrow. "In what way?"

My eyes refused to meet his. "She was delicate. I imagine it was difficult living with her. But I only saw them during the summers. I don't know what they were like the rest of the time."

He took another drag of the cigarette and dropped it on the ground, crushing it out under his heel. "Uh-huh. Well . . ." He fished in his pocket and pulled out a crumpled business card and held it out to me. Then he smiled and shook my hand.

"Miss Mercier, it's been a pleasure. And please send my regards to your father."

My hand stilled in his, then dropped to my side. "My father? How do you know my father?"

His fists formed little balls in his pockets. He looked at me, his expression grim. "I was one of the uniformed cops who responded to the emergency call when your mother was killed."

"Oh," I said, my voice small, suddenly smelling blood and feeling the weight of the darkness around me.

I must have looked odd, because I felt his hand on my arm, steadying me. His voice was solicitous. "Are you all right?"

"I'm fine. Can I get in my car now?"

Gently, he led me to my side of the car and held the door open. "Are you sure you're okay? I could drive you home."

"No, really—I'm fine. I just felt a little light-headed for a moment. It's probably the heat. I'm not used to it yet." My hands gripped the steering wheel, my knuckles white.

Lieutenant Houlihan crossed his arms on the car door and leaned in the window. "One more thing. Have you heard from Xavier Williams?"

"No, I haven't. Not since I left four years ago. Why?"

He examined his fingernails closely. "We'd like to question him, but nobody seems to know where he is." He raised his eyes to mine. "It's just odd that they would disappear at the same time."

My head pounded, keeping rhythm with the flashing blue police light. "I'm sorry I can't help you further, Lieutenant Houlihan. I'll be sure and call you if I think of anything." I waved his business card in front of him.

"Yes, you do that." He removed his arms and I raised the window, turning the ignition simultaneously with the other hand. My tires squealed as I pulled out into traffic and headed home.

Gary and I sat next to each other on the piano bench, sipping punch and watching people. Soft music from a live band drifted through every room, only the resonant beat audible over the din of people talking. I tried eating some of the hors d'oeuvres, but everything tasted bland. I found myself nibbling on crackers as I sat at the bench, crumbs scattered on my black dress. Gary had tried to get me to pick a more colorful hue, but I was drawn to black. When I'd stepped out of the dressing room at Maison Blanche, Gary whistled, and I knew that I had found the perfect dress.

Laughter erupted from a corner of the room and we both turned to see Lacy, stunning in an ice blue sheath dress, her figure as slim as it had been before she had Johnny. My gaze traveled over her shoulder and I saw Wes, and our eyes met. I looked away, whispered an excuse to Gary, and left for the sanctuary of the kitchen.

Trays of food brought by the caterers sat on the counter by the oven. Piles of plates, scraped clean, towered in stacked rows. I sat at the kitchen table, still clutching my glass of punch, and watched as two waiters scurried in with more plates and put another platter in the oven to heat. They slid out the door without a word, leaving me in silence, the low roar of people mercifully blocked by the swinging door.

I shut my eyes, listening to the distant hum of voices until I detected an acrid odor creeping through the closed oven. I turned my head to see a coil of dark smoke eking its way out of both sides of the door. I popped out of my chair, rushed to the door, and opened it. I coughed as my face and shoulders were immediately engulfed in the smoke. Without thinking, I stuck my hand into the mayhem and grabbed the tray to yank it out. As my fingers made contact with the metal, I screamed—but didn't let go. It was as if I didn't at first realize what was burning my fingers.

I finally let go of the tray, dropping it on the open lid of the oven door and hearing it clatter onto the ceramic floor, the puffed pastries somersaulting like fat cats. My eyes smarted from the smoke and the pain, and my mouth opened in a silent wail. The kitchen door swung open and Wes stood in the doorway, tall, dark, and like an avenging angel with the oven smoke swirling around him.

"Aimee! What happened?"

I looked at my hand, now red and shiny and reminding me of a tomato without its peel. I clutched the wrist with the other hand and held it up to him.

He rushed into the room, the door swinging shut behind him and fanning the smoke in fat puffs toward us. I coughed and leaned against the counter, my hand throbbing. He grabbed me and spun me around to face the sink. He stood behind me as he turned on the cold-water tap and then, holding my hand in his, held it under the cool stream.

I flinched as the water hit my wound, and pulled my hand away. Gently, Wes guided it back under the water, using his other hand to soften the flow by splaying his fingers under the tap and then letting the runoff drip from his hand to mine.

I sagged against him and raised my eyes to the window over the sink. I saw the reflection of his eyes as we regarded each other. His face was curved and distorted from the old glass, only a ghost of the real man. I wanted to reach and touch the man in the glass, but knew he would be cold and lifeless against my pliant fingers, his warm flesh unobtainable to me.

"It hurts." My voice was barely more than a whisper.

"I know," he said, and kissed the top of my head.

I closed my eyes and leaned into him, listening to the hollow sound of water hitting the metal sink.

Eventually, he shut off the tap and led me back to the kitchen table. Then he grabbed a handful of ice from a bucket left behind by one of the waiters and wrapped it in a kitchen towel. Pulling out a chair, he sat in front of me and held the ice pack on my hand, his large hands cupping mine.

"I'm sorry." His voice cracked and I found I couldn't look at him.

"It's not your fault. I was just careless. . . ."

His hand squeezed mine, forcing me to look up.

"That's not what I mean—and you know it."

I nodded. "I know." I swallowed, looking for words. "I can't stop the way I feel about you, Wes. I try, but I don't think it will ever stop."

He started to speak, but I raised my other hand to silence him. "What hurts me most is that you were able to let me go so easily."

His eyes rounded in shock. "Easily? My God, Aimee, it was the hardest thing I've ever had to do." He leaned toward me, his hands now covering mine. "I'll never get over you, Aimee. It will always be you."

I tried to pull away from him, remembering the hurt and betrayal, his sudden and inexplicable change of heart. "Then tell me why. Then maybe I could make my head and heart understand."

He was silent for a moment. "You need to know about Gary."

All was quiet in the kitchen as we contemplated each other, the sounds of the party distant and inconsequential to us. "What about him?"

"Gary's not as healthy as he would like us to think. His heart's not very strong." He squeezed my hands. "He loves you, Aimee. Do you think you could try to love him back?"

Before I could answer, the door swung open and Lacy breezed into the kitchen, followed closely by Gary. Gary held the door with his arm as Lacy stood, icy and blue, with her arms folded over her chest.

She looked at me but spoke to Wes. "You've been gone a long time." She clenched her lips, her bright blue gaze moving from Wes, then to me, and then to my swaddled hand, still held in his.

"She had an accident." Wes gently moved my hand to my lap and slid his chair back. Without a word, he stood and moved to Lacy as Gary stepped forward and sat down where Wes had been. He picked up my hand and unwrapped the towel. Ice slipped out and hit the floor, dancing on the ceramic tiles.

Lacy and Wes left the room but neither Gary nor I turned to look or say good-bye.

Gary spoke softly. "Are you okay?"

My lip trembled as I looked up at Gary. "Don't you dare be nice to me now—I'll start crying again."

"Not a problem," he said, moving his chair closer so he could lean back while still holding my hand. "Your boobs are too big and are practically falling out of your dress."

I sat up, shocked. "What?"

He grinned his most endearing grin. "Don't feel like crying anymore, do you?"

I leaned forward and hit him on the shoulder with my good hand. Then I sat back in the chair again, suddenly self-conscious. "Are they really?"

His grin this time was nothing but lascivious. "Oh, yes. But you'll never hear any complaints from me."

I felt my face break into a smile. "I don't know if I should slap you or hug you."

He put his hand to his forehead. "Oh, baby—how 'bout both?"

I laughed outright now, relieved at the sound. I wasn't sure I still remembered how.

My grandmother entered the kitchen, her brows knitted together. Her face uncreased as she spotted me. "There you are, Aimee. I've been wondering where you had disappeared to. You've been neglecting your hostessing duties."

She paused as she regarded my wrapped hand. "What happened?"

"I burned it." I showed my palm to her, the side of it now covered in a thin, watery blister.

Gary stood. "She's not feeling well. I thought I might walk her home now, if you think it's okay."

Grandmother looked at me, sympathy in her eyes. "Certainly. You do look tired. I'm sure Gary's father won't mind if I take over." She bent and kissed me on the cheek, then left, the sound of her sensible heels strong and purposeful.

We exited through the back door and walked slowly to my grand-mother's house, pausing on the garden path as a large palmetto bug skittered by in front of us. I had a great aversion for the giant insects and Gary usually teased me about it. But not tonight.

Mrs. Guidry's garden wilted with neglect. The wind rustled the dead leaves on the vines as they clung tenaciously to dried stalks. Shriveled brown blooms bowed toward the tired grass, returning to the earth from which they had sprung. I shut the gate behind me, staring at the lifeless fountain, the little boy still and alone in the wrecked garden. My hand lingered on the wrought iron as I recalled the woman who had once given this place life and wondered if the new life she had found was as barren now as the garden she had left behind.

"Sit with me for a while." I indicated the swing on my grandmother's wraparound porch. Gary held it still for me as I sat and then he joined me in the dim glow of the porch light. We swung in silence, listening to the night sounds of the city and the creak of the chain. A frog croaked from the Creole box shrubs, hopefully dining on fat, juicy mosquitoes. The scents of late-summer oleander and phlox hung in the humid air, enfolding us like a blanket. A storm-borne breeze carried with it the smell of rain. It picked up the leaves of the magnolia tree, the streetlight creating moving shadows under the long branches.

There was something about the moving shadows that made me think of my mother, a deep memory that stayed hidden and wouldn't be dislodged. I turned to Gary. "Do you still think about your mother?"

He clenched his hands, and then relaxed them. "Yeah. I do. All the time. I didn't tell you, but a few years ago I hired a private investigator to find her. I just couldn't believe she would go off like that and never contact us again. Wes and my father were furious when they found out—it's like they wanted to write her out of our lives just like she had written us out of hers. Not that it matters anyway. The PI never found anything."

"Did he interview Abe Holt?"

"I never talked to the PI about it, but Wes did. Said most PIs were in it for the money, so he took over the investigation because he knew how to deal with him. Wes told me the PI interviewed Mr. Holt, and that Mr. Holt admitted to having an affair with my mother, but that she'd abandoned him shortly after they left New Orleans and he hadn't heard from her since." Gary clenched his jaw. "I don't blame her, you know. Life with my father would have sent even a saint astray. I just don't understand why she would never write to me or call me."

I reached my good hand toward Gary's, and rested it on his. "I'm sorry." He turned his head slightly but didn't move. "How is your heart?"

He didn't look at me. "Besides being broken in two, you mean?"

I elbowed him in the arm. "I'm being serious, Gary."

"I know. So am I."

We faced each other. The light illuminated him from behind, casting his face in shadow. "What do the doctors say about your heart?"

He shrugged. "Basically nothing. I need to take care of myself and not overexert. Take my medicine. That sort of thing. I could live forever."

"Could you have another heart attack?"

He nodded. "Yeah. If things really go wacky again, my heart rhythm can be thrown off and I could have another attack." He shook his head. "But I won't. I'm really being careful—taking my medication, exercising, really watching out for myself. I'm trying to keep my emotions in check—things like that."

A mosquito landed on my forearm and I slapped at it, creating a dark smear on my skin. "I'm glad. And you certainly seem healthier than I've ever seen you."

"That's because I am. Med school will be hard on me, but I can do it. And I really want to be a doctor. I figure I've been around hospitals all my life—why not?"

I smiled, imagining Gary in a white coat and stethoscope. "Your handwriting is certainly bad enough to qualify you."

He bumped against me with his shoulder. "You're one to talk. I don't think your handwriting's changed since kindergarten."

I opened my mouth to retort, when I noticed a thick shadow across the street. "Shh," I whispered.

Gary followed the direction of my gaze just as the shadow disappeared. It had moved so quickly I was sure it had been just my imagination.

"What is it?"

I sat back. "I thought I saw somebody—but it was nothing. Probably a stray cat."

Gary had moved up to the edge of the swing, his feet firmly planted on the floor of the porch. I had slid up to the edge, too, and our thighs were pressed against each other. I turned my head to say something and realized his face was only an inch from mine. We stared at each other for several long moments, not saying anything. And then his lips touched mine, soft and gentle. His kiss didn't make my heart beat faster, or my blood heat, but there was something comforting there, something warm and familiar. Something mine.

His hand touched my good hand, and I realized that his fingers were pressing against the Cracker Jack ring he'd given me four years before. "Marry me, Aimee. Let me love you the way you deserve to be."

I thought of Wes, and how he was gone from me forever, and Ray Von's words about the different shades of love. I did love Gary, maybe even enough to make me forget Wes. And maybe even enough to make Gary happy. I kissed him back, hard, and his arms went around me, and my decision settled on me as tight and fitted as the lid on a firefly jar.

"I will, Gary. I'll marry you." The words didn't scare me like I thought they would but soothed me instead like a mother's hand on a fevered forehead.

"I love you, Aimee."

I smiled back at him. "I love you, too, Gary." I reached my arms around him, squeezing tightly. "I love you, too."

We stayed on the porch swing for a long time, our hands clasped, not speaking, watching as partygoers left the house next door and heavy clouds moved languidly over the moon, hiding it from view. Eventually, Gary stood, realizing as guest of honor he should probably be there to say good-bye to his guests. He kissed me one more time, then left.

Eventually, I stood and let myself into my grandmother's house. As I shut the door, I looked through the leaded glass window and saw the empty swing swaying in the wind and the first raindrops beginning to darken the deserted walkway.

CHAPTER 21

Their understanding
Begins to swell, and the approaching tide
Will shortly fill the reasonable shores
That now lie foul and muddy.

—WILLIAM SHAKESPEARE

Julie

I stood in the quiet foyer of the house on First Street and put my over-night bag beside me on the rug. It was a Wednesday evening in late February and I was tardy for my meeting with Trey because I'd had to leave Beau at Carol Sue's. He and Charlie had been invited to the same birthday party the following day, and Carol Sue had errands to run in New Orleans and could bring him back afterward.

Beau had hugged me good-bye, then run off to play, while I'd just stood in Carol Sue's kitchen, devastated. I'd slid Monica's red hat from my purse and placed it on the kitchen counter in case he needed it, then made sure Carol Sue had all the phone numbers she might need, in-cluding poison control and both the Louisiana and Mississippi highway patrols. I'd been in the process of looking up the phone number for the coast guard when Carol Sue opened the door and asked me to leave.

"In here," Trey called from the living room.

Trey and Aimee sat opposite each other on the two sofas, each holding a drink. Standing there amid the paintings and antiques I recalled that this was the room where a young Aimee had first met Gary and Mrs. Guidry. I wondered if everything had remained the same in the elegant room after all those years, and if Aimee remembered it, too.

"Sorry I'm late. I had to drop Beau off at Carol Sue's."

"We know. Carol Sue called to let us know, and to make sure I had a drink waiting for you when you arrived." Trey stood and moved to a brass-and-glass drink cart, where a bottle of wine stood open. "Wine okay or would you prefer something stronger?"

"Wine is fine," I said, moving toward the sofas. Aimee had moved toward the center of hers, so I had no choice but to sit on the one Trey had just vacated. He returned to the sofa and handed me my glass before sitting down beside me, his knee touching mine. I felt suddenly very aware of his being so close.

I took a sip and tried to relax. "The Hardie board arrived today for River Song. It's even earlier than everyone anticipated, so that's good. They should be able to start siding the house in the next week or so." I took another sip, if only to stop my rambling. "I wasn't really happy about not using real wood, but I have to admit that this stuff looks like the real thing. And it's made of cement, so bugs won't like it, and neither will water."

Trey leaned back against the cushions and stretched one long arm across the back, and I could feel his fingertips brush my shoulder. "And Hardie board won't splinter in a storm or need painting every year. Something any Biloxi resident could appreciate."

I wondered if he included me in the "Biloxi resident" category, and it surprised me that I would care. I still used my New York driver's license, and all of my mail was being forwarded to a post office box in New Orleans. But I'd been building a house in Biloxi for nearly five months while working at the Ohr museum and renting another house there, and I felt as if I'd earned the right to be referred to as a resident. Ever since my trip to Deer Island with Trey, I'd felt a softening around the heart as I exited the interstate onto the peninsula and drove along Beach Boulevard, seeing the boats at the marina and the smudge of the barrier islands in the distance, thinking about my dolphin as it swam in the sound. I'd found myself several times standing on the shore, searching for the sign of a telltale fin or ripple against the water's surface.

I cleared my throat. "Well, I'm glad it looks like wood, and I'm glad we did white again with black shutters—and not just because that's how it used to look. It's just so clean and crisp." I closed my eyes, remembering my early mornings and evenings at the building site. "The house will be a beautiful canvas for the light from sunsets and sunrises." I opened my eyes to see both Aimee and Trey watching me.

Aimee looked down into her glass, a small smile brightening her face. "Monica used to say that. She said River Song inspired her as an artist because of the way the light played with it."

A clock chimed, reminding me that it was past dinnertime. I knew it was Kathy Wolf's day off and didn't smell anything cooking. I set my half-empty glass on the table, afraid to drink more on an empty stomach. "I haven't eaten, and if either one of you is interested, I could see what I can whip up for dinner."

Aimee and Trey glanced at each other, and it occurred to me that they were probably talking about me before I'd arrived. "What's wrong?"

Trey sat forward in his seat and placed his glass next to mine. "Nothing's wrong. I got a call from my father today and he wants to meet you."

"Johnny?" I couldn't think of anything else to call him, because of Aimee's stories, although I realized he was a man in his fifties by now and I should probably be referring to him as Mr. Guidry. "Why does he want to meet me?"

Again, Aimee and Trey exchanged a glance. "He wants to thank you for bringing Beau home. But I think his phone call was prompted by my poking around in those old police files. Somebody must have called him."

"But why?" I asked, confused.

"Because he's got a lot of connections, and old acquaintances feel obliged to let him know when somebody's poking around in anything related to his family. Even if that person is his son," he added, as if anticipating my next question. He took a sip of his drink and I waited impatiently for him to continue.

Instead, Aimee spoke. "Trey called an old friend in the NOPD to gain access to my mother's case file as well as Caroline's. Apparently, all the old files were lost in Katrina. What wasn't ruined by the wind and water had to be destroyed later, because they were contaminated and held a potential health risk."

"So there's nothing left?"

She shook her head. "No. Nothing is left of anything that wasn't stored electronically, and those weren't."

"Then why would Johnny be concerned enough to call if there was nothing for Trey to see in the files?"

"That's exactly what I wondered, too, which is why I agreed that we'd meet with him tonight, and we can ask him in person. Unless you have other plans."

His smile was so smug that I almost lied and said I did. But cruising the Internet's missing persons files probably didn't meet anybody's definition of "other plans." I stood. "Fine. Just let me clean up and put a dress on."

Trey stood, too, and his face was split in a huge grin. "Actually, where we're heading, you might want to throw on your oldest jeans." He didn't elaborate.

"Then let me carry my bag upstairs and I'll be right back. And can we grab something to eat where we're heading?"

"Not at Miss Mae's. It's cash only and no food, but it's got the cheapest beer in town. We can swing by Domilise's for some po'-boys first."

"I'll let you explain what that is on our way over. I'm so hungry right now that as long as it's food I'll eat it. I'll be right back." I ran upstairs and returned quickly, then climbed into Trey's truck.

He glanced at my clean blouse and shook his head. "I hope those sleeves roll up, because eating a fried shrimp po'-boy can get messy."

"So what's a po'-boy?"

"I guess you'd call it a submarine sandwich, but they're much better down here, mostly because we like to put fried things in them. Just make sure you order yours dressed—that's lettuce, tomato, and mayonnaise—but if you want pickle and onion, you have to ask."

I settled back into my seat. "How about I let you order for me?"

"Will do." He shook his head, smiling to himself.

"What is it?"

"I feel like I'm in law school again. There's nothing cheaper than dinner at Domilise's and drinks afterward at Miss Mae's. Those are some good memories."

"I think you just called me a cheap date."

He pulled the truck in to park on a side street and I found myself blushing as I realized that I'd just defined our outing as a date. "For the record, I did not. Remind me to take you to Galatoires for lunch or Commander's for dinner to make it up to you."

I scrambled out of the truck before he could come around to let me out. "That's all right. I probably don't have anything to wear to those kinds of places."

We were stopped under a hand-painted sign that read, DOMILISE'S PO'-BOYS & BAR, and had a little fleur-de-lis in the bottom left corner. Trey looked down at me, frowning. "Before I met you, I'd never met a woman who wasn't at least an occasional shopper. But I've never once seen you with a shopping bag, except for something for Beau. You don't like our shops here?"

I stood still for a moment, without words. Monica had noticed it, too, but had never asked why. It was understood that it was something I never looked at too closely, like the reasons I'd kept Chelsea's hairbrush and why I accumulated collections of things that held no real meaning to me.

He put his hand on the restaurant door. "Last time I checked, Julie, it was okay to ask for more than one thing. It's okay to want."

A young couple, holding hands, pushed through the door, making Trey and me step back. He placed his hand on my back, and for a brief moment I wanted to lean into him, to thank him for understanding that part of me, for making me feel less alone. Instead I stepped forward and led him into the restaurant.

The walls were wood-paneled, the plates paper, the kitschy decor of photographs and handwritten menu on the wall definitely homegrown, and I don't think I'd ever tasted anything so good. We washed our po'-boys down with Barq's root beer, something I'd never tasted before but definitely something I could get used to. I sat in a satisfied stupor, hoping Trey would let me stay where I was for a little longer.

He stood but held a hand up. "Hang on—I want to get a to-go bag for my dad. He doesn't always remember to eat."

As we left the restaurant, a rectangular neon sign over the doorway of a squat brick house across the street caught my attention. The sign read, MADAME AVERY'S PALM READING, but the "a," "m," and "e" weren't lit, so it read, MAD AVERY. I laughed and Trey followed my gaze.

"Ever had your palm read?"

I grimaced. "Once, at the state fair. I didn't want to, but Chelsea did, so we went together. The woman told us that we would both lead long, happy lives and have lots of children." I laughed despite myself. "I think we actually believed her." I didn't tell him that for a long time after Chelsea was gone I'd wondered if we had somehow made ourselves vulnerable to what came later, that being assured of good fortune had made us careless.

Trey glanced at his watch. "Come on. It's still early, and my dad needs to get a few drinks in him first to take the edge off. Let's go see Madame Avery."

I resisted. "It's just a scam, Trey. She'll just take our money and make something up."

"I know. But it will be frivolous and fun—two words I think are missing from your vocabulary."

"And don't forget shopping," I added as he took my hand and pulled me across the street until we stopped at the doorstep under a short overhang. "You're paying."

He knocked on the door, then smiled down at me. It was like looking at Monica's face with the expression she wore before showing me a new painting. But her eyes had always held uncertainty and trepidation, whereas Trey's showed only confidence and conviction. I wanted to know how he'd managed to hang on to both after the events of the last five years.

An extremely tall woman with very dark skin and amber hair opened the door. She wore a smart skirt and blouse right out of a Talbots shop window, and when she smiled she revealed even, white teeth. She didn't look at all like the palm reader from the carnival.

"Are y'all here for a palm reading?"

Trey propelled me in front of him. "Yes. She is."

I gave him an annoyed look as Madame Avery led us through a tiny, dark kitchen into an even darker room in the back of the house. It looked like a normal office except there were blankets over the windows, and instead of a bed there was a card table in the center of the room covered in a white tablecloth, with two folding chairs pulled up on one side and a single chair facing them. Unlike my last palm-reading experience, there was no crystal ball or silk tablecloth or cardboard stars hanging from the ceiling. And Madame Avery herself wasn't even wearing multiple earrings and bracelets, so nothing jangled as she walked.

She flipped the switch that lit a dim ceiling fixture over the table, then motioned for us to sit down before sitting across from us. She smiled and looked so normal that I could have been in a doctor's office or job interview. "It's twenty-five dollars for a reading," she said.

I gave Trey a knowing look and waited for him to pull out the cash from his wallet and slide it over.

Madame Avery placed the money in the corner of the table, then took my hand, her own feeling like warm leather. She straightened my fingers and stared at my palm and I waited for her to start murmuring gibberish. Instead, she used a short fingernail to trace a line bisecting my palm. "This is your lifeline. It's long and unbroken, meaning you'll have a very long life."

I shot an I-told-you-so look over at Trey, but he just widened his eyes at me. I looked back at Madame Avery. "And I'll have lots of children."

Her dark eyes met mine over our hands, but she just smiled before returning to examine my palm. She frowned, a line creasing between her eyebrows, and I rolled my eyes as I waited for her to tell me about a dark stranger.

When she spoke, her voice was so quiet that I had to lean forward to hear her. "I see a journey, a wandering path that doubles back on itself, bringing you to the beginning again." She shook her head. "You have been searching a long time." She lifted my palm as she sat back, holding it up so the overhead light could illuminate the pale pink skin. Slowly she raised her eyes to mine again. "You are close to finding what you seek." She leaned forward, our foreheads nearly touching. "If you haven't already."

I swallowed a lump in my throat, hoping no one else could hear it in the quiet room.

"Your hand is always open to give." She took my hand in both of hers and slowly curled my fingers until they formed a fist. "You must remember to receive, too." She squeezed my hand between hers before placing it gently on the table, then sliding back her chair. "That's all you need to know. Thank you for coming. And tell your friends."

I wanted to make a glib statement about how twenty-five dollars for five minutes seemed a bit steep, but I couldn't push the words from my lips. Trey touched my shoulder, reminding me to move. I stood, not bothering to slide my chair under the table, and quickly left the room, eager to leave and escape from Madame Avery's cool, watchful eyes. I let Trey say good-bye as I stood outside in the cool evening air, taking deep, gulping breaths as if I'd just run a mile.

"You all right?" he asked.

I nodded. "It was just stuffy in there, that's all."

He regarded me closely, his eyes warm, but said nothing. "Come on; let's go meet my dad."

I walked quickly toward the truck, eager to leave Madame Avery and her black eyes as far behind me as possible.

As we drove down Annunciation Street, I saw an old lady walking three poodles, each one with fur dyed in the Mardi Gras colors of green, gold, and purple. I turned to Trey. "What was the name of your dog?"

"How'd you know I had one?"

"I saw his framed picture in one of your storage boxes and a leash in Monica's. A yellow Lab, I think?"

Trey nodded. "His name was Jax—after Jax beer, which used to be brewed here. First and only dog we ever had. Aimee gave him to Monica and me, but he had to live with Aimee, because our mother didn't want dog hair everywhere."

"And you never got another one?"

"No. Monica was too devastated when Jax died, so Aimee and I decided to wait before getting another dog. But then Monica left, and I guess I was waiting for her to come home so we could pick out one together."

We were silent for a while, listening to Marc Broussard on the radio singing about going home to the delta. "I'm thinking of getting a dog for Beau. Charlie has two cats and Beau's always talking about them.

But there's something about boys and dogs that I think goes together. What do you think?"

His cheek creased as he grinned. "I think it's a great idea. I was actually going to bring it up, but then changed my mind."

I looked at him in the dark cab of the truck, passing streetlights illuminating his face in fits and starts. "Why did you change your mind?"

He shrugged but didn't look at me. "Because I thought it would make it seem like you were putting down roots, and I know that's not what you want."

I wasn't sure what to say to that. It wasn't that he was right, but, I realized, it wasn't that he was completely wrong, either. "Dogs are pretty portable," I said.

"So are little boys," Trey added quietly as he pulled into a spot at the curb on Camp Street. We walked a block to the corner of Magazine and Napoleon and stood in front of a corner building with The Club Miss Mae's lit in neon orange over the front door. It was only eight o'clock at night, but there was a young man wearing topsiders and a polo shirt lying on the sidewalk against the building, a bottle of Dixie Beer cradled in his arms.

"Nice place," I said.

"It can be," Trey replied as he held the door open. "Especially if you're on a budget and don't want to spend more than a buck fifty on a drink. Or if you have a hankering for a drink at four o'clock in the morning. Miss Mae's is open twenty-four-seven—which is nice if you're in law school and studying until three in the morning."

"You come here often, then?" I asked as I stepped into the dark interior, the air heavy with cigarette smoke and stale beer.

"Not anymore," he said curtly, and I looked up at him, then followed his gaze to the long bar, where a man in a leather jacket sat with his forearms on the bar. A glass filled with amber liquid sat in front of him, two empty shot glasses next to it.

We walked toward the bar as my eyes adjusted to the dark, taking in the requisite neon bar signs on the walls, the Foosball table, a jukebox.

The place was nearly empty, and I thought it had less to do with it being a weeknight and more to do with the relatively early hour.

We stopped behind the man at the bar. "Dad?" Trey touched the man's shoulder.

He turned around and his face was pale under the fluorescent lights, his dark hair threaded with gray. He smiled with an achingly familiar smile as he slid from his chair and stumbled. Trey grabbed his arm and held him steady before the man embraced him tightly. They were about the same height and build, yet it didn't seem like Trey had any problem propping up the older man.

Johnny turned to me, his face so much like Trey's but fuller, the skin creased with lines caused by more than just age. "And you must be the girl who brought Monica's little boy to us."

"This is Julie Holt, Dad. Remember? She's Beau's guardian, and part owner of River Song."

He nodded as Trey helped him back on his stool.

I reached out my hand to shake his. "It's nice to meet you, Mr. Guidry."

He took my hand, but instead of shaking it, he raised it to his lips and kissed the back of it. The three-day stubble on his chin tickled my skin, and his blue eyes sparkled as they regarded me. "Call me Johnny. Everybody does." Still holding my hand, he looked over at Trey. "You didn't tell me she was such a looker."

Trey took my arm, forcing his father to release his grasp, and settled me onto another stool. He dumped the to-go bag from Domilise's on the bar. "Brought you dinner, since I figured you hadn't gotten around to eating yet. This might soak up some of the booze."

Johnny eyed him with amusement. "I hope it's none of that fried crap. You know how health-conscious I am."

Ignoring him, Trey asked, "How's Deidre?" He pulled a third stool between me and his father and sat down.

Johnny waved his hand, a gold ring on his pinkie. "No idea. Haven't seen her in a few months. I'm seeing Clarissa now."

Trey raised his eyebrows. "Well, if Deidre doesn't mind you dating other women while you're still married to her, stay married. It would be a lot cheaper than another divorce."

Johnny lifted his glass. "Amen to that," he said, and took another sip.

I looked on in stunned fascination. Trey and Monica were nothing like their father, except for the thick, wavy hair and straight noses. But as I watched Trey and Johnny interact, it occurred to me how much influence Aimee Guidry had had over her grandchildren, and how strong she must have been for Trey and Monica to have turned out as well as they had.

A bartender approached, and Trey ordered a Dixie beer for both of us, despite my request for a Coke. He leaned over and, speaking quietly, said, "You'll need the beer when talking with Johnny. I always do."

I raised my eyebrows, but let it go at that. Johnny lifted a finger and the bartender placed an ice cube in his glass, then added two shots from a Jack Daniel's bottle.

Trey took a swig from his beer. Plopping the bottle down on the scarred wooden bar top, he said, "So, Dad, what did you want to tell me in person that you couldn't tell me over the phone?"

"Nothing much. I just wanted to meet the beautiful Julie. The way you and Aimee have described her to me, I thought she'd have a halo and wings." He looked up at me and winked. "Just didn't expect her to be so gorgeous, too."

Trey leaned forward to block Johnny's view of me. "That's enough, Dad. Why don't you tell me why you felt the need to drag us here on a Wednesday night?"

Trey sat back on his stool as Johnny took a small sip from his glass. "Just wanted to know why you've developed this sudden interest in old family history, that's all."

I could tell from the belligerent look on Trey's face that I was going to need to intervene. Placing my hand on Trey's arm, I interjected,

"Because Aimee, Trey, and I think that there might be some connection between Monica's running away and Caroline Guidry's disappearance. We know that Monica had done some research into the family of the artist who'd painted the portrait before she left. The artist, Abe Holt, was my great-grandfather. The rumor after Caroline disappeared was that she ran away with Abe Holt."

He nodded slowly, his bloodshot eyes sharp. "But what about Aimee's mother? Why would you be digging that up? It's got nothing to do with Monica."

"Probably not," Trey said. "But while we were trying to find police records it made sense to see if we could turn up anything. For Aimee. She's lived all these years not knowing, and I think it would give her some peace to finally have an answer."

Johnny nursed his glass for a long moment. "Why are you doing this? None of this will bring Monica back."

"No," I said. "It won't. But we feel we need to know, to understand what drove her away. Beau will want to know when he's older."

After a long moment, Trey spoke quietly. "Aimee and I need to know that it wasn't because of us. It's the thing that haunts us both, not knowing that. To constantly wonder." Trey slid his beer across the bar and signaled to the bartender to bring another.

Johnny slammed his drink down. "And if you know, then you'll know who to blame, and what good will that do?"

Trey shook his head. "I'm not looking for blame, only understanding. I loved my sister, and she was trying to tell us something with her disappearance. Whatever her reasons, I don't blame her or anyone else. I want to know so I can say good-bye to her."

I looked at Trey as if seeing him for the first time, his skin smooth under the bar lighting, his eyes distant, and I had the strange urge to put my arms around him, to lay my head on his shoulder to show him that I understood the need to know, to understand that in the vagaries of the world there are times when there is no blame, and in its stead only circumstances and unexplained absences. I suspected that he'd known this all along; it was how he got out of bed each morning.

"So what did you find out from the old records?" Johnny asked.

Trey began peeling the label off of his beer, reminding me to take a sip of my own. "The same thing you probably already found out. That everything was lost during Katrina."

Johnny nodded, but didn't look at either of us. "So that's that."

"Not exactly." Trey studied his fingers as they slowly and methodically pulled strips off the Dixie beer label. "I spoke to Mom today—her twice-yearly phone call to see how I'm doing—and we got to talking about how I had been trying to find those old case files. And she said the most interesting thing to me."

I frowned. He hadn't mentioned any of this to me, and I wondered if it was because he wanted to surprise his father, or because he hadn't wanted me to know in advance.

"Careful what you say, son. Family is family."

"I know. Which is why I need to bring this out in the open."

"Do you want me to leave?" I asked, starting to stand.

Trey put his hand on my arm. "No. You're Beau's guardian and part of this family now. Unless you want to leave."

I settled back on my stool, my eyes steady as they met his. "No."

I watched as a tic began in Johnny's jaw, just like Trey when he was angry. I looked back at my warm beer bottle, trying not to laugh at the irony.

"So what was so interesting?" Johnny asked.

"Mom told me that after Monica left, you went digging into those same case files, and you found that Aimee's mother's file was missing completely and Caroline's file held only a couple of pages of noninformation. Like somebody had been messing around with them."

Johnny drained his glass. "What about it?"

"So it made me wonder. Why would Monica's disappearance send you into those files?"

"Same reason as you, I guess. I was curious. My only daughter had run away and took that painting of my grandmother. I thought there might be a connection."

Trey and I exchanged a glance. "We were interested because of Julie's connection to the artist. We didn't think there was a connection with Caroline's disappearance. Why would you?"

Johnny shook his head slowly. "Don't do this, Trey. You should let the dead rest."

"Why would you make that connection?" Trey demanded again.

Johnny swiveled on his stool and glared at his son. "Because when my mother died, she told me something."

"Lacy?" I asked.

"Yes. My beautiful mother, Lacy. Did you know that I was in the car wreck that killed her?"

I shook my head. Trey and Monica never talked about Lacy. I hadn't even known she was dead.

Johnny continued. "I wasn't driving. She was. Everybody thought she'd died right away, but she didn't."

Trey tensed on the stool next to me, his hand squeezing his empty beer bottle.

"She lived long enough to tell me something I didn't want to hear."

A loud group of college students burst into the room, but their laughter seemed distant and faint, as if the only voice in the room were Johnny's.

"What did she say, Dad?"

Johnny looked at us, one after the other. "She told me to ask my father to tell me why he'd married her, to tell me everything. That all the secrets were like a curse on the family."

"And did you?" I asked quietly.

He shook his head. "No." His gaze met mine, his eyes piercing. "Have you ever wanted the truth so badly that it blinds you to everything else?"

Air left my lungs as Trey's hand crept into mine and stayed there.

Johnny continued. "I'm not that strong. I wanted to know, but I was afraid of what I might find." He raised his glass. "Good ol' JD made it so that I wouldn't have to think about it."

"Until Monica left."

He nodded. "Yes. My only daughter ran away without saying good-bye, and it forced me to remember what my mother had said about secrets."

"I don't understand," I said.

Trey stood, bringing me up with him. "So after you found out about the missing files, you went to see Wes. To finally ask him what Lacy was talking about."

"Yep. And that's when I saw that the portrait was missing, and I figured that whatever I was trying to find out, Monica had figured out on her own. But it was too late to ask Wes about it."

"Because he'd had his stroke," said Trey.

Johnny nodded. "And then the dementia. Sometimes I wonder how lucky he is not to have to remember any of the bad stuff."

I stared at him, confused. "Wes? Wes is who Aimee visits in the nursing home?"

Johnny looked at me oddly. "Why wouldn't she? He's her husband."

I shook my head, not understanding. "But I thought she married Gary."

Trey put his hand on my arm. "Hold on, Julie. Aimee will want to tell you herself."

I glanced between the two men, suddenly eager to leave.

As if reading my mind, Johnny stood, gripping the counter tightly to hold himself steady. He looked at Trey. "You're a smart boy, son; I'm sure you can take it from here. There's just one more question you need to ask yourself."

Trey stared back at his father, a small crease between his eyebrows. Finally, he said, "Wes was the last one to look at those files. Aimee told us that he'd gone to see if he could find anything and he said there wasn't any new information. He didn't mention that one was missing.

He must have been the one to take them. But why? And what did Monica discover?"

Johnny tapped his forefinger against his forehead, his gold pinkie ring twinkling. "Just like your old man, Trey." Then he fell back onto his stool and signaled the bartender again. But I saw something in his eyes, something sad and desolate that belied his offhandedness. It made me think of Monica and how well she'd hidden her hurt from me, and it was suddenly obvious from whom she'd learned how.

"I'll see you around, Dad." Trey turned to leave.

"Good-bye, Johnny," I said, still focused on his sad eyes, Trey already tugging me toward the door. We'd almost reached it when I stopped. "Just a second." I dug into my wallet and pulled out Beau's preschool photograph, the one of him with the Thomas the Tank Engine sweater his mother had found in a consignment shop. I placed it on the bar and slid it over to Johnny.

"This is Beau. You should come see him. He looks just like Monica and I think he's the most wonderful little boy in the world. He's sweet, and smart, and funny. . . ." I stopped, realizing I sounded like a used-car salesman. "You should come see him," I finished.

He picked up the photograph and blinked rapidly as he looked at his grandson for the first time. I touched his forearm, wishing there were more I could say.

"I loved my daughter, Julie. Despite what you might think or have heard, I loved her. And I will mourn her until the day I die." He looked up at me, his eyes wet. "Can I keep this?"

"Of course." I squeezed his hand, then left, suddenly feeling exhausted. I stepped out of the bar into the cool February evening, gulping air like I'd been held underwater for a very long time. I was disoriented and turned until I found Trey, and he put his hands on my shoulders, steadying me.

"Thanks for doing that, Julie. For sharing Beau with him. I don't think I could have." Then, before I realized what was happening, or maybe because I wanted him to, Trey leaned down and pressed his lips against mine. I felt like I was underwater again, but this time I didn't need air to breathe or legs to stand, because I was breaking up through the surface, seeing the tall pine trees and the old oaks on Deer Island. And I felt Trey's warmth pressed against me, fluid and sleek, and when my eyes closed again, I saw the Katrina tree with the pod of dolphins, their hard bodies stretching into the sky.

CHAPTER 22

Eye: The roughly circular area of comparatively light winds that encompasses the center of a severe tropical cyclone. The eye is either completely or partially surrounded by the eyewall cloud. —NATIONAL HURRICANE CENTER

Julie

Our ride home through the New Orleans night was silent, as I was busy thinking about why Trey had kissed me and why I'd wanted him to. I assumed he was busy wondering what his conversation with Johnny had uncovered, and why Wes would have hidden the files. And what would have made Monica leave so suddenly with the portrait.

As he parked the truck, Trey turned to me. "I'd like a drink before I turn in. What about you?"

Swallowing, I said, "Sure."

"I'll meet you in my study. I want to check on Aimee first."

I nodded, then made my way to the study, glad for a few extra moments to compose myself. The boxes I'd brought from Carol Sue's office were still there, the insides spread out on the table like a dissection. I was about to go over and examine them again when I heard the sound of metal scraping hard earth coming from the garden.

Moving to the window, I pulled the curtain back to peer outside. From my vantage point, I didn't have a clear view of the whole garden, but I could see the carriage house and half of the garden shed. Xavier had pulled everything out of the shed and stacked it all on the grass. I heard the sound of metal scraping dirt again and strained to see around the corner.

"Don't mind Xavier. He's always worked at odd hours. I think he's an insomniac."

I started at the sound of Trey's voice. I turned to face him, as uncertain around him now as a twelve-year-old girl with her first crush. "I think he's getting ready to paint the shed. Seems like a big job. He's not exactly young, so I'm surprised he didn't jump at your offer to help."

Trey looked past me toward the shed. "Yeah, me, too. I'll ask him again tomorrow—assuming he doesn't stay up all night to finish." His eyes met mine again. "What would you like to drink?"

"Just water," I said, my head still a little fuzzy from the beer I'd had at Miss Mae's.

Trey turned and headed for the door. "I think I'll join you. Be right back."

While he was gone, I moved over to Monica's box again, peering inside to see what I'd left behind. I spotted the small vinyl photograph album again, its edges warped and curled, and pulled it out. Carefully, I used my little finger to unstick the cover from the first page, the clear plastic sleeve adhering to it as if it had been glued shut. I eventually pried it apart and found myself smiling at the photograph of a young Monica in her Sacred Heart uniform, standing with Aimee and an attractive older man on the front steps of the First Street house. Monica held a blue ribbon in one hand, and a framed watercolor landscape in the other. Her smile showed two missing front teeth.

"That's Wes," Trey said behind me as he handed me a glass of water with a wedge of lemon.

I nodded my thanks and took the drink. "And you're going to make me wait for Aimee to tell me how she ended up with him, aren't you?"

Trey raised his eyebrows but didn't say anything.

Sighing, I turned back to the album. "If it's all right with you, I'm going to see if I can salvage these photographs and put them in an archival-safe album. And then I'm going to give it to Beau. He doesn't have any photographs of his mother and I think he'd like that."

Trey took a sip of his water. "He gets a kick out of Monica's portrait in the parlor. He thinks it's funny that she was once a little girl."

"Me, too," I said softly as I reached into the box again and grabbed a handful of metallic green, gold, and purple beads. "She used to always decorate our apartments for Mardi Gras. I have no idea where she found the beads or the King Cake, but we always had them."

"Mardi Gras day is March eighth this year. I thought you and Beau might like to see a parade or two."

I nodded as I sorted through the crumbled petals of old corsages. "Carol Sue said we should see the Biloxi Mardi Gras parade—it's smaller but less wild. And it goes right in front of Walker's building on Howard Avenue. He's got a balcony we can sit on, so I don't have to worry too much about Beau."

"You wouldn't have to worry about him regardless. You're not the only adult watching out for him, you know."

"I know. Sorry. I guess it's a habit where he's concerned."

"You're a good guardian, Julie."

I ducked my head, staring into the box so he couldn't see my face. "And you're a good uncle. I think Beau's done pretty well for himself."

I listened to Trey's footsteps as they crossed to the desk. "Have you thought about what you're going to do with Beau once River Song is completed?"

I kept my head down. "I'm not used to planning that far ahead."

"Because that might make you actually stop and think about your life for a moment." His words were spoken softly, taking the sting from them. "But it's not just your life anymore."

Finally, I looked up at him, acknowledging that I'd thought the same thing but had been unable to voice it. "Beau's well-being is my priority right now. I'll think about the rest of it when I have to."

I turned back to the box, spotting something dark and round in a corner. Lifting it out, I stared at it. "It's a coconut with paint and glitter on it."

Trey took it from me and held it with deference in his hands. "But not just any coconut. It's a prized Zulu coconut—handed out only at the Zulu parade on Mardi Gras morning. It's kind of a coveted item." He tossed it in his hand. "Maybe it can be the decor inspiration for one of the rooms at River Song. It wouldn't be historically accurate, but I think Monica would approve, anyway."

I stared at him, just for a moment wondering what it was like to think ahead and make plans as if the life lived now would continue uninterrupted, to have the kind of strength and resilience required to rebuild after a storm. "I have to admit that I haven't given any thought to the interior yet. Other than the recycled-wood floorboards, anyway."

"Yeah, and that conversation took only three weeks." Trey placed the coconut on the table and returned to leaning against the desk.

"I wanted to get it right, that's all. The new River Song is going to be there for a long time, so we might as well fight for what we want."

When he didn't say anything, I looked up to find him staring at me, a small smile making his cheeks crease. "What?" I asked.

"Never mind." He finished his water, the ice cubes clinking in the glass. "So what did you think of my father?"

I leaned against the table and stared into my glass. "He seemed lost. And I think he's been that way for a long time. At least since his mother died."

"I'd never heard that story before. He could have been making it up."

"I don't think so. He wouldn't have told us about Lacy if he wanted to hide anything from us." I thought for a moment. "Do you think if we visited Wes, we'd be able to get any kind of an answer?"

Trey shrugged. "It wouldn't do any good. He doesn't really recognize anyone anymore, and before the stroke he never spoke about his parents. Just Gary and Aimee, that's all. He'd get agitated if anybody strayed too far into the past."

"Do you think he was covering up for somebody? Like his father? Gary seemed to think his parents' relationship was toxic. Maybe Wes found out his father had something to do with his mother's disappearance. And what about Xavier? He disappeared on the same night as Caroline. The detective in charge of the investigation seemed to think that he might know something."

Trey swirled the ice around in his glass. "Just don't say that in front of Aimee. She considers him her great protector for some reason. It used to irritate my grandfather, because Wes couldn't stand Xavier, and I got the feeling that the dislike was mutual."

I thought for a moment. "Ray Von told me that Xavier worked for your family since Camille. Where was he between the time when Caroline disappeared in 1956 and Camille in 1969?"

"Finding himself, according to Aimee. All I know is that that's when Ray Von began to distance herself from Aimee. As if Xavier's absence during that time were somehow Aimee's fault." He raked his fingers through his hair, much like Beau did when he was tired. "Like I said, Aimee won't stand to hear anything bad about Xavier. He's certainly devoted to her now, but neither one likes to talk about the past."

Trey's gaze lingered on me for a long moment, and I looked away. Turning toward the computer, I asked, "Is it okay if I use this right now?"

As if I hadn't said anything, he said, "Why do you care, Julie? Why does any of this matter to you?"

I moved the mouse and the monitor came to life with the background photo of Monica and Trey at the beach. It was a perfect moment in time, a touchstone to a happy life that ended abruptly, ten years before Monica took her last breath. I saw Aimee's shadow in the picture, her arms raised to hold the camera, encircling Monica in an embrace. "Because some things should never be forgotten. Whether it's a memory we should learn from or a memory of something precious, sort of like life's rewind button. Sometimes that's all we have left." I paused, seeing the innocent child still visible in both Trey and Monica.

"Johnny called you brave; did you realize that? Because you're prepared to face the truth. I think he's right. I don't think that's what I would have called you when we first met, but I think he's right."

Embarrassed, I turned back to the monitor. "I don't know what I am any more, but I'm pretty sure it's not brave." I studied my nails, short and unpolished. "I think brave describes people who come back to devastation but see only the possibilities. I'm not like that at all."

I clicked on the Internet Explorer icon and waited for it to load.

"Julie?"

"Yes?"

"Did you mind it when I kissed you earlier?"

I was glad he couldn't see my face. "No."

"So you wouldn't mind if I kissed you again sometime?"

I shook my head. "No."

"Good."

Keeping my eyes on the monitor, I waited for him to approach, but instead heard his footsteps walking away. "Good night, Julie. Don't forget to set the alarm before you go to bed."

The door clicked shut, and I realized that I was smiling.

I had just launched the FBI Web site when I heard a shout from upstairs. Alarmed, I jumped out of my chair and ran up the stairs to Aimee's room. A thin light showed from under her door, and when I knocked, the door opened silently into the room.

The dim light came from a silver fleur-de-lis night-light plugged in near the baseboard on the wall opposite the door. It cast long shadows over the bed and walls, the tall arms of the four-poster bed seeming to hold captive the bed's occupant.

"Aimee?" I peered into the alcove and saw her propped up on her pillows, her skin shiny with perspiration. "Are you all right?"

"The light. Please."

I flicked on the bedside lamp and she seemed to relax. "Would you like me to call Kathy?"

She shook her head. "No, I'm fine. It was just a nightmare. Could you please pour me a glass of water? It's right there on my nightstand. I'd get up and do it myself, but this bed is so damned high it would take me twenty minutes just to get out of it."

Her fingers fidgeted in agitation as she watched me. I waited while she drank from her glass, her hand shaking slightly. When she was finished she handed it back to me and I placed it back on the table.

"Would you like me to stay a little while?"

She gave a delicate shrug, but her face showed relief. "Just for a little while. I want to hear about your evening."

"About meeting Johnny?"

"Of course." Her eyes sparkled.

I found myself staring up at the ornate ceiling medallion. "He's not what I expected."

"No. Poor Johnny. I tried my best, but he was always Lacy's son. He's still sweet, but life really hardened him around the edges."

I leaned toward her, my elbows on my knees. "He told us something. That Lacy said something right before she died."

Aimee's knuckles whitened as she clutched at the bedclothes, but her expression didn't change. "What was it?"

"That he needed to ask Wes to tell him the reason he married her."

Aimee took a deep breath, her fingers still clutching at the blanket. "We all thought it was because she was pregnant, but Johnny wasn't born until almost two years after they were married."

"Then why? He loved you, and he knew you loved him. He must have given you a reason why."

Her eyes seemed to darken. "He said it was because of Gary. That he and I could never be together because Gary was too fragile to be hurt like that. And if Wes couldn't have me, then it might as well be Lacy."

Leaning forward, I said, "And I discovered it's Wes you visit in the nursing home. But what happened to Gary?"

Closing her eyes, she relaxed against her pillows. "I'm getting there. But first tell me—what did Johnny find out?"

"He didn't start looking for the answer until Monica disappeared, when it was too late, because Wes couldn't answer his questions. All he discovered was that your mother's case file was missing, as was the majority of Caroline's file."

Her fingers fidgeted with the edge of her blanket. "He never mentioned that to me. But what does it mean?"

"There's no way of knowing, since we don't know who last handled the files. All we know is that Wes looked at your mother's file when you asked him to. But that was almost seventy years ago—they could have disappeared anytime between now and then."

"Yes," she said. "They could have."

She looked pale and I poured her another glass of water.

"I came up here because I heard you shout. Were you having a bad dream?"

Aimee nodded once. "I don't have those dreams that often anymore, but when I do . . ." Her voice trailed away. "I don't remember much this time except . . . except the smell. I suppose it's always been there, but I've never really paid that much attention to it."

"Where are you in the dream?"

Her blue eyes met mine, small and shimmering in the dimly lit room. "In my mother's bed."

I sat back in the bedside chair. "And what is it you smell?"

"Sweat. It's not my own . . . but it's familiar. Like I know the person, but it's not someone I think I'm afraid of. And there's another . . ." Her voice trailed away.

Her hand lay empty on the blanket, grasping at air. I placed my hand in hers and she squeezed it. "It's my mother's perfume. I smell her perfume. I remembered her putting it on that night before she went out."

I sat still for a long moment, listening as night settled into the bones of the old house. "And that's all you remember about your dream?"

Aimee nodded. "I think there's something else, but every time I try to think about what it is, it eludes me. I just can't help but think it's important."

"It'll come to you. Don't think about it too hard. It'll come back when you least expect it."

She settled back into her pillow, releasing my hand, her eyes regarding me closely. "I have to tell you more about Gary."

I sat back in my chair. "I'd like that," I said. "If you're not too tired."

She gave me a lopsided grin. "Pretty soon I'll have all the time in the world to sleep. But for right now, there are more important things to do."

I reached over and refilled her glass from the pitcher, then waited for Aimee to tell me about Gary, and why she hadn't been surprised to hear that the two case files from two separate investigations into the Guidry family were missing.

CHAPTER 23

The lowest ebb is the turn of the tide.
—Henry Wadsworth Longfellow

Aimee

1961

The skies on my wedding day sent fat drops of rain down to earth, soaking everything and making the overhanging oaks on St. Charles Avenue weep on our procession as we drove beneath their canopy on our way to Holy Name Cathedral. Ray Von told me that rain on a wedding was a guarantee that my marriage would be full of tears. I ignored her, knowing that the success of my marriage would have nothing to do with the weather.

We'd planned on spending our brief honeymoon at River Song, and by the time we reached Biloxi shortly past midnight, the weather had cleared. Gary had been too tired to drive, and he'd quickly fallen asleep in the passenger seat. As I pulled into the driveway, he still slept soundly, so I decided to open up the house and move our bags in without disturbing him. As I stepped out of the front door after depositing our last load inside, I looked past the old oak tree and across the lawn to the sound. The full moon created a path of gold light across the water, and the gentle lapping of the surf on sand brought me to the pier. I stood at the edge and wrapped my arms around me in the chill of the night, remembering the hot summer days of our past. It all seemed so very long ago.

Something splashed beneath me, and I looked into the dark water, feeling the first tremors of fear. Above, the moon bathed everything in its glow, but in the places its golden arms couldn't reach, the darkness held. I shuddered and backed away, cautiously picking my way up the pier, afraid to turn my back on the dark places. I bumped into something solid and screamed.

"Shhh, Aimee. It's only me."

Gary's arms went around me, transferring his warmth to my shivering body.

"Oh, God, Gary. I feel so stupid. It's only the dark. . . ."

He kissed me on the temple. "It's not stupid." He held me for a while until my shivering subsided. Then he said, "Come on," and led me down the pier to the house.

He closed the door behind us, shutting out the night, then took my hand. "Let's go upstairs."

Suddenly shy, I pulled away and began methodically turning off the lights.

"That can wait, Aimee. Come upstairs with me."

He pulled on my hand and led me up the steep, narrow stairs to the large master bedroom, and I tried to erase all thoughts of Mr. and Mrs. Guidry in this same room.

The moonlight flooded the space with a fuzzy brilliance, blurring the edges of the world around us. I kicked off my shoes and slid down my stockings. The gold band on my finger felt warm and heavy on my skin as I walked into his arms and spread my hands across his back.

He kissed me, and the blood pounded in my head to the cadence of the surf outside. I felt the tug of the zipper at the back of my dress and then the cool air caressing my bare skin. I reached up to hold the dress in front of me, afraid to let it fall. He tugged but I wouldn't release it, feeling embarrassed to let him see me.

He settled the dress on my shoulders and rezipped it before saying, "Don't go away. I'll be right back."

I heard him running down the wooden stairs and out the front door. Within minutes it slammed again, and his feet raced up the stairs. He stood in the doorway, holding a bottle of wine, a corkscrew, and two glasses. "From your grandmother," he said, wearing a wide grin.

We sat on the bed, sipping wine and talking. We spoke of the old summers, and this place, and all the happy memories we had. Gary spoke of our children, and how we would spend each summer here with them and their friends until we were old and gray. We spoke of our future grandchildren, too, and how we would take them fishing on the pier and listen to them whispering on the sleeping porch.

The talk of children prompted me to bring up something that I hadn't had the courage to ask, the wine making me much bolder than I would have been. "What about your heart, Gary? I mean . . ." I looked down into my glass. "I mean, do your doctors say it's okay to . . . to . . . you know . . ."

"Have conjugal relations?" He threw back his head and laughed. "My doctor said if I was strong enough to run up stairs, I was strong enough to have sex. And if I was strong enough to run up two flights of stairs, then I could have sex twice."

I laughed, too, feeling the alcohol from the wine race to my head, relaxing me. I took his glass from his hand and placed them both on the nightstand. Then I stood and let the dress fall from my shoulders. Gary stood, too, and slid the straps of my slip down my arms.

He took a deep breath. "Aimee . . ."

I pulled back, worried at the tone in his voice. "What's wrong?"

"Nothing, sweetheart. I just wanted you to know that you'd make a horrible voodoo queen, because your spells fail spectacularly."

"What do you mean?"

He kissed me slowly and then said, "I'm glad to report that both balls are present and accounted for."

I laughed softly, smelling his champagne breath, remembering that long-ago summer day on the levee when I'd told both him and Wes what I'd hoped would happen on their wedding nights. "That's a good thing, since it would be hard to fill this house with children without them."

He kissed me again and then we lay down on the bed, the moonlight and the water an unbroken cocoon around us.

The sun woke me the following morning as it streamed across the bed, lighting on Gary's head and coating it with bright highlights. He lay on his stomach, his left arm stretched around me. I moved on top of him, kissing him gently on the neck and smelling sweat and stale champagne.

He rolled over, toppling me from my perch and pinning me under him in a twist of sheets. With a low growl, he yanked the sheets out from between us and threw them on the floor. I closed my eyes, hiding myself from the intensity of his gaze, and felt the heat of his kiss on my belly.

We made love through the morning and early afternoon, tracking the time by the slant of the sun against the wall. Finally, we rose, and fixed something to eat in the kitchen. I stood barefoot, wearing only his shirt, while I made sandwiches. He stood behind me, crunching on an apple, a hand constantly touching me.

He nibbled at my neck, pulling at the shirt and baring my collarbone. He paused and spoke, his breath hot on my skin. "Did you think about Wes when we were in bed together?"

I turned in his arms, pushing away from him, the counter cutting into my back. "Why would you say that?"

"I'm not blind, Aimee. I see the way you've always looked at him. The way you still do."

I stepped forward, pressing my forehead into his shoulder. "I married you, Gary. Isn't that enough?"

He pushed against me, his arms pinning me to his chest. His voice was low and seductive, his lips almost brushing mine as he spoke. "Just making sure. Because I want all of you."

I smoothed the hair off his face, then slid my hands down to rest on his naked shoulders. "You do have all of me."

He laughed, making his chest rumble. "Good. Now can we have something to eat?"

I cuffed him on the side of the head and resumed making sandwiches, glancing at Gary now and then and wondering how much of what I said was true.

As we ate our sandwiches, Gary said, "Wes had a strange request for me."

I kept chewing, trying not to show too much interest. "What was it?"

"He asked that I make sure Xavier stayed away from you. That he might be dangerous."

The food in my mouth felt suddenly very dry. "Why would he say that? I haven't even seen Xavier since the night of the Comus Ball." I looked down, remembering the feeling I had of somebody watching me, waiting for me.

"He didn't say. But I think Wes believes Xavier might have helped Mother leave with that artist fellow. Who knows?" He reached over and took my hand, squeezing it. "That's all in the past. All we have now is our future. Together."

I smiled, but my appetite was gone. I continued to eat without tasting anything, hoping that Gary was right.

We left three days later to return to our lives in New Orleans. As we pulled the car out of the driveway, dusk had begun to fall, robbing the earth of its colors. The sun leaked red and orange into the sound, bathing the house in fiery light. Gary drove, his right arm around me, and I watched the house disappear in the rearview mirror, an icon for the family we would one day have. I gave a sigh of contentment and leaned on my husband's shoulder, ready to begin our life together.

"I get to sit in the front seat!"

I slung my purse onto the floor of the car and looked at Johnny.

"No, sir. Uncle Gary believes that it's safest for little people to sit in the back, and I think he might be right."

The little boy scowled, his lower lip protruding as far as it would go. "My mommy lets me."

"I'm not your mommy, and it's my car. Either sit in the back or we're not going to go see *101 Dalmatians*."

His eyes widened as if to determine whether I meant it. I nodded, and he jerked open the back door, then climbed in.

I leaned into the backseat. "I'm just trying to keep you safe, sweetheart." I placed a kiss on top of his head, then closed the door.

"Where's Uncle Gary?"

"I don't know—he said he was right behind us. Hang on a second and I'll go find out." I ran up the steps of the Guidry house, still unsure whether I was enough of a member of the family to simply walk in. Gary and I had our own apartment on Carrollton, but Gary still called this house home. I had my own key, but had never used it in the months since my marriage. I rang the doorbell and waited for someone to answer.

After a few minutes, I rang again before opening the door myself.

"Gary—why didn't you answer the door?" The door closed with a small click behind me. "Gary! We're going to be late."

A small groan came from the parlor and I ran inside. Gary lay on the sofa, a forearm thrown over his face. "I'm here. Sorry. Couldn't quite manage to get the door."

I raced over to him, kneeling in front of the sofa. "Gary—what's wrong? Do I need to call the doctor?"

He lifted his arm. "No, I'll be okay. I just took one of my pills but it takes a few minutes." His arm fell back over his face.

His skin was chalky white and mottled like the marbled mausoleums in the cemetery. I sat down next to him and picked up his hand, his skin clammy. "Are you sure I don't need to call the doctor?"

"Only to set the broken bones in my hand. You're squeezing it too tight."

"I'm sorry." I hastily loosened my grip, smoothing my fingers over his hand. "I'm worried about you."

His eyes closed as he talked, his breathing slowing and his color returning. "I'll be fine—I just overexerted myself wrassling with Johnny. He may be small, but he's tough." He smiled. "I can't wait for a dozen of my own."

"I can't wait to see you give birth to them. The things you must be learning in med school." I nudged him slightly with my elbow.

"I'll be happy to start with just one." His eyes opened, and he reached his hand up to touch my cheek.

I held his other hand and brought his palm to my lips and kissed it. "We're only just married, Gary. We should wait."

The front door flew open, followed by a slam and the running of small feet. Johnny stood in the threshold, a bundle of energy and tousled hair. "Come *on*! We're gonna miss the movie!"

Gary shook his head. "Sorry, bud. I'm not feeling great. Would you mind going with just your aunt Aimee? She can be your date."

Johnny's brilliant blue eyes brightened. "Okay. But you get to take me again another time."

"Sure, bud. Maybe next weekend."

"Will you be all right, Gary? Do you want me to drop you off at home first?"

He waved me away. "I just need to rest—I'll be fine."

I kissed him gently, his eyes already closing. Then I stood and held out my hand to Johnny. "Come on, handsome. Let's go."

Wes pulled into the driveway behind my car as we stepped out of the house.

"Daddy!" Johnny ran to his father, arms outstretched, and was caught and lifted high in the air.

Wes rumpled Johnny's hair. "How's my favorite guy?"

"I'm taking Aunt Aimee on a date to see *101 Dalmatians*. Wanna come?"

Wes glanced at me and I shrugged. "I don't mind if you don't."

He looked confused for a moment, then said, "Why should I mind? There's no reason why you and I can't take my son to a movie."

"Right," I said, looking at everything except his face. "No reason at all." I thought of Gary asleep on the couch, and wondered if he'd mind. "We'd better hurry if we don't want to miss the beginning. I know how you men are if you do—you're totally lost for the rest of the film."

Both Wes and Johnny gave me identical smirks, making me laugh.

Wes walked toward his car. "We'll take mine, since I'm parked behind you."

Without complaint, Johnny hopped into the backseat. I slid into the front passenger seat, feeling like an impostor sitting in Lacy's seat, stealing a few hours of her family.

As we drove, Wes glanced over at me. "Marriage suits you, Aimee. You're practically glowing."

I felt the telltale heat on my face. "Thanks. Gary and I are very happy."

He was silent for a moment, but I didn't look up. "I'm glad for both of you."

We rode the rest of the way in silence peppered only with the occasional question from the backseat.

We sat in the front row at the movie theater, the large box of popcorn on Johnny's lap in the middle. Once, Wes and I reached inside the box at the same time, and our hands touched. I jerked back as if I had been stung. I spent the rest of the movie sitting on my hands to make sure it didn't happen again.

Afterward, we took Johnny out for hamburgers and a chocolate malt. He kept up a constant chatter, full of questions and commentary, so Wes and I didn't have to make conversation. I was in midbite of my cheeseburger when Johnny asked, "How does a baby get in a mommy's tummy? Donna Peacock's mommy's going to have a baby and she said that God put the baby in there, but I can't see how."

Wes coughed and I nearly choked on my food. We looked at each other, then at Johnny. "Ask your mother," we said simultaneously, and then had to stifle our laughter. At that moment, Johnny spilled his chocolate malt all over himself, the floor, and me, fortunately offering us a respite from answering the question.

I waited outside the restaurant on Napoleon Avenue while Wes took Johnny to the restroom to try to clean the little boy off as much as possible. It was one of those perfect spring days that New Orleans doles out sparingly, with cerulean blue skies and almost no humidity. My hair stayed in soft waves around my shoulders instead of kinking up in tight curls; my skin was soft instead of moist. I felt almost glamorous. I sat down on a bench facing the wide median and the streetcar tracks for the old Napoleon Avenue line that had stopped running nearly ten years before.

"Miss Aimee?"

I swung around, my breath hovering in my mouth. Xavier stood in the alley beside the restaurant behind me, his eye a lonely point of light in his dark face.

He stepped back farther in the shadows when he heard my gasp. "I'm not going to hurt you."

I stood and walked closer to him. "I know that. You just shocked me, that's all."

His eye darted around nervously. "I saw you with that little boy, Johnny. And Wes. Where's Gary?"

"He wasn't feeling well, so he stayed home."

"My mama says he doesn't have much longer."

A fly landed on my forearm, and I swatted it away. "Don't say that, Xavier. Your mother isn't a doctor."

Several passersby paused to stare at me talking with a black man, then ambled on. "I'm taking care of you, Miss Aimee. You don't need to be scared of the dark anymore. I'm watching out for you."

I moved closer. "Have you been following me, Xavier?"

"You need to be careful. You don't always know what some people will do to keep a secret."

"What secret?"

"Mr. Guidry . . ." he began but then stepped back as a boisterous throng of young people emerged from around the corner on Dryades Street, the leader carrying a football that he'd occasionally toss into the crowd and then catch as it was tossed back to him. After they passed I looked back at the alley, but Xavier was gone.

I searched for him in every direction, calling his name, but he was nowhere to be found.

Johnny and Wes emerged from the restaurant, and I smiled at them, feeling the prick of gooseflesh on the back of my neck as we walked toward the car, sensing Xavier's gaze on me and wondering how he'd known that I was afraid of the dark.

The chirping of a cricket awoke me. I turned to Gary but felt only cold, empty sheets. I sat up with a start, seeing a shadowy silhouette by the window. I relaxed when the shadow turned toward me, and my night-light illuminated Gary's face.

I slid out of bed and joined him on the window seat. The cricket sang nearby, its lonely call unanswered. I reached for Gary's hand, entwining my fingers with his. His were stiff and unforgiving, but I didn't remove my hand. He'd barely spoken to me after my return from the movies with Wes and Johnny.

Gary's eyes glittered in the reflection of the moonlight. "Ray Von says a cricket in the house is bad luck."

"Ray Von says a lot of odd things. I don't pay any attention to her."

"Maybe you should." He turned back to the window.

I slid closer to him on the seat, repositioning myself to rest my back against his chest. "I saw Xavier yesterday. Outside the restaurant—Wes and Johnny didn't see him. He said that he was watching out for me."

"Maybe he has a crush on you. It doesn't seem too uncommon."

Ignoring his jibe, I said, "Lieutenant Houlihan has been looking for him, but I'm not sure if I should let him know that Xavier is here. He's hiding for a reason, but I can't help him, because he won't tell me anything. He said your father's name, but then he disappeared before he could tell me more."

Gary shrugged. "Wes and my father don't tell me anything. Except that Wes thinks Xavier is dangerous. Maybe you should tell the lieutenant that you saw him."

I closed my eyes, listening to the cricket sing, the strident notes drifting in the dark night. I changed the subject, not wanting to argue. "Why aren't you in bed?"

He shifted behind me. "I couldn't sleep. Thinking too hard, I guess."

I snuggled close to him. "Thinking about what?"

His voice was close to my ear, low and deep. "About how I wish you would light up when you look at me the way you do when you look at Wes."

The plaintive cry of the cricket came closer this time, almost to the window seat.

"That isn't true." I reached behind me and touched his cheek, feeling the prickly stubble of his beard. "Please let it go. I can't move on if you keep dragging me back into the past."

He turned his head into my palm and kissed it, his lips warm and wet. He didn't say anything, but faced the window again with a deep sigh.

I stood and held my hand out to him. "Come to bed with me."

He looked up, his eyes hidden in dark pools of shadow. In a fluid motion, he stood and pulled me down with him onto the floor. His caresses were rough and tender at the same time, bruising and arousing. I felt his love for me, and it touched my soul and erased all thoughts of Wes from me for another night. I fell asleep in Gary's arms, listening to the cricket's solitary call as the black night faded into purple morning.

CHAPTER 24

A storm surge is a large dome of water, often 50 to 100 miles wide, that sweeps across the coastline near where a hurricane makes landfall. —NATIONAL WEATHER SERVICE

Julie

I dreamed I sat on the porch at River Song, the way it had once been before the storm had come and taken it away, leaving behind only memories and a scarred oak tree. I looked beside me and saw my sister, Chelsea, and she smiled back at me. She was the nine-year-old girl I had known, but her eyes were older and wiser, and when I looked closely, I realized they were Monica's eyes.

The rough rope of the hammock rubbed my legs and the metal hooks creaked as Chelsea and I rocked back and forth, keeping rhythm with the sound of the surf.

"Look," she said, pointing at Deer Island covered in brown, dead trees. I closed my eyes, not wanting to see, and then I heard Trey's voice telling me to open them again. And then I was lying on my back on the sand with Chelsea next to me, the trees green again, rippling in the warm breeze. The sound and smell of the sea were stronger now, the sky a sweep of crystal blue dotted with clouds as we stared upward.

"Look," Chelsea said again, and I searched the sky to see what she saw.

I smiled when I spotted her cloud, the long nose and dorsal fin identifying the dolphin as it floated in perpetual grace, poised to splash through the water's surface.

"I see it," I said, laughing at how obvious it was and wondering why I'd never recognized Chelsea's clouds before. "I see it," I said again to Chelsea's retreating back as she stood and walked to the edge of the shore. With one last look toward me, she waved, then dove into the unseen depths of the dark water, disappearing from sight.

I called her name, but my voice wasn't frantic, as if my dream self knew Chelsea was near even though I couldn't see her. But I felt the heavy weight of my own loneliness, its cause more than just her absence, my awareness of it just beyond my reach.

Something splashed nearby, loud and crashing, and I jerked up in bed to find Beau with his face very close, his mother's eyes staring into mine. He carried the red hat, but he wasn't sucking his thumb. I suddenly realized that it had been a while since I'd actually seen him doing that.

"Who's Chelsea?"

I sat up and flipped on the bedside lamp, then looked at the clock glowing on the nightstand. "It's four o'clock in the morning, Beau. What are you doing out of bed?"

"You were talking to somebody named Chelsea."

I pushed my hair out of my face, imagining I could still hear the sea and smell the salt air. "Chelsea was my sister."

"She's not your sister anymore?"

I blinked slowly, not understanding at first. "Yes, of course. She's just . . . not around anymore."

"Like Mommy."

I smoothed his hair back from his forehead, noticing how long it had gotten, and how much lighter it was from all the time he now spent outdoors with Charlie and Trey. I imagined that Monica's hair had looked that way, too, until she'd moved to the city and her airless apartment, feeding herself on the memories of bright sun and moving waves. *What happened, Monica? What happened to take you away?* "Yes, Beau. Like your mom will always be your mom."

"And Chelsea will always be your sister." He balled his hand into a small fist and pressed it against my chest over my heart, as I'd done to him on the day we'd buried his mother. "She'll always be right here, even if you can't see her."

I stared at him for a long time, wondering when he'd grown so smart. Then I leaned forward and kissed him on the forehead.

Beau grinned up at me. "Are you thinking I'm wonderful again?"

I laughed, then tousled his hair. "Yeah. And pretty smart, too. I think you're going to be ready to start kindergarten in the fall."

He rolled his eyes. "I can already read. I don't see why I have to go to school, since I'm already so smart."

It was very hard not to laugh. We were distracted by the sound of something being dragged on the lawn beneath the window. I climbed out of bed and followed Beau to look outside.

Xavier had set up a floodlight to illuminate one side of the shed, and he was in the process of moving the contents of the shed that had been stacked against the outside out of the way so he could paint. A sprained hand and then bad weather had postponed Xavier's painting the shed and it appeared that he had decided the job had waited long enough. Paint cans, one opened, stood in the grass, a wide brush resting on top of one of the closed cans. A shovel lay facedown several feet away, and I wondered if the sound of it falling and hitting a can were what had awakened me.

"Isn't it easier to paint in the daytime, when you can see better?"

I looked down at Beau. "Forget kindergarten. I think you're ready for high school." I peered out the window again. "I'll go ask him. But I want you to go back to bed first. Charlie and her mother want to be at Dr. King's office as early as possible before the Mardi Gras parade, and I don't want you to be Mr. Grumpy, because you're sleepy. Miss Aimee's coming with us, and she'll probably be in the car at eight o'clock, blowing the horn for us to hurry."

He smiled at the image, but his eyes were solemn. "Okay. I'll try. But I think I'm too excited to sleep." He gave me a quick hug, then ran back to his room through the connecting bathroom. After he'd gone I turned back to the bed and realized that he'd left the red hat. I picked it up and started walking toward his room to return it, but instead placed it on my bedside table, where it would be if he came back for it.

Using the light from the night-lights placed strategically in the hallway, I found my way to the kitchen. After disarming the alarm, I stepped out into the garden; the smell of freshly turned earth and paint entwined with the odd, decaying, sweet scent of New Orleans at night hit me like a wall.

I found Xavier perched on a ladder, methodically swiping strokes of white paint on the shed's siding. He froze when I called his name softly, the brush held aloft in midstroke.

"You should be in bed sleeping, like normal people," he said gruffly.

Crossing my arms over my chest, I said, "I could say the same about you."

He carefully placed the brush across the can and stepped down off the ladder. "Can't sleep. I figure I might as well get something done instead of wasting time in front of the television."

"But painting? Isn't that a little hard to do at night?"

He shrugged. "I could paint blindfolded, pretty much. This way it'll be dry enough in the morning that I can start moving everything back inside."

I nodded, surveying all the heavy boxes and equipment that sat stacked outside. "How old are you, Xavier? Seventy-five, seventy-six?"

"Around there."

"I'm impressed. I don't think I'd have been able to do all this work by myself."

"Did you need to ask me something, Miss Julie? Because I've got work to do."

I hesitated only for a moment, not knowing whether I'd have the opportunity or the courage to ask Xavier again. "The night Mrs. Guidry disappeared, you disappeared, too. I understand that Wes Guidry thought you might have helped her leave with my great-grandfather. The rumor was that they ran off together, but we haven't been able to find any evidence to support that. I thought that maybe you would know something, and I'm wondering if Monica might have asked you about it, too."

Xavier didn't move, but his eye glittered in the light from the spotlight. "What is the good in dragging up all of this old history? It didn't help Miss Monica, did it?"

I paused, knowing he expected me to back away, that raising the specter of Monica would get me to stop asking. But I'd had too much experience searching for answers that eluded me. "So she did ask?"

He didn't answer right away, and we stood silently facing each other as something dark and small darted out from the eaves of the old house, its wings fluttering like a breath. Finally, he said, "She did. She stood just where you are now and asked the same question as you are right now."

He turned his back to me and began climbing the ladder. "I told her to go ask her grandfather. That if there was anybody who could answer her questions, it was him."

I watched as he slowly dipped his paintbrush back into the can, then began to swipe it back and forth over the boards of the shed.

"And did she? Did she go ask him?"

The smell of paint overtook the scent of freshly turned earth, an incongruous smell in a garden at night. The wet paint shone in the floodlight, the center of brightness in the middle of so much dark, like being in a dream where stepping outside the circle meant waking up.

He stopped moving his arm for a moment. "I don't know. Next thing I heard was that Monica had gone and then Mr. Wes had his stroke."

I stared at his back, going over his words, and wondered what I was missing. "He had his stroke the same day?"

Xavier nodded. "I guess. I didn't see Miss Monica leave. All I know is that my mama came out of the house yelling for me that Mr. Wes had fallen over in his room and she needed my help to move him to the couch while we waited for the ambulance."

"So you were with him—right after he had his stroke? Did he say anything to you, anything about Monica and why she would have left so suddenly?"

Xavier turned his head slowly, his single eye bright against the darkness of his face. "He didn't say anything to me." He waited a moment, as if he had something else to add, then turned back to his painting. "It's late, Miss Julie. You need to go back inside and get some sleep."

Realizing that he wasn't going to tell me anything else, I said good night and turned back to the kitchen door. I hesitated at the threshold, noticing that the door was cracked open and all the kitchen lights were on. Slowly I pushed the door open and heard the beep of the microwave before I saw Aimee placing a teaspoon each of cocoa powder into two mugs. She turned and smiled as I entered the kitchen, then popped open the microwave door and pulled out a steaming pitcher of milk.

"I couldn't sleep, so I made myself some cocoa and, when I heard you talking outside with Xavier, thought you might like some, too."

I slid into a chair at the table. "Thank you. I'd love some."

She held up a clear plastic bag. "Marshmallow?"

"Yes, please."

She dropped two large marshmallows into each mug before pouring the steaming milk on top. She stuck spoons into the mugs and placed them on the table. "I'm guessing Xavier woke you up, too."

I stirred slowly, waiting for the marshmallows to melt. "Yes. Beau, too, but I'm hoping he went back to sleep. He's got a big day ahead of him."

Aimee nodded. "He sure does. Monica would make such a big deal of Mardi Gras. She'd decorate River Song with streamers and wreaths and anything she could find in Carnival colors. She was always hoping that one day she'd be Queen Ixolib."

"Who?" I blew on my mug, watching the steam rise.

"It's Biloxi spelled backward, and she's the queen of the Biloxi Mardi Gras." Aimee took a small sip from her mug. "Just imagine—by next Mardi Gras we'll be able to decorate River Song again."

I thought of the newly sided house with the bare yard and shutterless windows, trying to imagine what would happen once it was completed, but couldn't. It was nearly finished, its new elevation giving a panoramic view of the sound from the front porch, still without rockers or hammocks. Yet when I pictured the house in my mind, I saw only the empty lot and the scarred oak tree standing like a sentinel on the front lawn.

Aimee's eyes were soft as she regarded me through the rising steam. "You haven't thought that far ahead, have you?"

I shook my head. "No. Although I have started looking into schools for Beau in the Biloxi area. He'll have to start school in the fall regardless of where he or I end up." It was the first time I'd acknowledged, even to myself, that Beau and I could end up in two completely separate places. I took a quick sip of my hot cocoa, burning my tongue and hardly feeling it.

She raised both eyebrows, and I continued speaking to prevent her from saying more. "I actually looked at St. Martin's in Ocean Springs. It's still a boarding school, but they have day students, too. Isn't that where Xavier went?"

"Yes, it was. It used to be a private blacks-only school during segregation. Even back then it was highly regarded. One of the few black college preparatory schools."

I frowned into my cocoa, staring at the reflection of the overhead lights in the flat surface. "I was surprised by how high the tuition is. Has it always been so expensive?"

"I really don't know, although I imagine so because of its reputation. Why do you ask?"

"Well, I just wondered how Ray Von could afford to send him there. Do you know how long he attended?"

She was silent for a moment. "Not exactly, but I do know he was sent there right after my mother died. I remember that only from what Gary told me when I used to grill him about what he remembered about my mother's murder. Xavier was about nine, and from what I've been told, he thought my mother was an angel because she was kind to him. Maybe that's why they sent him away to school after she died—I don't know. Regardless, I think Xavier might have graduated high school there sometime in the early fifties, and then came back to New Orleans to live with Ray Von, and would do odd jobs for Mr. Guidry."

"Until the Comus Ball, when Mrs. Guidry disappeared and then he dropped out of sight, too."

She shook her head, her hand cupping the mug between them. "Not completely. He thought I needed protection, although he's never told me from whom. Even today if I ask him, he'll just tell me that he's keeping me safe because my mother isn't here to do it for me. I think it stems from his devotion to her."

"And then he reappeared after Camille and has been working for the Guidrys ever since."

Aimee nodded, then placed her spoon inside her empty mug. "Wes hired him. Wes was injured during Camille; have I told you that? And Xavier saved him. Anyway, Wes said he needed help around the house and hired Xavier. Ray Von retired and we bought her the house in Biloxi. And it's been that way ever since."

I stood and picked up her mug. "Want some more?"

She nodded and I poured more milk in the pitcher to heat it. "You haven't told me about what happened during Hurricane Camille or how you ended up with Wes."

We both turned at the sound of the ladder being moved. Aimee continued looking at the kitchen door leading out to the garden as she spoke. "No, I haven't. But I think it's time I told more of my story. I think we're getting close."

"Close?"

"To finding out what it was that Monica knew that we can't seem to see. I told you when you first got here that if we put our stories together we could figure it out."

I opened the microwave door. "But we seem to have more questions now than we did when we started."

"Life is like that, Julie. But having questions doesn't necessarily mean that you don't already know some of the answers." Her blue eyes regarded me steadily as I realized she wasn't talking about Monica anymore.

I poured the steaming milk over cocoa and marshmallows in each mug and placed them on the kitchen table. Then I sat down across from Aimee and prepared to listen.

CHAPTER 25

However long the night, the dawn will break.

—African Proverb

Aimee

1962

The hot spring erupted into a scorching summer, the humidity heavy and intrusive, its thick fingers reaching through window blinds, under doors, and through the light cotton of the suits I wore to work at the art gallery. The pungent odor of the Mississippi wrapped itself around the city like a big snake, a redolent ribbon of muddy water.

Gary had finished his first year of medical school with high marks, but the grind for him hadn't ended. He was working in a research lab at the medical center for the summer, his hours just as long and arduous as they were when he was in school. He came home in the evenings exhausted, having little more energy than what it took to eat his dinner and watch our favorite shows on television. Most nights he fell asleep on the sofa, and I left him there, covered by a blanket, while I slept in our bed alone.

Gary's birthday fell at the end of July, and I asked my supervisor for the entire weekend off to surprise Gary with a trip to River Song.

I slipped into the lingerie department at Maison Blanche during my lunch break, looking for something to keep Gary awake and to bring back memories of our honeymoon.

I also had an idea for part of his gift. I remembered the portrait painted of Mrs. Guidry wearing her Comus Ball gown, the one Mr. Guidry had relegated to the attic. I'd never asked why, and could assume only that it was too painful for him to look at. But Gary had been close to his mother, and if he wanted to hang it on the wall in our apartment, I was sure I could convince his father to let Gary have it.

I used my key this time without ringing the bell, knowing Wednesday was the day off for the help. Poking my head through the door, I called, "Hello! It's Aimee. Anybody home?" I didn't really expect an answer. The men would be at work and Lacy was rarely home.

Dust motes rose in the shaft of light from the open door. I waved a hand through them, watching them tumble against one another, then closed the door behind me. "Hello!" I called again, and no one answered.

I climbed to the top of the stairs and faced the attic door. The phone rang, and by instinct I raced to a nearby bedroom to answer it, only to get a dial tone when I picked up the receiver. I hung it back in the cradle, and looked around me, realizing I must be in Wes and Lacy's bedroom. A large four-poster bed commanded my attention in the middle of the room, its bedspread covered with wildflowers and vines. I caught myself wrinkling my nose at the femininity of it, wondering how Wes could stand it. A man's undershirt and socks lay in a heap on the floor by the bed. In that regard, the two brothers were very much alike.

I turned my head and spotted a desk and chair. As I lifted the chair to bring it back to the hall with me, I noticed the top of the desk, covered with photos of Lacy and Wes. There were a few professional photographs of Johnny, but the others were candid shots of his parents at various functions. The two made a handsome couple, but I couldn't help noticing how Lacy always appeared to be clinging to Wes, red fingernails gripping his coat jacket as if she were trying to prevent him from running away. His smiles in all the portraits were the same, thin and small, his eyes flat—with only one exception. In the picture of Wes holding his newborn son I could feel the joy displayed on his face. I touched the frame, feeling only the cold glass under my fingers.

I dragged the desk chair down the hallway and used it to prop open the attic door. It had a propensity to close and latch on its own, and I had no intention of being locked in the attic until somebody came to find me. Brittle light showed at the top of the stairs from the attic window as I carefully climbed the narrow, steep steps.

The heat sat in the enclosed area like a living entity, the force of it hitting me in the face as I stood on the top step. I hardly recognized the attic—it looked completely different from the last time I had been there. Most of the boxes and furniture had been moved to one side of the room, leaving a large empty space in front of the window. A pillow and some blankets were stacked against the wall, the bottom panes of the window wiped clean.

I looked around, wondering if I would be able to find the portrait. I spotted an old armoire and noticed the top drawer was cracked open. Out of curiosity, I walked over to it and slid it open. A bright yellow flashlight rolled toward me, and I picked it up and flicked it on, surprised at the strong beam it shone on the wall.

After replacing the flashlight, I continued to glance around the attic, looking for discards Gary and I could use in our apartment. Gary's mother had attempted to redecorate parts of the house in the new, modern style of bright colors and chrome, placing priceless antiques up in the attic. I made a mental note to ask my father-in-law about some of the pieces I spotted gathering dust.

I walked around the perimeter of the room, searching through various framed artwork leaning against the walls and furniture. I'd almost given up when I discovered an old desk in the far corner, with a rolled-up rug in front of it. After shoving aside the rug, I began opening the desk drawers, finding them filled with old photographs and papers. When I got to the largest drawer on the bottom, I tugged on the pull, but something inside caught, preventing me from opening it. Carefully, I reached my hand inside and felt the corner of something hard, like wood. Excited that I might have found what I was looking for, I pressed down on the edge of the picture frame and gently pulled the drawer open.

My heart thudded as I found myself staring into the face of Caroline Guidry, looking exactly as she had when I'd last seen her nearly seven years before. The alligator pendant pinned to her breast glittered, almost succeeding in taking over the focus of the portrait. But a look into Caroline's eyes convinced me that she would never have allowed herself to be upstaged.

The sound of footsteps on the stairs spun me around, and I saw Mr. Guidry, a soft smile on his lips.

"Aimee—what a delightful surprise to find you here. Since you and Gary moved across town, we hardly seem to see you." He glanced at the portrait I held, his smile dimming. "What's that?"

Despite having known him all of my life, and even being married to his son, I felt uncomfortable around my father-in-law, like waking up each morning to find yourself in the wrong bed. "I was looking for a birthday gift for Gary. I remembered this portrait of his mother, and if he wanted it, I was going to ask your permission to hang it on the wall in our apartment."

He stared at the portrait, but didn't move to take it from me. "I should have destroyed it years ago. I don't know what made me keep it."

"I'm glad you did. I think Gary would like to have it."

He turned his back on me and walked to the window, facing out. "I'm sorry, Aimee, but I don't think that's a good idea. You realize, of course, how delicate Gary's health is. Seeing this reminder of his mother and her abandonment could only put stress on him. Stress that he doesn't need right now." He faced me again, his face dark. "I'm sure you understand."

I swallowed, the oppressive air weighing heavily on me and making me sweat. I forced a smile. "I really don't think—"

"Dad? Are you up here?"

We both turned at the sound of Wes's voice and watched him approach. "Hello, Aimee. I saw your car outside and knew you were here somewhere." His eyes softened as he looked at me, and I hoped Mr. Guidry didn't notice.

I smiled. "Hi, Wes."

He looked at the portrait in my hands and immediately frowned. "What are you doing with that?"

Surprised at his reaction, I said, "I thought Gary might like it for his birthday."

He was shaking his head before I even finished speaking. "It's out of the question."

Mr. Guidry stepped forward and took the portrait from me. I wanted to resist but realized my efforts would be futile. "That's what I was trying to tell her. How it wouldn't be good for Gary to be reminded of his mother's abandonment every time he saw it." A glance I couldn't decipher passed between them.

Wes nodded. "He's right, Aimee. We have to think of Gary." He moved to take my arm, leading me toward the stairs. "Let's go downstairs. Gary's been mentioning how he'd like a new satchel for school. The straps on his old one are just about worn through."

Knowing I couldn't argue with both of them, I headed toward the stairs.

"Did you find anything else? Anything else that belonged to my wife?" Mr. Guidry asked as he stood next to the desk where I'd found the portrait.

I shook my head. "No. Are you looking for something in particular?"

"No. I just try to ensure that Gary doesn't run into unpleasant reminders of his mother. It's best that he forgets her. That we all forget her."

I watched as he placed the portrait into the drawer and I caught a last glance of her blue cat eyes. I continued down the stairs, unaware of Wes's hand on my back and anything else besides what other reasons Wes and his father could have for wanting to forget Caroline Guidry.

"Happy birthday, handsome." I leaned over Gary and kissed his still-sleeping lips.

He groaned, shielding his eyes from the open window with a bedsheet.

"Time to rise and shine, Gary. We've got birthday plans."

Without warning, he reached up and grabbed me, pulling me back into the bed. "So do I, Mrs. Guidry—so do I." He nuzzled my neck, his sleep-warmed body radiating heat.

"But I'm already dressed."

His lips vibrated with a throaty chuckle as he nipped at my jawbone. "That can be fixed pretty quick." He slipped his hand to the zipper of my skirt, then stopped. "Ow." He sat up, rubbing his arm. "My arm's killing me; I can hardly move it."

I sat up with alarm. "What's wrong with it?"

He continued to rub it, his fingers kneading it like unresponsive dough. "It's nothing. I must have slept on it funny. It'll go away." He slid his legs over the side of the bed and stood up, his need to undress me forgotten. "I'll go take my shower now."

"And I'll go and make you a breakfast to knock your pants off."

He raised an eyebrow. "Always trying to seduce me, aren't you?"

I threw a pillow at him, then admired his retreating backside as he walked to the bathroom, still rubbing his arm.

He picked at his breakfast, barely touching the grillades and grits I had so painstakingly prepared for him. He excused himself to lie down for a while and I loaded the car.

I stood in the doorway, car keys dangling from my fingers, and watched him try to find the energy to pull himself off the sofa. "Gary, when was the last time you went to see your heart doctor?"

He sent me an apologetic grin. "I've just been so busy lately, I've missed a couple of appointments. I promise I'll call next week."

"I'm thinking we shouldn't go away this weekend. Is there any way you can schedule an appointment today?"

He pushed himself off the armrest and stood, a bit shakily. "No way. It's Friday. They're out golfing." He walked toward me and kissed me on the cheek. "Look, I've got my medicine to get me through the weekend. A few days of rest and relaxation are probably all I need anyway, but I promise I'll call on Monday. I'm fine—really."

He kissed me again, this time on the lips, and led me out to the car. He slid into the passenger seat, and I drove the hour and a half to Biloxi. We spent the rest of the day lying in the hammocks on the front porch and playing cards. I got up occasionally to fix drinks or bring snacks from the kitchen, but mostly we stayed in the cocoon of the wide front porch overlooking the sound, watching the white gulls and skimmers.

I didn't realize when darkness fell, and when I moved to stand, Gary stood, too. A cool breeze danced off the sound and waltzed with the bushes up against the house. "Come on," he said, holding his fingers out to me.

I clutched his hand, following him across the sandy lawn. I gazed warily at the hazy moon, wondering whether it would extinguish its light and throw us in complete darkness.

Gary stopped on the sandy bar running alongside the water, then lay down with the surf lapping at his feet. Hesitantly, I joined him, heedless of the wet sand in my hair. We stared up at the black sky, at the moon and her stars, and let the breeze caress our cheeks. The water was warm on our feet, seductive as it licked our skin, and as soothing as a lullaby.

"Do you know what the Eskimos say about the stars?"

He turned his face toward me and I shook my head.

"They say they're openings to heaven. The love of our lost ones pours through them and shines down upon us to let us know they're happy."

I reached for his hand, all gritty and wet, and squeezed it. "I like that. It makes me think of my mother, that she isn't truly lost to me."

He didn't answer, but turned his face back toward the sky. After a while, he said, "Wes still loves you, Aimee."

I propped myself up on my elbow, watching the blue cast of his skin deepen as a wisp of cloud drifted in front of the moon. "Please don't, Gary."

Almost as if he hadn't heard me, he continued. "I think he knows the biggest mistake he ever made in his life was letting you go. And I still don't know why. I've thought about it a lot, and I still can't figure it out."

"I don't want to talk about it—none of it matters anymore."

He sat up and faced me. "But it does, Aimee. It matters very much. You and Wes have sacrificed so much for others' happiness—including my own. I hope the time will come when you two will be able to put what you want first."

"You're scaring me, Gary—what are you saying? That you don't want to be married to me?"

He touched my face, his fingers as gentle as the warm breeze. "Oh, no. Being married to you has been the best part of my life." He looked out into the sound for a moment, then turned back to me. "I just want you to be prepared. If something should happen, I want you to go for what *you* want for a change."

"But it's you I want. We're married, remember? Till death do us part and all that. I won't leave you—ever."

I couldn't read his expression, but he leaned forward and kissed me. "Let's go sit on the pier."

He rubbed his arm again as we walked up the pier, the wood timbers dry and grainy under my bare feet.

We sat in lawn chairs at the edge of the pier, our hands entwined between us. We watched the moon hover on the horizon and climb slowly in the night sky.

"I'm thirsty." His voice sounded strained and brittle.

"I'll go get us some hot tea with lemon—I'll be right back."

I stood to leave, but his hand pulled me back. The moon illuminated his grin. "Aren't you going to kiss me good-bye?"

I bent to give him a small kiss, but felt his hand on the back of my head pressing me into a deeper one. I kissed him back, then lifted my head. "I'll hurry," I said.

I walked down the pier and heard him call after me, "I love you, Aimee."

Stopping, I turned around. "I love you, too." I waved, then jogged the rest of the way to the house.

In the cozy kitchen, I bustled about making a tea tray. I filled the kettle with water and stuck it on the stove, then arranged an assortment of cookies on a plate. The water seemed to take forever to boil, and I reminded myself of the old adage that a watched teapot never boils. To make the waiting time productive, I ran upstairs and began unpacking our suitcase. I carefully folded everything in the drawers and arranged our toiletries in the bathroom, our toothbrushes touching in the toothbrush holder. Feeling romantic, I drew a heart on the mirror with toothpaste, our initials inside.

I bounded down the stairs, surprised I hadn't heard the kettle yet. It steamed and rocked on the burner, telling me the water inside was boiling. With a hot pad, I lifted the pot and placed it in the middle of the tray, then loaded two cups and saucers. Balancing it carefully in one hand, I opened the door and very gingerly picked my way across the lawn and road to the pier.

As I reached the base of the pier I called out, "Gary—I'm back. Could you give me a hand? Sorry it took so long, but I think the little knob on the kettle might be broken and I got distracted waiting for it to whistle."

He didn't turn around. I stopped and called again. "Gary!"

His name evaporated in the night air, like tiny droplets from a crashing wave. The water lapped at the pier, its rhythm smooth under my restless feet. I watched Gary, the breeze lifting his hair slightly, his hand, the one I had been holding, motionless beside him.

"Gary, I could use some help here. . . ." My breath caught as I remembered something about heaven and stars.

My scream echoed off the water, through the darkness under the pier and all around me. The tray slid from my hands, the china breaking in a thousand pieces, the kettle bouncing on the pier and spraying my legs with scalding splashes of water. I stepped on the broken china as I ran to him, the sharp edges tearing at the tender skin of my feet. But I felt nothing—nothing except the cold, inky darkness that had suddenly thrown its black cloak around me, consuming me completely.

CHAPTER 26

Strike: For any particular location, a hurricane strike occurs if
that location passes within the hurricane's strike circle, a circle
of 125 nautical miles diameter, centered 12.5 nautical miles to
the right of the hurricane center.

—NATIONAL HURRICANE CENTER

Julie

Trey drove us to Biloxi, Aimee beside him and me in the back with
an exuberant Beau bouncing up and down in his seat. I hadn't
taken him to any of the New Orleans parades, still uncomfortable with
the thought of losing him in a crowd. Beau had begged to go next year.
I'd evaded answering him, unable to imagine myself here or anywhere
in a year's time, and hoping that watching today's parade in the con-
fined space of Walker King's balcony would be enough.

Trey had to drop off a repaired air compressor at the work site in
the Ninth Ward neighborhood on our way out of town. As we drove
through the city, so many of the sights were new to me yet seemed
familiar, too. In my time spent here, I'd discovered that New Orleans
was a city of contrasts: of decay and luminescence, of tradition and the
unexpected. It was a European city with a tropical climate, English

gardens filled with banana trees and roses. The more time I spent in the city of Carnival and floods, gumbo and Sazeracs, debutante queens and transvestites, the more I realized that Monica's stories had ceased to be hers; they were becoming mine, too.

As we waited in the truck while Trey and two men moved the air compressor, I got a good look at the neighborhood that had received so much attention following Katrina. It reminded me a lot of what I'd seen in Biloxi: empty lots, concrete slabs, houses with patchwork repairs, doors still with the orange paint markings. But like Biloxi, too, I saw the signs of renewal—new homes with small grass lawns, porches with rocking chairs and children's toys, thin tree saplings, long and spindly like adolescents. The sound of hammering and the fresh smell of lumber filled the air, making me think of River Song as it rose like a phoenix out of the sandy grass.

Trey motioned to me as he approached the truck with an attractive black woman in her late twenties wearing a T-shirt with the words MAKE IT RIGHT stamped over the number nine. I stepped out of the truck as Aimee rolled down her window and called out to them.

"Good morning, Ms. LeBlanc. You're making good progress." She indicated the frame of the house in front of us, the foundation raised on tall pilings, a recurring theme I was beginning to recognize along the Gulf Coast.

The young woman smiled broadly, revealing large white teeth. "Yes, ma'am. My sister and her husband have been working on the house just as hard as me. I guess they're tired of me and my children camping out in their living room." She laughed loudly, the sound contagious as we found ourselves laughing, too.

Trey introduced us. "Carmen, I want you to meet Julie Holt. She's the one who's been bossing around the workers in the Biloxi house and who I've been trying to get down here to lend us a hand. Julie, this is Carmen, an Iraq War vet. She came home to a bit of a surprise. Her house had to be demolished because of all the water damage."

"Luckily, my kids were living with their aunt and uncle out in

Metairie while I was deployed, so they were safe. Lost everything, though." She laughed again, and it was genuine, with no trace of bitterness. "Sometimes I guess you need to lose everything before you realize what's really important. My mama actually calls it a blessing." She rolled her eyes like a teenager instead of the war veteran she was, and I found myself smiling.

She shook my hand in a firm grasp. "It's a pleasure to meet you. Next time I'm in Biloxi, I want to come see your house, though I feel like I've been in it, with how much Trey talks about it. About you, too. The man can't stop talking about you and how you saved his sister's house and how much he's learned from you about dedication." She shook her head. "It's one thing to want to rebuild and work hard at it; it's a whole different kind of faith when you rebuild while thinking you're doing something temporary until the next storm."

Trey and I avoided looking at each other, so I couldn't determine who was more embarrassed. I looked around me at the eager faces and at the bright newness of the nearby houses standing proudly on their pilings and found I could no longer think of the people who lived here and rebuilt as shortsighted or egotistical. They were mothers and daughters and sons and fathers; they were families regaining so much more than furniture and clothing and old photographs. The word that came to me now was "defiant." Because a person had to be defiant to be able to stand amid the wreckage of her life and instead of shaking a fist, pick up a hammer.

We said our good-byes and headed back to the truck. As we merged onto the interstate, I remembered Monica's photo album. I'd stuck in my purse. I pulled it out and handed it to Aimee in the front seat. "You asked to see this, so I brought it with me. I haven't had a chance to find out which photographs I can salvage, so I hoped that maybe you could pick out your favorites and I'd start with those. I'd like to have a scrapbook ready for Beau's birthday."

She took the album from my hand. "Thank you, Julie. I'll see if I can easily pry any loose while I'm at it." She immediately bent over the photographs, pausing at each page as she brought the album close to her face to see the photos better. I watched as she carefully slid a finger into one of the plastic slots and began to slide it back and forth.

"Julie? Why didn't we have any snow this winter?"

Beau's questions distracted me for the rest of the ride, so I forgot all about the album and was surprised when Trey stopped the van. He dropped off Aimee, Beau, and me as close as he could get us to Howard Avenue while he went to park the truck in the driveway of my little house. Aimee seemed unusually subdued, although she insisted she felt fine and was looking forward to the parade. I wondered if seeing the photographs of Monica had made her nostalgic, and I hoped I'd done the right thing by showing the album to her.

Crowds of people lined the parade route. I saw a lot of children, a lot of painted faces, and most everybody wore all three Mardi Gras colors. I'd never thought that purple, gold, and green went together, but now I couldn't seem to imagine one without the others.

We passed through a family dressed up as the TV Simpsons, and almost tripped on three dogs appropriately decked out in Carnival gear, including feathered masks perched over their ears.

We let ourselves into the back door of Walker's dental office, then up the stairs to a space used for storage. Boxes were stacked against one wall of the room, clearing out a wide expanse of carpeted floor in the middle. A temporary bar had been set up on the other end of the room, with large tubs filled with water bottles, juice boxes, and soft drinks for the younger set, and a keg and a cooler with wine for the adults. Music blared from an old-fashioned portable radio sitting on a card table, a babble of voices coming from the wide balcony that stretched across the entire front of the building.

Aimee walked over to greet Carol Sue's parents as Carol Sue and Charlie came over to say hello, bringing with them an older couple. "Julie, I've been dying for you to meet Sandra and Ted Davis. Their house stood about two blocks from River Song and looked pretty much as bad after Katrina except that they didn't even have any trees left.

They've been watching what you and Trey are doing to your house and you've inspired them to rebuild."

I wanted to shake my head, to hold my hand up in protest, to tell them that it wasn't "my" house, but stopped. I thought again about Carmen LeBlanc and her hope and excitement, of her defiance of accepting the way things were, her courage to change them. I looked into the open faces of the Davises and saw the same thing I'd seen on Carmen's, and Carol Sue's, and all the other people I'd met since coming here. It was the familiar look of those searching for what they had lost, searching for their place in this world that settled in their bones like an old friend. It was a look I remembered seeing on Monica's face from the first moment I met her.

"Thank you," I said instead. "Although I can't really take any credit for it." I took a deep breath. "It was all Monica's inspiration."

Trey approached with a steaming Styrofoam bowl of what looked like chunky soup and rice and handed it to me with a plastic spoon. "And shortsightedness, don't forget."

I blushed, remembering what I'd said to him the first time he'd brought me to Biloxi. I didn't reply, suddenly unsure of what my answer should be. I looked down at the bowl he'd handed me. "What's this?"

"Gumbo. Another neighbor here, Susan Sands, makes her special gumbo every year for Walker's Mardi Gras party." He indicated a petite blonde with perfect teeth. "Her husband's a partner in Walker's dental practice."

I took a bite and closed my eyes to really appreciate the mix of flavors, including something so spicy it made my sinuses tingle. "This is wonderful. I'll have to get her recipe."

"Luckily, she's got a good memory. Lost all her recipes in the flooding after Katrina. Not that it stopped her from making her gumbo from her FEMA trailer for the 2006 parade." He lifted his beer bottle in salute in Susan's direction.

I took another bite. "I'm glad. This would be a shame to be forgotten."

"Julie! Come look!"

I turned my attention to Charlie and Beau, who were standing out on the balcony with Walker and Aimee and several more adults. I made my way to stand behind them and looked over the railing to see a line of floats slowly careening their way down Howard Avenue. As the floats passed, the crowd reached up their hands as goodies were tossed at them, the rising motion like a giant wave.

"There are so many floats! I didn't think it would be this big."

Trey came to stand behind me. "We're about at the pre-Katrina number of floats now—twenty-something, I think. Half of them were destroyed by the storm. The guy who makes them got busy right away, saying he couldn't stand to watch a parade full of floats he didn't make." He took a draw from his beer. "The number of spectators is still down, but growing every year. If you parade a bunch of floats and promise to throw stuff at people, they will come."

Trey took my empty bowl and disappeared for a moment before returning to hand me a beer and juice boxes to Charlie and Beau. Two stools had been set in front of the balcony railing for the children, high enough for them to see over, but not high enough that they could fall, although I kept checking to make sure. They were waving their juice boxes at the floats, watching as the throngs of bystanders below us reached up with open hands as cups, beads, and leis were tossed into the crowd.

Beau faced me. "Why's everything in purple, gold, and green? I don't even like purple."

I remembered asking Monica the same question and recited her answer verbatim. "Purple for royalty, gold for power, green for faith. Seeing how Mardi Gras is all about royalty, with kings and queens and their courts, and that tomorrow marks the forty days before Easter, it kind of makes sense, don't you think?"

He thought for a moment. "I guess purple's okay."

I hid a smile as Beau turned back to the parade, a frown on his face.

In a lowered voice, I asked Trey, "Are there any tricks to getting the good stuff—like the T-shirts and stuffed animals?"

A wide grin split his face before he answered, making me fairly confident I'd asked a pro. "Getting the good throws takes cunning, speed, and fine motor skills. Doesn't hurt to be tall, but in my experience"—he glanced over at Charlie and Beau—"some of the most vicious throw-catchers are small, innocent-looking children who use their size and agility to outmaneuver us older, more sedentary paradegoers."

I looked at a frowning Beau, anticipating his next question. "How are we going to get any goodies thrown to us up here? They're never going to see us."

"You have to be real obvious. Lean over a bit and shout, 'Throw me something, mister.'"

Walker stood behind us and nudged Trey with his elbow. "In New Orleans, the ladies have a special way of getting a bunch of the good loot, but this is a family-friendly parade."

"What do you mean?" I asked.

Trey and Walker shared a look. Clearing his throat, Trey said, "Let's just say that even though we would probably appreciate the view, let's keep your shirt tucked in, all right?"

I stared at him. "They don't really . . ."

"They do," Walker and Trey said in unison, before they both took long sips from their beer bottles so they wouldn't have to say any more.

With a quick glance at Beau and Charlie to make sure they weren't jumping too high on their stools, I peered over the balcony, where the red-and-white uniforms of the Biloxi High School marching band paraded past, their banner proudly displaying their Indian chief mascot. Girls holding flags strutted in front of the band members, a jaunty rendition of "When the Saints Go Marching In" blaring from shiny trombones, trumpets, and tubas.

I stretched my neck to see what came behind them and spotted a large float in the shape of a dune buggy painted in the three Mardi Gras colors, with a huge banner on the back proclaiming the rider the grand marshal. Huge tricolored flags fluttered from the back of the float, every edge outlined in sparkling purple, green, or gold streamers. An older woman and man wearing black T-shirts sat on high seats toward the front, their arms draped in beads that they'd pull one by one to toss into the crowd.

I watched as the man leaned forward into a box at his feet and pulled out two necklaces with large, pearly beads. They were moving slowly under our balcony, completely oblivious to the two children above them.

Standing on the bottom rung of the railing, something I'd explicitly instructed the children not to do, I leaned over as far as I could and screamed, "Throw me something, mister!"

The man looked up at me and I pointed at the two children. He nodded briefly, then drew back his arm and threw the two necklaces up in the air toward us. I saw both children reaching through the railing, their arms too short to catch them. Without thinking, I leaned over and grabbed both necklaces as they'd begun their descent, feeling strong arms around my hips holding me on the balcony.

I stepped back, holding up my prizes. "I got them!"

Trey's face was very close to mine. "I'm glad. Because I'd hate to see you fall to your death for nothing."

"Me, too," I said quietly before stepping away to give the children their necklaces, thankful I'd caught both of them so I wouldn't have to do that again.

My cell phone buzzed from the back pocket of my jeans. I pulled it out and looked at the screen to see who was calling. The noise of the crowds and the people near me on the balcony shrank to a pinpoint of sound, the bright sun outside suddenly dimming as I stared at the familiar number.

"What's wrong?"

I heard Trey's voice in the vacuum of sound and turned toward it. "Can you watch the children? I need to take this."

He nodded and I quickly made my way to the stairs. I closed the door behind me and sat on the top step before flipping open the phone. "Hello?"

"Julie, hello. It's Detective Kobylt."

"I know." My voice sounded strange to my ears. Calm, normal. "What's up?" For a brief moment, I thought that maybe he was calling me to tell me that his daughter had given birth to his first grandchild.

"I have some news for you."

The sounds from the party and parade had burst to life again behind the closed door. Of all the times I'd imagined this phone call, this scenario had never crossed my mind.

"I'm listening," I said, my voice sounding like it belonged to somebody else. I remembered my visit to the palm reader and my hand began to shake. *You are close to finding what you seek.*

"We've found something."

I paused. "A body?"

"We've found remains of what preliminary reports are telling us is a young girl between the ages of nine and fifteen. It's only skeletal remains, and we're thinking they've been in the ground for a long time."

"Seventeen years?" I asked, my voice slightly more than a whisper.

"It could be. It's still too early to know for sure, but it looks about right."

"Where did you find . . . her?" I couldn't call the loose scattering of bones I imagined by any name. They were only bones.

"Look, Julie, I don't want to tell you all of this on the phone. This is hard for you, I know."

"It's all right, Detective. I know that if I lived closer, you would be at my front door right now. But I need to know. I need you to tell me everything that you've found."

I heard him swallow into the phone. "At Oakham State Forest—about twenty-five miles from your parents' house. We've had a lot of washout lately because of all the rain, and a woman walking her dog found a bone."

No, no, no, no. No, Chelsea. Not alone like that, in the middle of the woods. She would have been so scared. I pushed the panic down, forcing my voice to remain normal. "Anything else that might identify the body?"

"That's why I'm calling you. I was wondering if you could fly up here. There're fabric samples that were salvageable but not immediately recognizable as anything your sister might have been wearing, as well as a few other items. I was hoping if you saw them up close, instead of a picture, you might have a better chance of identifying some of it."

"What about dental records? You have Chelsea's, right?"

There was a long pause. "The skull wasn't found with the body. It could have been removed prior to burial, or animal scavengers could have gone at it at some point; there's no way of knowing. I'm sorry, Julie, but you're pretty much our last hope at identifying these remains. We're trying to see if there is any trace DNA on anything, but time and the elements have pretty much made that impossible."

I didn't hesitate. "I'll come. I'll take the first flight I can get and will call and let you know. It might not be until tomorrow morning."

"That's fine. I'll pick you up at the airport if you need me to."

"Thank you." I said good-bye, then closed the phone and shut my eyes, waiting for tears that wouldn't come.

I didn't know how long I'd sat there until I felt the door open behind me. Trey sat on the step next to me. "Is anything wrong? I was starting to get worried that you'd developed a sudden aversion to parades or something. And Beau caught a plastic cup that he's eager to show you."

Looking at him, I said, "I need to go to Massachusetts. They think they've found Chelsea." My voice was matter-of-fact, but my hand was shaking so badly that I dropped my phone.

Trey picked it up and placed it on the step behind us, then put both of my hands between his, steadying them. "I'll come with you."

It wasn't a question and I was glad: glad that I didn't have to fall apart with the gratitude I felt in knowing I wouldn't have to make this trip alone. "Thank you," was all I could manage.

We found Carol Sue and explained the situation to her, and without asking she took charge of Beau and told me not to worry about anything, that everything would be taken care of here.

I found a subdued Aimee sitting by herself on a folding chair on the balcony, her legs crossed neatly at the ankles, her hands in her lap, facing the parade but not appearing to see it. Her eyes seemed focused somewhere else, as if all the noise and colors right below her didn't exist.

"Miss Aimee?"

She blinked, then looked at me for a long moment until she seemed to recognize me.

"Are you all right?"

With a brittle smile, she said, "Of course. It's Mardi Gras. I've always loved the parades."

"Are you sure? Is it too warm out here for you?"

She shook her head. "No, dear. Everything is fine."

I sat down in an empty chair next to her. "I have to fly to Massachusetts—they've found remains that might be my sister's. Trey's going to come with me, but Carol Sue will take you to her parents' and then drive you home tomorrow, if that's all right."

Aimee touched my shoulder, her eyes warm but distant. "You go. Don't worry about me, or Beau. You do what you need to do. We'll be here when you get back."

"Thank you." I bent to kiss her cheek, then stood, but she held on to my hand.

"You're stronger than you think, Julie. This will be hard, whatever the answer, but you'll handle it. You always have."

I tried to smile. "I wish I could believe that."

We said good-bye; then Carol Sue gave me an extra-tight hug. "Call me as soon as you know anything. Anytime, day or night. I'll answer on the first ring."

I hugged her back, unable to trust my voice with words.

Trey and I said good-bye to Beau, then walked silently through the dissipating crowds, kicking discarded wrappers and cans left behind by the spectators, and I resisted the impulse to pick up dropped beads, no longer sure why I'd ever wanted to collect things.

Climbing into the passenger seat, I spotted the photo album that I'd given to Aimee. When I picked it up to move it so I could sit, two loose photographs, ones I imagined Aimee had managed to pry loose from the album sleeves, slipped out.

I recognized the first photograph, one of Monica doing a cartwheel on the beach, but I realized that I hadn't seen the second. It had something stuck around the edges, as if it had been adhered to the back of the first photograph and Aimee had managed to pry them apart.

Settling into the seat, I placed the photographs on my lap and reached for the shoulder strap of my seat belt. It snapped back suddenly, but I barely noticed the loud clank it made as the buckle hit the inside of the car by my head. I was too intent on looking at the photograph Aimee had found, a photograph of an older Monica taking a picture of herself in the hall mirror I recognized from the foyer in the First Street house.

She wore a red cardigan that I recalled as one she still wore when I knew her, and a silver watch on her wrist that Aimee had given to her on her eighteenth birthday. Her left hand, holding the camera between her index finger and thumb, had the remaining three fingers splayed awkwardly, as if to show off the wide gold ring on her third finger. And there, on the left side of the cardigan, the dark green of the brooch like a stain on the red of the sweater, was Caroline Guidry's alligator pin, the ruby eyes winking from the flash of the camera.

CHAPTER 27

I walked beside the evening sea
And dreamed a dream that could not be.
The waves that plunged along the shore
Said only: "Dreamer, dream no more."
—GEORGE WILLIAM CURTIS

Aimee

Gary's funeral was held on a Thursday. I don't remember if it were sunny or cloudy. I no longer saw the need for the sun to rise each day and considered it a personal affront that it did.

Visitation at the funeral home was held the night before, and I was pleased for Gary to see the sizable crowd, the men in their dark suits and the women with their gloves and veils. He had been a very social person in life, and it was fitting that his friends would gather around him in death.

I was last. I knelt and tried to say a prayer for Gary, but no words came to mind that hadn't already been said. I stood, reached into my pocket, and pulled out the Cracker Jack toy ring and placed it in the coffin, my hand brushing the black wool of his suit. I picked a piece of stray lint off his lapel and smoothed his tie as the dim light from the candles reflected off the rosary held in his hands, the black beads hard and immovable under stiff fingers. The burnished oak of the coffin gleamed gold, and the aroma of wax and polish wafted heavy in the dim interior. I moved aside my veil, then bent and kissed Gary on the forehead, his skin cold and firm against my lips. *Good-bye, Gary. I loved you, you know. I really did.*

The funeral Mass was said at Holy Name Cathedral, the place where we had stood together on the altar such a short time before and professed our love for each other until death did us part.

He was laid to rest in the Guidry family tomb at Lafayette Cemetery No. 1. I stared at the open tomb, and remembered Gary and me visiting the cemetery long ago. He'd told me how he imagined that when it was his turn to be laid to rest here, he'd smell like roasting pork in the hot tomb under the Louisiana sun. It had shocked me then, as he'd intended, but I found my lips lifting in a reluctant half smile. Only Gary could make something awful into something funny.

I looked up and saw Wes watching me, a small smile on his face, and I knew we were both thinking of Gary and how he used to make us laugh.

The immediate family stood with the coffin while the priest sprinkled holy water over the tomb. Johnny held my hand, his feet dancing in the grass, and I wondered absently if his mother had remembered to take him to the bathroom. We chanted three Hail Marys and three Our Fathers, our words battling one another in the humid air as we struggled to speak in unison. The priest's voice rose as we said the last prayer. "Eternal rest grant unto him, O Lord, and let perpetual light shine upon him. May his soul and all the souls of the faithful departed, through the mercy of God, rest in peace. Amen."

My gaze slid to the tomb next to the Guidrys', and I read the epitaph for a young man who had died more than a century before. I squinted, trying to read the words, dim with age:

The light of other days have faded,
And all their glories past;
For grief with heavy wing hath shaded,
The hopes too bright to last.

My knees buckled slightly, and I straightened, my eyes blurry. Something small drifted from the sky, and I reached out to capture it. A dead butterfly, its pale yellow wings almost translucent, settled in my outstretched palm. I blew on it gently, watching the frail wings flutter, then collapse. It was a beautiful thing, even in death, and I didn't want to let it go. I looked up and saw several people staring at me. I lifted my hand and blew hard, and watched the delicate insect lift and soar. I turned my head before it fell again, as if by my not watching it fall, it would forever fly upward and never touch ground.

A hand brushed my arm, and I jerked my head to find my father drawing me away. "I'm not ready to go yet. Can you give me a few moments, please?"

With an understanding smile, he hugged me briefly, then left. Wes took Grandmother's arm, and Lacy and Johnny followed them. I turned away from the direction everyone had gone, and walked. I passed decaying tombs, their stucco coverings long since ravaged by time, revealing the stacks of brick beneath. I paused in front of the tall white classical structure of the tomb built by the Société Hospitalière, the figure of an angel holding a cross at the top, towering over the cemetery, keeping watch.

"Miss Aimee."

I twirled around, and found myself face-to-face with Xavier. His face was wet with sweat and tears, his ruined eye weeping. He grieved for Gary, too, and my heart ached a little less because of it.

Before Xavier could move, I hugged him. He was at first stiff and unresponsive, but then his arms went around me, squeezing tightly. Abruptly, he put me away from him.

"No, Miss Aimee. I can't be seen with you. I just wanted to make sure you were okay. Gary's not here to look after you anymore."

"I'm fine, Xavier. Or I will be." I looked closely at him, at his rumpled and dirty clothes, and wondered where he'd been sleeping. "It's hot out here. Why don't you come back to the house? You can see your mother and we can talk."

He didn't answer right away, and then I remembered the cleanly swept attic, the stack of folded blankets. The flashlight. "You've been staying in the Guidrys' attic, haven't you?" I didn't wait for him to answer. "Why?"

Xavier's gaze darted up the path. "I have to go now."

"Who are you hiding from?"

His green eye was cold and hard as he answered. "I was there when your mama got killed."

I recalled the smell of sweat in the room, knew that it wasn't mine or my mother's, but remembered that it smelled familiar, too. The sun seemed hotter, the air harder to breathe. "So you saw . . ."

He shook his head. "No. It was dark and I was hiding under the bed."

I tried to force my question through dried and cracked lips.

Xavier continued. "I was living with Mama in the guesthouse, but we didn't have ice. It was so hot, and I just wanted a cold glass of water. So I was in the kitchen in the big house getting a glass of ice when I heard your mama and Mrs. Guidry start shouting at each other in the parlor. I was scared. I knew I'd be in a heap of trouble if they found me. But I was scared, too, because I'd never heard your mama raise her voice before."

He glanced around to make sure we were still alone, then swiped his face with the bottom of his stained and dirty shirt. "I heard somebody getting slapped, and then your mama left to walk home alone. She was always so nice to me, and I didn't think it was safe, so I followed her home. But the thing is, the whole time I felt like somebody was behind us, following us, but I couldn't see anybody. I was only nine years old and didn't know what to do. So I went in the back door that I knew your grandmother unlocked when she was babysitting so she could go outside to smoke a cigarette. I saw her asleep on the sofa in the living room, so I snuck upstairs to see if you were all right. But you weren't in your room."

I felt the press of the heat against my chest, smothering me. "I was in my parents' room. I always slept there when my father was away." My voice was quiet, the words heavy in the leaden air.

"I heard your mama coming from the dressing room and crawled under the bed so she wouldn't see me."

"And you were there. . . ." I couldn't finish.

Xavier nodded. "I didn't see anything, because I'd fallen asleep under the bed. But somebody thinks I did."

"Who does, Xavier? Who thinks you saw?"

Instead of answering, he said, "Ask Mr. Guidry why he sent me to that expensive school, Miss Aimee. But be ready to hear the answer. Sometimes not knowing is easier."

"My mother's wedding ring was taken that night. Do you remember seeing it at any time that evening?"

Footsteps crunched on gravel, and Xavier took off in the opposite direction, quickly vanishing behind a crumbling tomb.

I turned toward the footsteps and saw Wes, his jacket held by a finger over his shoulder, perspiration staining his shirt. "Aimee? Are you ready to go now? We're all waiting."

I nodded, still shaken by what Xavier had told me. I didn't have the strength to make room for my mother's death amid the overwhelming grief for Gary, and tried to push aside Xavier's words. I tucked my hand in the crook of Wes's elbow and allowed myself to be guided out of the cemetery, wondering what else Xavier hadn't told me.

Cars lined both sides of the street as the limousine pulled up in front of the Guidrys' house. A large wreath, festooned with black ribbons, crowned the front doors. I sat in the back between Grandmother and

Mr. Guidry, Wes and Lacy facing us. Johnny bounced from side to side, excited to be riding in such a big car.

Food covered every flat surface in the downstairs. I had never understood this society peculiarity, as if a full stomach might push out some of the grief. But the combined smells nauseated me, and I found a seat in the parlor and sat down without a plate. Wes eventually wandered in, carrying Johnny, a lost expression on Wes's face. He sat down and the little boy reached for me. I sat him on my lap, facing me, and held him tightly, noticing again his strong resemblance to his uncle. I squeezed him tighter and kissed the top of his head.

"How are you managing?"

I looked up at Wes and saw the dark purple marks under his eyes. "About the same as you, I expect." I swayed with Johnny in my arms, my eyes squeezed shut. I opened them again, willing away the tears. "Some of his last words were about you, you know."

He lifted his head, his eyes moist.

"He said . . ." I looked away, realizing that I couldn't tell him, that the words would be too incriminating.

We were interrupted by a group of Gary's friends who had sought me out to offer their condolences. Johnny's eyes, drooping with exhaustion, stared up into mine. "Is Uncle Gary in heaven?"

Without answering, I said, "Let me show you something." I stood and walked through the house and outside with Johnny, his solid body heavy in my arms. Wes followed and shut the back door behind us. We sat on the garden bench, the early evening sky displayed before us, the stars peeking through the lavenders and pinks of the sunset.

"Do you know what your uncle Gary told me?"

He shook his head.

"He said that the stars are openings to heaven, and that their light is the love of people living in heaven shining down on us."

He tilted his head back, his little mouth open slightly, and pointed a pudgy finger toward the sky. "Do you think Uncle Gary is watching us now?"

I kissed Johnny's forehead. "Oh, yes, Johnny. He is. I know he is."

Wes stood behind us, and we sat on the bench until the last shades of lavender had shifted to gray, and the cicadas sang to the deepening gloom.

As the months following Gary's death passed, I began reclaiming my days little by little. I'd returned to my grandmother's house, not able to stand to be in the apartment I'd shared with Gary. I would stuff my grief into a little compartment in my heart so I could go to work and appear like a normal person. But in the evenings, I would kiss my grandmother good night and go to my room to quietly fall apart where nobody could see. The grief eventually became manageable, but the guilt did not. And when I finally fell asleep, my cheek sticking to the wet pillow, Gary refused to be summoned to my dreams.

The days grew shorter and the nights longer as autumn approached, and we all welcomed the cool respite from the pressing heat of summer. The verdant foliage and brilliant colors of the summer gardens faded to hues of brown and beige as dead blooms littered the ground and scattered with the cool winds. Halloween loomed on the horizon, and Johnny came over every day after I came home from work to check on the progress of his shark costume. Before Gary died, I had promised Johnny I'd make one for him, and he held me to it. I was glad, in a way, for it gave me something to occupy my thoughts, and it brought Johnny to me on a regular basis.

I didn't see Xavier again, and when I checked in the attic at the Guidrys' house, everything had been put back and the blankets were gone, as if he'd never been there. Ray Von denied any knowledge of his whereabouts, claiming that if he'd been living in the attic she hadn't known about it. I didn't believe her and I didn't really think that she ex-pected me to. I felt uncomfortable in her presence, feeling her watching me carefully, as if waiting for me to shatter. Or to finally see something that was hovering on the perimeter of my vision.

I still hadn't approached Mr. Guidry with what Xavier had told me about the night my mother died. *Sometimes not knowing is easier.* Easier than what? Not knowing at all? I didn't know if I'd have the strength to handle an ugly truth, and so began my long dance with avoidance.

On Halloween night, small white skulls and hanging skeletons mixed with draped Spanish moss on the iron railings and porches of the houses on our street, casting the old Victorians and Greek Revivals in an even eerier light than usual. Clusters of costumed children had already started their rounds as I walked next door to collect Johnny and take him trick-or-treating. His parents had a party to attend, and I, as usual, had no other plans for the evening.

Wes opened the door when I knocked, the hood of Johnny's costume clutched in one hand. "Thank God you're here," he said, pulling me into the house. "We can't seem to figure out how this is supposed to go."

Johnny stood in the middle of the foyer, his face in a deep frown.

"Well, if it weren't on backward it might fit better. Don't you know a shark's fin goes on the back?"

Wes gave me a sheepish grin. "Oh. I guess you're right." He squatted down on his haunches. "Come here, Johnny; let's fix you up."

Johnny stepped out of the costume and Wes adjusted it so it went back on properly. He stood and handed me the hood. "Here. He won't let me put it on."

I walked over to Johnny and knelt in front of him. "Why don't you want to wear it? Don't you like it?"

He looked down at his feet, now cleverly disguised as flippers. "I don't want people to laugh at me."

"Laugh at you? This thing is so scary people will be running from you. Maybe if you scare them enough, they'll drop their candy and you can pick it up." I poked my head through the hood, the felt shark teeth dangling in front of my face.

Johnny laughed and snatched the hood off of my head and put it on his own. Wes and I pretended to be afraid, but I had to put my hand over my mouth to hide my smile.

I held out my hand to Johnny. "Okay, Johnny—ready to go ruin your teeth?"

Wes grabbed a jacket off the chair and opened the front door. I stared at him in surprise. "Aren't you and Lacy going to a party tonight?"

His eyes were devoid of expression. "It was a party at one of Lacy's friends'. I thought trick-or-treating with Johnny would be more fun."

A sense of unease settled on me. I looked at Johnny. "Well, then—there's hardly any need for both of us to take him."

Johnny's face fell, and he stamped a flipper. "No—Aunt Aimee, you promised!"

"I know, but that's because I didn't think your parents would be here to take you. But now that your dad's here . . ."

"Noooooooooo!" Johnny fell in a dramatic heap on the Oriental carpet, his arms and legs pounding the floor.

Wes got down on all fours and crawled over to his son. In a firm voice he said, "If you stop your whining and calm down, perhaps if you ask Aunt Aimee nicely, she'll say yes."

Johnny stilled, then turned to his side, facing the wall, his shark fin protruding from his rounded back. After a moment, a sullen and muffled voice said, "Aunt Aimee? Could you please take me trick-or-treating with my daddy?"

I looked at Wes, and he shrugged, as if to tell me it was up to me. I went over to Johnny and picked him up from the floor. "Okay, bud. We'll both go—but at the first whine, I'm coming back home." I stilled for a moment, realizing I had called him by Gary's nickname for him. He didn't seem to notice.

The light had dimmed outside, bringing out more trick-or-treaters. Pint-size ghouls and goblins, with the occasional princess or angel, raced up every walkway, their bags rattling with their loot. Wes and I stood at the front gates and let Johnny approach each door with whatever crowd of children happened by.

"You never told me what Gary said to you on the night . . . when he died. You said he spoke of me."

I looked up into the black sky, seeing overhead the branches of an old oak tree, looking like arms embracing the night. "I don't think you really want to hear it."

"Really? Was it bad?"

I found the courage to look him in the eyes. "No. But it was about us—you and me."

His voice was quiet. "What did he say?"

I looked down at my feet, not sure I could tell him.

Gently, he said, "Whatever it was, Aimee, I can take it. He was my brother, and I loved him. I'd like to know what his last thoughts were about."

I looked directly into his eyes. "He said that you still loved me."

Johnny came whooping down the walkway. "Look! Cherry! My favorite!" He waved a cherry lollipop in front of his face as he ran past us and down the sidewalk to the next house.

Wes pulled on my arm as I went to follow. "And what did you say?"

I paused for a moment, trying to read what was in his gaze. "I told him that it didn't matter anymore."

He stared at me for a long time before Johnny raced past us, and we had to hurry to catch up.

As we approached the next house, I turned to Wes, eager to change the subject. "There's something I've been wanting to ask you."

Wes looked up expectantly, the streetlamps reflected in his eyes.

"I saw Xavier at Gary's funeral." Wes stiffened, but I went on. "He told me that he was in the bedroom when my mother was killed. He didn't see anything, but he also told me that somebody thinks that he did, and that if I wanted to know more, I needed to ask your father about why he paid for Xavier to go to St. Martin's. Does any of that make sense to you?"

Instead of answering, he asked, "Have you mentioned this to my father?"

I shook my head. "I didn't want to bring up my mother's death so soon after Gary. But with you, it's easier." I felt my cheeks heat and was glad it was dark.

Wes took a deep breath. "Are you sure you want to hear this? It has nothing to do with your mother's death. I don't know why Xavier wants you to think that it might."

Wes shoved his hands into his pockets as we followed Johnny to the next house. "Xavier found out a long time ago that we share a father. That's why he was sent to school."

I was sure my face registered my shock. "Your father and Ray Von . . . ?"

"It's one of the reasons my mother left with me and Gary all those years ago. I suppose she tried to live in denial for several years but in the end decided she couldn't live with an unfaithful husband and his bastard. I didn't know until recently, after my mother disappeared. My father told me—thought it was time for me to know. It makes sense, though. Why Xavier wants to be part of the family, to be your protector. That's why we think he helped my mother get away with that artist—so that Ray Von might take her place."

"Are your father and Ray Von still involved?" I stifled an involuntary shudder.

He shook his head. "Oh, no. There's been nothing there for years. I don't really know why she stays with us, especially now that Xavier isn't around to remind my father of his obligation to her."

I stopped walking, and when I spoke my voice was hard. "He's your half brother and he's been living in your attic and on the streets and who knows where else. Don't you have an obligation to him?"

Johnny's reappearance interrupted my questions, and we jogged to keep up with him, his fin shaking as he ran. As we paused at the next house, he said, "I'm not obligated to him because Xavier betrayed our trust. He was responsible for taking our mother from us—from Gary. You know what it's like to lose a mother. If you found out somebody you knew was to blame for your mother's absence, how forgiving would you be?"

His eyes glittered with the reflection of the streetlight, his voice serious, as if he weren't asking a hypothetical question. I thought of all the years without my mother, of my father's grief and how I remembered her mostly by the scent of her perfume, the same scent that had lingered in her room and remained still in my memory. And of my fear of the dark and all things that lurked there.

I met his eyes. "I wouldn't be," I said, uncomfortable with the hatred I felt for a person whose face I'd never seen.

He looked at me with a hooded gaze. "Then you understand why I want you to stay away from Xavier. Have you told the lieutenant that you've seen Xavier?"

"No. I can't believe that Xavier is guilty of anything besides looking the way he does. He's a gentle soul, Wes. I know it. I can't believe he had anything to do with your mother's disappearance."

"I think you're wrong about him. Just the fact that he lurks around but doesn't make his presence known tells me that he's up to something, that he might even be dangerous. If he did help my mother leave, who knows what else he might do to force us to make him part of this family?" He paused. "But I'm glad you didn't tell the police you'd seen him. I don't want him talking to them."

My mind spun as I grabbed Johnny's hand and brought him across the street. As he galloped up to the door, I turned to Wes again. "Why don't you want him talking to the police?"

He watched Johnny hold out his bag at the opened door. "Because I think this family has had enough scandal. His parentage would be fodder for months. Just let him be, and tell him that you don't want to see him again if he shows up."

I didn't want to argue, knowing that on the subject of Xavier we would never agree. But I still had questions about Ray Von. "What happened to his face? I thought his father did that to him."

"From what my father told me, Ray Von left after she found out she was pregnant and got married to a longshoreman. He was nice when he was sober, but a mean drunk, and he was drunk most of the time. He died in the house fire he set while Ray Von and Xavier were sleeping. Ray Von turned to my father for help, and she came back to live with us." He shoved his hands deep in the pockets of his trousers. "I have no idea how my mother reconciled herself to the idea for as long as she did."

"I don't think she really did. I overheard an argument between your parents. It was the night before the Comus Ball, when I was staying at your house."

A dog barked nearby, its sound shrill in the chilly autumn air. "Well, then. That could explain why she wanted to leave." He let out a soft breath. "I wish Gary had known that. It might have made it easier for him, knowing there was a reason that had nothing to do with him."

We walked quietly to the next house, following a more subdued Johnny, whose heavy candy bag now dragged on the ground beside him. As we waited for him, I turned to Wes, the darkness making it somehow easier to put words to the black thoughts that wouldn't rest. "Xavier told me that our mothers were arguing the night she died. Have you ever heard that they were at odds about something?"

He shook his head. "No. According to my father and from what I remember, they were the best of friends—or more like mutual admirers, I should say. Your mother appreciated my mother's sense of style and intellect. My mother, well, she liked everything about your mother that wasn't her: her happy family life, her gardening, her voice—all those domestic things that my mother could never get ahold of. She pretended to feel nothing but disdain for women like that, but I think she was envious. It set her apart from the society she longed to belong to. But your mother was so kind to her, as if she really appreciated my mother's uniqueness. I think that's why they were such good friends, even though they were so completely different."

"The alligator brooch Caroline used to always wear—my mother gave that to her, you know. I'd like to think that they were real friends." I walked on ahead to grab Johnny's hand. "Are you ready to go home now? I think you've got enough candy to rot every single one of your teeth—even these long, sharp ones." I jiggled the shark teeth of his costume.

He giggled. "Can you carry me?"

"Sure, bud." I hoisted him up, and Wes took the candy and shark hood.

A sleepy voice on my shoulder said, "Uncle Gary used to call me bud. I like it."

"Me, too," I whispered back.

When we reached the Guidrys', I put Johnny down.

Wes stretched, then casually leaned on the gate. "The evening's early. Do you want to come in? We could help Johnny count his loot. He doesn't know how to count past eighteen."

I wanted to say yes, thinking of the empty room waiting for me at my grandmother's house, but held back. "I'd love to, but I can't. I'd better go home."

His eyes were still and somber. "Home to what, Aimee?"

I bristled at the truth in his words.

"I'm sorry—I didn't mean that the way it sounded. Please come in. Johnny and I would enjoy the company."

I turned away, not wanting him to see the panic in my eyes. "I can't, Wes. I really can't."

"All right. You win." Handing Johnny the candy bag, Wes said, "You go on inside. I'm going to walk your aunt Aimee home."

Johnny gave me a quick peck on the cheek, then ran to the house, his hand already busy digging into the candy.

My voice sounded higher than normal. "That's really not necessary. I can make it next door by myself." I indicated the deserted sidewalk with my thumb.

"Not when I know that Xavier has been following you. I'd feel a lot better seeing you home."

"Wes, I've told you before—I'm not afraid of Xavier. And I can walk home alone." I forced a smile. "Good night." I turned on the sidewalk, but he pulled me back.

His face was only inches from mine. "Why do you avoid me, Aimee? Is it because of what Gary told you?"

"No." I pulled my arm free and turned away again.

He caught me this time with both arms. "Then what is it? Don't you know that I grieve for him, too?"

I started to cry, ashamed at my tears, and wondering if it were possible to cry from sheer guilt.

His hands brought me closer to him, his voice earnest. "Don't you think it would be easier if we grieved together?"

"No!" I said again, trying to pull away from his grasp.

"Why?"

I put my hands on his chest, pushing away. "Please. Don't ask me to tell you."

He lifted my chin, his eyes hard and angry. "Gary's dead, Aimee. There can't be anything worse than that."

I jerked back, hitting him in the chest with the balls of my fists, making him stagger backward. "Yes, there can be." I hit him again, almost blinded now by the dark and the tears. I shouted at him, wanting to share the pain with the only other person who could understand it. "I have to live with the fact that I never loved him like I love you. And I can't forgive myself for that—I'll never forgive myself."

We stared at each other in stunned silence, aware of the enormity of what I had just said. A leaf fell from an old tree, drifting slowly to the ground. I turned and ran down the deserted sidewalk, not stopping until I had reached the end and rounded the corner onto St. Charles Avenue. I didn't need to look behind me to know he didn't follow.

And when I closed my eyes that night to sleep, I dreamed of the alligator pin with the ruby eyes, and smelled Shalimar perfume mixed with the coppery scent of blood.

CHAPTER 28

In the middle of the journey of our life I came to myself within a dark wood where the straight way was lost.

—DANTE ALIGHIERI

Julie

I stared out of the rental car window as we passed through familiar streets of my old New England hometown: the grocery store, my elementary school, the stark white Presbyterian church with the steeple that leaned slightly from a storm nearly one hundred years before. Chelsea had said it was a good thing, as if God were showing us that He was accepting of our human imperfections. I had come to think of it as His avenging finger, bending closer to the earth.

But this place of leaden skies and shell-less asphalt was alien to me now, and I found myself listening for the bark of skimmers and the relentless surf, and the soft accents and dropped consonants I'd begun to accept as familiar.

I glanced at my watch. "We've got a little time. Take a right at the next street. I want to see our old house."

Trey nodded. "I was in my study late last night and heard you on the phone with Aimee. What were you talking about?"

I told him what she'd told me about Gary's death and funeral, Xavier being in the room when Aimee's mother was killed, and what Wes had said about Xavier's father.

Trey shook his head. "So Xavier is my great-uncle. I can't believe that he's never told me. I guess we can ask him, or Ray Von, if Wes was telling the truth. Regardless, it's not that hard to prove." He shook his head again. "And he's never said anything about him being a witness to a murder."

"It might have been in the police report, but I guess we'll never know."

Trey strummed his fingers on the steering wheel. "I've been thinking about the picture of Monica with Caroline's brooch."

"Me, too. I wanted to ask Aimee about it last night, but she seemed to only want to talk about Gary so I figured it could wait until later. But I admit I'm intrigued about that pin. It was assumed that Caroline had taken it with her, but what was Monica doing with it? In all of the years I knew her, I never saw it. And I didn't find it when I went through her effects after she died. Unless she sold it at some point, which I doubt. But why would she have sold the pin and not the portrait?"

Trey flipped on the blinker and turned. "What I want to know is, where is it now?"

"I was just thinking the same thing." I sat back in my seat and stared out the window again. "Pull over to the curb when we get to the next block. It's the second house on the right."

Despite the chilly temperature, I lowered my window to get a better look at the nineteen sixties split-level I had called home for the first twelve years of my life. The small maple sapling my father had planted now dominated the side yard, and the shutters had been painted red instead of brown. An unfamiliar SUV sat in the asphalt driveway, and bikes lay scattered on the walk leading to the front door.

I'd always imagined that when we found Chelsea we'd bring her back here. As I sat watching, a woman came out the front door of our house with a small child on her hip and walked to the SUV. My breath came out in white puffs of air, expelled like old dreams. This wasn't our home anymore. Somebody else's family lived here now, with their lives and little dramas played out much like, I imagined, ours had once.

Watching the woman strap the child into a car seat, I realized that I'd always pictured this house the same, with our furniture and bikes, with our minivan in the driveway. But time had relentlessly moved forward; the house had changed. We had changed. Yet still, I'd dreamed that it waited for us. For a family that no longer existed.

Trey touched my cheek, and when I looked down at his finger I was surprised to find that it was wet.

"Are you all right?"

The woman started up her car and began to back out of the driveway. I looked at Trey, not sure how to answer. I was all right; I was sitting here, next to him, breathing and whole. But something had been shaken loose inside of me, and I felt too much pain to see through the settling dust. I managed a nod, then pressed my fists against my chest as if I could hold in all the grief I'd kept there, hidden inside the dream of a house and family that I realized now had disappeared with Chelsea all those years ago.

Ignoring my protests, Trey put the car in park and reached for me, enveloping me in an embrace of down jackets and comfort. He didn't say anything, and I was glad, because I knew he understood the journey, knew that the road to find the missing was never smooth or well-defined, and had no clear destination.

Eventually we pulled apart and he kissed me on the forehead. "Are you ready now?"

I wiped my face with the sleeves of my jacket and nodded. I told him where to drive, then leaned back in my seat with my eyes closed, and found myself straining to hear the calls of the skimmers and brown pelicans.

The police station sat on the edge of the town green in the old courthouse building. The courthouse, a midcentury monstrosity of modernism and tiny windows, sat across from its elegant past, its windows squinting at the police station as if to pick a fight. At least, that was what Chelsea had said, and I'd agreed even though I'd never told her.

We parked in the lot behind the tall brick police station with the Gothic cornices. I was still staring at a broken pediment over the rear entrance when Trey opened my door.

"Are you ready?"

I nodded and climbed out of the car. Inside the building, nothing had changed. Old metal radiators still spewed hot air along the walls, creating pockets of warmth in the tall-ceilinged reception area. Vinyl-cushioned benches, ones that didn't look like they'd been replaced since I'd first sat on them seventeen years ago, sat in the same L-shaped pattern on light blue and cream linoleum squares. A bulletin board filled with "most wanted" posters hung to the right of the two front double doors, a new generation of unsmiling faces staring out at me. An older woman with glasses on a chain around her neck looked up as we entered.

"May I help you?" Her vowels held the flat twang of the Northeast, and I paused for a moment, as if translating from a foreign language.

"We're here to see Detective Kobylt."

"Just a moment." She pushed a button. "You have visitors, Detective."

"I'll be right there." Even the sound of his voice calmed me. I knew that, having him and Trey with me, whatever the outcome of this visit, I was going to be okay.

When he entered the room I at first didn't know who he was. I'd always pictured him looking like Detective Johnson, the original detective on the case. He'd been old, gray, and bearded so I was surprised to find a trim and fit man in his late fifties with blond hair that barely showed any white.

I almost held out my hand to shake his as I approached, but when he opened his arms I stepped into his embrace as if we were old friends. I introduced him to Trey and we made small talk for a moment, but the specter of the reason for my visit hovered close.

Finally, the detective said, "I've got an interrogation room reserved for us, and the box of materials is already in there. If you're ready, we can go look at it now."

I felt Trey's hand on my shoulder. "I'm ready," I said, surprised at how strong my voice sounded.

We climbed wooden stairs painted the same mint green I remembered, and stepped into a large room filled with cubicles, the only difference being the larger number of desktop computers since the last time I'd been there. Detective Kobylt led us down a small hallway at the rear of the room, where three doors were lined up on the right-hand side. He stepped in front of us, then opened the third door before stepping back to allow us to enter.

The room was sparse, with a square wood-veneer table in the center and two chairs pulled up on each side. A white cardboard box with a lid sat in the middle of the table, making me think of Monica's stories of holy relics stored in church altars. I'd expected it to be larger—large enough to hold all of the years between then and now. But this was just a box used to hold reams of paper instead of what belongings remained of a girl left in a state park more than a decade before.

Detective Kobylt pulled back two chairs and indicated for us to sit. He then moved to the box and slowly lifted the lid. "We've already taken as much forensic evidence as we can from everything in here, so if you need to touch anything you're free to do so."

Very slowly, he began taking things out of the box and laying them on the table in front of Trey and me. I felt light-headed, as if I were watching this from the vantage point of the ceiling, or the two-way mirror at the end of the room. As if this composed young woman sitting at the table watching the detective remove things from the box were somebody else; as if all this were happening to somebody else.

The first thing he placed in front of me was a four-inch square of what looked like it had once been a sweater with wide pastel stripes. Next to it he placed a rainbow-hued shoelace, a tight knot at one end, encrusted with dried dirt. A small red patent-leather purse with a dull brass handle came next, followed by a lace-edged ankle sock, the lace wilted and brown.

I touched them all, the stiff hardness of the material, the slippery softness of the purse, and stared closely at these remnants of somebody's life, willing them to be recognizable. But Chelsea had been wearing my favorite gray Harvard football sweatshirt when she disappeared. She might have been wearing a sweater underneath, but she didn't own a pastel-striped sweater. I knew this with certainty, because Chelsea wore all of my hand-me-downs and I hated stripes.

And Chelsea never had pocketbooks or lace ankle socks. My sister had loved science, math, and painting. These were not hers, could never have been hers. And as I placed the shoelace back on the table with shaking fingers, I was no longer sure whether I should be relieved or disappointed.

Both men were watching me. I shook my head. "These aren't Chelsea's." I explained why and watched the detective's shoulders fall. I stood and took his hand. "They aren't Chelsea's, but they're somebody's. I hope you find out whose, so the family will know."

Detective Kobylt shook his head. "I was so sure . . ." He let out a deep breath. "And here you are, trying to make me feel better." He hugged me tightly, and my world seemed to refocus itself.

Gently, he put me away from him. "This isn't your sister, Julie. But maybe this is a clue to finding her. This victim and Chelsea are about the same age, and one was found and the other went missing in the same geographical area. This gives us something, at the very least." He looked from me to Trey and back again. "I'm just sorry to have dragged you up here."

I shook my head. "I'm glad we came. We know for sure now that it wasn't Chelsea, and I got to meet you finally."

He smiled sadly. "Still . . ."

"And I'd do it again. Anything to help you, all right? Don't hesitate to call me if you need me to come back."

He nodded, then led us to the reception area. My palms were slick with sweat, my hands shaking as he placed them both again in his. "I won't forget Chelsea. I'll keep looking."

"I know," I said. "Thank you."

We hugged again and said our good-byes; then Trey and I left. We walked out the back door into a day filled with heavy gray clouds, an icy misting rain beginning to fall. But I turned my face skyward, sensing the sun that lay behind the clouds and feeling a lightness I hadn't felt in a very long time. As we walked toward the car I pressed my hands against my chest again, feeling a hollowness there, an emptiness that had been carved not from the passing on of a burden, but instead from the opening of a void that waited to be filled.

We sat in the car, but Trey didn't start the ignition right away. "Are you okay?"

I took a deep breath, my lungs suddenly seeming to have more room to expand. I breathed out slowly and we watched as it came out in a cloud of white. "I don't know." I took another breath. "I really don't know. But I'm glad you came."

"Me, too." Trey leaned over and kissed me lightly before starting the car.

My cell phone rang and I saw it was the house phone in New Orleans. I picked it up, surprised to hear Aimee's voice.

"Julie?"

"Yes, Aimee, it's me." I looked at my watch, calculating the time in New Orleans. "It's only two o'clock in the afternoon. I didn't expect Carol Sue to have brought you home so early. Unless nobody felt like partying last night and you all got to bed early."

Her voice was agitated, distracted. "I needed to get home. I've got things to do that can't wait."

"Did Beau come with you?"

"No, he stayed with Carol Sue." There was a long pause, and I was beginning to wonder if she'd remembered that she was the one who'd called me. "That photograph of Monica. I left it in Trey's car."

"Yes," I said. "I found it."

"Did you see?"

"The pin?"

"Yes." She breathed into the phone. "And the ring. My mother's ring was taken off her finger when she was killed."

I straightened. "Yes, I remember. Do you know how Monica got them?"

She didn't answer right away. Finally, she said, "I need to tell you my story of the night Hurricane Camille hit Biloxi."

I focused on breathing deeply, trying to tamp down my impatience. "But that was way before Monica's time."

"Yes, it was," she said slowly, as if already thinking back on the summer of 1969. "But I think I figured out where the jewelry's been all this time."

"All right," I said. Then I sat back in my seat and began to listen.

CHAPTER 29

In saffron-colored mantle, from the tides of ocean rose the morning to bring light to gods and men.   —HOMER

Aimee

1969

My life developed a sameness to it, a routine I found outwardly comforting. It was as if I believed a placid external life could smooth the wrinkles of my conscience and make them go away. They never did.

My father died, and I went up to Philadelphia to the funeral and to pack up what few possessions he had. My parents' wedding photograph that had sat on his nightstand for all of those years now sat on mine.

We saw the Guidrys often, especially Mr. Guidry, who seemed to latch onto me as his last connection to Gary, and that touched me. Gary's relationship with his father had never been a smooth one, yet I found some comfort knowing Mr. Guidry grieved for his youngest son. He'd gone through the attic for Gary's baby pictures and given them to me. I treasured them, along with my wedding ring, which I still wore.

And Johnny became the son that I wished I'd had. He was an intelligent and sweet boy who enjoyed building with blocks, then knocking them down with swift, harsh kicks. I supposed this was natural for a child with an innate curiosity about how things worked, but whose mother seemed more interested in social appearances, and whose father spent more time at his office than he did at home. Johnny came over almost every day after school, and I'd give him a snack while we talked or built log houses or just sat on the front porch absorbing the heat of the day. He needed companionship almost as much as I did.

Wes and I avoided each other, although it was usually he who'd come to claim Johnny on Ray Von's day off. We kept our conversations on neutral ground, avoiding the minefields of our thoughts and feelings. But I looked forward to those meetings, rushing through my life until the next time he'd come to my grandmother's house to collect his son.

I didn't see Xavier again; Ray Von said he was working on a lumber barge on the Mississippi River and making good money. With him away, Ray Von seemed almost relieved, and was less hostile to me. But when I asked her to send my regards to Xavier and wish him well, her expression would harden, so I learned to stop asking.

I never visited River Song during those years; the memories were too painful. But I knew Wes, Lacy, and Johnny visited it often, always with large groups of friends and their children, as if they needed the distraction of other people. I was glad for Johnny. The beach and the beautiful white house held so many possibilities for a young boy, a place of refuge by the water where the days seemed longer and the stars at night brighter.

I still worked at the same gallery on Royal Street, but had been promoted to manager, and had even been allowed to go to several estate auctions on buying trips. I loved my work, and was good at it, but it never filled the void completely. Looking back, I realized that my life had become much like the hot Sahara wind blowing into the Atlantic: deceptive in its obscurity, yet spawning the seeds of a great storm more than a thousand miles from its inception.

On a Saturday morning in the middle of August, I woke up to

a red-tinted sky, remembering something about a red sky at morning, sailors take warning. By the time I'd dressed for work and was in my car headed downtown, the sun blazed in a perfectly blue sky, the trees barely ruffled by a calm breeze. If a storm brewed somewhere, the placid houses and people I passed on my way to work were blissfully unaware.

Traffic converged on Lee Circle, and I braked quickly to avoid a beat-up sedan, a collection of Mardi Gras beads dangling from its rearview mirror. I turned on the radio and listened to the weather report. A tropical storm named Camille had hit Cuba, and was expected to head out into the Gulf of Mexico, gathering strength as it veered toward the Florida panhandle. I expected we might get some wind and rain from Camille, but the panhandle was far enough away from New Orleans that I wasn't too concerned.

At the beginning of the hurricane season in June my grandmother and I had attended a Mass to pray to Our Lady of Prompt Succor, as native New Orleanians did, to protect us from hurricanes. Almost three months into the hurricane season, I felt some relief knowing that we were halfway through.

I noted again the dirgelike movement of the leaves on the trees and flipped to another station to find music instead of the incessant chattering about the storm. Still, I planned to close the hurricane shutters on the house and move the outdoor furniture inside when I got home after work. Grandmother had left for her yearly cruise with her girlfriends, and Aunt Roseanne was taking her own vacation, so it was up to me to make sure the house was stormproofed.

Around noon, the gallery owner stuck her head in my office.

"Aimee, have you been listening to the weather reports?"

I shook my head, my pencil poised over a column of figures.

"Camille is in the gulf. The National Hurricane Center has issued a hurricane watch all the way from Biloxi to St. Marks, Florida. You have a house in Biloxi, don't you? They're still saying it'll hit the panhandle, but I'm closing the gallery so everybody can have a chance to fill their tanks with gas and join the rest of the city at the grocery store to buy bread and milk and get ready for their hurricane parties."

I thought of River Song and the last time I'd been there with Gary. I'd always thought of it as a haven, but now could see how vulnerable it seemed so close to the water, its glowing white facade as delicate as a seashell. "You don't really think we'll get hit, do you? We get warnings like this all the time, but it always seems to turn and go somewhere else."

She shrugged. "Not always." With a wave she disappeared out the door.

Before I could put the pencil down, the phone rang. "Hello?"

"Aimee, it's Wes." He paused a moment, and I listened to the sound of my breathing in the receiver. "Have you been listening to the news?"

"No, but if it's about the hurricane, I know all about it. We're closing the gallery, and I'll be heading home as soon as I finish some paperwork."

"Good. I'll help you secure the shutters. Then I want you to come to our house to ride out the storm."

"Do you really think that's necessary?" A feeling of unease took root in the pit of my stomach.

"Yeah. I do. It doesn't look good. The thing's growing in the gulf, and they're saying that the winds are already about one hundred and sixty miles per hour. If it hits, we're in big trouble. Even if it doesn't hit us directly, we'll get some serious winds and more water than this city knows what to do with. They're not evacuating New Orleans, but I want to know you'll be safe."

"All right. I'll give you a call when I get home. When will you be there?"

A phone rang in the background. "I'm going to stop and pick up Johnny from school. Then, depending on traffic, I should get home around three."

"Fine. I'll see you then."

"And, Aimee . . ."

"Yes?"

He paused. "Never mind. We'll talk later."

I cleared my throat, staring at my wedding ring on my finger. "Okay. Later, then."

I hung up the phone, my heartbeat almost audible. The traffic was heavy as people headed home to prepare for the worst. Within an hour and a half, I had made it to my grandmother's front steps. Next door at the Guidrys' house, the tall shutters—decorative on houses in other parts of the world—had been closed over the thick antique glass windows and bolted.

I quickly changed into blue jeans and a blouse, then called next door, hoping Wes would be the one to answer. He wasn't.

"Hello, Lacy. It's Aimee. Wes told me to call to get some help shuttering my windows. Is he home yet?"

She paused. "He's picking up Johnny and hasn't returned yet." She didn't say anything about taking a message to have him call me back.

"Well, never mind then. He'd also mentioned riding out the storm at your house, but I think I'll be fine over here." I looked out the window, where thick clouds had begun to obscure the blue.

"Yes. I think you're right. Good-bye, Aimee."

I heard a click and then the dial tone before I hung up the phone.

I spent the rest of the afternoon getting the house ready, then ate a TV dinner watching the news. Hurricane Camille was now just two hundred miles south of the Mississippi River, and the hurricane watch had been upgraded to a hurricane warning for the entire Gulf Coast. They were advising evacuation of low-lying areas.

I called next door to see if they'd remembered to call a neighbor in Biloxi to board up the house and move the furniture to the upper stories. I tried three times throughout the evening, and received a busy signal each time. I wondered if Lacy had placed the phone off the hook, and how much embellishment she might have added if she'd relayed my earlier phone call to Wes, as an explanation for why he didn't try to call me.

A soaking rain fell overnight, and when I awakened on Sunday morning, the skies hung low and gray, the saturated earth oozing water into the humid air. I reached for the phone again but hung up without dialing. If there were an emergency, I could always walk next door.

I went to Mass, noting that it was nearly as crowded in the church as it was on Easter and Christmas. I'd always thought that the people who attended Mass only on the high holy days reminded me of students who studied only for the final exam. A hurricane, I supposed, was no different.

I spent my day alternating between moving valuables to the upper stories of my grandmother's house and watching the news. The roadways moving away from the Gulf Coast were packed with would-be vacationers, station wagons stuffed full with suitcases strapped on top, sedans and coupes all heading away from what forecasters were now saying would be a direct hit somewhere along the coast. By five o'clock p.m., the pictures of the approaching hurricane sent me to the phone again.

It rang before I could pick it up to dial.

"Hello?"

"Where is he?" Lacy screamed into the phone. "Is he with you?"

"Wes? No. I haven't even talked to him since yesterday morning. Why?"

She was sobbing so hard that she was nearly incoherent. "Because he's gone! He left an hour ago without telling me where he was going, and he hasn't come back. His car isn't here either."

"Calm down, Lacy. Did you ask Mr. Guidry? He might know."

"He's not here either. An old widow—a client of his, near the river bend—needed his help to board up her windows, so he left a couple of hours ago. Ray Von is gone, too—she went to her sister's house in Chalmette first thing this morning."

Her voice was rising again, and I kept my voice calm. "Is Johnny with you?"

Lacy sniffed loudly into the phone. "Yes. It's just the two of us, and I don't know what to do."

"Lacy, your house is shuttered and the Garden District is on higher ground, so you and Johnny should be safe. Let me make a few phone calls to see if I can locate him and then I'll come over and we'll ride out the storm together, all right?"

She didn't hesitate. "Yes." A pause. "Thank you."

I hung up the phone, then grabbed my address book and began calling numbers. Nobody answered at his office, and the few people I reached at home had not seen or heard from him. I called Lacy back to see if she recalled the name of the client whose house Mr. Guidry had gone to, but she couldn't remember. I'd been hoping that he might at least know where Wes could have gone.

I turned off the television, needing the silence to think. Rain pelted the windows and the roof, and a strong wind bent the trees in the garden, stripping the flowers of their petals. I had my hand on the phone, getting ready to call Lacy to tell her that I was coming over and would let myself in with my key, but stopped. The last time Wes had disappeared had been after the Comus Ball, and he'd gone to River Song. But then he'd gone to escape the turmoil of the aftermath of his mother's disappearance. This time he was moving toward the source of turbulence and confusion, and the heavy weight of dread settled firmly on my shoulders.

I picked up the receiver and dialed the phone at River Song. I let it ring ten times before hanging up and trying again. This time Wes answered on the second ring.

"Wes. Thank God. Lacy and I have been eaten up with worry. Why didn't you tell anybody where you were going?"

"Because I didn't want anybody to stop me. Somebody had to come down here and get River Song ready for the storm. I have to run to the store still to get some supplies and food in case I can't leave for a while. It's going to be bad."

I closed my eyes, listening to the staccato beats of rain against the window. "You shouldn't be there. They're evacuating."

"I know. But there are things I need to take care of here. Things that nobody else knows to do."

His voice sounded odd to my ears, and I wondered if it were because of the bad connection. "Are you all right, Wes? You sound . . . different."

"Did you talk with Lacy?"

"About what?" I almost screamed into the phone. I wanted him to tell me that he was headed back to New Orleans, not ask me about his wife.

"I can't talk any more, Aimee. I've got to take care of things." He paused for a moment. "All truths rise to the surface eventually."

I gripped the receiver tighter. "What are you talking about? There's a hurricane heading toward Biloxi. You need to leave now."

"I can't. Go stay with Lacy and Johnny and keep them safe."

For the second time in as many days, I heard the line click and then the sound of the dial tone. I hung up and dialed the number again, each number on the rotary dial seeming to take longer and longer than the last. I got a busy signal the first few times I called, and then nothing but empty air. If the phone lines were down, it was only a matter of time before the power went out, too.

One last time, I picked up the phone. "Lacy, it's Aimee. I found Wes. He's at River Song getting it ready for the hurricane." I paused. "Did you argue before he left?"

Fresh sobs erupted into the phone, but when she spoke her voice was harsh. "You could say that."

"He didn't sound like himself on the phone, and I'm worried."

Her laugh was soft and unexpected. "You have no idea how worried you should be. You're so naive, Aimee." She sniffed. "You have no idea."

"You're not making any sense, Lacy." The rain slapped against the side of the house. I looked around at the nearly empty rooms, devoid of paintings and furniture I'd moved upstairs. My aloneness resonated within the walls, echoing with each drop of rain.

"Aimee?" Lacy's voice sounded hoarse. "Are you there? Are you coming over?"

I hope the time will come when you two will be able to put what you want first. Gary's words came to me with so much clarity that I imagined the world around me became brighter. There was nothing for me here, in this house, in this city. Everything I loved was at River Song, with Wes.

I cleared my throat. "He shouldn't be alone," I said, my voice trying to sound convincing for both of us. "I'm going to drive to Biloxi, see if I can get him to go to a shelter."

"No," she hissed. "I'm still his wife. I should be the one with him."

"You've got a son, Lacy, and you need to stay with him. Stay here with Johnny. Hopefully Mr. Guidry will be back home soon. If not, you're safe where you are."

"Please don't go." Her voice pleaded now, but I wasn't sure whether she didn't want me to go because she didn't want me with Wes or because she was afraid to be alone.

"I promise we'll be in touch as soon as we can find a working phone. Stay with Johnny. He needs you."

Without waiting to say good-bye, I hung up the phone. Grabbing a raincoat and umbrella, I ran out to my car in the teeming rain and headed toward the highway. Despite the open road in the direction I was heading, I didn't go as fast as I wanted to. The roads were slick, the wind strong, and I had no intention of being blown off the side of the road.

The traffic flowing in the opposite direction was heavy but moving. I imagined that most of the full-time residents of the coast would remain in their homes as a point of pride. Since Biloxi was about twelve feet above sea level, most people considered themselves safe once they'd taped up their windows. I hoped that many of them were watching the news and the predictions for the ferocity of this storm and heeding the evacuation advice. But even I, who had grown to love the area as if I were a native daughter, would have to be convinced of impending danger before I would leave.

They'd closed Beach Boulevard and I had to drive through back roads to avoid the barriers and come up to River Song from behind. I parked on the street that lined the side of the house and opened the car door. The wind snatched it out of my hand, and for a moment I thought it would blow off its hinges as I wrestled with the wind to get it closed again. I'd left the raincoat and umbrella in the car. Neither would be any match for the sheets of rain that soaked the world around me.

I crossed the yard to the front walk, my feet sinking in sand and grass, my shoes saturated. I saw Wes's car in the drive as I ran to the front porch, now bare of rocking chairs and hammocks. A brand-new shovel with a sticker tag still attached to the light wood handle lay faceup near the door.

Rain battered my back, and I didn't stop to knock but pulled open the screen and opened the front door. Stepping in quickly, I shut the door behind me and leaned against it. The wind howled outside, almost blocking out the sound of the blood rushing in my head.

Something hit the side of the house with a loud wooden slap, making me jump. The shutters rattled like a band of drunks, hitting against the window frames in a haphazard pattern. The lights flickered, and I dreaded the inevitable moment when the lights would go out for good.

"Wes! It's Aimee."

Footsteps pounded on the stairs. When he appeared at the bottom, his eyes widened. "What in the hell are you doing here? I told you to stay in New Orleans."

"I was worried about you. You didn't sound like yourself when we spoke, and then you weren't answering the phone."

"The phones are out."

"I told Lacy I would get you to a shelter. You shouldn't be here. We shouldn't be here." *For more reasons than a simple hurricane.*

The front door groaned, its hinges straining with the pressure. "There's no time." He took my hand, but there was no warmth. "We need to finish securing the shutters. With the wind and rain it's taking me five times as long to do each one."

He dragged me up the stairs after him. The bedroom where Gary and I had stayed was dark from the closed shutters, and I was grateful I wouldn't have to go in there.

"In here," Wes called from the sleeping porch, and I quickly followed. I wanted to talk to him, to ask him what he'd meant when he talked about the truth rising to the surface. I wanted to know whether it had anything to do with what he'd wanted to talk to me about when we'd spoken on the phone earlier, but darkness came like a door shutting as the wind and rain increased their fury, erasing all thoughts but survival from my head.

We struggled with each window, the rain pouring in as we opened each one to access the shutters, the wind fighting, and sometimes winning, against our efforts to pull them shut and bolt them from the inside over the windows. We'd managed to close the four on the porch and had moved to the front bedroom when I saw headlights moving across the lawn.

We both stared at the window as the ceiling light flickered twice.

The driver's door opened and a woman stepped out.

"Lacy," Wes said through clenched teeth.

And then the passenger door opened and Johnny leaped out of the car and struggled to close it. Giving up, he ran to the porch, his mother close behind him.

"Dear God," Wes said, as he headed toward the stairs and the lights went out, throwing us all into a black abyss.

I struggled to find the flashlight Wes had given me earlier that I'd stuck inside the waistband of my blue jeans. My fingers were slippery and cold, and I fumbled for the "on" switch, managing to turn it on and head for the stairs behind Wes, my shaking hand creating a dancing orb of light.

We both aimed our flashlight beams at the two sodden figures inside the front door. Johnny ran to me when he saw me, and I put my arm around his trembling shoulders.

Wes stood, shaking his head at Lacy. "Why are you here? And why did you bring Johnny? Why did you bring our son?"

His anger rolled down his skin in the rivulets of water. Johnny clung tightly to me as Lacy looked up at Wes and swiped her wet hair off of her face. "Because I didn't want you here, alone with her. And I didn't know what you would do with . . ." She stopped and glanced at me.

All truths rise to the surface eventually. I stared at Lacy and her limp hair, no longer feeling sorry for her. *She knows*, I thought. Whatever it was that had drawn Wes to River Song, Lacy knew.

The walls and windows of the house shuddered and moaned, the wind screaming. Wes shouted, "The hurricane's hitting at high tide. Go! Upstairs, go! We don't have much time."

Pushing Johnny in front of me, I headed for the stairs with Lacy close behind me. When I reached the top I looked down the stairs and saw Wes waiting on the bottom step.

"Wes, you've got to come, too."

He shook his head. "Go to the interior upstairs bathroom and get in the bathtub. I've got something I've got to do first."

"No!" Lacy screamed. "It's not worth it." She started down the stairs, but I grabbed her blouse, pulling her back.

"You can't, Lacy," I shouted over the sound of the storm. "Don't do that to Johnny."

Her jaw stiffened as she made up her mind. She looked at her son and her face softened. Glancing back at Wes one more time, she took Johnny's arm and ran the rest of the way up the stairs.

I stood near the top, torn between safety and Wes. "Where are you going?"

"It's just something I need to do. So I can sleep at night. So . . ." He stopped. "Be safe, Aimee." He took a step backward. "I love you. I never stopped."

I was too angry to respond, too scared of the cloying darkness with only the thin beam from my flashlight to illuminate what lurked in the corners. I stayed where I was long enough to watch him disappear from my sight and listen as he wrestled with the front door to open and then close it again. I watched from the window at the bottom of the stairs as he crossed in front of it on the porch, bent over at the waist, then leaned down to pick something up before disappearing from my view.

I took the stairs two at a time, losing a shoe but not wanting to take the time to retrieve it. The bathroom door was shut, and when I turned the handle it was locked. Banging on it hard, I shouted, "Lacy, let me in!" I banged on it again, my mind searching for the possibility of finding a room without a window in a beach house built to enjoy views of the sound.

It took only a moment for the door to open inward, and I stumbled inside the small room.

Lacy, with her hair flat against her head and her makeup washed away, looked like a child who'd just lost her favorite doll. "I'm sorry, Aimee. I thought you'd go with Wes."

I closed the door and locked it again, although I wasn't sure what I really thought I could keep out. Johnny, who, at eleven years old, was almost as tall as I was, sat in the empty bathtub, his arms wrapped around his knees, his face turned to me as if I had all the answers. The tub was small and couldn't accommodate all three of us.

"Lacy, get in with Johnny. I'll sit here on the floor next to you and wait."

"To get rescued?"

I looked at Lacy, resisting my impulse to shake her. Everything she'd been raised to be had no bearing here, in this island of a bathroom in the middle of a hurricane. I touched my forehead to the cold porcelain of the tub, feeling unprepared to be anybody's last line of defense.

"What do we do now?"

I looked up at Johnny and put my hand on his arm. "We wait. And pray. There's nothing else we can do. And if the water rises to the second floor, we go up to the roof. Hopefully your dad will be back soon, and he can help."

A soft sob came from Lacy, and I wanted to shout at her to stop, that she was scaring Johnny and not helping. Instead I placed a hand on her shoulder and left it there for a moment. "This house has survived bad storms before. There's no reason to think it won't again."

They looked at me with identical expressions of hope tinged with realization, and I had to look away. The beam of light from my flashlight dimmed. I knew spare batteries were kept in the kitchen, but I wasn't leaving the bathroom. "I have to save the batteries, so I'm going to turn off the flashlight until we really need it."

I held my thumb over the switch and turned it off, throwing us into inky blackness. Things continued to bang and slap against the house, the sound of the straining walls muted in our makeshift shelter. A booming crack rent the night outside, cutting through the sounds of the raging wind. It was followed by an almost deafening crash that shook the floor beneath us. I stood, frozen with fear, listening to the walls wail and for Wes's voice, and waiting for the virulent thing that crouched in the darkness to find me.

Nobody spoke, and I thought for a moment that Lacy and Johnny might have fallen asleep. But then a hand reached for mine, and I felt the wedding ring on the third finger. "Thank you," Lacy said, and nothing more before she let go of my hand and she melted into the darkness. I wasn't sure if she were thanking me for being there or for not following her husband outside.

A shout cut through the night, and I strained my ears, wondering if it had been my imagination. I stood, feeling Lacy and Johnny turning their heads toward me. I heard it again, closer this time, and flicked on my flashlight. "Did you hear that?"

They both shook their heads.

"I heard somebody shout. It might be Wes. He might need help."

Johnny stood but I waved him back. "No. You two stay here. I'll go see."

I didn't wait long enough to hear any protests. Unlatching the door, I stepped into the upstairs hallway. A shutter had come loose on the sleeping porch, and wind and rain streaked inside through the broken glass. I glanced down the stairs just in time to get out of the way as

Xavier ran toward me, half carrying, half dragging Wes. The flashlight beam caught a jagged tear of red cutting through Wes's scalp and forehead, diluted blood dripping down the side of his face.

There was no time to think or be surprised. I took a step back and opened the door. "Put him on the floor. I'll wrap his head with towels."

Lacy threw her hands over her mouth and stared in shock. Johnny reached over and grabbed a beach towel from the rack and folded it up like a pillow to place under his father's head as Xavier laid Wes on the floor beneath the pedestal sink.

I took a hand towel from the ring beside the sink, then sat down and pressed it against the gaping wound on Wes's head. He seemed to be unconscious, which was probably a good thing. Any aspirin that was kept in that bathroom wouldn't be enough.

"What happened?" I asked Xavier. The knees of his blue jeans, as well as the front of his shirt, were covered in mud. Aiming the dim beam of light at Wes, I saw that he was, too, and that his hands and nails were embedded with thick, dark mud. "What are you doing here?"

He jerked his chin toward Wes. "My mama told me he was coming down here, and I knew that was bad news. So I came, too, and found him outside. One of those limbs on the oak out front broke off and hit him in the head. Good thing I found him."

He stood and backed away to the door. His hand was fisted, holding something inside. "It's going to be all right now. I don't have to run anymore." He put his hand on the doorknob and began to turn it.

"Xavier, no. You can't go. It would be suicide."

"Don't you worry about me, Miss Aimee. I've got a place to go."

"Let him go, Aimee. Let him go. He knows what he's doing."

I turned to look at Lacy, who stood in the bathtub, her back pressed against the wall. A look passed between them that I couldn't decipher. *All truths rise to the surface eventually.*

"Would somebody please tell me what's going on here?"

But Xavier had already slipped through the doorway, closing the door behind him, and Lacy resumed her hunched position in the bathtub with her son.

Terror took root in my belly as the deafening roar of the wind and debris pummeling the house tore at my ears. I did what I could for Wes, changing towels when the one on his head became soaked with blood. He regained semiconsciousness and asked for water. But nothing came from the taps. I could have laughed: all the rain and water outside but not a drop to drink.

Lacy kept asking about Wes, but stayed in the tub. There was no room for her to move anyway, and I wanted to keep my hand on his chest to make sure his heart still beat. I had never seen such darkness—no streetlights, no moonlight, nothing but seamless black in the windowless room. We began to pray out loud when we heard a sound like that of an approaching train, a loud booming whistle followed by the crack of torn wood and shattering glass. Wes flinched under my hand and Lacy cried out, but Johnny and I remained silent, realizing that our shouts wouldn't be heard.

The wind grew stronger and louder, slicing now through the cracks under and around the door, and I wondered if another window had broken. The deceptive calm of the eye passed over us, and I had to press Lacy back into the tub so she wouldn't leave the room.

Eventually the rain stopped its unremitting pounding, the wind its brutal pulse. Lacy and Johnny fell asleep, but I forced myself to remain alert, to press my hand on Wes's chest, to listen for anything that would tell me that this was all over.

I knew dawn had arrived by the gray light that crept through the cracks around the door. Wes still slept fitfully, but he'd survived the night. I stood, my neck and shoulders stiff from sitting on the floor for so many hours, leaning against the sink.

"Are we safe?" Johnny's voice cracked from his dry mouth.

I didn't know how to answer that, unsure that I could believe I'd ever be safe again.

Johnny's words woke his mother, and she sat up, blinking, trying to recall where she was. Her eyes fluttered to her husband. "Is he . . . ?"

"He's all right for now. The bleeding's stopped and he was awake about twenty minutes ago asking for water. But we need to get him to a hospital as soon as possible."

They both stood in the tub, looking and waiting for me to open the door. I hesitated only a moment. Turning the knob, I pulled the door toward me and found myself standing under a predawn sky under what had once been a roof.

Dim gray light touched the remaining walls, the trees outside, and my outstretched hands, the amount of darkness and light equal. Ray Von had a name for this: *entre chien et loup*—the light in which one couldn't distinguish between a dog or a wolf.

The light gradually brightened as I stood there, realizing how lucky we were. The roof was gone from most of the house, the only part remaining over the bathroom and hall closet, clinging in places like fingers of Spanish moss. Turning around, I said, "Lacy, stay with Wes. Johnny, come with me to find help." I continued down the stairs and found my shoe where it had fallen, yet the couch that had sat in the living room had been blown through the window and now held court, right side up with all of its cushions intact, in the middle of the front yard as if it had always been there.

I saw the oak tree, its limbs stripped bare, a white streak on its side where the bark had been stripped away. Lacy's car rested on its roof beside it, twisted beams, a dead cat, and tree limbs scattered around it. But it had survived. We had all survived. We'd never be the same again, but we had survived.

The sun broke over the horizon, illuminating a clear blue sky, an odd sky devoid of clouds or birds. We walked down the steps and outside to a ruined world. River Song still stood, battered and worn, but she was still standing. What was left of her white siding gleamed in the sunlight like a beacon of hope. A wind chime jangled and I admired its tenacity.

"Look up," I told Johnny, and he did, his mouth open. "Remember that, all right? When everything you're about to see is too much, look up and see that the sky is clear and know that everything is going to be all right."

I took his hand and led him carefully down to the debris-strewn beach, beginning to run toward the sound of wailing sirens, watching as the sun rose again on a new day over land and air that had been wiped clean. And only once did I stop to wonder what Wes had been doing under the oak tree before I realized that it didn't matter. That nothing mattered except that we had survived the storm.

CHAPTER 30

*To him that waits all things reveal themselves, provided that
he has the courage not to deny, in the darkness, what he has
seen in the light.* —COVENTRY PATMORE

Julie

Once we'd boarded the plane back to New Orleans, I gave in to exhaustion and fell asleep on Trey's shoulder. I dreamed I was at River Song again, but this time I was standing on the pier, looking at the house from afar. There were people all over the lawn and they were celebrating something, but I couldn't tell what. The house sat proudly on new pilings; the old oak, surrounded by a shoofly, glowed resplendent with green leaves, its arms casting cool shade on the people beneath on the sandy grass.

Chelsea stood on the front steps, beckoning me. I followed her through the front door, but I was no longer in Biloxi but was instead standing by myself in the foyer of the house on First Street. The cloying smell of perfume filled my nostrils, taking over all of my senses.

Then I heard the chanting of the doomed Pascagoula tribe as they marched into the river, past the carved Katrina tree of the swimming dolphins, and I opened my eyes just in time to hear the pilot announce our descent into New Orleans.

I pressed my forehead against the window, watching as the tall buildings in the distance grew larger, the odd feeling of coming home settling temporarily in my heart, as if I were trying it on like a new coat.

Closing my eyes again, I tried to conjure Chelsea, but all I could see was the dead oak trees reborn as marlins and pelicans and dolphins, their smiling eyes watching me, waiting for me to understand. As the plane touched down on the tarmac, I was still wondering what they were trying to tell me.

It was almost midnight by the time Trey parked his truck in front of the house on First Street. Kathy Wolf met us on the front steps, wringing her hands, her forehead creased with worry. We ran up the steps to meet her.

"What's wrong?" Trey asked.

"Everything's all right now. She told me not to call you, or I would have—"

"What happened?" he asked, cutting her off.

"She was in a car wreck. She's okay—just a little shaken up, and she has a bad scrape on her forehead from the air bag."

"She was driving?" I asked. "What did she hit?"

"Just a mailbox, thank goodness," Kathy said. "No other vehicle was involved. But her car had to be towed." She shook her head in agitation. "She took the car keys from my purse. It never occurred to me that I needed to hide them."

Trey made to move past her, but Kathy stopped him. "She's resting now, Trey. The doctor gave me something to give her so she could have a full night's sleep."

"Did she tell you where she was going?" I asked, my mind reeling with all the questions that stacked up in my mind like storm debris.

Kathy pursed her lips. "She wanted to see Wes. She said she had to show him something. I told her that it was too late, that because of the holiday visiting hours were limited and I would take her tomorrow. She left while I was in the laundry room and couldn't hear her."

Trey and I looked at each other, the same question in our minds.

"Kathy, any idea what she wanted to show Wes?" I let my overnight bag, packed just in case I'd needed to stay overnight in Massachusetts, slip to the porch floor.

She shook her head. "Like I said, she sort of sneaked out, so I have no idea what she might have brought to show him."

"Do you know where they towed her car?" Trey asked.

Kathy nodded. "Yes. They took it to the dealership out on Airline Highway. It's not totaled, but it will take them a couple of weeks to fix it."

"Do you happen to have a spare set of keys?" Trey asked. "I want to look inside the car and trunk."

"Actually," Kathy said, "Billy Crandall at the dealership was nice enough to box up everything and drop it off. It's in the utility room."

I was nearly out of breath chasing Trey up the stairs to the second floor and to the end of the hall. He threw open the door and flipped on the light, illuminating a small room with a large washer and dryer, a drying rack, a set of cherry cabinets over the appliances, and a large folding table up against the opposite wall. Sitting on top of the washing machine was a cardboard box, its ends folded in on themselves.

With one firm pull, he opened the box. Scattered inside were the usual personal items found in a car: a box of Kleenex, a road map of Louisiana, a rosary, a pair of slip-on tennis shoes—for times when Aimee needed to get out of tight heels, I supposed. But propped up against the inside of the box so it wouldn't get damaged was a loosely wrapped package of the same size and shape as Caroline Guidry's portrait.

Trey pulled out the package and unwrapped it, revealing Caroline Guidry's blue cat's eyes and the alligator brooch with the pointed tail and ruby eyes.

My gaze met Trey's. "I guess Aimee was my anonymous buyer." I shook my head. "But why was she taking this to show Wes?"

He looked back at the portrait, a crease between his brows. He was silent for a moment. "For the same reason Monica did. To confront him. Because they'd both discovered something that convinced them that he knew something about Caroline's disappearance. And maybe more."

I stared hard at the portrait, my thoughts churning. "That picture of Monica wearing the gold band and pin—that's what made her go see Wes. Aimee was acting odd when I spoke to her at Walker's, and that was right after she'd seen the photograph." I leaned toward Trey, lowering my voice. "Aimee knows that the only thing missing from the murder scene was her mother's wedding ring. That's why they thought it was a robbery."

Trey shook his head slowly. "It's not robbery if that was the only thing missing." His eyes met mine. "That's personal." A tic had started in his jaw.

"What are you thinking?"

"That Monica found out something terrible, something she couldn't live with. Something she must have confronted Wes about. And she didn't confide in me. She just left without any explanation. As if she couldn't trust me with the knowledge."

I thought of the Monica I'd known, the woman for whom truth and fairness ruled everything she did. The woman who was loyal and trusting to a fault. I shook my head. "No, Trey. It wasn't because she didn't trust you. She did what she did to protect you. And Aimee, too. Whatever it was she'd discovered she knew would hurt you and Aimee in a personal way. The only way she could protect you and preserve her integrity was to leave."

Trey placed the portrait on top of the washing machine, his eyes thoughtful. "My grandfather hasn't recognized any of us in years, and has been pretty much unresponsive to any sort of conversation. I'm thinking Aimee just hoped to elicit some kind of response by showing him the portrait." He paused for a moment. "I'm thinking she's always known something. She hung that damned portrait in the hallway all those years even though she knew her husband hated it."

Softly, I said, "I guess she and Wes had their own 'don't ask, don't tell' policy regarding unpleasant truths. She loved him, and didn't want to lose him like she'd already lost Gary, and not after having nearly lost each other during Camille. But seeing the ring and the pin in Monica's photograph was somehow proof that Wes was complicit in something. And maybe was responsible for Monica's leaving. After all this time, Aimee was ready to know the truth."

I continued, "What if Wes had the ring and brooch? We can assume they were hidden together, because that's how they were found. Remember how Aimee found him at River Song after his mother's disappearance? What if he hid them then? Which would explain why Wes went to River Song to dig something up before Camille, realizing how serious the storm was and wanting to make sure his secret remained safe."

Softly, Trey said, "If he was so desperate to hide the pin, then I'd have to think that Caroline didn't give it to him willingly. That he had it because she was unable to resist."

"But why take it at all?"

His voice was hard when he answered. "Because it would have been identifiable. Wherever Caroline Guidry showed up, dead or alive, she would have been noticed or recognized because of that pin."

I thought for a moment, remembering Aimee's recounting of the hurricane, almost feeling the bullet-sharp rain on my face. "Xavier must have taken the ring and pin when he found Wes. Aimee said that Xavier was holding something when he left them after bringing Wes upstairs during the storm. Something he said would make him safe."

Trey nodded. "Like insurance. And he hid them all of those years. Until Monica somehow found them, and knew what they were and what they meant to her family. Why they'd been hidden."

I could almost hear the puzzle pieces sliding into place—all of them except the part that would explain why. "Then she went to Wes to confront him, probably to get him to tell her the truth of what happened to his mother, and to convince him to tell Aimee and maybe even the police—because that's the kind of person she was. She must have given him the ring and brooch or he took them from her.

"But she took the portrait because it was hanging in the hallway outside his room, and was a sort of proof that the pin had belonged to Caroline and that she was most likely wearing it on the night she disappeared."

I thought of the gentle girl I'd known being forced to face the ugly fact that those she loved had been complicit in something as evil as murder. Of possible matricide. I touched Trey's arm, not sure who needed the comfort more. "Being Monica, she held out hope that she was wrong. She found me, wishing for the chance of discovering that her great-grandmother really had left with the artist. That I would know something to validate Caroline's presence in Abe's life through my family history."

Trey's eyes were dark as they regarded me. "Which you didn't, but it was sort of a lucky break for Monica anyway, since it brought you together."

"One of her few," I said. I looked at Trey, not seeing him but instead seeing a summer night in the garden and smelling the scent of fresh paint. I grabbed his arm. "Xavier said he was the one who went to move Wes after his stroke while Ray Von called for the ambulance. If Wes had the jewelry after his argument with Monica, Xavier could have taken back the ring and brooch then, and returned them to their hiding place."

It was Trey's turn to follow me through the house as I ran down the stairs to the kitchen and out the back door. We stopped in front of the shed, the new paint glowing in the dusky light. "Aimee told me Monica loved to garden, and would hang out here with Xavier just like Beau does."

I slapped at a mosquito without looking, a newly honed instinct. "Nobody goes in this shed except for Xavier. When he painted it, he had to take everything out and find a new hiding place. And remember how he didn't want you helping him?" I stood back to allow the faint light to illuminate the grass by the side of the shed. "He's been digging at night—we heard him, remember? And so did Beau and I."

I got down on my hands and knees and began feeling the earth, searching for a bump or mound of grassless dirt.

"Over here," Trey said, indicating something with the toe of his shoe. I stood and walked to the back corner of the shed. A small hole gaped in the dark earth, a pile of dirt next to it.

We both knelt before the empty hole. "Do you know where Xavier lives?" I asked.

He stood and held out his arm to pull me up. "We don't need to know. I don't think he dug it up to hide it again."

For the third time, Trey and I walked through the grand house and up the stairs, our steps slower this time, as if we both realized that understanding what Monica had wanted to keep hidden to protect those she loved would never bring her back.

The door to Aimee's room was open, her bed unmade and empty. I stilled a growing panic, something I imagined I'd always feel when not finding somebody in the place I expected them to be. I stepped back into the hallway, Trey behind me. "Miss Aimee?" I called, looking down the hallway and noticing that the attic door was ajar.

We walked quickly to it and pulled it open. Xavier sat on the step, a shaft of twilight from the window behind him creating a halo around his head. His ruined face shone wet. "She knows," he said, his voice so soft that I had to lean forward to hear. "All these years I tried to protect her. But today she told me that it was time she knew the truth."

Trey stepped from behind me. Gently, he asked, "What did you tell her?"

"Nobody else should have to see what I saw." He put his head in his hands. "I lied. I lied when I said I didn't see anything that night her mama was killed. I didn't stay in the Guidrys' kitchen like I said. I saw Mrs. Guidry. . . . She tried to kiss Mrs. Mercier, but not in the kind of way a woman kisses her friend, you know?"

He looked up and I sat down next to him, putting my hand on his shoulder. I watched Trey, wondering if he could smell it, too: the suddenly strong and overpowering scent of perfume, of Shalimar.

Xavier continued. "Mrs. Mercier slapped her, hard. I knew it was hard 'cause I could see the red handprint on her face. And then Mrs. Mercier left. I followed her to her house, and I was hiding under the bed like I told Miss Aimee, and I didn't lie—I didn't see anything. But I heard somebody come in, and somebody stopping by the side of the bed, but I swear I didn't see who killed her. It was too dark. But . . ." He let out a deep, shuddering breath.

"But what, Xavier?" Trey prompted.

His gaze traveled from me to Trey. "I heard something hit the floor and it rolled under the bed."

"The wedding ring," I said, pinpricks of static electricity beginning to creep up my arms, the scent of perfume so strong my throat convulsed.

"I wasn't sure, but I put it in my pocket, then waited until I was alone and then I left. I was so scared of being caught that I didn't look at the bed when I crawled out from under it and didn't stop running until I got back home. I didn't know that Mrs. Mercier was dead until the next day, when the police came to the Guidrys' house. I didn't want to get in trouble with the police, so I gave the ring to Mr. Guidry so he could talk to them. I was so scared, thinking the police would think I'd done it, since I was there. Instead, Mr. Guidry sent me away to school like my mama wanted, and because I was his blood kin. I thought it was because he was trying to protect me."

"No," I whispered. "It was because he thought you knew something and was trying to buy your silence."

Trey looked at me with a question, but the thoughts whirling around in my head wouldn't settle long enough for me to have an answer.

He nodded. "Until that night at the ball. Mr. and Mrs. Guidry came home early with Wes in his car. I guess he'd already dropped off Miss Lacy, because she wasn't with them. They were shouting at each other. I was in the kitchen waiting until everyone came home to lock up the house. Usually everybody's been drinking, so somebody has to remember to do it.

"Mrs. Guidry was telling her husband that she was leaving him, and was going to tell everybody the truth about how it was his fault that she liked women the way that she did. And Wes was begging her not to leave, that it would kill Gary if his mother left, but she didn't even seem to hear him. It was like she was out of her mind. And then she ran out of the house, and I went to the garden to see.

"She was just walking down the street in her gown. It was Mardi Gras night and nobody else was around, just her in the middle of the street. And then Wes . . ."

Trey cleared his throat, as if he weren't sure he could push enough air out to form words. "What did Wes do next, Xavier?"

"Wes got in his car and started following his mama, trying to get her to get in and go home and to stop talking crazy. And then she stopped walking and turned around and she was standing right in front of the car. She said something to him and Mr. Guidry was coming from the house to tell her to be quiet, but it didn't matter. She was out of her head with drink and her craziness, talking about how she was tired of secrets and wanted everybody to know the truth. Then she yelled something at Wes, something I couldn't make out. And then he . . ." He swallowed thickly, shaking his head. "I heard the engine rev, and then I saw Mrs. Guidry was under the car."

I closed my eyes, seeing it all in my head, hearing the sound of crunching metal and of a body hitting pavement.

"What did she tell him?"

Xavier shook his head. "I don't know. But it was enough to make him crazy, too."

We were all silent for a moment; then Trey asked, "What did they do with her body?"

"Mr. Guidry—he saw me and told me that I had to help them or I would be arrested. This was before blacks had any rights, and he didn't have to tell me that I could be in a heap of trouble. So I did what he said. And Mr. Guidry gave Wes something in a little bag and told him to hide it with that alligator pin she always wore where nobody could ever find it. We put her in the trunk of the car and drove to Mississippi. Then we dumped her in a swamp between here and Biloxi, and I thought he was going to throw in that bag and the pin. But he didn't."

"Then you dropped him off at River Song and took the car so the police couldn't find it and see the damage on it. And then you disappeared." Trey's voice was flat, as if he were reciting a prewritten speech.

"I dumped the car in Alabama, made sure nobody'd ever find it. Wes gave me money to disappear, but I didn't go far. I was afraid for Miss Aimee. Afraid she'd figure it all out and that she might get hurt if she did. I saw what those two did, you see. I saw it and I was afraid for her. What they might do to her."

"But Wes loved Aimee," I said.

Xavier's green eye regarded me with steely ice. "He loved his mama, too."

I was silent for a moment, trying to push away the grief that seemed to seep from the walls. "That's why your mother wrote to Aimee when she was in Pennsylvania, to get her to return so you'd come back. She knew you'd gone away because of her."

Xavier nodded. "And I could never tell her. I figured the fewer people who knew the truth, the safer they'd be. But then Camille came, and I took the ring and the pin because I knew that would make them afraid I'd go take the evidence to the police. I didn't. They were my blood kin. So I stayed and started working for them, and Mr. Guidry died. And all was fine again."

"Until Monica found the ring and the alligator pin."

His head dropped, and I saw his hands, still clasped in front of him. "I should have thrown them in the swamp. I would have, if I'd known what would happen. My mama always told me that all truths rise to the surface eventually."

I looked at Trey, remembering Johnny, and what his mother had told him before she died. "Lacy must have seen Mrs. Guidry die. She must have returned to the Guidrys' house to talk with Wes, to try to get back together again. And she saw him kill his mother. That's why he married her and not Aimee. Because he was afraid she'd talk."

"But who killed Aimee's mother?" Trey asked.

"I don't know. But I think the answer has to be here." Xavier opened his hands, and I stood, mesmerized by the bloodred eyes in the alligator brooch, the gold ring nestled against it in Xavier's calloused palms. The light made the red eyes glitter, but all I could see was the pointed tail of the reptile, sharp enough to break skin, and I smelled the distinctive scent of Shalimar.

I opened my hands and Xavier let the two objects fall slowly into my cupped palms. I let out a quick breath, my discovery like a punch to the chest. "Where's Aimee?"

Xavier turned his head, indicating the top of the attic stairs and the room beyond with the single bulb hanging from the ceiling illuminating the space. I looked at Trey. "Stay here. I need to talk with Aimee. I think it would be easier for her if it were just the two of us now."

Slowly, I climbed the stairs, not sure what I expected to see. I found Aimee sitting on a sheet-covered wing-backed chair, a white satin gown spread over her legs and cascading onto the floor. A trunk was beside her, its lid open.

"Aimee?"

She was looking out the window at the blackened sky and didn't turn when she spoke. "This was my mother's wedding dress. I'd hoped that one day Monica would wear it."

I approached and gently closed the trunk lid before sitting on it. She finally looked at me, her eyes larger and bluer under the white bandage on her forehead.

Aimee smiled. "Are you here to find out what happened after the hurricane?"

"You married Wes," I said.

"Yes. He'd asked Lacy for a divorce, figuring that Johnny was sort of his leverage, that Lacy would never let it be known that Wes was a murderer because of how it would affect her son and their position in the community. That's what he'd wanted to tell me when we spoke on the phone that morning. That's why she chased him down to River Song with Johnny, to try to change his mind." She shrugged. "Camille brought a change of heart, I suppose. Being near death does that to a person."

She faced the window again, the lights from the city casting the distant sky in purple. "We were very happy in the years we had together. We had our difficulties, of course—all families do, but we had a good life. We had Johnny, and then his children, and I thought that if we could just keep looking toward the future we wouldn't need to dwell on the past." She smiled softly to herself. "And then I gave that Abe Holt book to Monica and told her the old rumor about how Caroline had run off with the artist. Monica was such a romantic, and I thought she'd enjoy telling her friends about the family connection." Her voice hitched on the last word.

Gently, I prompted, "But being Monica, she had to get to the bottom of it, find out the whole truth of what really happened, and was curious when she couldn't find anything to substantiate the rumor."

Aimee nodded. "It wasn't until after you arrived here and I knew that Monica had given you the portrait that I started putting some of the pieces together. I figured that Monica must have hit a dead end looking for Caroline until she found the brooch and the ring and confronted Wes. He must have told her the whole story, expecting her to understand why they couldn't tell anybody else. Which, knowing Monica, he should have known wouldn't sit well with her. That's why she felt she had to leave. She couldn't live with herself and keep the secret, yet she wanted to protect her family from such an awful truth."

"When did you know that Caroline Guidry killed your mother?"

Her eyes met mine. "I didn't. Until today, when Xavier showed me the alligator pin and the wedding ring. That's when I remembered that my mother wasn't the only one who wore Shalimar." She swallowed. "It must have been what Caroline shouted at Wes before he killed her.

It's the only thing I could think of that would have sent him into such a blind rage."

I opened my hands, the two inanimate objects in my palm more powerful than if they'd breathed air. I studied the pointed tail on the ridged back of the alligator, wondering if too many years had passed to find DNA evidence. Tears pricked at the back of my eyes. "Monica was an optimist. Despite all the evidence she'd found, she took the portrait and found me, hoping I'd have some information regarding Caroline being with Abe, living with my family. Hoping to find out that she was wrong. That her family wasn't what she'd discovered them to be. And that her grandfather hadn't been holding on to a secret all those years."

Aimee was silent for a long moment as we watched a yellow butterfly settle on the window glass, its wings beating in slow motion, making me wonder why it was out at night. "We lie to ourselves and to those we love sometimes because we think it will protect them. Just like I did, and Wes did." She turned to look at me, her blue eyes dark. "Just like your mother did."

I started to pull away but she placed her hand on my arm. "Your father and your brother chose to believe that Chelsea wasn't coming home. But your mother chose to believe she was, and she taught you to believe, too. It gave you purpose to your life, a reason to go on. It brought you here and to River Song. To us." She smoothed her hands against the creamy satin of the gown, the blue veins on her hands like sharp arrows. "Sometimes, Julie, we search and search, looking for what has been right in front of us all along."

I waited for the hurt and anger to wash over me, for the denials to spring to my tongue. But the weight that had begun to shift while I was at the police station in Massachusetts shifted more, carving out more room in my chest. I wanted to cry and laugh and shout, all at the same time, but I couldn't. Instead I breathed in deeply, filling my lungs, feeling lighter still.

"Thank you," I whispered instead, not sure if she heard me but knowing she understood.

Aimee touched my hand. "Give those to Trey. He'll know what to do, and I'm all right with that. Even if Wes is found guilty, there really isn't anything they can do to him."

I nodded and stood, sensing her need to be alone for a little longer. "Thank you," I said again, louder this time, so that Monica, Chelsea, my mother, and all those who had brought me to this place could hear.

Something tapped on the glass, and we both looked up at the window, watching as a cluster of yellow butterflies hovered together, suspended, it seemed, by sheer force of will in the dark night. And then, as quickly as they had appeared, they flew off, leaving only the view of black sky and the memory that they had ever been there at all.

CHAPTER 31

It is only in sorrow bad weather masters us; in joy we face the storm and defy it.   —AMELIA BARR

Julie

Death and loss, they plague you. But so do memories. The memories I have of my lost sister and of Monica are still fresh—full and ripe like summer fruit. I imagine they always will be. But there is room now in my heart for more memories, carved by a letting go that I could find only by coming home to a place I'd never been. I think Monica knew that, and that was why she brought me here. Unable to heal herself, she'd chosen to heal me instead.

On my way back from buying supplies for the housewarming party, I head down what has become my favorite stretch of Beach Boulevard, the long blocks between Gill and Rodenberg avenues where three Katrina trees stand interspersed with tall, leafy oaks.

There're an egret, a dolphin, and a pelican: all solitary statues with resolute expressions hewn from solid wood. Sometimes I'll park the car to get a better look at them, to touch them so that perhaps I can better understand why I feel such affinity for them. I'm in no rush to figure this out. I've decided that Beau and I are staying in Biloxi at River Song, and it's hard to imagine a time when I doubted this outcome.

I've begun to take for granted the blue-painted Katrina lines on telephone poles around town showing the various heights of the storm surge, and names like Tchoutacabouffa, Atchafalaya, and Bogafalaya, now roll easily from my tongue as if I've been saying them my whole life. And the five-o'clock train whistle has become as familiar to me as wearing shorts in February and the sound of water rolling toward shore. I think this is a good thing.

As I pull into the drive, Trey steps out onto the wide lawn in front of River Song, the white house with black shutters now standing on new pilings. A swing hangs from the old oak in the front yard, and hammocks and rocking chairs on the wide porch creak in the breeze. If Monica drove up now she'd recognize her beloved house, new, but old, too, as if the yarn of years and memories has been unwound and tucked into the new joists and wooden beams, preserved for more generations.

Trey kisses me, then takes the bags from the back of the van. I smell the wood smoke from the barbecue pit in the backyard, a whole pig spinning slowly on a spit. We've invited everyone we know to share in the resurrection of River Song, of building up what had been torn down, of restoring hope where there'd been only fragmented memories. Among the two hundred or so guests, Carol Sue and Walker King, newly engaged, will be here, and Kathy Wolf is driving down with Aimee and Xavier. Even Ray Von has promised to come. We're having a mini ribbon-cutting ceremony with Steve and Julia Kenney from Kenney-Moise Homebuilders officiating. I don't know if Monica would have wanted all the pomp, but there's so much to celebrate.

On the day the last of the construction equipment had rolled away, Ray Von came to see me to deliver the note Monica had included with the portrait of Caroline Guidry.

"She stuck this into the note for me, but told me not to give it to you until I thought you'd decided to stay. And I guess now is as good a time as any." Without further explanation, she'd handed it to me and watched as I read.

Dear Julie,

Please tell Aimee and Trey that I'm sorry, that I never stopped loving them. Looking back, I've seen that I could have trusted them more. But I was young and headstrong, and I made my choice. By welcoming you and Beau into their lives, I know they've forgiven me.

I'm giving you my two most precious possessions—Beau and River Song—because I know you will be more than just their caretaker. If I'd told you in advance what I wanted you to do after my death, you would have reasoned your way out of it. Forgive me, and know that I love you like the sister I never had.

Survival is like a stone wall, and kindness is a door. You have taught me this.

MMG

I keep the note in my purse, wrinkled now so that it's almost illegible. But I keep opening it, trying to understand what she was trying to tell me. *Survival is like a stone wall, and kindness is a door.*

Johnny is coming to the barbecue today, too. Even Trey agreed that he should be here. Before sunset, a small group of us will kayak over to Deer Island and bring Monica's ashes to sprinkle into the sound. It will be a homecoming of sorts, a return to a place that she never completely left. I hope that Johnny's presence here will be a forging of new bonds with his son and grandson. Monica would have wanted that, and I can't help but think that she'd planned it all along.

Trey is working on Wes's defense and getting him declared incompetent to stand trial, but we've managed to keep it out of the media and the prosecutor's office is moving very slowly on the case. Johnny hasn't acknowledged it, but I don't doubt that he might have had a hand in that. We're all hoping that the preparation for the case outlasts the number of months Wes has left.

Trey takes my hand, leaving the bags on the kitchen table, where an assembled team of cooks has already taken over. "I want to show you something."

He leads me upstairs to the sleeping porch, where everything smells new, and evidence of Beau's and Charlie's presence is everywhere, with discarded sandals, sand toys, and pajamas littering the floor. I leave them there, thinking that the presence of children makes River Song the home Monica always imagined it should be.

Trey brings me to the last twin bed against the wall. "Lie down here and face the ceiling."

I look at him with a question but lie down anyway. I watch him go to the farthest bed against the opposite wall and lie down, too.

And then, as if he is lying next to me and whispering in my ear, I hear, "I like you a lot, Julie Holt."

I jerk my head at him in surprise, amazed at the acoustic marvel that Kenney-Moise has been able to re-create the way Aimee and Monica had remembered. And, apparently, Trey.

"I like you, too, Wesley John Guidry the Third," I whisper, turning my head to see Trey as a slow grin spreads over his face. We look at each other across the room and the three beds between us, imagining the years of stored secrets of children that still seem to live in the long, windowed room at the back of the house.

The front screen slams and the pounding feet of children race up the stairs, and I listen for the creaks on the second, ninth, and twelfth steps and I picture Monica laughing at my attention to detail. Charlie and Beau appear, already dressed in their bathing suits, with Carol Sue eventually appearing at a more sedate pace. Jax II, Beau's new puppy, races from behind her and jumps on me, giving my face a good cleansing with his pink tongue.

On the day Beau neatly tucked his mother's red hat into the bottom drawer of his dresser to "save it for later," I'd cried, amazed at this child who'd suffered so much loss but could figure out how sometimes you need to leave things behind if you're going to move forward. The next day, I brought home Jax II.

I adopted him from a shelter, imagining he'd be a good hunting dog for Beau when they were both old enough to go out with Trey. Trey had been kind in telling me that a cocker spaniel–poodle mix wasn't necessarily a good hunting dog, but would certainly make a good companion for a young boy. And Jax II never stops showing his gratitude every time he sees me.

Beau scoops up the little dog and begins bouncing on the bed. "You said we could go swimming when you got back. Can we go now? Huh? Can we go now?"

I sit up slowly, resigned to fulfilling my promise made under duress while packing up our things from the rental house. It had seemed far enough in the future at the time that promising to go swimming with Beau as soon as we were settled at River Song had seemed like a small thing.

With a sigh, I sit up and go to my bedroom in the front of the house and pull on my new bathing suit—purchased while on a forced shopping trip with Carol Sue to New Orleans. I hadn't had a bathing suit since I was a child, and Carol Sue thought that it was time now that I'd planned on taking up permanent residence in Biloxi.

We wait while Trey changes, and then we lug coolers and chairs down to the beach, where I prepare to sit and watch the children, making sure they don't go out too deep. I don't trust the bright orange inflatable armbands to keep them safe. Even Jax II has a doggie life vest, at my request. Maybe in time I'll be less protective of those in my care, but old habits die hard.

Trey stands in front of me, his hand extended. "It's your turn," he says, pulling me to a stand.

"For what?"

"To go swimming. You can't own a beach house and not swim. That's just wrong."

"I don't own all of it," I say petulantly, a smile forcing its way to my lips.

Carol Sue and the children watch as Trey brings me to the reaching surf, and I resist the impulse to step back as it laps at my toes. We stand there for a while until Trey tugs on my hand again. "You ready?"

I look into his smiling eyes and nod; then he takes me a little farther until the water reaches just above my knees. It's the color of iced tea, but I can see the sand and my toes on the silty bottom, the water warm on my legs.

"It's shallow for a good bit, so we'll just stay here for your first time, all right? But you need to get your hair wet for this to count."

I look at him with a question and he moves closer.

"Give me your hands and lean back, and when you're ready let me know and I'll let go. All you need to do is hold your breath and close your eyes. I'll be right here the whole time."

We stand that way for a long while, the sun beating down on us, the happy shouts of the children and the dog's barks sounding so far away. Realizing he's not going to let go until I tell him, I nod and his fingers slip from mine and I fall backward.

After the initial splash, I'm surrounded by utter silence except for the sound of water rushing in my ears. I open my eyes, seeing a murky sun and the shadow of Trey, and I'm comforted. I feel a little as if I'm dying, my thoughts clear, past conversations replaying in my head. *Moving on doesn't mean forgetting.* I remember Aimee saying that as we looked at the Katrina memorial, and I understand. Finally, I understand.

I push up to the surface, and suddenly I know what Monica meant, what the Katrina trees have been telling me: that our lives are spent searching for what makes us whole, for the things that make surviving worthwhile. I stand in the surf and see Monica's house—my house now—and the old oak tree standing out front, its trunk and limbs scarred and gnarled, but its branches full of new leaves. We are like old friends, the tree and I: survivors of storms.

I fall back into the water, a laugh on my lips as I go under once more, the liquid arms holding me. Then Trey's hands find mine, and he pulls me up, and I smell the salt air and see River Song and Beau and know that I am whole again.

Karen White is the award-winning author of thirteen previous books. She grew up in London but now lives with her husband and two children near Atlanta, Georgia. Visit her Web site at www.karen-white.com.

The Beach Trees

KAREN WHITE

A CONVERSATION
WITH KAREN WHITE

Q. The Beach Trees *touches upon real current events, such as Hurricane Katrina and the BP oil spill. Was it difficult to balance the detailing of some of the devastation caused by these events with the fictional narrative you were creating? How much of the tragedy that happened to the fictional characters was based on real events, and how much of it did you create?*

A. There are many parallels between the devastation of the Gulf Coast and protagonist Julie Holt's life. It was necessary to delve into the realities of the despair faced by those who have lost so much. When we first meet Julie, her life is as wrecked and as desolate as the Biloxi beaches, wiped clean. She believes she has lost everything worth losing, as hurricane survivors often feel, yet as Julie meets the survivors of Katrina, she begins to learn that great loss isn't necessarily the end.

All of the personal stories of the characters were borrowed from composites of survivors' stories. I spent days poring over firsthand accounts of Hurricanes Camille and Katrina to give my fictional characters realistic reactions and emotions.

Q. How did you first hear about the Katrina trees art? Have you been able to see them in person?

A. For research, I subscribe to a newspaper archive service, which is very helpful when digging up facts about a particular setting. I read so many stories about these trees, and then was blown away by the photos I found in books and on the Internet. There's a wonderful quote from the mayor of Biloxi, about how the trees were like making lemonade out of lemons. It was this outlook from many survivors that I tried to re-create in the book.

I haven't seen the Katrina trees in person but plan on visiting soon.

Q. What made you decide to use the Gulf Coast as the setting for The Beach Trees*?*

A. I lived in New Orleans for four years during college (I graduated from Tulane University) and fell in love with the city, and my father is from Biloxi (Class of 1950 from Biloxi High School), so it wasn't too far of a stretch for me to come up with the setting. In the spring of 2005, I'd actually started a book set in New Orleans and then Katrina hit—making me change the setting to Charleston. (That book became *The House on Tradd Street*.) Katrina was so monumental that I knew it needed to be front and center in a book, and "The House on Coliseum" (the original title) didn't have room for it, so I waited until the right book came along.

Aimee's story, however, is taken from a book I wrote a long time ago and never published. It was set in New Orleans in the 1980s (a familiar decade for me), so I had to rewrite almost all of it, and I'm so glad I found a book in which to tell her story.

Q. *There are two different first-person narrators in* The Beach Trees. *Was it difficult for you to go back and forth between Julie and Aimee and their stories?*

A. I've written books using this method a few times before and found I enjoyed it. It allows me to get inside the heads of the two protagonists, permitting me to see where their story lines intersect. I love the unexpected surprises they always have in store for me.

Julie and Aimee are so different, I never had trouble knowing whose head I was in. Plus, they're from different generations, so their thoughts and experiences were completely separate which helped a lot.

Q. *Between the two, did you have a favorite narrator and story line? Who was your favorite character in the entire novel?*

A. It's hard to choose between Aimee and Julie, but I'd have to say Julie, if only because she had such a long way to go from when we meet her until the end of the book. She learned a great deal about letting go, and I admire her strength and tenacity. But I don't think she could have done any of it without Aimee as her mentor.

As far as my favorite character, I'd choose Carol Sue. She's like the sister I never had—a great contemporary mentor and friend for Julie. Having not grown up with a sister, I find the need to create them for my protagonists in my fiction.

QUESTIONS FOR DISCUSSION

1. Why do you think Monica willed everything, including Beau and her beloved beach home, River Song, to Julie—especially since she still had family living? What were her intentions, and what was she trying to say? What are the repercussions for Julie?

2. How does Chelsea Holt's disappearance shape Julie's life? What emotions still haunt her, even after almost twenty years?

3. What significance does the portrait of Caroline Guidry with the alligator brooch hold to each member of her family? Are the sentiments diverse? What clues does it hold within it?

4. Do Aimee's flashbacks fill us in with an objective history of the intertwined Guidry and Mercier families? What critical clues does Julie glean from them to advance her investigation?

5. How does the search into the past—and for loved ones, including Caroline, Monica, Chelsea, and Aimee's mother—influence the trajectory of the characters' lives, psychologies, and their relationships to one another? How do secrets come to define and haunt the Guidrys?

6. What motivates Julie to dig through old case files and artifacts to connect the dots between the two families? Do you think she was foolish not to let sleeping dogs lie? Would you want to know the truth, especially if it were unsavory? Is this doggedness a beneficial trait, or are there costs for Julie? How does she end up untangling the mystery?

7. Why do you think the residents of the Gulf Coast continue to rebuild after numerous tragedies—most recently from Camille, Katrina, and the BP oil spill—on the same plots of land that remain highly vulnerable? What might tie them to this place? What is the significance in rebuilding?

8. How does Julie's life mirror Aimee's? Both assumed a form of guardianship—of Johnny and Beau—and both seek answers to the unexplained tragedies in their lives, but what sets them apart? What do they offer to each other?

9. Do you think Aimee and Wes did the right thing in loving each other from afar, keeping their feelings secret to spare Gary's heart? What were the consequences?

10. What did you think happened to Caroline? And who did you think killed Aimee's mother? Were you shocked by the revelations? What kept the secrets airtight for so long, and what is at stake with them no longer being held?

11. What were Ray Von's and Xavier Williams's roles in the scandalous events? Do you think Xavier did the right and necessary things? Do you think he was effective in shielding Aimee?

12. What do you think the next chapter at River Song holds for Julie, Trey, Beau, and the rest of the Guidry family?